ALAN R. MULAK

The Innkeeper

and Other Short Stories

BALBOA.
PRESS

A DIVISION OF HAY HOUSE

Balboa Press books may be ordered through booksellers or by contacting:

Balboa Press
A Division of Hay House
1663 Liberty Drive
Bloomington, IN 47403
www.balboapress.com
1 (877) 407-4847

Because of the dynamic nature of the Internet, any web addresses or links contained in this book may have changed since publication and may no longer be valid. The views expressed in this work are solely those of the author and do not necessarily reflect the views of the publisher, and the publisher hereby disclaims any responsibility for them.

The author of this book does not dispense medical advice or prescribe the use of any technique as a form of treatment for physical, emotional, or medical problems without the advice of a physician, either directly or indirectly. The intent of the author is only to offer information of a general nature to help you in your quest for emotional and spiritual well-being. In the event you use any of the information in this book for yourself, which is your constitutional right, the author and the publisher assume no responsibility for your actions.

Any people depicted in stock imagery provided by Getty Images are models, and such images are being used for illustrative purposes only. Certain stock imagery © Getty Images.

Print information available on the last page.

ISBN: 978-1-9822-0845-5 (sc)
ISBN: 978-1-9822-0847-9 (hc)
ISBN: 978-1-9822-0846-2 (e)

Library of Congress Control Number: 2018908230

Balboa Press rev. date: 07/25/2018

Dedication

I dedicate this collection to my daughter Michelle who continues to be one of my most loyal supporters. Everybody needs someone like Michelle.

Table of Contents

Introduction

I love reading and writing short stories, which of course says something about the length of my attention span.

This book contains twenty-two short stories. Some are long enough for you to put your feet up and settle into a comfortable chair while others are so short, they can be read as the coffee pot perks.

Some of my readers – that's you – ask me where I came up with my ideas. My ideas came from you. We are all worthy of a story that in some cases, is mighty entertaining. Thank you for sharing.

The work contained herein is fiction. I made up every word, each character, and all the locations. Any actual person or place that corresponds with my fictional writing is purely accidental and unintentional.

As always, I never deliberately set out to hurt anybody, so if any of my words sting or offend, I sure am sorry. It was by accident.

Enjoy!

The Innkeeper

Illustration by Gina Ash

Chapter One

Old Friends

"When was it you died?" the old man asked.

"What's that?" Josh replied.

Harold Wilson, resident Innkeeper and affectionately known as the 'Old Man' by the staff, held up the registration form and pointed at the empty space in the upper left-hand corner. "Look here," he said, peering over his glasses. "This space is empty. They will return this form if it isn't filled in correctly. Blasted bureaucrats."

Josh sat back in the oak chair and rubbed his chin. "Well let's see," he said, squinting his eyes. "It was May of 2014, and I was putting away the Christmas ornaments…"

The old man raised his gray eyebrows. "In *May?*"

"Can't rush these things," Josh replied, continuing to squint back in time. "It was after my son's birthday because we had gone to their house for dinner the week before. Terrible dinner as usual. Terrible. His wife is a real looker, but a God-awful cook. I fed my food to the dog under the table. So, let me think…that means it was about the tenth or eleventh I'd say."

Josh, in the prime of life, sported a head of bushy, dark-brown hair, a round face, and eyes always ready for mischief.

The old man picked up a pen and said, "Let's call it the tenth, just to put something down here. Ok?"

Josh smiled. "Fine with me."

The old man inserted the date and studied the registration form. "Everything else looks in order. And I see you are here for the poker tournament. So, you'll be staying with us for three nights? Correct?"

"Unless I win big, then I'll stay for the championship. I'm feeling lucky. Put me down for another night."

"No problem, no problem," the old man said, making notes on the form. He then took it and placed it in the outbox, atop several other forms. Sitting back in his chair, he removed his reading glasses and cleaned them with a handkerchief. "Good to see you again Josh," he said. "It's been a while."

Josh nodded. "I'll say. It's been since 1975, when we were playing softball in Westfield, Pennsylvania."

"Those were good times," the old man said. He pushed a few unruly strands of gray hair off his forehead, replaced his glasses, and then folded his liver-spotted hands. "How did it happen?" he asked.

"What's that?" asked Josh. "My death or us playing softball?"

The old man laughed, deep wrinkles emanating from the corners of his bright eyes. "Both. But first, I'm interested in your death. There are some strange rumors about that, as I'm sure you know."

Josh crossed his legs and brushed some stray ashes from a previous cigar off his pants. He took a fresh cigar from his shirt pocket. "Can I light up?"

"I'm sorry, but no. You'll have to go out on the porch to smoke. Some of the guests complain. You know how that goes."

"No problem," Josh said. "My death. Well, it's really quite simple. I was on the stepladder in the garage, tucking away the last box of Christmas lights, when I couldn't quite reach the remaining spot in the rafters. So, I stood on the top step, you know, the one that says, "Do Not Stand Here," and presto, the ladder kicked out and down I went."

"So," the old man asked, "your wife didn't push you?"

"Nah," Josh replied. "She wasn't even home. Now, she would have, if I gave her the chance, but nope, it was all my stupidity." Josh thought for a moment, again squinting into the past. "Remember all that bullshit people used to say about your life flashing in front of your eyes when the time comes?"

The old man nodded.

"It's bullshit," Josh said with a grin. "Me? When I was on my way down, headfirst, heading for the concrete garage floor, I was thinking...this is going to hurt like hell!"

Both men laughed.

"And about us playing softball together," Josh continued. "That last year we played, we did all right. Better than all right. We were good."

The old man smiled again. "Champions, if I recall correctly."

"Do you remember that last out, when Walmsley hit the long ball to left field?"

The old man nodded. "I'll never forget it. The ball must have gone four hundred feet."

"It was the longest out in history, I bet." Josh said.

A moment of silence passed between the old friends.

"You look good, Josh," the old man said.

"Thanks." Josh opened his hands, palms up. "Harold. Let me ask you something. Why are you still an old man?"

The old man shrugged. "Waitin' for Mary."

"But..."

"The Age Adjustment Forms are such pains in the ass, I only want to fill them out once. Once Mary arrives, we'll tackle it together."

Josh nodded. "And how's she doing?"

The old man shrugged again. "She's living in one of those active adult communities. Last time I checked she's still going strong: playing cards and line dancing and running around a court chasing some kind of whiffle ball with a ping pong paddle. They call it pickleball." He laughed, showing his remaining teeth. "Get this. She still buys that Catholic crap about heaven and hell. She's in for a real surprise."

"Weren't we all!" After a pause, Josh continued. "Do you worry," he asked in earnest, "if she's going to find someone else? You know, some guy to replace you."

The old man frowned. "Happens all the time. As Innkeeper, I see it all too often. Breaks everyone's hearts. Sad. Really sad." He shook his balding head slowly. "I worry some, but I'm counting on the fact that we had a really good thing going. Just have to wait and see."

Josh rolled the cigar he had been holding between his fingers, giving it an appreciative sniff. "Mary is special. Nobody could play the piano and sing 'You Are My Sunshine' like her. She was, and probably still is, a class act."

Silence.

Replacing the cigar into his pocket, Josh asked, "When did you pass?"

"Four years ago, last week. Right out of the blue, the old ticker just quit. The only meds I was taking were for blood pressure, I had most of my own teeth and I could walk all day, but bingo, one morning I got up out of bed and my knees buckled. I was dead before I hit the floor."

The old man straightened some papers on his desk then asked, "So Josh, what age did you choose?"

Josh beat his fists on his chest like Tarzan. "Twenty-five...this one. This was about the best it was for me. I had a full head of hair and was in reasonable shape. It's good to be young again. You ought to try it," Josh concluded with a wink and a laugh.

The old man held up his hand. "My turn will come but, like you with your Christmas ornaments, no need to rush these things."

Both men started to get up from their chairs when the old man snapped his fingers and said, "Oh, I almost forgot. What form of payment will you be using?"

Josh again took out his cigar and held it between his fingers. "Work it off." He replied.

"Night shift or day shift?" The old man asked.

"Night works for me."

"Great," said the old man, making a note on Josh's registration form. "Want to start tonight?"

"You bet."

The old man turned toward a man sitting quietly in a nearby overstuffed Club chair, reading the newspaper. "Hank," he called. "Your night shift help is here."

Hank put down the paper and looked at Josh over his reading glasses. "Glad for the help," he said. "When do you want to start?"

Josh shrugged. "Can I smoke my cigar?"

"Yep," Hank replied, and then asked, "Can you play cribbage?"

"Is the Pope Polish?" Josh retorted.

"Nope," the old man replied seriously, "not anymore. This one is from Argentina."

"No shit?" asked Josh.

The old man shook his head no.

"Well then, let me try again. You bet I play cribbage! You got a board and cards?" Josh asked.

Hank laughed and held up a small picnic basket. From within a muffled sound of drink glasses clinking against a bottle could be heard. Clearly, there was more than a cribbage board and cards within. "Always prepared."

"Then how about now?" Josh said.

"Let's get to it," Hank said and got up. The two men shook hands, pulled on sweaters, and left by the huge, richly carved front door with the brass knockers.

Chapter Two

The Inn

A short time later, with the early spring dusk creeping out from between the buildings, Harold Wilson, the old man and resident Innkeeper, dressed in a threadbare topcoat and matching Stetson hat, took his afternoon walk. He paused after shutting the massive doors behind him, buttoning his coat. The extra-wide wraparound porch was empty except for Josh and Hank, a short distance away, talking softly and playing cards. Josh's cigar smoke wafted by, triggering memories of camping trips and poker games. The old man smiled. Those were good times.

He walked down the wide wooden stairs and paused again on the sidewalk, looking back at the three-story Victorian house with yawning single pane windows, now dark as the sky above. The shutters and shingles were old but in decent shape, he thought. They weren't flaking or peeling and really had not faded with the passing decades. The slate roof, with two spires and three turrets all reaching for the deepening sky, was also in excellent shape. Oh sure, there was some moss growing on a few of the lower shingles but, all in all, it was quite acceptable. In fact, the entire house was passing through the years without any outward signs of aging. No one in town had yet noted this rather peculiar phenomenon. In fact, most of the town folk hardly noticed the house at all. It sat on a corner lot directly across the street from the new library – the pride of the taxpayers. People came and went all day and every evening from the brick and stone building, built to the exacting and ridiculously tight standards set by the historical committee. It continued to be a beehive of the town, fully utilized, sensibly designed. Curiously, with all the activity at the library, the large old house across the street seemed to be ignored, and to some extent, was overlooked even more.

Harold knew the grand old home had been built in either 1839 or 1847, depending upon which "historically accurate" account you read. At first, it was called the West End Inn, being literally on the edge of the New Hampshire wilderness. When the trains were running, it did a brisk business, but after the Civil War, the train arrivals were less frequent as vacationers continued on to the Green Mountains of Vermont. Eventually, the automobile extinguished passenger train travel altogether, and the old Inn was closed. Sometime around World War I, the Masons moved in and used the old building for meetings and initiations and all the other secretive activities associated with that ancient organization. Like many of the old associations, the Masons faded, and by the early sixties, went the way of the passenger train. The Inn sat empty for a number of years until, in 1983, it was purchased by an unidentified buyer for an undisclosed amount of cash.

Since that time, the landmark building slipped into obscurity, much the same way the miles of stone walls had essentially faded from notice by passing sport utility vehicles, crammed with families headed for 'pay as you go' outdoor adventures. The walls were still there all right, defining property borders of now-defunct farms and pastures, but had become an inconspicuous part of the New England landscape like maple trees and mountain laurel.

But the Inn, from time to time, drew the attention of opportunistic yet wildly imaginative 'historical experts,' offering 'Ghost Tours of Haunted Buildings and Graveyards.' This became big business in the fall when scores of 'leaf peepers' find their way to the pumpkin festivals and best apple pie contests that mark the onset of autumn. Open-sided tour buses crawled by every day, the intercom extolling the supernatural sightings and paranormal activities associated with the dark and spooky building. The fact that the visit always failed to produce even a disembodied moan or two did nothing to dampen the enthusiasm of these modern-day ghostbusters. Tourists paid their money just the same.

Occasionally, a Jehovah's Witness selling salvation, or a Girl Scout selling cookies, mounted the steps and utilized the brass knockers, announcing their presence. No one answered and eventually, the peddlers moved on. Sometimes, Century 21 left their card in the door, or Verizon dropped their latest offer in the mail slot but, for the most part, the Inn was ignored.

Taxes and utility bills were always paid in full, right on time. The grass was mowed in the summer, leaves were raked in the fall, and walks were shoveled in the winter. If anyone ever wondered who tended to those chores, they would have been unable to come up with an answer. But no one ever wondered.

Chapter Three

Madam Zelda

Harold Wilson was a man who thrived upon routine, and his afternoon walks were always the same. He would head down Main Street, passing by the glitzy boutiques, new age pottery shops, and outdoor cafés, then turn down Millwork Alley, an aging section of town not yet touched by gentrification. About halfway down on the right, he would go around back and enter the shop where Roselyn Clumpowski, also known as Madam Zelda the Psychic, met with her clients who pined for communication with their departed loved ones. Sometimes, when he arrived while Zelda was in session with a customer, the old man would slip into her crowded, dimly-lit séance chamber - the only source of illumination being an LED light cleverly hidden inside her crystal ball that cast ghostly shadows onto one and all - and take a seat in the back of the stuffy, incense-perfumed gathering room. On those occasions, Madam Zelda would break her trance and place two ring-covered hands on her orb. Then, in a ghoulish, baritone voice she would announce, "A messenger from the other side has joined us."

The old man would always smile and say something like, "Hi Roselyn. Good to see you again. How's it going?" The clients, all holding hands and trying to remain in their dream-like state, could not, of course, hear the old man.

Zelda would then hoarsely intone, "Oh, Messenger from the other side, gathered here are the grieving children of (here, Zelda would insert the name of some poor sap who recently died) seeking comfort in their recent loss. What news have you of their dearly departed father (or whatever he was) for them?"

The old man would then take out his pocket notebook, put on his reading glasses and, having done his homework, give a report about the person in question, usually lying about the departed waiting saint-like to be joined with his loved ones. Often, the departed would actually be playing golf in Scotland or gambling in the Caribbean, but the old man knew he shouldn't report the truth. It just wouldn't fly. Then as a kicker, he would always add a factoid or two that only the immediate family would know, such as, "Remember to take care of my roses out back, they need fertilizer," or "Tell your mother to stop hitting the bottle of brandy she's hiding under the bed," or "Tell my brother in Cleveland that I am well aware he stole all of Mom's silver and he'll suffer for that soon." The clients would always gasp, some bursting into tears upon hearing such disclosures, the detailed information giving renewed credence to Zelda's performances.

After a few minutes, the old man would tire of the emotional outpouring, rise, and say to Zelda, "When you wrap it up, I'll see you in the living room. Don't hurry. I know where you keep the scotch." Then he'd leave and Zelda would announce gravely, "The portal to the other side has been shut." And magically — by a switch activated with Zelda's shoe — the lights would slowly come up, indicating the session was over.

Once her astonished clients had departed, Zelda would join the old man. He always made himself at home: drink in hand, seated in the Lazy Boy chair, watching sports on the big screen tube.

She was an enormous woman of about fifty who really was as advertised: a psychic. For some reason neither she nor Harold could figure out, she could actually see the old man in his present dead state. Once they had gotten over their initial shock and surprise, they had struck up a friendship, and a working relationship. She provided him with names to be investigated, which provided her with credible information for clients. In return, Zelda kept him in top-shelf scotch and Cuban cigars.

Once the sessions were over, she would plop her generous girth down onto a leather couch and begin the process of removing her outfit: silk turban head wrap, scores of twinkling rings, oversized dangly earrings, and finally, using super strength makeup removing wipes, clean her face of the caked-on brightly colored cosmetics.

When the Zelda outfit had been put back onto the shelf for another day, Roselyn Clumpowski would emerge. Supper was generally a pizza from the local Domino's, and together, they would enjoy a fattening, greasy dinner together, washing down the sausage and mushroom special with more than a few beers. Harold didn't worry about calories or cholesterol because, after all, he was already dead. Roselyn didn't worry because she didn't worry.

After supper, they would sit and chat amiably – usually about sports and upcoming clients - and eventually, round about nine or so, the old man would thank his host and take his leave.

Chapter Four

Intruders

Later that night, just after midnight, Josh was stretching his legs. On this, his first night on the job, his assignment was to patrol the property and perform the tasks of a night watchman. It was boring work and he strolled around the house, staying on the wraparound porch, humming *You Are My Sunshine*, and chewing on a cigar. It was then he spotted them. There were four dark figures, keeping to the shadows, approaching the Inn. They were about two blocks away but were walking at a brisk pace straight toward the house.

Swiftly, Josh doubled back to where Hank was seated, reading the sports section of the evening news.

"Hank," Josh whispered. "Somebody's coming."

The two men crept around the corner to the back part of the porch. Sure enough, four human forms were coming their way. As Hank and Josh watched, the group passed by a street light and the men could identify the gender of the figures: there were two young men and two young women. They wore baggy jeans, piercings, chains and spiked hair, along with leather jackets and fingerless gloves. They all appeared to have purple hair, but in the low light, it was hard to tell. The group stopped at the bottom of the steps leading to the dumpster in back of the Inn. There, they opened a bag and took out several extra-large cans of spray paint. Hank mumbled, "God damned kids," and gave Josh his newspaper. "Watch this," he said, and then he walked down the steps, carrying hedge-clippers in his right hand. The four youths were shaking up their paint cans, and quietly trying to figure out where they should start with their artwork. They took no notice of Hank.

Hank walked right up to the nearest artist, reached over to the paint can and, with the clipper, cut off the plastic nozzle. Bang! The plastic nozzle flew off into the night, the pressurized paint filling the air in an orange haze. Hank repeated the procedure on the other cans and each one, in turn, BANGED, sending its contents out in an expanding cloud. In seconds, all four would-be vandals were coated with fluorescent paint, spitting it out of their mouths and clawing it out of their eyes. Screaming various versions of "What the fuck!" they stumbled backward, then turned and ran blindly away, yelling as they went. Josh couldn't make out exactly what they were shouting, but it was something like "Told you!" and "Haunted!" and a variety of obscene expletives.

When Hank came back up the steps, Josh looked him up and down. Although he had been in the middle of the chaos, he wasn't wearing a drop of paint.

"Well," Hank said rather matter-of-factly, "I don't think they'll be back anytime soon. Come on, I'll beat you in a game of cribbage."

Chapter Five

New Arrivals

It was well after noon when Josh emerged the next morning. He and Hank had dutifully fulfilled the tasks of night watchmen, chasing away the intruders but mostly playing cards and drinking single malt whiskey until eight in the morning, when they turned in. Showered and dressed, Josh followed his nose to the kitchen on the first floor. Delicious fragrances of baking loaves of bread and perking coffee were drifting up the stairs.

The vista from the sweeping grand staircase that flowed from the second floor to the first was impressive. Ornately framed portraits of long-gone Masons lined the walls, softly illuminated by yellow shafts of firelight coming from a vigorously snapping fire in the massive fireplace. A stately grandfather clock stood guard alongside a grand piano. Floor-to-ceiling draperies and various tapestries depicting days gone by covered the walls and the polished oak floor was covered with several oriental carpets. A scattering of overstuffed chairs and leather sofas completed the plush decor.

But none of that caught Josh's eye. Instead, he stopped in his tracks and took hold of the polished banister to study the two young women who were seated across from the registration desk where Harold sat. They looked to be in their early twenties, one a blonde, the other a redhead. The two were dressed in short, tight skirts, silky loose-fitting blouses, and dangly bracelets with necklaces to match. Although it was hard to tell from where he stood, they appeared to be shapely. One woman, the blonde, had her long legs crossed and was absently bobbing her six-inch heels. The redhead was filling out the registration form. Josh felt a heat rising from within, something he hadn't felt for quite some time. Neither woman was beautiful, but both were— well, hot.

And there was something else. They seemed vaguely familiar. There was a nebulous déjà vu sensation about the two women that harkened back to... He stared some more, but his brain, like a Rolodex madly flipping through all the entries, could not settle on a hit. The Innkeeper looked up from the desk.

"Ah, good morning Sunshine," he called to Josh. "Be a good lad and come on down here and carry our guests' suitcases to their room. They'll be staying in room six, right next to yours."

Josh looked over his shoulder to see if Harold was talking to someone else.

"Yes, Josh. I'm talking to you," he said. "There's no way my wobbly knees can make those stairs."

One of the young women, the blonde, spoke up. "That's hardly necessary," she said, reaching across the desk and touching the old man's arm. "We are more than capable of carrying our own..."

"Nonsense," interrupted the old man. "Social niceties shall be observed here as long as I'm the Innkeeper."

Josh made his way down the remaining stairs to the desk. "No problem," he said, picking up the two suitcases. Now he was able to get a closer look at the women. He had seen them before. Somewhere. Sometime.

"Have we ever met?" Josh blurted out.

The redhead laughed. "Sounds like a pick-up line to me."

The blonde stood and extended her hand.

"I'm Judy Johnson."

The redhead followed suit. "And I'm Linda Vincent."

16

An *explosion* of recognition went off in Josh's brain. He took a backward step, dropping and nearly stumbling over one of the suitcases.

"You," he stammered, pointing his finger back and forth between the two women, "weren't schoolteachers by any chance, were you?"

They exchanged looks and then laughed.

Linda Vincent folded her arms across her breasts, tilted her head, long red hair falling over her shoulder, and said, "And you Master Joshua, were a mischievous devil that tested my patience every single day when I had you in second grade at the Scranton Elementary School."

Judy Johnson covered her mouth. "Oh my God, you're right." She pointed a finger at Josh and, with a smile of recognition, announced, "And I had you in third grade. If I recall, you spent a fair amount of time seated front and center where I could keep a close eye on you."

"Miss Vincent? Miss Johnson? But…" Josh sputtered, blatantly looking both women up and down, "But…"

Linda raised her pencil thin eyebrow. "But what? Perhaps you don't recognize us because the last time we met, we had become, shall we say, full-figured?"

Judy guffawed, "Fat. Go ahead, say it. We were two fatties."

"And," Linda continued in mock indignation, "we were well on our way to becoming spinsters."

"We were indeed," Judy added.

"But," Josh said. "You, both of you, look, well…"

No words came out. The two women looked at Josh who was looking from one to the other, mouth open. Harold, the Innkeeper, sat back in his chair, grinning. Hank, who was over in his overstuffed Club chair, reading the newspaper, put down the sports section to watch the proceedings.

The fire snapped in the fireplace and the grandfather clock's ticking suddenly became much louder.

Finally, Linda said, "I'll take that as a compliment."

The old man pointed at the suitcases. "Now Josh, if you don't mind..."

Snapping out of his daze, Josh pocketed the key to room six, picked up the two travel bags, and turned toward the stairs, saying, "If you ladies would follow me."

Judy narrowed her eyes, smiled, and took Josh by the arm. Then she looked over her shoulder at Linda and said, "Things are going to be different this time around."

It was eleven p.m. when Josh crawled into bed. He was due to meet Hank at midnight on the porch for another shift of night watchman duty and was hoping a quick nap would help carry him to dawn without becoming too drowsy. Sleep deprivation is a serious side effect for third shift workers.

He was just drifting off when his door quietly opened then closed.

"Hello?" he said, reaching for the table lamp, but before he could switch it on, a hand took his wrist.

"Shhh," said a woman's voice.

Then he felt someone slide under the covers and move to him. Then he felt someone else slide under the covers on the other side of the bed, and press against him.

"What's going..." Josh began, but a finger pressed against his lips.

Both bodies were nude and now intertwining around his.

The woman's voice on the left whispered, "Like I said, things are going to be different this time around."

Josh was two hours late reporting to Hank on the porch. Hank studied him evenly, his eyes bright in the glow of his cigar.

"Sorry I'm late," Josh said lamely, avoiding Hank's gaze. "I, ah, overslept."

Silence.

Hank sipped his drink, ice cubes clinking in the glass. "It was just after midnight and I figured you might be sleeping so I went on up to your room and was about to bang on your door, but then I heard what sounded like moaning from within and bed springs squeaking. And I'm not sure, but I could swear I heard a woman's voice saying something like '*oh God, oh God.*'"

Josh exhaled and studied his hands.

"But then," Hank continued, "I figured you must be been havin' some sort of dream, so I decided to let you sleep."

Josh looked at Hank, and even in the darkness, he caught a barely perceptible grin and the twinkle of his eyes. "Yeah, it was just a dream," Josh said. "But it was a *really* good dream."

Chapter Six

Spring Training

"Come with me," the Harold said, pulling on his cardigan sweater. "Let's take a walk."

Josh, his hair mussed, slumped in his chair, looked up from his third cup of black coffee and blinked a few times. "Why?"

"There's someone I want you to meet."

A few minutes later, the two men were headed into town. It was an unseasonably mild spring afternoon and the first migrating robins had arrived, noisily announcing their presence. The sun seemed to be awakening after a winter of lackluster efforts.

The old man shot a sideways glance at his companion, who was clearly struggling to keep up. "You know, Josh, my old friend, even at twenty-five, there are limits."

"Not for those two."

"You might try putting a lock on your door."

Josh shook his head slowly. A week had passed since Linda and Judy had arrived, and between working the graveyard shift and nightly double fornications, he was about spent.

"When are they due to check out?"

The old man laughed. "I'm afraid I have some bad news for you. They have decided to stick around and work as housemaids during the upcoming busy season."

Josh stopped in his tracks. "Are you shittin' me? They're going to kill me."

"Too late," the old man replied. "Which brings me to a related matter."

They resumed walking.

"Your application to stay on as a handyman has been accepted, but before you start your new job, I've got a temporary assignment for you. I need you to fill in for me at the reception desk."

Josh frowned. "Why? Where are you going?"

"Clearwater, Florida. The Phillies are starting spring training in a few days and I want to take in all five weeks of it."

Josh stopped again. "Five weeks? You're leaving for five weeks?"

The old man straightened. "What's the matter with that? Can't I take a vacation once in a while?"

Josh grabbed the old man's arm. "Of course you can. Sorry. It's just kind of a surprise."

They resumed walking. As they did, they passed a house with a dog tied up out front. The dog rose and tail wagging, came out to meet them. The old man stopped to scratch the dog's ear.

Josh pointed at the dog. "Hey, I thought the living couldn't see us?"

"Dogs can. And cats, and birds. In fact, all living things can, except for fellow humans. To that end, there are a few rare exceptions, which, by the way, is where we are going."

As was the routine, the old man slipped into Zelda's dimly lit chamber and took a seat against the rear wall. Zelda, in the midst of one of her sessions, cast a hypnotic glance their way, but then, for the briefest of moments, her eyes grew wide and then went back to their dreaminess.

The old man leaned toward Josh. "She sees you."

Josh pointed to the people seated around the table, holding hands, and whispered, "Can't they hear you?"

"Nope."

Zelda, in her ghoulish, baritone voice, announced, "Two messengers from the other side have joined us."

The old man said, "Hi Roselyn. Good to see you again. How's it going?"

Josh pursed his lips. "I thought her name was Zelda."

"Nope. It's Roselyn."

One of the clients, an obese man wearing a New York Yankees baseball cap, let out a disgusted sigh. "Oh come on," he said derisively, "do you expect us to buy this shit?"

Zelda, unfazed and entirely composed, asked, "Oh Spirit from the beyond, we have among us a non-believer. What message should I pass on to him that would have him cast aside his doubts?"

The old man had removed a notebook from his pocket and was swiftly flipping through the pages. Then he stopped and muttered, "Gotcha." To Zelda, he said, "Ask him about the phony business he set up to dupe the IRS. It's known as Organic Dental Supplies, Inc."

Zelda, eyes closed, rubbing her crystal ball like she was massaging the head of some bald guy, moaned, and said, "Our messenger inquires as to the veracity of Organic Dental Supplies, Inc."

The eyes of the fat man in the Yankees cap flew wide open, his mouth moving noiselessly like some fish flopping around in the bottom of the canoe, gasping for air. Finally, he squeaked, "What da fuck?"

Zelda, on a roll, continued. "And our messenger says if further proof is required, he could see to it that the IRS receives a, shall we say, anonymous tip."

"Oh Jesus," the fat man croaked. "Okay, okay, I believe."

After that, the meeting ran its course and, as always, ended with the customers filing out, thoroughly drained and bewildered.

Once the session was over, Zelda came bustling into the living room, then halted, hands on her hips. She looked at Josh. "Who are you?"

Harold, feet up, drink in hand, said, "Ah yes. Roselyn Clumpowski, may I introduce you to Josh Matuszak. Josh has recently joined me at the Inn."

Josh stood and shook Roselyn's multi-ringed hand.

"You could have warned me you were bringing a guest. I almost fell off my chair."

The old man sipped his scotch. "My apologies. But you handled my faux pas just fine."

The psychic plopped down onto her leather couch and began the process of removing her outfit, thus morphing from Zelda to Roselyn. Pizzas were ordered, delivered, and the unhealthy feast commenced.

Reaching for a third slice, Roselyn said, "Nice work with that prick of a brother-in-law."

Harold chuckled. "When I spoke to the deceased, he warned me about him. In fact, he asked me to somehow get word to the IRS and nail his plump behind."

Between bites, she handed the old man a piece of scented stationery, covered with handwritten names. "New clients," she said.

The old man studied the list. "Which brings us to why my friend Josh has joined us. I'll be away for at least five weeks, and although he doesn't know it yet, he'll be filling in for me."

"Where you going?" she asked.

"Florida. The hapless Philadelphia Phillies will be holding their annual spring training and I want to watch all their games. I believe it's called the Grapefruit League. For a Phillies fan, I am well aware it will likely be another abysmal season, but hope springs eternal."

Josh sat back. "Timeout. I've got about a zillion questions, and since I'm hearing my name tossed around as your replacement, I think I have a right to know what's going on."

Roselyn and the old man exchanged amused looks. "Shoot," said Harold.

"First of all," Josh began, pointing at Roselyn. "How can you see us and nobody else can?"

The old man refreshed his scotch and added two ice cubes. "That's a very good question. The simple answer is I don't know."

"Me neither," Roselyn said, taking another slice. "Just is. And in fact, I'm a little surprised I can see you." She chewed thoughtfully for a minute and then continued, "Never knew I could until one day, I spotted Harold strolling down Main Street. I was sitting in an outdoor café and noticed him making his way up the cobblestone sidewalk, among all the tables with local yuppies who were drinking nine-dollar-a-glass cheap wine. I watched carefully as he moved among them: no one looked his way even though he was passing just a few feet from the customers. As he swept by, everyone pulled on their jackets and sweaters, complaining of a sudden chill." She looked at the old man and smiled. "So, when he came near me, I asked him to join me, and we've been friends ever since."

Harold held up his drink glass to toast their friendship.

"And," Josh said, "What about this list of names? And that notebook you're carrying in your pocket. And what's this about me filling in for you?"

"My, my. You ask many questions," the old man said, smiling. "The last one first. I want you to man the registration desk for me. It's easy as pie. I'll fill you in later. Now about the list of names, when we first met and I learned about Roselyn's profession, I offered to help. After all, most of her clients are interested in learning about the recently departed which, my dear man, like it or not, includes us. So, I snooped around and discovered that there exists what is commonly known as a DRD, which stands for Directory of the Recently Departed. The DRD has a website and most members can be contacted via email or texting, and they don't mind chatting on the phone. I've found just about everyone is more than willing to divulge virtually any earthly secret because, after all, none of us need anything from our past life anymore. In the case you witnessed this afternoon with Madame Zelda, he (the departed) told me all about his troublesome brother-in-law. Good thing. It came in handy." He looked at Roselyn and smiled.

"Damn right," she said, wiping crumbs off her double chin.

"So where do I come in?" Josh asked.

"This list," the old man held up the sheet of stationery, "is the new clients. I'd like you to investigate them for me and assist Roselyn here," he nodded her way, "in her sessions. In return, you can eat all the fattening pizza your heart desires, compliments of our hostess."

Josh opened his mouth then shut it. It didn't seem like a promising deal to him.

The old man guessed what he was thinking and winked, "One never knows when one will need a connection to the living."

While walking back to the Inn, Josh peppered Harold with questions. So much so that by the time they started up the steps to the Inn's front door, the old man had fallen silent. Josh started to ask more about the DRD, and then he looked at his friend and shut his mouth. The twinkle had left the old man's eyes and his shoulders were stooped.

"Hey, you okay? Josh asked.

The old man stopped before opening the massive front door and without turning, said quietly, "I miss Mary."

Chapter Seven

Up Into the Wild Blue Yonder

The next weeks, with Harold away, the tasks at the registration desk were anything but easy for Josh. The paperwork was murder. It seemed that the recently dead are a bit behind in using all the features of a computer, so many submitted handwritten applications and registrations in triplicate. Plus, details and forms and thoroughness were Josh's perennial weak area.

The big event during his first week on the job was the arrival of a group from a WWII B-24 bomber reunion. Nine guys, looking young and WWII'ish, showed up, ready to party. Josh assigned them to the third floor, and it took him all day to grind out the registration information. One unexpected side benefit of the Air Force reunion was that he was sleeping much better. Linda and Judy had also noticed the arrival of the flyboys and had found other beds to sleep in.

The fact is, Josh's relationship with the two former spinster school teachers had evolved into something more meaningful than getting sweaty and humping the night away. They met each morning for coffee and breakfast and often took a walk together later in the day. They called themselves "Three's Company," based upon the TV sitcom that aired back in the seventies, and they hung out together when their Inn tasks permitted. There was much about their new situation as RD (Recently Departed) that they didn't understand so together they tried to make sense of where they were, why, and how. One afternoon, they were out for a stroll and found themselves in an old forgotten cemetery containing fading granite headstones dating back to the early eighteen-hundreds. As they drifted about, reading the markers, Judy asked, "Why aren't these people here among us right now? Where are they?"

Linda tilted her head and looked all around. "You're right. Where is everybody?"

They both turned and looked at Josh as if he might have the answer. He shook his head no. "Don't know. That's a very good question."

Judy bent over and pulled a handful of weeds that were growing around a headstone. Upon straightening, she shrugged, "Maybe, we're just passing through."

Linda opened her arms. "But to where?"

"And to what?" Josh asked.

The three amigos exchanged looks, locked arms, and started back to the Inn. Josh ended the topic by stating, "Let's ask Harold when he returns."

Together, they made little progress sorting out all the mysteries and almost none of their questions were answered, but nonetheless, they became fast friends.

The morning after the flyers departed, Josh was enjoying an early morning cup of coffee with the ladies when he brought up a worrisome topic.

He sipped his coffee, and then put down his mug. "Can I ask you guys something?"

Linda and Judy, a bit frayed from a long night of amorous farewells, exchanged surprised looks. "Sure," they said in unison.

Then Linda added, "You have nothing to worry about."

Josh blinked a few times. "Oh?"

"Judy and I have decided we need to take a few nights off if you get my drift."

Judy blushed. "Just a temporary time out."

Josh laughed. "Not to worry. I'm just now catching up on my sleep. But that's not what I wanted to discuss." He suddenly became serious. "It's about Harold. I'm worried about him."

Linda pulled her long red hair into a ponytail. "How so?"

"He misses his wife terribly."

Judy opened her hands, palms up. "I'll bet there's a lot of that going around. It's one advantage of being single." She tried a weak smile and then sighed. "You're sweet for being concerned, but I think there's nothing that can be done other than wait."

"After all," Linda said, still fidgeting with her hair. "Time is on our side."

"I know, I know, but watching the old man is gut-wrenching."

Judy touched his arm. "You're a good friend."

Josh sat quietly for a few beats, and then said, "What if Mary knew he was patiently waiting for her? I'll bet that would put his mind at ease. And maybe hers as well."

Linda frowned. "You're making an assumption that she..."

"I know I am," Josh interrupted. "But I'd bet on it."

Judy sat back. "Okay, perhaps you're correct. But how are you going to do it? You can't just pick up the phone and give her a call."

Josh nodded and squinted his eyes. "I can't, but I know someone who can."

Chapter Eight

A Favor Por Favor

Josh took a seat against the rear wall of Zelda's dimly lit chamber and cleared his throat. Zelda, who was deep in the midst of one of her sessions, briefly opened her dreamy eyes and announced, "A messenger from the other side has joined us."

Josh waved hello but said nothing.

A woman seated to the right of Her Immenseness, Darleen somebody, was sobbing inconsolably. She asked imploringly, "Madam Zelda, please ask the messenger if my Harvey arrived safely."

Josh checked his notes. Harvey had not only arrived safely but was, at this very moment, drinking some kind of tropical drink on a topless beach on St. Maarten island in the Caribbean.

Josh gave her a thumbs up.

Madam Zelda went on and on for a few minutes about how Harvey sends his fondest regards and will meet her at the gate when her time arrives.

The woman on the other side of Zelda, apparently Harvey's twenty-something-year-old daughter from a woman other than Darleen, was a bit more pragmatic. "Zelda," she said evenly, "ask my father if he intended to have the trust he left me in his will administered by his latest wife."

Promptly, Darleen stopped sobbing.

"Oh, Messenger from the other side..." Zelda began but was immediately interrupted by a suddenly dry-eyed Darleen.

"Hold it right there," she said. Then, leaning across the séance table, Darleen continued, "We've been over this fifty times. I'm the executor. You'll get what I give you."

The daughter also leaned across the table so that she and Darleen were nearly nose to nose over Zelda's crystal ball. "If *my* father wanted you in charge of *my* trust, why didn't he tell *me* about it? It's in my name, not yours."

Darleen's face flushed with anger. "Because he knew you'd blow it like you've done with everything we've ever given you."

The daughter yanked her hand away from Zelda's and stood up. "What's this *we* shit? You never worked a day in your life. That was Dad's money and he meant it for me."

Darleen also yanked her hand free and jumped to her feet. "It's always the same with you. Gimmie, gimmie, gimmie."

"Me?" the daughter shouted with rage. "Me? You're the money-grubbing gold digger!"

"And you're a worthless little whore!"

"Bitch!

"Slut!"

The daughter tried to pick up Zelda's crystal ball to throw at Darleen, but Zelda beat her to it, wrestling it away from her.

Darleen stormed out the back door, followed by the lovely daughter, and they resumed shouting insults in the parking lot.

Zelda got up and closed the door. "Well," she said. "How about some pizza?"

They were deep into the second meat lover's special when Josh broached the subject. He took a healthy swig of beer then said, "I need to ask you a favor."

Zelda, now Roselyn, looked up. "A favor?"

"Not for me," Josh quickly replied. "It's for Harold."

Roselyn sat back and wiped her chin. "Go on."

Josh stood and paced around the room for a few laps, then began. "I'm worried about Harold."

Roselyn cocked her head. "Oh?"

Josh sat in the Lazy Boy chair where Harold normally sat and explained his concerns. He finished with, "He misses Mary terribly and worries that she might forget him, and I know that's just the way these things are, but then I got to thinking, maybe it doesn't have to be this way."

"Oh?"

Josh leaned forward and with some energy began. "What if you were to take a little trip down to South Carolina where Mary is living in one of those active adult communities, and just have a little chat with her? You could tell her that, as crazy as this sounds, you see Harold on a regular basis and he's still madly in love with her and waiting patiently..."

Roselyn held up her hand in a stop position. "For her to die, so why don't you hurry up and croak? Is that what you want me to tell her?"

Josh shrugged. "Well, maybe not that indelicately..."

"Let me ask you something," Roselyn said. "What if before you died, someone approached you and said there was someone near and dear to you waiting on the other side. What would you have thought?"

"Well," Josh stammered.

"You would have thought the person was some kind of whack job and sent him or her packing. Such a visit might not go as expected. This is a totally bogus idea, fraught with opportunity for bad endings."

Josh's shoulders sagged. "I was just thinking about Harold and how he'd be relieved if..."

"If he knew she knew he was here waiting for her? That would ease his pain. Correct?"

Josh nodded glumly.

Roselyn sighed. "I've grown very fond of Harold. He's the kindest man I've ever met, and I too, have noticed his growing anxiety and seeming depression. It's only natural for people like you and me to try to sooth those we love in a time of need."

Josh stood. "You're right. This is crazy. I'm sorry I brought it up."

"Sorry?" Roselyn asked. "I'm not. I think it's brilliant. Harold is worth the risk."

"What?"

Roselyn folded her hands on her lap. "Book us on the first flight out. Make sure we get the row with two seats in the emergency exit door row."

"Us? But I can't…"

"Of course, you can. Fat people like me often buy two airline seats so they can spread out. No one will give us a second look."

Chapter Nine

Carolina Lakes Adult Community

Other than a comical fiasco at the security metal detector - Josh kept triggering the alarm which caused the agents to search and fondle Roselyn repeatedly – their travels went smoothly. At the Charlotte airport, they rented a car and drove the thirty miles south to an active adult community called Carolina Lakes Adult Community.

The ambulance was just leaving by the time they reached the house belonging to Mary Wilson. Four women stood in her driveway, weeping, consoling each other. Roselyn slowly rolled by, but then went around the block and headed out.

Josh asked, "Where are you going?"

"Home."

"But, we've come all this way. Don't you want to find out…"

"The ambulance didn't have its lights on."

"So?"

She cast a patient glance at Josh and continued. "You don't have to be a psychic to figure out what happened. If an ambulance is in a hurry like they are when a person is having a heart attack or stroke or something, the blue lights will be flashing and the siren wailing. When the person is dead, there's no need to make a fuss.

And those women in the driveway — they weren't standing there for their health."

"Oh."

Silence.

After a few miles, Josh asked, "What do we do now?"

"Go home."

Chapter Ten

More Reunions

Back at the Inn, the pile of work awaiting Josh had grown to a small mountain. By the time he once again slid behind the registration desk, it was a foot high. Most of what he had to deal with were two reunions: twenty-six men from the now-defunct major league baseball team, the Washington Senators, and twenty-four women from Smith College's class of 1952. Clearly, the two groups had come ready to party and seemed to really like each other. By noon, the noisy affair was well underway and the Inn was in a state of bedlam.

Linda and Judy were doing their best to help move the groups upstairs to their rooms on the third floor but seemed to have no effect on the mob. Like an ocean whirlpool pulling in all the nearby flotsam and jetsam, they were soon sucked into the party and disappeared.

For a while, Josh circulated with a fist full of registration forms, trying to match the errant paperwork with the offending guest, but this proved to be a hopeless task. Finally, completely frustrated, Josh quit trying. He got up from his desk and strolled among the crowd, where, more than once, a partier asked him where he played and what number did he wear on the back of his uniform. At one point, he spied Linda and Judy surrounded by Washington ballplayers and Smith alumni, all with champagne glasses in hand, laughing at some story which was lost in the din. Josh sighed. The best he could do was instruct revelers to move it upstairs at the first break in the action, but it was no use.

As he made his way across the long great room, he noticed a young couple seated at the piano, off by themselves. They looked to be about his age. She was a pretty blonde with eyes so blue they could be seen from across the room, and he was a skinny, clean-cut kid with a mop of unruly, light brown hair. The two were singing, staring into each other's eyes. She was playing the keys and he had his arm resting upon her shoulder. Moving purposefully, Josh drew near, and as he did, he could hear the unmistakable notes from the lovely, timeless song, *You Are My Sunshine.*

Nasty Jake

Jake was an Araucana Rooster who lived in a chicken coop with seventeen egg-laying hens. In my sixty-six trips around the sun, I had never met anything as mean and nasty as Jake. He and I got off to a rocky start and our relationship went downhill from there.

We first met three years ago when visiting our daughter's small farm in Ludlow, Colorado. In addition to the poultry, she had three pigs, a couple of steers, a small flock of turkeys, and one delightful dog named Cricket.

One morning my daughter asked me to gather eggs. "Okay," I said, "I'll give it a try." Here's the drill; with a basket in hand, go to the coop, shoo the hens off their nests, take eggs, then wipe feet and deliver fresh eggs. Nothing to it. She didn't tell me about Jake. While I was bent over, reaching into the nest boxes, Jake silently stole up behind me and took a quarter-sized chunk of flesh off the back on my leg causing me to leap in the air, bang my head on the roof of the coop, and drop the basket, breaking all the eggs. I whipped around and there was Jake, strutting just out of arms reach. Grabbing the nearest thing I could find – the chicken's water dish – I hurled it at his head, narrowly missing, but sending him scurrying for his life. He stopped running and from a safe distance, fixed me with his black beady eyes, swearing at me in low guttural clucks. Wasting no time, I picked up the manure shovel and set off after him. In addition to being mean, Jake was quick. A few minutes later, panting hard, blood running down my leg, I gave up. That's how Jake and I met and we never again turned our backs on each other: he knew I would throttle him at first opportunity and I knew he would take another chunk out of me if he had the chance.

Twice, when he was arrogantly sauntering across the drive, I nearly got him with the farm truck. Another time, when no one was looking, I tried to spray him with wasp and hornet killer but he was on to me and kept just out of range. Then I nearly succeeded by running electric wire onto his favorite perch, atop which he would crow at dawn's early light. It would have worked except my daughter caught me lurking near the fuse box in the pre-dawn darkness, getting ready to run 120 volts through her miserable rooster. She interceded on his behalf and Jake received a stay of execution. He was after all, very good at doing what roosters do best. Plus he was extraordinarily effective at protecting his harem from all sorts of chicken-loving creatures that live in the wilds of Colorado.

The final episode with His Nastiness took place late one night when I was left alone to tend the farm while everyone went on a three-day river rafting trip. This was to be time for me to get some writing done on my novel. I promised my daughter I wouldn't kill Jake while she was away and all went smoothly until four in the morning of the final night of my watch.

I was awakened out of a sound sleep by the family dog, Cricket's, incessant barking. He was standing on the foot of my bed, excitedly hopping on all fours as he sounded his alarm.

"Okay, okay," I said, grabbing a flashlight and pulling on my jeans. "Let's go take a look."

I flipped on the backyard spotlight and peered out the window. There was a large black spot with a shiny nose and two bright eyes, standing at the edge of the lighted barnyard: a bear! Now, it is important to point out that all bears are big and strong. Some are bigger and some are stronger but even the lesser *ursidaes* are not to be trifled with. I had been warned that bears have a fondness for fresh chicken and I may be called upon to shoo them away. The details of precisely how I was to do this were a bit vague but so is everything in Colorado. I had not been given any sort of bear-shooing device such as a bazooka, so it was up to me to improvise. On my way out the door, I grabbed the hockey stick – a relic from college days - that was standing in the corner. If all else failed, I could shoot a few slapshots at it.

I started out across the yard, yelling and waving my hockey stick. Cricket was no help and proved to be a sniveling coward that stuck to my backside like a moon shadow. Mysteriously, the bear continued to hang back. Stopping at a safe distance, I discovered why. Anchored directly in front of the intruder was none other than Mr. Nasty, Jake the rooster. He was all puffed up and muttering loud threatening clucks like some poor sap inflicted with Tourette's syndrome. The bear seemed to be confused and would come no further.

Then, it dawned on me: this was the opportunity I'd been dreaming about. With a little luck, the bear would tire of the charade, pounce upon Jake, and make the world a happier, safer place. And best yet, I would not be responsible and could, with a clear conscience, report the facts of the case to my daughter, and how it was not me that snuffed out the poor, unfortunate (but deserving) Mr. Jake.

"Come on bear," I urged, my voice filling the silence of the night. "Do it! You can take him!"

Cricket whimpered.

Jake muttered.

I picked up a stone and hurled it at Jake, hoping to drive him into the bears drooling jaws. No dice. Jake simply sidestepped my effort and shot me a loathing look that said, *I'll get you for that.*

The hens, located behind Jake in the coop, were awakening, clucking with alarm.

It was a standoff.

Then, and I grudgingly have to give him credit, Jake fluffed up every feather on his bony body and charged the bruin. The effect was astonishing: the bear turned and ran away, its progress being marked by the crashing of branches as it retreated.

I dropped my hockey stick, cupped my hands around my mouth and yelled, "Come back you yellow-bellied, stinking coward!" But all I could hear was the fading sounds of the bear's departure.

Cricket stopped whining. The hens stopped clucking, and Jake strutted with renewed arrogance. I threw down my hockey stick with disgust.

Two hours later, the sun came up and so ended my watch.

Epilogue: The following night, the cowardly bear, wanting no part of a crazed roster, chose a neighbor's chicken coop to raid. Unfortunately for the bear, the neighbor had a loaded rifle under his bed. At about three A.M., I heard a single shot. So much for Mr. Bear.

Finally, about a month later, Jake tried the same stunt, this time with a Mountain Lion. The results were quite different, and as a result, the world is a wee bit kinder.

The Day Joey Lonzack Saved Me from Getting My Arms Pulled Off

Joey Lonzack and I met in the principal's office at Belcher Elementary School. We were in first grade at the time, and we had pooped in our pants. Our mothers were being called to come fetch us and take care of the necessary clean-up business. We would both be given a stern warning about the severe consequences of future pants-filling, and then brought back to school to resume our day of memorizing the alphabet or learning addition. The practice of returning a child to his or her classmates after a biological accident was thought to be part of the toilet training process— sort of a potty-training post-graduate refresher course, I suppose. Back then, it was believed that if youngsters were shamed by having to face classmates who had clean underwear after their own smelly adventure of having parents called in, the embarrassment would plug them up once and for all. Well, it didn't work that way for me and Joey. True, we didn't poop in our pants anymore (at least, not that I can recall...but then again, that was 57 years ago,) but from that day on, we became fast friends and remained so for all of Joey's rather brief life.

Joey and I became inseparable, had numerous adventures, and learned some of life's lessons together. One of our earliest escapades occurred after watching Walt Disney's <u>Swiss Family Robinson</u>. This was the movie where the castaways washed up on some Pacific Island and had a boatload of fun. After oohing and aahing through the entire film, we built a raft and launched it into the murky, opaque waters of the Chicory River.

I suppose the life lesson we learned at this juncture had something to do with planning. For example, did we really have a destination in mind? Well, no. Did we have oars to get back to shore? Nope. Were we just upstream from the outflow of a Hidden Valley Chemical Plant, the worst polluter of the Connecticut River Valley in all recorded history, dumping millions of gallons of dangerous chemicals into the sluggish river? Yep. All the same, the day started well enough and off we went.

Fortunately for us, a passerby spotted us drifting toward the toxic soda fountain and called the police, who called the fire rescue squad, who launched several small boats to come fetch us. There were flashing lights and bullhorns and a growing crowd of people. The local TV station was on hand to capture the dramatic rescue for the 5 o'clock news. I recall being quite interested in all the activity on shore. Both Joey and I agreed that they seemed to be mobilizing to pull some poor sap out of the river. At one point, we called to the nearest boat, asking the occupants if they wanted help. After some Abbott and Costello 'who's on first' exchanges…

> *Hello on the raft! Are you injured?*

> No, are you?

> *What?*

> Are *you* hurt?

> *Of course not. We meant you. We're coming to rescue you two.*

> Why?

> *Because you are in danger!*

We are? Us?

...the motorized, rubber rescue boat fleet - and this is a quote – "plucked us from certain painful death" and brought us to shore. Our abandoned raft, alas, was allowed to float downstream into the abyss, never to be seen again.

Needless to say, we had to answer some questions. We, of course, had no good answers and our parents were reprimanded for our careless and dangerous behavior. My father, stung by the accusation of irresponsible parenting, was motivated to administer punishment to fit the crime. I was sentenced to a week of hard labor cleaning out the chicken coop at my uncle's farm. Although the odor of aging chicken waste products is well beyond words, my Aunt Cecilia took pity on me and made sure I was well-fed with her baked goods...also beyond words to describe. Lunchtime parole was heavenly. She could do more wonderful things with Cortland apples than there are stars in the sky, and I think I ate them all during my time in the pen.

I don't recall what Joey's punishment was but, in any event, we both survived to once again set off on a new adventure.

Our next life lesson had to do with the hazards of becoming an entrepreneur. It was about a year or so after the Great Rafting Adventure (as it soon became known,) and somehow, we learned of a unique opportunity to line our pockets with enough coins to keep us in Rexall soda fountain banana splits for the balance of the summer.

Some people invest in precious metals or the stock market. We were about to invest in golf balls. Here's how our new scheme came to be. Joey's Uncle Stan, a roaring but harmless drunk, who, much to our amusement, regularly passed out and fell off his chair, was regaling us with a fantastic tale about a mystical force existing in the horseshoe-shaped pond surrounding the 18th tee at Chicory Country Club's Public Golf Course. According to Uncle Stan, this force would capture even a perfectly struck golf ball and suck it into the pond, never to be seen again. The bottom of the pond, he concluded, must be covered with golf balls!

Now this information by itself is curious, but not terribly exciting. However, toss into our recipe for a quick fortune the fact that the nearby driving range was paying fifty cents per pound for used golf balls, and bingo, Joey and I were in business.

It wasn't long before two skinny kids stood on the 18th tee of CCC, swatting mosquitos and staring at the pond. We were equipped with swim fins, underwater masks, fishing nets, and two burlap bags. Although our planning skills had clearly improved since our raft trip, we still had a way to go. For example, the pond we were about to enter was covered with green slime and choked with some sort of tentacle-like algae. Even worse, there were living things in the pond, such as snapping turtles, leeches, and water snakes. And did I mention the mosquitos? They were in the, "Oh my God!" category.

I remember asking Joey, "What do you think?"

"Are you scared?" he asked.

"No," I lied. "You?"

"Nope," he lied. "Well, let's get to it."

And with that, we entered the slimy muck hole and started kicking around. Not surprisingly, the bottom *was* covered with golf balls, and soon both of our burlap bags were half full. Once again, our lack of foresight came to bear. For example, burlap gets heavy when soaked…especially when half-filled with golf balls. Furthermore, every movement we made in the water was impeded by a thick coating of green yuck covering us from our heads to our flippers. The depth of the pond was about 'stand-on-your-tiptoes' deep. If you stood on your tiptoes and pointed your flippers down into the muck, you could barely push your face above water for a breath. Still, we were ringing up some hefty profits. Then, a series of events conspired against us.

First, as the golf course was adjacent to a local farm, at night when the course was closed, a squadron of dairy cows was allowed to come down to the water's edge to drink. When they showed up for their nightly refreshment, they didn't pay much attention to us at first, idly watching us as we grabbed a breath of air then dove back down into the pond. Then, according to the story Joey told, something enormous and wiggly found its way into his shorts, resulting in a swift attack of the panics. Like a penguin escaping from a killer whale, Joey leaped from the pond onto the shore…among the cows…and began flailing like a madman and screaming incoherently. The cows may not have enjoyed a skinny little kid flopping around nearby, but a green-slime covered UFO (unidentified flopping object) was terrifying. The herd, thinking they were being attacked by the Creature from the Black Lagoon, turned and fled. So far, so good. No harm done. However, the farmer, who had taken a pleasant evening stroll down to the pond to check on his herd, was bowled over and trampled by his frightened milk trucks, resulting in a waffle-iron pattern all over his body. Upon recovery from his stomping, he called the police.

About the time the officers arrived, a tadpole had been located and extricated from Joey's private parts, and we were just wrapping up our job well done; hauling two large sacks of golf balls from the water. Two of Chicory's finest stood waiting for us as we strained and grunted our loot up from the pond. There they stood; neatly pressed uniforms, donut crumbs on their bulging bellies, grinning like the proverbial Cheshire cat.

"All right boys," one of them said. "Let's go for a ride to the station."

I looked at Joey, he looked at me. In a flash, we were off. The policemen decided to pursue us. Big mistake. Skinny little kids, motivated by the fear of capture, can move REALLY fast. Plus, we were light enough to hop from grassy hummock to grassy hummock without tumbling into the swamp. Plus, we knew where we were going. Plus, we were unimpeded by decades of beer and burgers and (of course) free doughnuts. Plus, the police had none of these advantages and very soon, were wallowing in black, greasy swamp ooze that made short work of their clean uniforms.

Our one mistake was doubling back for our cache of golf balls. That's when we got nabbed.

Fortunately for us, and much to the chagrin of the two slime-covered policemen, the night shift supervisor at the CPD (Chicory

Police Department,) thought the whole escapade was hilarious. We were turned over to our parents (again,) but we were not charged with anything. Of course, we still had to face parental sentencing. My sentence this time was the pig yard at my uncle's farm. And Joey was directed to join me. We had to shovel out the entire pen and, using a wheelbarrow, move the decaying pig poop out to the tobacco fields. Actually, it wasn't such bad duty. Pigs can be kind of fun to ride (although they don't think so) and once again, Aunt Cecilia accepted the challenge of fattening us up with her scrumptious baked goods.

Following closely on the heels of that brush with the law, we found ourselves about to learn another lesson.

This time we discovered gravity.

The summer was in full retreat and school was fast approaching. One of the last carefree summer evenings found Joey and me on the hill behind the Chicory Department of Public Works (DPW.) We were lying on our backs, looking up at the night sky. It was a warm August evening and life was pretty good at the time. Joey, declaring he had to relieve himself, got up and wandered off into the semi-darkness.

"Hey!" he yelled. "Come take a look at this."

In the moonlight, Joey had stumbled over an enormous tractor tire. Why or how this mammoth tire found its way to the *top* of the hill behind the DPW yard I have no idea, but there it was. Without any forethought, we grabbed hold of the rubber beast and, with a fair amount of grunting and groaning, stood it up. It was bigger than we were! What a cool toy! Now, what in the world could we do with it? But, before any bright ideas popped into our mostly empty heads, gravity interceded. The tire, acting on its own, started rolling. We actually tried hard to grab it and arrest the downhill motion but that effort was futile. Off it went.

We stood frozen, watching the six-foot-diameter, incredibly heavy tire gathering momentum as it rolled down the hill. The moon provided enough light to follow its progress. It was heading straight for the DPW Quonset Hut Vehicle Repair and Maintenance Shed.

When it struck the back wall, it passed right through without even a pause. It reminded me of the Wiley Coyote and Road Runner cartoons where when one of them runs through a wall, it leaves an outline-shaped hole. The hole in the wall of the shed was a perfect rectangle. In the next nanosecond, loud crashing sounds reached our ears as the tire passed through the shed destroying anything in its path, before exiting out the far side.

We had seen enough. Employing our legs – since we obviously hadn't employed our brains - we took off at high speed in the opposite direction, never pausing until we reached Joey's house, where we hid in his backyard, panting heavily, listening for police sirens. When none came, we decided the coast was clear, so I slunk home and slid into my bed as if nothing had happened. To this day, I have never returned to that hill. For years, I wouldn't even go near the DPW end of town. I can only imagine how confused the DPW workers were on the next day when they showed up for work. As for the tire, as far as I know, it's still rolling along, flattening everything in its path.

Finally, I need to tell you how Joey saved me from having my arms pulled off.

In the last summer of our time together, Joey and I, being too young for real jobs, hired on as tomato pickers at Kroysonovich's Vegetable Farm. There is no need to sugar-coat the job…it was slave labor for low wages. The work was grueling but paid slightly better than my old newspaper route.

Commercially grown tomatoes are not staked up neat and tidy-like but are allowed to sprawl on the ground. This means harvesting is back-breaking work, either from hands and knees or hunched over. As a result of my time in the fields, I have a special place in my heart for migrant workers. But there we were, picking 'slicer' tomatoes and hauling the wooden storage carts to the end of the row to complete the next step of the process of making BLTs.

Among the unfortunate souls who were toiling at this task was a particularly cruel human being named Bobby Heinkel. We called him (behind his back) the 'Troll.' He was huge, dim-witted, and as mean as they come. I hated the Troll. One time, he hurt my dog, Duffy, hitting him with stones until Duffy yipped and cried out from a cut above the eye. I grabbed the turning fork and went after the Troll, and I would have stuck him if parents didn't intervene. We had several other exchanges of a similar nature. Needless to say, we became enemies. The Troll would have liked to get his wart-covered hands on me and perhaps remove a limb or two, but so far, I'd been quick enough to stay out of arm's reach.

Joey, too, had a score to settle with the notorious bully. One time while Joey and I were fishing at Fuller Brook, the Troll ambled by and stomped Joey's bicycle into a pile of twisted metal tubing. From that moment on, Joey and I vowed revenge.

But before we dive into the 'big event,' there is another important player in this tale: Mrs. Kroysonovich. She, the farmer's wife and neighborhood crazy person, was the supervisor assigned to oversee us kids in our slavery. "Mrs. K," as we called her, was constantly mumbling to herself in a voice that was borderline Tourette's syndrome, using a vocabulary laced with many words that I personally wouldn't use for a few more years. She always wore a dirty cotton dress, never combed her Medusa hair, and may have weighed 85 pounds when constipated. As a supervisor, she was vicious. Mrs. K dragged along a high-pressure water hose and would blast anyone fooling around, not working, or committing the most serious of crimes — eating a tomato. She was absolutely convinced we were eating all the profits and she was determined to catch us in the act.

A word about the punishment. It wasn't just a squirt of the hose. It was a three-minute blast with enough pressure to knock you off your feet. If it hit you in the face, you would always come away with a bloody nose and a black eye or two. It was no fun, and she was very willing to blast away.

So, there we were; me and Joey in one row, the Troll two rows over. Mrs. K was nearby, but focused elsewhere, scanning her slaves in hopes of peeling back someone's skin. This is when I hatched my plan. It was to be a pre-emptive strike in hopes of triggering a nuclear war.

I located a particularly rotten tomato – there were plenty to choose from, as sprawling plants lose about one-third of the fruit to rot – and held it in my hand. It was perfect — smooth, red skin on the bottom, black fruit rot on the top, full of juice. I caught Joey's eye and nodded towards the Troll. At first, his eyes opened wide, frightened of the potential consequences, but then his face broke into a wide smile and he nodded back.

As a young man, I played my share of baseball, often at third base. To play third base, you must have a good arm. Throwing the ball all the way across the baseball diamond requires some accuracy and a fair amount of oomph. Never, in all my years as a ballplayer, did I throw anything with greater accuracy or more oomph than I did that day in Kroysonovich's tomato field. Even now, if I close my eyes, I can still see the hefty slicing tomato, tumbling in slow motion, ejecting some of the rotten juices like a comet streaming towards the sun, heading for the Troll's head.

The impact was something to behold. I suppose it made contact somewhere between his cubby ear and tiny evil eye. Wherever, for one blissful moment, the Troll's head dissolved into an explosion of tomato puree!

Joey, quick as a rabbit, jumped to his feet and shouted to the warden, Mrs. K., "Look! Bobby Heinkel is eating tomatoes!"

Mrs. K, trigger happy as always, turned and saw all she needed to see...and let loose a blast of high-pressure water that took the Troll off his feet.

The Troll, being slow as...well, slow as a troll, had no idea what hit him.

Joey and I ducked back down to the path between rows of tomatoes and held our sides laughing. It was a magnificent sight! *Cel-e-bra-tion* time! The fast action by my friend, Joey Lonzack, saved me from certain dismemberment. I owe all my limbs to him.

Once the mess was sorted out, the punishment was administered, and the Troll was banished to the shed for the rest of the summer. The shed, usually spoken of in a hushed tone, was a most unpleasant place to be. It was a wooden garage where crates of tomatoes were stacked, awaiting delivery trucks to take the fruit to market. The shed had no ventilation, was infested with black biting flies, smelled of fruit rot, and was crawling with maggots. It was a perfect place for the Troll.

What happened next? Here my memory drifts into the fog of fifty years. Nothing much, I'd guess. The Troll was no longer part of our daily toils. In fact, rumor has it he is serving time in the State Penitentiary for multiple DWIs, but I haven't verified that. Joey and I picked tomatoes for the rest of the summer until school - Joey's final school year - sprang us free from servitude.

Shortly after school began, I learned one more lesson. I learned about leukemia. One day, for no apparent reason, Joey Lonzack got sick and died. Now, I think I have come to understand (or at least accept) the cycle of life and death, but the randomness of Joey's illness will forever be a mystery to me. Why Joey? Why not me? Why not his very unpleasant, bullying brother? And who made that decision? Was it totally random, like the flip of a coin, or is there some kind of a master plan? Even today, fifty years later, I have no answers to those questions.

Yet to this day, I still grow a garden in my backyard, and every year, I plant at least one Big Boy Tomato plant. Sometime in late August, I go snooping around the ripening fruits and find one with lots of rot. Then, in the privacy of my own backyard, I pluck and hold the fruit with its smooth red skin on the bottom, black fruit rot on the top, and full of juice. Then I fling it as far as I can. And think of Joey Lonzack. And smile.

A Kiss is Just a Kiss

The public address system interrupted my perusal of the New York Sunday Times. "American Airlines Flight 603 to Kansas City is 50 minutes behind schedule and is now expected to arrive at 2:06 at gate 16."

A few people seated close by mumbled something unpleasant and drifted off towards the lounge. Others slouched down and closed their eyes.

I sighed, returned to my newspaper, and decided to give the crossword puzzle a try. Recognizing my ineptness with word puzzles, I took out a pencil – and eraser – and dove in. One across: the midwestern state. *Hmm.* K-A-N-S-A-S. Next, one down: Hawaiian king. *Forget that one.* Two down: TV actress _____ Dickinson. A-N-G-I-E. Three down: slang for kissing. N-E-C-K-S.

I stared at the paper but the puzzle swam and faded. Suddenly, I was a sophomore at Central High in Salina, Kansas, on my way to pick up Angie Porter for a date – my first, her first. Dad's weathered pickup bounced along the dirt road as I tried – unsuccessfully - to harmonize with the Beach Boy's.

My older brother had briefed me on the finer points of dating. Go to the front door, shake hands with the father, don't stare at his daughter's body, talk about corn, promise to drive safely and be back on time, call him sir, etc. But he never mentioned an anecdote for the terror that was growing inside me.

I was about to abort my mission and turn back when there I was, at Angie's house. Mustering my courage, I pulled into the gravel drive, narrowly missing the light post. I was heading for the front door when the screen door flew open. Out stepped a little girl. It was Angie's little sister, aka: The Demon. She held her doll by the hair and glared at me.

"You fly's open."

Death, swift merciful death, please take me. I looked down, only to discover the barn door was closed.

"Made ya look! Made ya look!" she jeered. She was already missing her front teeth, probably the result of a similar stunt with a previous suitor. A woman came up behind her.

"Jamie Lou, go fetch your sister." She looked at me a smiled kindly. "You must be Kenny. Come in. How's your mother?'

My briefing was designed to prepare me to converse with fathers. This was a mother. I was on my own.

We stood in awkward silence.

"So," I began. "You're Angie's mom."

She smiled again. "Correct."

"How's the corn crop?"

Before she could answer, Angie came down the stairs. Her melon-colored hair was curlier than it usually was in algebra class.

"Hi, Kenny."

"Hi, Angie. You look..." *Don't look at her body!* I stared at the ceiling. Angie and her mom looked up at the ceiling to see what I was looking at.

"...nice."

We drove in silence past a zillion acres of corn. The Beach Boys had been replaced by those long-haired British guys.

"Do you like those guys?" I asked.

"They're okay."

"I think so, too."

Silence.

"Still want to go to the movie?"

"I saw it last week. My mother made me take my sister (the demon) while she went to the dentist."

"Do you want to see it again?"

"Only if you do."

Considering the two dollars admission I'd pay, I opted out. "That's okay. What else could we do?"

The Everly Brothers crooned on. Finally, Angie asked, "Wanna go parking?"

Once my larynx resumed functioning, I croaked, "Sure. Have any place in mind?"

"Take your next left."

I did. It was a grass-covered cattle lane.

"Go way over to the left, right against the fence. That way, we can't be seen from the road."

I nestled the pickup tight against the wire fence and turned off the ignition. The daylight was fading and the crickets were tuning up. A few horses were grazing in the pasture. Then it hit me.

"I thought you said this was your first ever date?"

"It is."

"Then how'd you know about this spot?"

"My sister's a senior."

Except for the crickets, all was still.

Angie broke the silence. "How'd you do on the algebra test?"

"Eighty-eight."

"Really? Me too."

More silence.

Under the cover of darkness, I felt emboldened. "What else did you sister tell you?"

"What do you mean?"

"Well, I don't know. I mean, did she...I don't know." So much for boldness.

"Kiss?"

"Yeah. That's it."

Angie slid across the seat until she was right next to me. She smelled good. I was terrified.

She asked, "Have you ever kissed a girl?"

"Do mothers and aunts count?"

"No. I mean real girls."

"Sure," I lied.

"Really?"

It was then, at the age of sixteen, I did something I hadn't done since I turned twelve. I told the truth.

"No. I never kissed a girl. I bet I'm the only sophomore in Kansas that's never been kissed."

After a pause, Angie said, "You're not the only one."

Although it was dark, I looked into Angie's face and could see her eyes searching for mine. She was smiling.

"Well?" I said.

"Well?" she replied.

She closed her eyes and leaned towards me. I closed my eyes and leaned towards her. Unfortunately, with eyes closed, no one was navigating. We missed our targets.

Realizing our error, we both laughed nervously.

Trying again, Angie placed her warm hand on my face for guidance and then moved in for our first kiss.

It was at that moment that one of the horses decided to investigate the goings-on in the truck that hugged the fence. Loretta, the old mare, hoping for a scratch on the snout, stretched her neck and put her head through the open window.

Just as Angie's lips were making contact with mine, she briefly opened her eyes to ensure we were on target. Although she was a farm girl accustomed to animals, the effect of the unexpected guest at such close quarters was alarming. She screamed.

Several things happened simultaneously. Loretta reared up and retreated, denting the roof in the process. Angie involuntarily propelled herself across the front seat, slamming into passenger side door, cutting open her head to the tune of seven stitches. I tried to leap up from my seat, hitting the rear window jamb. That one was good for four stitches.

The newspaper had fallen from my lap during my nap. Someone was standing in front of me. There, in a finely woven business suit with leather attaché case in hand stood a woman with curly, melon-colored hair. Her smile was as warm as ever.

"Hello Kenny," she said, extending her hand.

I jumped to my feet. "This is unbelievable. I was just thinking about you!"

"Sure you were," she said laughing. "You haven't changed a bit."

Our eyes met. Although twenty-five years had slipped by, it seemed like just yesterday.

"Your freckles are gone," I stammered.

"Thank goodness. I hated them."

The public address system interrupted. "Last call for flight 603 to Kansas City."

Angie softly touched my cheek, and then leaned into me, kissing my lips.

"There," she said. "I've owed you that."

Our eyes locked one last time, and then she turned and went to catch her flight.

The Door in the Tree

Illustration by Gina Ash

Introduction

Mrs. Violet Harriett Thayer died on May 21, 2015. She was somewhere between 91 and 95 years old, depending upon which story you believed. She took a perverse pride in being the oldest resident of Sherryshire, Massachusetts, and to ensure her first place status, she would skip over the even numbers now and then. The records of her birth, which likely occurred sometime in the 1920s, went up in smoke when the town hall burned to the ground in 1930.

Her body was discovered by her hairdresser, who had dropped by as usual on Monday morning to administer the weekly shampoo and set. Violet sat unmoving in her chair, a look of disgust permanently etched on her wrinkled, weathered face. The medical examiner figured she had been dead for about twelve hours— she probably expired right after the Boston Red Sox lost yet another game on their recent road trip out west. The word around town was that Violet, a lifelong Boston Red Sox fan, simply couldn't take any more lack-luster efforts by those "over-paid pathetic prima donnas," and simply died to avoid watching them get swept by the Oakland A's.

A widow for at least twenty years, she had lived alone, stubbornly refusing to move out of the drafty old (circa 1722) mansion. She had become something of a town icon, uniting the townsfolk in a joint effort to look after their colorful, often surprisingly profane, unofficial mayor. Valued at an estimated five million dollars, the acreage, colonial house, two barns, and everything therein, had been left to the historical society. And that was that. Violet's life was over, and all of her worldly possessions had been passed on to a worthy cause. There was nothing unusual about any of the proceedings, with one exception: the sudden appearance of a door in the tree.

Chapter One

Locking the door to the workshop and pocketing the key, I straightened my back and extracted my cane from the umbrella rack. It was pleasant to the touch, worn smooth by years of handling. When I first cut the ash sapling from the banks of the swamp out back and carved the gnarly grip, it was known as a hiking staff. Then it became a walking stick. Now, decades later, it has become my cane. Strange how simple trips around the sun have changed its function.

It was unusually hot for May and today was going to be another scorcher. I headed for the wrought iron bench in the deep shade of the ancient sycamore tree. Doug would be arriving soon with my morning coffee. Shuffling along, I took stock of my body. So far, no pain in my knee or hip, and my back pain was registering "low" on the back-o-meter. As they used to say in NASA's Mission Control, "All systems go." I lowered myself onto the bench and heard Doug's ancient Ford pickup truck struggling and straining to make it up the hill. If the wind was blowing my way, I'd smell it as well. Not today.

He pulled into the shady spot and killed the engine, which "ka-dunk, ka-dunked" a few times before exhaling noisily, expelling a significant cloud of smoke. Unfortunately for Doug, his arrival corresponded with the passing-by of Andi Lacy, the librarian, on her way to work.

Waving blue smoke away from her face, she coughed a few times, then shouted in her best witch's voice, "I thought you were getting rid of that heap of junk?"

Doug unfolded his lanky frame from the front seat, and with two coffee cups in hand, turned to face the screechy voice. "Oh, hi Miss Lacy."

"And how many times do I have to tell you, don't call me Miss Lacy. Makes me feel like the old maid I am."

"Okay, Miss...er...Andi"

"And what about replacing your truck? The citizens of Sherryshire are tired of the noise and smoke."

"I'm working on it. Savin' the best I can."

"And another thing," she stepped closer, the top of her head almost reaching Doug's chin. "You've got a book that's overdue."

"You mean the Chilton's repair manual for 68 Ford trucks?"

"That's the one."

"You mean someone else has come lookin' for it?"

"That's not the point. If everyone kept their books until someone requested them, our shelves would be empty."

Doug frowned, clearly confused. His mop of blond hair was still damp and uncombed from a recent shower. "Not sure I know where it is."

"Well you better find it and get it back to the library or else there'll be hell to pay."

"Yes, Miss Lacy."

She threw up her hands, shook her head, and stomped off towards the library.

As we do every weekday morning, Doug joined me on the bench and we sipped our coffees.

I adjusted my Ben Franklin spectacles and said, "A word of advice, my friend?"

Doug looked at me and blinked.

"Either arrive fifteen minutes earlier or fifteen minutes later. "You choose," I said. "That way you'll avoid the daily tongue lashing."

He nodded. "She sure seems to be crabby all the time."

"Don't take it personally. She's an equal opportunity crab."

I took out a twenty-dollar bill and slipped it into Doug's shirt pocket.

"What's that for?"

"Coffee. Forgot to pay you last week."

"Colin, that's way more…"

I smiled. "Keep the change. Call it payment for hand delivery. Maybe you want to put it towards your new truck."

He laughed his toothy country-bumpkin laugh, but then he suddenly became serious. Mouth open, he pointed. "What's that? Where'd that door come from?"

I sipped my coffee. "I've been thinking those exact same thoughts."

"Wasn't there last Friday," he said, staring at the door in the tree.

"Doug, there's a piece of paper tacked up on the door. I'll bet it's some kind of note. Would you mind fetching it?" I pointed my cane at a white envelope pinned to the door.

Doug walked to the door and cautiously, as if it might be hot to the touch, removed the white envelope, then came back and sat down.

"Go ahead." I said. "Open it."

He hesitated, then opened the small envelope and extracted a single piece of paper. It was stationery from the deceased Mrs. Violet Harriett.

"Read it."

Doug held the piece of paper, and in a halting voice – reading was not his strong suit – he read:

Warning!

Behind this door may be your deepest, darkest fear,

Or perhaps, your wildest wish held dear.

Open if you will, but what lies inside,

66

Only ye who opens will decide.

He frowned again. "What do you think that means?"

I took out my pipe and carefully packed it with English Cavendish tobacco. "What do *you* think it means?"

"Well," he said, absently scratching his head, "I think it means maybe something bad is behind the door, or maybe something good."

"Hmm," I said, between puffs as I lit my pipe.

"And maybe the person who opens the door will decide which."

I pursed my lips. "I think you've got it."

"But how's that gonna work?" said Doug. "I mean, is this supposed to be some kind of magic door?"

I puffed some more, then said, "I don't know. There's only one way to find out."

Chapter Two

Doug sat perfectly still on the bench beside me. The only thing moving was his oversized Adam's apple. Clearly, some internal conflict was in full battle within.

"Well," I said between puffs on my pipe. "Go open it."

He didn't move. "Do you think I should? You were here first. Maybe you should get to open it."

I chuckled. "I'm too old. Let me see that note again."

Doug handed me the paper, which I re-read.

"At my age," I said, "All my wildest wishes would surely kill me, and as for my deepest fears, I've already made peace with those demons. Oh, no mistake, they're still hanging around, but after all these years, we've figured out how to live with each other." I smiled and stared at Doug over my glasses. "You, on the other hand, have your whole life in front of you. Go ahead. Take a chance. Give it a try."

Just then a booming voice came from the parking lot. Pastor Balthazar, who presided over the local Lutheran Church, was striding our way. "Why don't I hear the lawn-mower running? We're not paying you to be sitting on your duff," he barked.

"Ah, Padre," I responded. "You're looking more rotund than the last time I saw you. Church living must be quite lucrative."

His heavily jowled, nearly-round face reddened. "It's *Pastor*, not Padre."

"And before you make any other pronouncements," I continued, "*you* are not paying Doug anything. You are merely a member of the board of this lofty historical society and thus have no fiduciary responsibility. I, on the other hand, am the executor of the will, sole legal counsel, and temporarily, president of the transition committee, which in fact makes me responsible for this estate and who gets paid for what."

He glared at me, hands on hips. "You lawyers..." He shook his head. "There are some people on the board that feel you have outlived your usefulness as legal advisor and should go back into retirement."

I smiled. "I'll bet you do." Rivulets of sweat ran down his face, dripping onto his bulging-at-the-buttons black shirt. He spied the door in the tree. "What the blazes is *that*?"

"Well Padre, we're not sure. We were just discussing it. It just appeared, as if by magic or perhaps divine intervention. That should be right up your alley. And this note was tacked up on it." I handed it to Balthazar.

"Is this some kind of joke?" he asked.

"Don't know. I was just urging Doug," I nodded his way, "to open it and see what's behind. Perhaps you'd like to give it a go."

Balthazar looked again at the note, and then said, "Well, if it will get the grass mowed, I'll be happy to open the bloody door, and we'll see how this is nothing more than someone's idea of a prank."

He took three steps toward the enormous tree and reached for the door handle, but just as his hand was about to touch the brass knob, he froze. The breeze that had been rustling in the leaves, stilled. From behind the door, Balthazar could hear a woman sobbing. Immediately, he was back in time, twenty-four years prior, one hundred pounds lighter, sitting on a bed with a quilted bedspread, alongside a young woman who held her face in her hands. He had his arm around her shoulder.

"I know this is difficult," he said, "but it's for the best. For both of us."

She removed her face from her hands. Her wet, blotchy face was a picture of misery. "How can you say that?"

Balthazar blustered for a moment, clearly not expecting such a question. "Well, well, neither you nor I are ready for an illegitimate child."

"Why not?" She said between sobs. "You've been saying all along your marriage is barren and without love. Here's your chance to start over. It will be *our* child."

"Oh, come on, Andi. Think about what you're saying. How would it look? The new pastor divorcing and fathering a child from one of the parishioners in the first two years of his tenure."

"Is that what I am?" She forcefully removed his arm from her shoulder. "Merely one of your parishioners? I thought you said I was your first *true* love. What happened to that?"

"Look, I know you're upset, but the Lord tests us in a variety of ways..."

"Oh, I see. Now it's the Lord who got me pregnant? And speaking of the Lord, what about all that *abortion is murder* crap you're always preaching from the pulpit?"

"Well," Balthazar abruptly stood and began pacing around the bedroom. "That's the church doctrine. I have to support their stand. This is different."

Andi stopped crying and stiffened. "How so?"

"I mean...how would it look?"

"How would *what* look?"

"You having *my* baby. It's not the right time. Don't you understand?" He turned and faced her, wringing his hands.

"No, I don't, but here's what I do understand. You came on to me and lured me into your bed. Then you got me pregnant. Now you want me to go to some doctor in Providence to have an abortion, so no one knows what you did. That's what I understand."

"Well, when you put it that way..."

Andi looked out the window. Resigned and calmer now, she asked, "What time will you be picking me up tomorrow?"

"Well," Balthazar stammered, "I won't be picking you up. I hired a driver..."

Andi stood. Although she was a full foot shorter, suddenly she seemed to tower over the cowering Balthazar. "What?! You hired a driver?!"

"Try to understand. How would it look if...?"

Through gritted teeth, Andi said, one word at a time, "I don't give a flying fuck how it looks. You're nothing more than a miserable, sniveling coward. How could I have ever thought otherwise? What a fool I've been."

"Now, there's no need for..."

Andi picked up a handheld mirror from her bureau and brandished it in his face. "I swear to that God you're always talking about, if this was a gun, I'd blow your fucking head off right now."

"Hold on, and try to be reasonable. We all make mistakes."

"Mistakes? Get out of my sight." She paused, regained control, and then said with great solemnity, "I promise you this; I will haunt you till the day you take your last breath. You will come to rue the day you ever touched my flesh. I swear to God."

Balthazar turned and fled. And as he did, he could hear her renewed sobs from behind the bedroom door, just as he could at this moment in the present, from the behind the door in the enormous Sycamore tree.

From where Doug and I sat, we watched Balthazar pause before touching the doorknob. Then his face went white, and then green like the color of a day-old bruise. The note fell from his other hand, fluttering to the ground. Sweat fairly oozed from his face.

"Hey Padre," I called. "Are you okay? Maybe you better come sit with us."

He staggered backward a few steps, muttering something about, "Got to go, important business." Then swaying like a drunkard, he shuffled away in great haste.

Chapter Three

Eyes wide, Doug watched Balthazar depart. Then he said, "What was that all about? He looked like he'd seen a ghost."

I nodded and fiddled with my pipe. "Perhaps he did."

We sat quietly for a few minutes, listening to the freshening breeze rustling the leaves. I packed my pipe but paused before relighting it. "Now, my friend, before we're interrupted again, why don't you go open that door."

Doug stood and took one step toward the door, but once again his progress was interrupted, this time by a loud crash and a woman's scream from the other side of the house.

Grabbing my cane, I hobbled along as fast as my legs could carry me. Doug ran ahead. By the time I turned the corner, he was pulling someone out from the forsythia bush. Clearly, whoever it was had fallen head first and all that could be seen were two legs sticking up in the air, flailing wildly. A muffled woman's voice pleaded, "Help! Help! Get me out of here!"

With a mighty tug, Doug extracted Mrs. Joyce Morgan from her predicament. When Doug released her, she plopped to the ground with a thud. Remarkably, except for a bloody scratch on her cheek and the appearance of being a bit dazed, she seemed to be all right. We went through the usual "Are you okay's?" Once I had determined that she was, in fact, unhurt, I stepped backward and lowered myself onto the porch steps. Then I noticed the old wooden ladder – usually used to pick apples from the tops of the estate's Baldwin apple trees – leaning against the house. The always stylish Joyce looked uncharacteristically disheveled: her blonde hair was mussed with twigs and leaves sticking out, she had grass stains on her stylish jeans, and one shoe and a sleeve from her white blouse were missing. I looked up at the window above the kitchen. There, attached to an errant nail, hung her other sleeve. And, strangely, she was wearing what appeared to be an empty backpack.

It took me two seconds to put together all the pieces. I already knew the answer, but I had to ask the question to make it look good. "Well," I said, "What on God's green earth were you doing up on that ladder?"

She grimaced, paused, and then lamely said, "Checking on the apple crop."

This was the end of May. The blossoms had just dropped. There were no apples, and we both knew it.

"Doug," I said, "Could you please run down to the drugstore and pick up some of those sanitized handy wipes? We need to clean that nasty scratch on Mrs. Morgan's face. I'll pay you for the wipes when you come back."

Eager to help, he was off in a flash. A moment later, the silence was broken by a fair amount of engine grinding and then vrooming, and finally, the unsteady roar of Doug's truck starting up. As the sound diminished down the hill, I smiled. "That boy needs a new truck." I paused, and then looked at Joyce. "Want to try again?"

As she pulled twigs from her hair, she said, "Whatever do you mean by that?"

"It doesn't take Sherlock Holmes to figure out what you were doing here."

She started to get up. "I think I'll be going."

"No," I said firmly. "Take a seat. Let's chat."

Reluctantly and somewhat gingerly, she sat back down.

"Why don't I give it a try," I said. "A few weeks back, when we were taking inventory of Violet's possessions, I noticed you lusting over the silverware. I don't know much about these things, but I'd guess they are sterling silver, antique, and worth a tidy sum. I also watched as you fondled the silver candlesticks. Remember?"

Joyce took a sudden interest in her fingernails. "I have no idea what you're driving at."

"You and I both know, as do all the board members, that this house will remain locked up and off limits until the estate is settled." I pointed to her sleeve flapping in the breeze, still attached to the second-floor nail. "That smoking gun hanging up there is a strong indicator that you were about to do some breaking and entering. You are in fact, damn lucky to be alive. How you didn't break your neck is beyond me. How am I doing so far?"

Joyce stared at me but said nothing.

I pursed my lips and let my words sink in. Joyce remained silent.

Trying another approach, I said, "Look, you're married to the mayor, president of the historical society, and you're the queen of all the social circles in our little town. What are you doing?"

Joyce shook her head slowly. "You have no idea how difficult my life is."

I waited but there was no more. "That's true I suppose, but serving time for common burglary most assuredly won't help."

Her eyes momentarily dampened, but that quickly passed. She set her jaw. "So, what are you going to do? Call the police?"

"You know me better than that. I'm a lawyer, not a policeman. But let's make sure we understand each other. Nothing in this house better go missing. Understood?"

She snickered bitterly. "Sure, sure, but you know what's going to happen? About six months after we move my historical society inside this fire-trap, the silver and candlesticks and anything else that can go out in a lunchbox will disappear. Some opportunist, maybe the plumber or UPS man will grab them. Happens all the time. Then what? You gonna have my house searched?"

I studied her face. No remorse. No regret. Only bitterness.

I stood. "It's hot here in the sun. Let's go around to the other side and sit in the shade. Doug should be back soon."

We no sooner plopped down on the wrought iron bench when she spotted the door in the tree. "What's that?"

"A door. Seems to have mysteriously appeared sometime over the weekend. And this was attached." I handed her the note which she read and reread with great interest. A change came over her face. In a twinkling, she went from an angry criminal awaiting sentencing to a prospector who just spotted a chunk of gold as big as his fist. Her eyes brightened, she sat bolt upright.

"I'd like to see what's behind that door," she stated.

"Go ahead."

Joyce jumped from her seat and stopped in front of the door, wringing her hands together in anticipation. She reached for the handle and almost touched it...almost. Then she saw them. Blue strobing lights, leaking out from the cracks in the wooden door. She had swiftly moved forward in time, to July 15 – the end of the town's fiscal year. The annual financial audit was complete, and the results were in. Hundreds of thousands of taxpayer dollars were missing or misappropriated. This had been going on for years, but now all indicators pointed in one direction. Bank records had been checked. Confidential testimony had been given. There was no doubt about it.

She watched the police cruisers pull to the curb out front. She turned from the front door, and there her husband, the Mayor, sat in his favorite leather chair. His tie was opened at the neck of his wrinkled white shirt, hair mussed, eyes glazed. His legs were crossed, shoes off, scotch in hand. The bottle on the end table was half empty. He was gazing off at somewhere only he knew. Or maybe it was nowhere.

"What the hell are you doing?" she shouted. "The police are here."

"I wanted to give you everything," he said absently. "It wasn't enough. It's never been enough."

"What are you saying?"

"All I ever wanted was to make you happy. This mayor shit, I did it for you. I'm no politician. In fact, I hate it and clearly, I sucked at it. Hell, I couldn't even take bribes without leaving a trail. And now, the good people of Sherryshire will understand why the budget couldn't be balanced. It's called embezzlement. Ah yes, what a slippery slope it is. It's so easy. No one ever asked any questions. They trusted me. Boy, I showed them." He shook his head slowly. "You know, I'm glad it's over." He smiled and took another huge swallow.

She stood in shock. "What will happen to me?"

"And thank you for your concern about me," he said sarcastically. "Me? I'll be going away. You won't have to pretend to be my loving wife anymore." He shook the glass, ice cubes clinking. "You? You will lose this house, the BMW, the furniture, jewelry, and in fact, most of the possessions. They belong to the bank and when the payments stop arriving...." He emptied his glass, and then refilled it. "Basically, you're fucked."

She turned away from her husband, moved the curtains to one side, and peered out. Two men in dark suits were walking up the driveway. Police were standing alongside their cars. The mobile van from WBZ –TV was parked down the street. Some talking head was interviewing the District Attorney. A small crowd of townspeople had gathered. And all the while, blue lights strobed in her face.

Joyce stepped back from the tree. In a small voice, she said, "Make them stop."

"Pardon me? What did you say?"

She stood as still as Lot's wife, staring at the door in the tree. Doug was returning, his truck backfiring as he made his way up the hill. He came running, sanitary wipes in hand.

"I got 'em," he said panting, holding up the box of tissues. He looked from Joyce to me then back to Joyce. "I got 'em," he said again.

Without a word, Joyce turned and walked down the driveway, took a left on the sidewalk and kept on walking.

Doug, mouth agape, looked at me for some sort of explanation.

I smiled. "You need a new truck."

Chapter Four

Hardly had Joyce turned the corner when the telltale crunch of gravel underfoot foretold of yet another visitor coming our way. At first, I thought it was Joyce returning, but to my surprise, the person who came around the corner was Andi. I was certain she was approaching to give Doug another earful about his truck, but once again I was wrong.

She held up a shoe box. "Earlier when I came by, I forgot to give these to you two lazy bums."

Doug accepted the box and opened it. The delightful odor of freshly made chocolate chip cookies filled the air.

In her piercing, witch's voice, she began speaking in eyebrow-raising rapid fire. "I made too many this morning when I couldn't sleep as long as I usually do, because we're having all those bratty school kids in today for lunch, and you have to feed them something or they'll complain to their pandering parents and then the library catches hell. And, since I had way more than necessary, and if you give the kids too many, they get all hyper and start running around and yelling, and then I have to get mean to shut 'em up, I decided to bring some over to you two. I figured maybe if I bribed you, you'd get some work done instead of sitting around, smoking your pipe and telling tales," she said, pointing a shaking crooked finger at me. To Doug, she said, "And you, being a dumbstruck audience for him, instead of mowing the grass and earning money to replace that damned truck.

By the way young man, you might try combing that hair of yours. You look like the scarecrow in Wizard of Oz. And tuck your shirt in while you're at it."

Doug quickly did so.

I laughed aloud. "How many cookies have *you* eaten?"

"I have to try my bakin' to see if it's edible, although chocolate makes me a bit buzzy."

"Just a *bit?*"

"And another thing," Andi continued. "What in the world did you do to Joyce Morgan? I just passed her on the sidewalk and she looked like she'd lost a battle with a hedgerow."

I cast a glance at Doug, winked, and said, "Something like that."

"Didn't say a word. Passed me right by like I wasn't there. Some people around here think they're better than others."

"Don't mind her. I think she had a lot on her mind."

Andi was fanning her flushed face. "Damn flashes. Chocolate does it every time."

I shuffled over and took her by the arm. "Come sit with me. You look like you need to get off your feet."

We settled down on the wrought iron bench, all the while Andi chatting rapid fire about the state of the library world and how the newer generation is too involved with their electronic media to give a fiddler's damn about the printed page. Then, abruptly, she stopped and pointed at the tree. "What's with the door?"

I shrugged.

Doug, who had melted into the shadows, stepped forward and spoke up. "Don't know much about it, Miss Lacy. Showed up this weekend. Check out the note that was tacked up on the front of it." He handed her the single sheet of paper which she studied.

"Whose idea is this?"

Doug held up his hands defensively. "I swear, I had nothin' to do with it."

She glared at me and I shrugged and shook my head.

"So, this door just magically appeared out of thin air?"

Doug and I exchanged glances but said nothing.

She jumped to her feet and straightened her blouse. "Well let's get to the bottom of this right now."

Andi walked across the longish grass and reached for the doorknob. And like her predecessors, her hand stopped short. Unlike her predecessors, she heard nothing and saw nothing from behind the door. But it was the silence – absolute, dead silence – that stopped her. Suddenly, she was back in time, twenty-three years prior sitting on a bed with a quilted bedspread. Alongside the bed was an infant's crib. It was empty. It was silent.

A week prior, when the adoption agency came for her son, she had turned them away, unable to release her child. On this day, she let him go. And now there was no sound.

She would no longer feel his tiny hands closing around her finger. She would no longer be able to silence his cries by pulling him close to her breast as they slept.

The agency had been kinder and more understanding that she thought possible. They gave her pills for depression, pills to help her sleep, and pills to dry up the milk in her painfully swollen breasts. But they could do nothing about her broken heart.

The silence was absolute.

Andi slowly turned from the door and fixed on Doug, who cowered back from the intensity of her stare. Her voice was steady now, measured and direct. "Stand up straight. You're starting to stoop, and it looks like hell. You're tall. Be proud of it."

Then she spun on her heels and strode back toward the library, gravel crunching under her feet.

Chapter Five

Doug watched her go. "This is really freaking me out."

"How so?"

"There's something about that door. Everyone acts really weird around it. It's starting to give me the creeps."

I took off my glasses, and with a red kerchief, gave them a cleaning. "All the more reason to go open it up and see what's behind it. You might want to do it quickly before someone else comes by."

He slowly shook his head. "Not so sure anymore."

I felt my shoulders slump. After a moment, I got to my feet. "All right then, I'll open it." I took a step towards the door, but Doug jumped in between me and the tree.

"Hold on," he said. "You said whatever was behind that door might kill you. You know what I mean, your age and all."

I smiled. "I was referring to some of my favorite sexual fantasies that might be, what was that...*my wildest wish held dear?* And yes, at my age it may be lights out, but what a way to go."

Doug looked grim. "Colin, I can't let you do that. I mean, what if..."

I put my hand on his shoulder. "I'm touched, but one of us has to open it. This has gone on long enough."

Racked with indecision, he shuffled from one foot to the other, then, he snapped his fingers. "I've got an idea. Give me some time to work up my nerve. How about I mow the grass, and when I'm done, I'll open it. And if I'm still freaked out, well then, maybe…"

I turned and sat back down. The day was warming up fast, and I could use a few minutes of quiet time. "Fair enough."

Doug bounded off, and soon I could hear the John Deere starting up and the mowing process begin.

It was a mesmerizing sound, like the humming of many bees, ebbing and flowing, and soon my eyes grew heavy and I was out. Seemingly an instant later, I awoke with a start. It took me a second to realize I wasn't alone. Seated next to me was the last remaining U.S. Postal Service mail carrier who performed all her duties on foot: Alice Menard.

"Have a nice nap, old man?"

I blinked a few times. "Just resting my eyes. How long have you been sittin' here?"

"About five minutes. I didn't know if you had died or were just taking a nap. Since I have to deliver all the estate's mail to you in person, I'm glad you're not dead. If you were, I would have been in a real quandary as to what to do with your mail."

"Glad to save you the trouble."

Alice, hair white as snow, pushing sixty but trim and firm, stretched out her long legs and rubbed her knees. "My legs are telling me to retire. Pretty soon, I guess." She nodded towards the door in the tree. "Some kind of practical joke?"

"Don't know. Doug and I discovered it this morning. This note was tacked to it." I handed her the sheet of paper.

Pushing a lock of hair from her face, she read it aloud:

Warning!

Behind this door may be your deepest, darkest fear,

Or perhaps, your wildest wish held dear.

Alan R. Mulak

Open if you will, but what lies inside,

Only ye who opens will decide.

I smiled and asked, "Want to give it a try?"

She pursed her lips and shook her head no. "Well, if this is somehow legit and not some prop for a YouTube video, someone else will have to open the door."

"Oh?"

She pulled her hair back and using a rubber band, tied it into a ponytail. Her deeply tanned, weathered face became strangely serious. "Here's my story. I've got a husband who loves me and holds me all night. My two adult kids finally found suitable mates and have decent jobs. Our four grandchildren are the joy of my life. We're all healthy and reasonably well off. No debt. No bills." She looked at me, her blue eyes searching my face. "I don't need anything. All my wishes have come true. And as for fears— at my age, they don't scare me anymore."

I nodded. "Well said. My feelings exactly."

Alice sat for several silent beats, and then said, "It's all about choices, isn't it?"

I folded the note and put it in my shirt pocket. "Are you referring to this note or…?"

"Life," she said. "Life is all about choices." Then she pointed at the tree. "We are who we are because of the choices we've made."

I raised my eyebrows. "Quite astute for a mail lady. Is that a famous saying by some philosopher?"

"Yep. Me."

I chuckled.

Alice stretched her legs again. "I'll bet some of our neighbors here in town would find some pretty interesting wishes and fears behind that door."

"Once again," I said, taking out my pipe. "You are correct." I related the attempts to open the door by Pastor Balthazar, Joyce Morgan, and Andi. And how they all failed. And how they all fled.

Alice nodded again but said nothing. We sat quietly for a moment, listening to the mower go back and forth. Then she gestured toward the note and said, "If I'm not mistaken, I believe that's in Violet's handwriting."

Adjusting my glasses, I made a show of studying the note. "Perhaps," I said. "You might be correct."

Staring at the door, she said, "I'd ask you how you're doing, but I already know. So maybe I'll put it this way. How bad are you hurtin'?"

My eyes suddenly moistened and I turned away, wiping them with the back of my hand.

I cleared my throat. "Sorry. Allergies."

"My ass."

I absently fiddled with my pipe for a minute or so and then began. "Violet and I go back, or I should say, *went* back, forty-four years. When we met, it was wildly exciting. After all, she was an older woman by ten years, give or take, and that in itself was a kick." I smiled, recalling those early days. "We had terrific sexual escapades, all hush-hush of course. I'd sneak in the back door after dark and slip out before dawn. Sometimes, we'd get away to a country inn for the weekend, going in separate cars, only to rendezvous in our room. The secrecy added to the erotic tension. Great stuff. We thought we were a well-kept secret, but I don't think so."

"You weren't."

"All the same, we believed it. But you know, after a while, I began looking forward to sitting in the porch swing together, watching the stars come out, sipping a glass of wine, as much as all the physical stuff. Over the years, our time together shifted from the bedroom to playing Scrabble or eating ice cream cones and simply holding hands and going for a stroll. It was wonderful." I looked at Alice. She was gazing at me. "You asked how bad I'm hurting? Violet's passing, it's like having a major part of me amputated. There's this huge hole in my body. And every morning I wake up, thinking this is a bad dream, but then I realize, it's not a dream. It's real." I paused, fighting off tears. "My life will never be the same."

She nodded, then reached over and touched my hand. "Why didn't you guys marry?"

"We talked about it. A lot. But that was always going to happen sometime in the future. Maybe we felt our life was so perfect, why take a chance and screw it up. I think the real answer is we simply never got around to it."

Alice and I fell silent again. The humming of the mower was the only sound. She pointed at Doug, "It's great you took him under your wing. He's a good kid."

"Yeah, he is. And you know, it was actually Violet's idea. She really cared for him."

Alice leaned closer, a bit conspiratorially, and said, "So does Andi."

I blinked. "You *know* about that?"

"Hey, us mail ladies don't miss a trick." Suddenly, she sat upright and turned to face me. "I almost forgot. Did you hear the news?"

"What news?"

"Our mayor has flown the coop."

"Bill Morgan?"

"Yep. He apparently took off sometime overnight. Left a letter of resignation on his desk. His secretary found it first thing this morning. The town is buzzing."

"And Joyce?"

Alice shrugged. "No word on her. Apparently, she's still around somewhere. A lot of us wish she had left with her husband."

I nodded.

"You don't look surprised."

"No, I'm not." I said. "I've been wondering how long Bill was going to remain our mayor. I figured he'd either take off or get thrown in jail. As for Joyce, she was just here, less than an hour ago."

"And?"

"She didn't say anything about Bill being gone."

Alice waited for me to continue, but I chose to leave it at that.

"I hear," Alice continued, "the police chief has ordered an investigation."

I chuckled. "That should be good. This will be a classic case of the fox guarding the chickens."

Alice stood, stretched, and shouldered her mailbag. "You take care, old man."

"You too."

Chapter Six

Lost in thought, I didn't notice Doug's approach. When I looked up, he was standing in front of me.

"I've decided I'll do it," he said frowning. "I don't want to, but I can't let you…you know."

I smiled, nodded at the door, and waved him on.

Much to my surprise, he covered the ground in three swift strides, grabbed the doorknob, and threw it open. Inside there was nothing dark and mysterious but instead, just the gnarly base of the tree. Attached to the tree opposite the door was a large brown envelope with Doug's name written on the front. Hands shaking, Doug took the envelope and came back and sat down alongside me.

He was breathing hard.

"Well," I said, "I think you better open it."

He took a deep breath, then did so, and pulled out the various papers from within. He frowned as he examined them. "What is this?"

I adjusted my glasses, gently took the pile of papers, and looked them over.

"It appears," I began, "that this is a title to a four-wheel drive 2015 Ford Pickup Truck, red in color, paid in full. And this document, let's see, is a receipt for three years' worth of auto insurance, also paid in full. And all this is made out to you."

Doug sat motionless, clearly stunned.

"I think my good man," I said, "all you have to do is drive down to Sherryshire Ford and drive away with your new truck."

"My wildest wish," Doug said quietly. "But how…?"

I shrugged.

He looked at me for a long minute and then narrowed his eyes. "You did this, didn't you?"

"I was merely following instructions."

He looked down at his feet. "I don't know what to say."

"Andi will be thrilled."

Doug laughed. Then he went serious again. "But what about the others, how weird they got around the door? How did that happen?"

I sat back and stared at the door. "I was surprised. I guess when you let your imagination run wild, anything can happen."

"Wow," he said. "What a day."

"Now, why don't you go fetch that truck? The raking can wait until tomorrow."

He smiled broadly, jumped to his feet, then – to my surprise and his I suspect – leaned down and gave me a hug. Gathering all the paperwork, he nodded and said, "Thanks."

I watched him go, blue exhaust smoke hovering in his wake, and listened to the roar of the engine grow fainter and fainter. When all was quiet again, I took out my cell phone and punched in some numbers.

"Ralph's Home Repair, this is Ralph speaking."

"Colin here. Please come take down the door you put up last night. Come after dark. Don't let anyone see you. And you can keep it or bring it to the dump. It's yours."

After a while, I got up, walked over and closed the door, then headed for the workshop. I took out the key and stepped in. There, pinned up on the wall, was a picture of Violet – my very favorite - in her younger years. She wore a Red Sox cap and was wrapped in a flowery boa.

"Well, Violet, I've carried out your final request. It's been quite a day, but then again, I'm sure you knew it would be. This was our final secret, our last bit of business. Now, all I have is our memories."

I closed the door to the workshop and pocketed the key. Cane in hand, I started home. And this time, I didn't bother to wipe away my tears.

The Mysterious Christmas Package

I was in the middle of emptying the dishwasher when my phone rang. I could see by the caller ID it was my editor from Massachusetts.

"Hi Dave, Merry Christmas."

"Yeah, same to you. Listen, I'm between classes and don't have much time but wanted to provide you with some feedback on your novel, specifically chapters seven and eight."

I leaned back on the kitchen counter. "Okay, shoot."

"Good stuff," he said. "Your characters are dynamite, the writing is crisp, and the story makes the reader want to stay up all night to see how it ends." But then he fell silent.

"But..." I asked.

"You and I are good friends so I think I can be brutally frank. Agree?"

I hate when people say this. "Fire away."

"Your sex scenes need work. Lots of work. In fact, they're rubbish. Start over."

I blinked several times.

"You still there?" he asked.

"Yeah. I thought they were..."

"Well they're not," he said. "You need to turn up the heat. Take a look at one of Ken Follett's novels. He writes great sex scenes. The best is in Lie Down with Lions. It'll make you need to take a cold shower. That's the type of scene you need to write."

90

"But," I objected lamely, "I thought I had…"

"You didn't," he said, again interrupting me. "Yours are like a Wikipedia description of human reproduction 101. And you resort to telling, not showing. Your readers are adults and enjoy a torrid tale from time to time."

"But…"

"Admittedly, sex scenes are damn tough to write," Dave said. "Many accomplished writers do a terrible job with them, but when they're done right, it's a wow."

"But…"

"Don't worry about what other people think," he insisted. "Chances are they'll think you're hot stuff because you're writing what they fantasize about."

"My mother won't," I said lamely.

"You might be surprised," Dave said. "Look, I gotta go. Re-write the sex parts and get them to me by this weekend," and then he was gone.

I was about to go look through the bookcase for a Ken Follett novel when I heard a thump at the front door. By the time I swung it open, a FedEx truck was driving away and there was a package at my feet. I picked it up and my eyes were drawn to the return label: Frederick's of Hollywood.

"What the …" I said aloud. "What kind of cosmic coincidence is this?"

Heading back into the kitchen, I poured a cup of coffee and stared at the parcel wrapped in brown paper. Frowning, I mused, "I didn't order anything from Frederick's and it's unlikely my wife did."

I took out a knife and opened the package. The only note was a card reading "Frederick's wishes you a Merry Christmas and is sure – *wink, wink* - you'll enjoy this gift." Pushing back the wrappings, I extracted the contents. The bra was silky and bright red, but enormous. I checked out the size – 38DD. Then I lifted the matching thong panties, size XXL. They were so big they could have been used for of one of those *trebuchets* used to hurl large projectiles at walled castles during a medieval siege. *What the fuck?*

For reasons I'll never fathom, I immediately assumed these two items were sent as some sort of secret message. My first thought was they were sent by Dave my editor, as kind of a not-so-subtle hint to write better sex scenes. But that didn't make sense. He was too cheap.

Then my scrambled brain jumped to another source: a girlfriend going back about forty years, well before I met my wife, Ann. She was big. Not Ann who is petite but the girlfriend. She was the shot put champion from UNH. Although when I thought back, I couldn't recall her being *that* big. Was this her way of surreptitiously contacting me and telling me...telling me what? That she was interested in reconnecting? This could go very badly, plus, she could break me like a twig.

Then the door opened and Ann had arrived. "Hi Honey, I'm home. Please give me a hand."

Quick as a flash, I threw the bra and panties into the dishwasher and slammed it shut.

As we carried in the sacks of groceries, I casually asked, "We're not buying each other Christmas gifts anymore, correct?"

"Correct. We stopped several years ago, remember?"

I nodded and we set to work putting away the food. Then Ann reached for the dishwasher and started opening it. I leaped forward and shoved her out of the way.

She looked at me, mouth agape.

"That's *my* job," I said defensively. "I'll empty it."

"I just wanted to get out my teacup."

"I'll get it for you."

Ann cocked her head slightly. "What's going on?"

"Nothing," I replied, my voice an octave higher than normal.

She stared at me for a long time and then, while leaving the kitchen, mumbled, "Have it your way."

My most immediate concern was to get rid of the extra-large intimates. I felt like I was in one of those TV crime shows where I yell at the screen and urge the numbskull actor to ditch the incriminating evidence. Now I realized it may not be that simple.

The opportunity presented itself when Ann's sister called. They were both long-winded. I knew I had about an hour.

My first thought was to throw the undies into my trash can. No good. Ann might peer into the container and I'd have some explaining to do. Then I came up with a brilliant idea; sneak the items into one of my neighbor's trash cans. Tomorrow was trash pick-up day and some of our more compulsive neighbors put their trash out to the curb a day early. Stuffing the bra and panties under my sweatshirt, I crept outside and looked both ways. The coast was clear. Sure enough, there were several trash cans already standing guard on the curb.

Now, one problem with living in an adult community is the dog walkers. They're always out. Doesn't matter what time of day or night, they're always there, following behind Fido, picking up his steaming crap with a plastic bag. I was about half-way to the nearest trash can when, from behind, came "Good afternoon."

I wheeled around, one bulbous bra cup slipping out from under my sweatshirt, and came eye to eye with Miss Crabby Busybody and her unpleasant little dog, Sunshine.

"Fine day," she said, her eyes on my bra. Sunshine strained on its leash, barking and snapping at me. I followed her eyes to the escaping garment and swiftly tucked it back under my shirt.

"Well, hello there Sunshine," I said, backing up a step or two. "Have you bitten anyone today?"

"Ho ho," Crabby said with a laugh. "She's really friendly."

"Looks it."

"She wouldn't hurt a flea. She just likes to make noise."

Sunshine was foaming at the mouth, trying to sink her yellow teeth into my ankle. I fantasized about kicking Sunshine like a soccer player booting a corner kick. I was envisioning Sunshine flying through the air toward the goal with her legs trailing behind like a

Russian Sputnik Satellite when Crabby adjusted her wire-rimmed glasses and asked, "What's that under your shirt?"

I groaned. Busted. "Oh that," I said, dancing away from Sunshine's lunges. "A surprise for my wife."

Crabby raised her eyebrows. "Looks to be a little large for Ann."

My mouth dropped open and I found myself wishing I was quick-witted and could conger-up some clever response that would knock Crabby back on her heels, but alas, I'm not so. Instead, I quipped, "Looks can be deceiving," and then beat a hasty retreat back home.

When I ducked back into the house – Sunshine following my every step with snarls and growls – I was met by Ann. Her arms were crossed across her chest. She stared at me with an intensity that would have curdled fresh milk.

"Let's see it," she said.

"See what?" I responded innocently.

"What you're hiding under your sweatshirt."

I let out a long breath, removed the massive, padded bra, and handed it over. Then I extracted the matching thong panties which dangled halfway to the floor and handed those over as well. Ann held them both up for examination. After an interminable minute or so, she sighed. "Clearly, these aren't for me so you're either having an affair with King Kong's daughter or you're giving serious consideration to becoming a transvestite."

I stammered for a moment and then launched into the explanation about the mystery package. "Honest," I said, holding up my right hand as if by doing so, it provided the Good Housekeeping Seal of Authenticity. "I'm not screwing around or becoming a cross-dresser. I have no idea where these came from."

"Where's the box these came in?"

I blinked a few times. *That's a very good question* I thought. "I think I threw it into the trash can under the sink."

We spread it out on the kitchen counter and Ann studied the address. "Unless you've changed your name to Alice Muller, this was delivered to the wrong person. And look, this was supposed to go to Forrest Hill, not Fort Mill. They got the zip code right though."

I felt my knees weaken a bit, put on my glasses, and read the label. "Well, I'll be damned," I whispered.

Within a few minutes, Ann had repackaged the gargantuan undies and re-addressed the package to Alice Muller.

Relieved, I watched with interest and finally said, "Maybe we should deliver this in person. Aren't you the least bit curious?"

Ann crossed her arms again, and held me in that *are you shitting me* gaze.

After dropping the mysterious package into the FedEx box, I sat at my computer and wrote my first really torrid sex scene, complete with sweat trickling down between rounded breasts, tongues probing, and backs arching. Thank you, Alice Muller, wherever you are.

The Serendipitous Arrival of the S. S. African Queen

Bill Flanagan awoke with a jolt and hit the stop button on his DVD remote. It was two-fifteen in the morning and just as he'd done every night for the previous two months, he had watched the movie *African Queen* nonstop. Reaching for the bottle of Gordon's Gin, he emptied the contents into his glass, and then tossed the empty into the corner to join the growing pile of dead soldiers. He relit his cigar and in the process knocked ashes onto his soiled bathrobe, the leather couch, and down onto the living room carpet. Blowing out the wooden match, Bill cast a bleary look for the ashtray, which was overturned onto the coffee table, contents well distributed both on the tabletop and spilling over to the floor. He frowned and scratched his grizzly, untrimmed beard. Grabbing a nearby empty Budweiser can, he slipped the match therein.

He closed his eyes and put his head back. As usual, sleep would not come.

It was then he heard her cough softly.

Bill blinked and sat up. Across the litter-strewn room, in the Queen Anne chair by the window, sat a woman. She wore a large flopping sun hat, a high-necked white linen dress with lace trim. Her hands were crossed, resting upon a bible which lay on her lap. She had high cheekbones, no makeup, and wore a stern face.

Then she smiled. "Well, good evening Mr. Allnut. Or perhaps I should say good morning."

Bill closed his eyes and shook his head. Then he opened them again. She was still there. "What the…? Who are you?"

"I think you know who I am but the way you've been drinking…" she narrowed her eyes, her face again becoming stern. "Perhaps you do not recognize me. My name is Katharine Hepburn but you may know me as Rose Sayer from the movie you've been watching."

Again, Bill closed his eyes. "Yeah, right, and I'm the Easter Bunny." He rubbed his forehead and muttered, "Oh man. I've gone around the corner." Then he opened one eye and peeked across the room. She was still there.

Katharine smiled and waved with her fingers. "Still here."

Bill groaned.

"In fact," Katharine said, "I've been here for three days."

"Three days?" Bill opened his eyes, thought for a moment, and then added doubtfully. "I haven't seen you."

"I've been invisible."

"Of course you have," Bill closed his eyes again, and then to himself, mumbled, "What the hell is going on?"

"For example, I was sitting right here three days ago when you received the call from your poker buddies. Remember that? They were wondering about you because you've missed the last two games."

Bill said nothing but kept his eyes closed.

"Then two days ago, one of your neighbors, the single woman with that shock of red hair, dropped off a casserole for you. She also left a voicemail on your phone. I believe the dish is still on the front steps. Too bad, I'll bet it was delicious."

Again, Bill said nothing.

"And yesterday, your daughter called. She was crying. You listened to the voicemail but instead of calling her back, you poured another drink."

Bill opened his eyes, scratched his beard again and frowned. "Laura called?"

"Yes. Your phone is on the end table. Go ahead and play it back."

He picked up his phone, went to voicemail, and played her message.

"Dad, this is Laura. Please pick up." Pause. "Please Dad," her voice cracking. "I know you're there, please…" She was crying. Pause. "I'm broken up about Mom's death and miss her terribly too, but I've got a baby who's due in a couple of weeks. He's going to need that crib you're making. Life is going on. I…" Pause. "I need you to be here this time." Pause. "I'm worried you're going to do something…" More crying, then she disconnected.

Bill stared at the phone.

"Mr. Allnut. You should call your daughter."

He said nothing for a long time, and then asked, "Why do you keep calling me Mr. Allnut?"

She smiled. "Seems fitting."

Bill tossed the phone aside, closed his eyes, and moaned. "I've lost my mind."

"No," Katharine said. "Actually, you haven't. You may be *trying* to pickle your brain but you haven't completely succeeded yet."

The effects of a fifth of gin finally caught up with Bill and he dozed into a fitful sleep. It was well after seven when he opened his eyes again.

"Shit," he said. "You're still here."

Katharine, who hadn't moved, just smiled. "Sleep well?"

"Gotta pee."

With difficulty, Bill got up, went to the bathroom, and then staggered into the kitchen. "Coffee. I need coffee."

The table was covered with stacks of unopened mail, dirty dishes, and empty beer cans. Rolled up newspapers, still in their clear plastic bags, were piled in the corner.

Bill stared at the coffee maker. "Shit."

"Excuse me?"

He frowned. "I'm out of coffee."

He turned. Katharine was seated at the kitchen table. "That's my wife's seat. She always sat there."

Katharine smiled.

"Well," she said, getting to her feet, smoothing her dress. "It's a fine morning for a walk. Let's go to the store and buy some."

Bill stared at her, folded his arms, and stated, "You're not going away, are you."

She smiled again. "Not yet."

* * *

Katharine was correct: it was a fine morning for a walk. The store was a few blocks away and for a time, they walked in silence. An elderly couple was approaching from the other direction.

They smiled and said good morning – Bill mumbled the same. He watched their eyes. They didn't even look at Katherine. After they passed, Bill said, "Excuse me."

They stopped and turned.

Bill pointed at Katharine. "You didn't say good morning to my friend here."

The elderly couple blinked a few times, then exchanged a wide-eyed look, and wordlessly, turned and kept walking. The old man shot a parting glance over his shoulder, making sure the grubby crazy man wasn't following.

"Told you," Katharine said.

"What the…?" Bill stood with his hands on his hips, watching the couple shuffle away, albeit at a quickened pace. Then he reached over and gently poked Katharine in the arm. "Why couldn't they…"

They walked the rest of the way in silence; Bill deep in thought, Katharine humming an old tune. As they entered the mini-market, Bill said, "This doesn't make sense."

The man behind the counter looked up. "Pardon me?"

Bill shook his head. "Oh, sorry. I wasn't talking to you."

The man cocked his head slightly and stared hard at Bill. It was almost as if he was thinking, 'Oh no, not another one of *those* guys.'

Katharine tapped Bill on the arm. "Perhaps it would be better if you didn't speak to me when we're out in public."

"Okay, I get it," Bill said resignedly.

The store clerk behind the counter continued to glare at Bill and watch his every move. When Bill bought a pound of coffee beans and then turned and departed, the clerk exhaled and shook his head, being clearly relieved to be rid of that crazy guy.

*   *   *

After two cups of coffee, Bill sat at the kitchen table, watching Katharine and she watched him. They said nothing.

Finally, Bill asked, "Where did you come from?"

She smiled. "Why, I'm right out of the movie *African Queen* of course. Your favorite movie."

Bill nodded. "Not *my* favorite, my wife's."

Silence.

Bill got up and poured a third cup. "Have I gone insane?"

Katharine laughed. "Not at all, Mr. Allnut." Then, shifting the topic, she asked, "What day does the recycle trash truck pickup?"

Bill scratched his head. "What's today?"

"Tuesday."

"Well, that would be today then."

Katharine stood, and waved her hand at the pile of newspapers. "I'd say this is a good place to start, wouldn't you?"

Bill sighed.

*   *   *

The green trash bin, full to capacity with empty gin bottles, beer cans, and unread newspapers stood at the curb. Bill backed away a step or two, wiped his hands on his pants, and said, "Wow."

"Wow?"

He pointed at the bin. "That's a powerful amount of drinking."

"It is that. And Mr. Allnut, you should refrain from speaking with me in public. Your neighbors are watching." Katharine pointed to a house across the street. In the front window stood the outline of a woman.

"Shit," Bill said, waving to his watcher. "Now it'll be all over the neighborhood."

"Not to worry Mr. Allnut. It already is."

*   *   *

Reluctantly and with significant urging, they next tackled the rancid casserole on the front steps. The contents were dumped into the trash and the dish washed and dried.

"Now," Katharine said. "We're going to return the dish."

"We are like hell," Bill said heatedly. "She's a nosey intrusive bitch who makes my skin crawl."

"That's a bit harsh."

"I call 'em like I see 'em."

"Perhaps she's simply trying to be neighborly."

"She wants a man, and any man will do."

"Well," Katherine said, after a moment's pause. "You could call her and if she's not at home, we could walk up to her house and leave it on her front steps, with a note of thanks."

Bill opened the kitchen cabinet next to the refrigerator and rummaged around.

"And the time has come for you to take a shower. And you need a shave."

Bill closed the cabinet and moved to the one under the sink. "I'll tell you what I need; I need a drink."

He continued searching to no avail.

"That's nice Mr. Allnut."

Bill flung open the pantry door. His search was becoming frantic, muttering, "Where the hell did I put that bottle?"

The rumble of the town trash truck could be heard from outside, and the clink of bottles being dumped.

Bill wheeled around, his eyes wide. "You didn't!"

Katharine studied her hands.

"What the..., you have no right..., get the hell out of here, now! I've had it!"

She smoothed her dress.

Bill's face was flushed. "You sit there, prim and proper, telling me what to do. You have no idea what I'm going through."

Katharine looked up and held his gaze. "That's where you are wrong Mr. Allnut. In fact, I believe I know exactly what you're going through." She paused, and then asked, "Have you ever heard of Anne Lamott?"

"Who?"

"She's a writer and I believe, a bit of a philosopher to boot. One time, when she was talking about her beliefs regarding death, which is of course what we're dealing with here, she said, *'It's so hard to bear when the few people you can't live without die. You'll never get over these loses. And no matter what the culture says, you're not supposed to.'*"

Bill closed his eyes, letting the words sink in. Then, ever so slowly, he moved to the kitchen table and plopped down.

"Ms. Lamott goes on to say, *'But their absence will also be a lifelong nightmare of homesickness to you.'*"

Voice trembling, Bill said, "It was ninety days from the afternoon she came home from her doctor's appointment until the end. Before that terrible, shocking day, life was just about perfect. Then, in the briefest of moments, it all changed. Now, every morning in that time between sleep and awake, I shudder at the bad dream that just haunted me. The dream I dream is one wherein my wife dies. I reach across to her side of the bed and it's cold. She's not there. Then I realize, it was no dream. My life has now become this bad, recurring dream. This is how I start each day."

They sat in silence at the kitchen table. While tears coursed his face, sunshine streamed in through the window in the back door.

* * *

Eventually, like a long train that has been at rest, Bill began to move forward. He showered and he shaved. Then, with Katharine by his side, he returned the casserole dish to the doorstep of the woman with a shock of red hair – she wasn't at home. They walked through the park, stopped at the market to buy a bag of groceries, then came home and made supper.

That night, Bill slept as he hadn't slept for months, as he did the next three nights.

* * *

The sun was peeping in through the kitchen window. Showered and shaved, Bill shuffled in and made the coffee. There were no dishes in the sink and the counter was devoid of life's detritus. While the coffee gurgled in the coffee maker, Bill swept the kitchen floor. Katharine was seated, as always, in Bill's wife's seat.

Katharine asked, "Do you miss drinking?"

Bill cocked his head. "An unexpected question for this time of day. Whatever happened to 'good morning' or 'did you sleep well?'"

Katharine smiled. "Okay. Good morning. Did you sleep well? Do you miss drinking? It's been almost a week."

Pouring a coffee, Bill took a seat. "Yes, and no. Yes because I've been really pounding down the drinks lately. No, because I never was much of a drinker. How's that for an answer?"

"Honest. Are you going to buy a bottle today?"

He chuckled. "With you by my side? Not hardly."

"Well, that brings me to my point Mr. Allnut. I'll be leaving."

"Oh?"

She shrugged. "The time has come."

They sat in silence for a few beats.

"You," Bill said. "Are not real, are you?"

"No."

"You're just a figment of my imagination."

"Yes."

He nodded. "When?"

She smiled. "Even as we speak I hear the S.S. African Queen chugging up the river. I'll be boarding momentarily."

He looked away, waiting for the panic to pass. It did.

She stood.

He stood and stepped towards her. "I know you're not real but..." He swept Katharine in his arms and gave her a tight hug. "Thank you for coming."

Katharine moved towards the door and paused. "What will you do today?"

Bill smiled through his tears. "Call my daughter. I have a cradle to deliver for my new grandchild."

"Goodbye, Mr. Allnut."

Then she left.

The Murder of Giovani "Big Cheese" Manicotti

Clean Feet Vineyards, makers of <u>RFG Table Red</u> and <u>Not Just For Women White</u> wines, is located just outside of Lotsa Grapes, California, in the heart of the Napa Valley. It has been in the Manicotti family for three generations and enjoyed a great run of successful years. Then one day, seemingly right out of the blue, Giovani decided to call it quits with the wine business and dedicate the rest of his days - and all of his fortune - to the Save the Noodle campaign. This movement, which has now gained national attention, is in response to a crusade sponsored by a group from Cambridge, Massachusetts called Stamp Out Carbs in Kids (or SOCK for short). The problem with the SOCK movement is those folks from Cambridge want to take all pasta and pasta products off the shelves, nationwide! This, of course, is what spawned the Save the Noodle counter attack. In the words of Save the Noodle president, I. Emma Fatso, "Those burned-out hippies need to stay away from my colander." Fatso, tipping the scale at an even 300 pounds, has clearly explored all of the virtues of a steaming plate of spaghetti.

Regardless, and for reasons not clearly understood, Giovani decided to trade his vineyard and fortune, for a key place in the ranks of the noodle lovers. As it turns out, this was a bad decision.

To his undying credit – well, actually his *dying* credit – Giovani made the decision to inform all the important people in his life face-to-face, over a grand and eloquent last supper. The deal to sell the entire vineyard was to be signed the following Monday.

Invitations went out and the Inn at the Vineyard was closed for this private party. The dinner and announcement were to be held on the following Saturday evening, but the fates (or at least one of the guests) intervened. Down in the wine cellar, Giovani was found dead on Sunday morning! The cause may have been natural causes but the knife in the chest gave rise to suspicion.

Police Inspector Sly LeDunn closed the Inn, sealed off all the exits, and sequestered all the guests to the library until the ongoing investigation was completed.

With everyone present, Sly, a moose of a man with a magnificently twirled handlebar mustache, resembling that of a lion tamer at the carnival, began.

"Thank you all for coming," Sly said, dropping a box of odds and ends at his feet. He clasped his hands behind his back and studied all those present.

Immediately to Sly's left, seated in an over-stuffed leather chair was Vita Vermicelli-Manicotti, Giovani's rather curvaceous grieving widow. In fact, she wasn't grieving much at all and was focusing her attention on filing her blood-red nails. On occasion, she'd toss back her head of wild, raven-colored curls, glare at the other guests, and then go back to her nails.

Standing to *her* left was Father Sardini, allegedly the deceased's best friend. A striking, tall, tanned man with dark piercing eyes and wizard-like bushy eyebrows, he was dressed in full priest garb. His rather unfocused demeanor was the result of the third (or was it the fourth) glass of red wine. A half-empty bottle of Cabernet was close by.

On two folding chairs immediately to Father Sardini's left were Hope and Antonio "Dizzy" Cannoli; the resident farmhands from Italy whose green cards had long expired. Hope, a former prostitute from Rome, may have quit the profession but retained the looks; from a plunging neckline to black fishnet stockings. But the expression she wore on her face was anything but sensuous. Her jaw was set, her eyes fixed, and her arms crossed over her ample breasts. If a word could describe her demeanor, it would be *seething*.

Conversely, her husband resembled the unfocussed family dog going for a ride in a car with its head out the window, tongue lolling in the wind. Dizzy looked a lot like a cornfield scarecrow: skinny and unkempt; certainly a bulb of low wattage.

And finally, to *their* left was a wiry, painfully thin woman in a business suit. She exuded all the warmth of a weasel. This was Angelina Anchovy, the family lawyer and long-time financial advisor to Giovani. Her hair was pulled back in a severely tight bun, her hands folded on her lap, and her legs crossed at the ankles. Her penetrating eyes flitted from person to person, while her lips, adorned with fire-engine red gloss, remained pressed together.

Sly cleared his throat. "Last night, Giovani Manicotti was murdered." He paused and looked from face to face. No noticeable changes. "He was found in his favorite chair in the wine cellar, located immediately below the kitchen, with a carving knife protruding from his heart." Again he studied the faces. No change. "One of you is a murderer." No changes. "And none of you are leaving here until I figure out who did it." He paused, and then asked, "Anyone care to confess?"

Silence.

Sly sighed. "Okay, let's begin. Sometime after dinner last night, when Giovani made the big announcement that the winery was soon to be sold, he *allegedly* drank too much and had to be helped out of the dining room by Father, er, what's your name?"

The priest hiccupped. "Sardini."

"Yeah," Sly continued. "Whatever. Father Sardini here helped the victim out the door and was last seen entering the wine cellar. Is that right Father?"

Sardini, flying several sheets to the wind, nodded, somewhat like a bobble-head. "Right."

"What did you talk about?" Sly asked.

The priest shrugged. "Nothing. I helped him into his chair and he promptly passed out."

"And then?"

"And then I left, came in, went to my room on the third floor, and turned in for the night."

"Did anyone see you?"

The priest shrugged again and stared at the cop, pie-eyed.

Sly shook his head. "I'll take that for a no. Now, a couple of things. We searched your room, Father, and found this under your bed." Sly held up a carpenter's auger. "Does it look familiar?"

The priest frowned and then shook his head no.

"Your fingerprints are on it."

The priest gulped down the remains of the wine is his glass. "I kneeled on it last light when I was saying my prayers. Quite painful. I simply shoved it under my bed, out of the way. That's why my prints are on it."

Sly nodded. "We found wood shavings on the floor next to the deceased. Someone had used this tool to drill a hole in the floor of the kitchen, which as you know is right above the wine cellar. Know anything about that?"

The priest again shook his head no.

Sly held up a length of surgical hose. "We found this in the bottom of the dried-up artesian well in the yard. It's got your fingerprints on it. Know anything about this?"

The priest swayed slightly and hiccupped again. "No idea."

"Then how come your fingerprints are on it?"

The priest refilled his glass and shrugged. "Don't know. I never saw it before."

"And just so you know father, the propane tank in the kitchen is empty. How do you suppose that happened?"

The priest frowned and shook his head. "No idea. I don't cook. Maybe ask one of them." He beckoned vaguely in the direction of the farmhands.

Sly took a notebook from his pocket, read for a moment, and then continued. "During our investigation this morning, when we found the deceased, a full glass of wine, clearly untouched, was on the table beside him. Anybody know anything out that?"

Vita Vermicelli-Manicotti, Giovani's not-so-grieving widow, looked up. "I brought that to him. You already know that because those were my fingerprints on the glass."

Sly blinked a few times, the curls on the end of his mustache twitching. "Care to elaborate?"

Vita sat up and defiantly cocked her head. "I always bring him a glass of wine before I go to bed. It's his nightcap."

"And what did he say to you?"

She shrugged then went back to filing her nails. "Nothing. He had passed out."

"Did you notice anything odd about him, like a knife sticking out of his chest?"

"I saw no knife when I brought him his wine, but then again, the room was dark."

Sly stared at Vita for a long silent moment, and then asked, "Why did you put the rat poison in the wine?"

Without returning his gaze, she nonchalantly responded, "I have no idea what you're talking about."

Sly shook his head, and then lifted a plastic bag from his evidence box. In it was a bloody knife. "Just so you know; your fingerprints are all over it."

She worked on her nails, and without looking up, she said matter-of-factly, "I cooked with that knife last night. I used it to carve the prosciutto. Of course, my prints are on it."

Sly frowned, and then shifted his attention to Antonio "Dizzy" Cannoli, the resident farmhand. "Got anything to say, Mr. Cannoli?"

Dizzy blinked a few times, clearly stunned by the question.

Sly removed another plastic bag from the evidence box at his feet. In it was a handgun with a silencer attached. "Look familiar?"

Dizzy cowered like a dog caught drinking out of the toilet bowl and smacked with a rolled-up newspaper. Sly, still holding the gun for all to see, continued. "Your prints are all over it. Care to comment? We found it hidden in the barn."

It was then Angelina Anchovy, the family lawyer, spoke up. "You will keep your mouth shut."

Stunned by the outburst, everyone swiveled in their seats toward Angelina. She stared at Dizzy and repeated, "As the family attorney, my client has nothing to say."

Ignoring Angelina, Sly spoke directly to Dizzy. "In the wine cellar, we found six empty shell casings on the floor, directly in front of the deceased. Oddly, there were no bullet holes in him. Apparently, someone missed their target from point-blank range. Got anything to say about that?"

Angelina shouted, "Keep that hole in your moronic head shut!"

Dizzy stated to cry and through his sobs, said, "My hands were shaking so bad, I couldn't hold the gun still. I just kept pulling the trigger…"

"Shut up!" Angela shouted again.

Suddenly, Sly shifted his gaze to Angelina. "And you Attorney Angelina Anchovy provided him with the gun, didn't you!"

She laughed. "You can't pin the gun on me. It was…"

"Stolen," Sly said. "That is true. But the silencer was ordered via a mail order source and sent to your shop in town, isn't that right Miss Lacey Leather."

Angelia looked away. "I have nothing to say."

Sly plowed on. "Yes, it's true. You are the Lacey Leather who runs the BSDM shop in the dodgy end of town. When you're not a lawyer, getting drunk drivers off on a technicality, your don your leather and tie up clients, like Dizzy here, for a night of perverse pleasure."

It was then Hope Cannoli, Dizzy's wife and a former prostitute from Rome, sat up in alarm. Staring at Dizzy, she exclaimed, "You WHAT?" Whack! She smacked him across the head, sending him sprawling on the floor.

Sly stepped across the room and restrained Hope Cannoli. "There'll be no more of that," he said, pushing her back into her seat. "And as for you Mrs. Hope Cannoli, you're not exactly lily-white yourself, are you?"

She folded her arms across her chest. "I don't know what you're talking about."

Sly reached into his book of evidence and withdrew a sheet of paper, put on his glasses and began to read. "Let's see...yes, here it is...you and the deceased and Father Sardini over there made several trips to the Caribbean in the past two years. I believe it was down to St. Lascivious Island where you three enjoyed each other's company. Correct?"

Hope looked away.

Sly, stroking his handlebar mustache, turned to the priest. "Where did you get that tan Padre? I'll bet if you pulled down your trousers, we'd have a hard time finding tan lines. Not customary behavior for a priest, is it?"

The priest stared back, lost in an alcoholic haze.

"And Mrs. Hope Cannoli," Sly continued. "You cleaned up after the party, didn't you? Which means, you, wearing the same rubber gloves you always wear when handling dirty dishes, could have taken the butcher's knife, the one covered with Mrs. Giovani's prints, slipped out the back door, ran down to the wine cellar, and stabbed the deceased in the heart. Then, you could have returned and finished the dishes. No one would have seen you as they were all still around the table in the dining room."

Silence.

Sly stepped back and leaned against the mantelpiece over the fireplace. "So there we have it. Each of you has motive and opportunity." He paused and then continued. "With the sale of the winery goes the luxurious lifestyle of Father Sardini and illegal alien Hope Cannoli. Further, the good padre knew he was to get fifty percent of the winery when Giovani dies, as he was named in the will. Supposed to go to the church but who's to say? Pretty good incentive to snuff out Manicotti I'd say. And Hope, going back to Italy may not be pleasant for you, so perhaps you'd stay on as a hired hand, which would be needed no matter who owns the vineyard."

Sly strolled over to the lawyer. "And you Attorney Angelina Anchovy or Lacey Leather or whoever you are today; you drew up the bill of sale for the winery so you knew what was coming. You also drew up the dead man's will and could charge a small fortune to execute the said will. You would make out quite well upon his death but if he sold the farm, you'd get nothing. Why not cash out? So you blackmail your man Dizzy over there to do your dirty work. Pretty tidy I'd say."

He turned to Vita Vermicelli-Manicotti, Giovani's rather curvaceous non-grieving widow. "And you Mrs. Vermicelli-Manicotti; I believe you were simply fed up with his cheating ways and decided to use all the commotion to make your move. After all, hell hath no fury and all that."

"So there you have it," he said, fingering his magnificent mustache. "Without an autopsy, we don't know how the victim died, but I believe I know exactly what happened."

He removed a glossy 8 x 10 photo of the dead man, who was seated in his chair with a butcher's knife sticking out of his chest, and held it up for all to see. "Note the total lack of blood from the wound."

So reader; with the information presented, who
was the murderer and how did they do it?

Solution:

After the dinner and big announcement, Father Sardini slipped a sedative into Manicotti's drink which caused "Big Cheese" to fade faster than usual. Sardini then wrapped his arm around Manicotti's shoulder and led him out of the house, down the steps, and into the wine cellar, taking care to close the door to the cellar behind him. Slipping back upstairs, while the dinner party was still in full swing, Sardini hooked up the rubber hose - which he had earlier stashed behind the kitchen propane tank – to the propane and ran it to the hole in the floor he had drilled earlier in the day. The hole had been hidden by the rug on the floor. He then turned on the tank and emptied the contents into the wine cellar. The gas displaced the air in the enclosed space and Manicotti was dead in five minutes. Then, Sardini removed the hose, slipped out of the kitchen again, ran down to the cellar, opened the door thus letting the propane escape, and checked Manicotti's pulse – which was gone. He then tossed the hose into the well, which unfortunately for Sardini had gone dry, and returned to the dinner party.

After the party broke up, his wife, Vita Vermicelli-Manicotti did, in fact, take a glass of wine – laced with enough rat poison to kill an elephant – to her philandering husband. He appeared to be passed out from previous drink, so she left it on the table with hopes he'd drink it when he came to. But since he was dead, he did not drink it.

No sooner had she left when Hope Cannoli, who had been watching from the shadows, slipped into the cellar and stabbed the "Big Cheese" with the butcher knife Vita had been using to prepare supper. She was wearing the gloves she always wore when doing the dishes. Then Hope ducked off into the shadows. But since he was dead, he did not bleed.

Sometime later, her husband, Dizzy, unsteadily strode into the wine cellar, raised the handgun, closed his eyes, and began pulling the trigger. Although he did considerable damage to the racks of 2007 Cabernet Sauvignon stacked against the fall wall, he missed his target with every shot. Nice shootin' Tex!

All the while, Attorney Angelina Anchovy (aka or Lacey Leather) slept the sleep of the dead.

Pedicure

Hello My Friends,

Recently, I experienced another personal first: I got a pedicure.

The explanation of this bizarre event requires a bit of history. When I turned fifty, my feet decided to go slightly reptilian and began drying up. No problem. I left them alone, they left me alone. Then when I turned sixty, my feet became full-blown reptilian. For the first time, began rebelling against their host – me – and formed deep, painful cracks. Still, no big deal. Smear with some sort of goo, wear socks, be happy. But since moving to Colorado where the air is bone dry and the ground is hot, open war has begun, and up until yesterday, my feet were winning. Jen, whose house we are currently living in while ours is being renovated, got sick and tired of watching me limp around, so on Father's Day, she gave me a gift certificate to Nails Supreme for a pedicure. You know, this makes sense. If the pedicurist removes the all the dry skin from my heals, the applied goo will actually do some good.

So, here goes. Yesterday, at 9 A.M. when the store was supposed to open, I stood outside Nails Supreme, gift certificate in hand, wearing a disguise of dark glasses and a large floppy hat to hide my face, waiting for the store to open. Being Colorado, it opened at 9:20. Sigh. Regardless, a diminutive Asian woman directed me to a seat.

118

The exact quote was *"You, take seat!"* – where I settled in for my new adventure. The Asian woman then busied herself in the shop, turning on a variety of vats and cauldrons yielding noxious fumes and a variety of buzzing noises. It reminded me of the laboratory in the movie Frankenstein. I cast a nervous glance around. The next thing I noticed was the choice of magazines. They all featuring nails and nail colors, wedding gowns, and some newsletter about a new cure for menstrual cramps. I took out my phone and settled for a game of chess but didn't get very far. Almost immediately, a rotund woman of perhaps 300 pounds, wearing a yellow tee shirt that read, "Guns Have Rights, Too!" and then in smaller print beneath, announced, "The Second Amendment Guarantees My Automatic Weapon," took a seat next to me. My first thought was to ask her if she'd ever actually *read* the second amendment, which refers to a *militia* bearing arms, not the average Joe Blow, but then, noticing her unusually large handbag – certainly big enough to house an automatic weapon – thought better of it. I smiled and went back to my chess game, but it was too late. She sized me up.

"You gettin' a pettie?" She barked with a lisp.

I didn't understand her question. I thought she asked, *are you getting pretty?* What kind of question was that? Did she think I was following in Bruce Jenner's footsteps? But as one of my cardinal rules is *never argue with gun-toting fat women*, I smiled weakly and said, "Maybe."

Unabashed, she plowed on. "My Norman had feet like a barnyard chicken. I kept after him to get a pettie, but he never did." She cast a glance at my feet.

Again, many questions popped into my head, but the most pressing inquiry was, *what do you mean **never** did?* That sounds like past tense to me. Did you shoot him? Do I have feet like a chicken? Are you going to shoot me?

119

I felt the need to respond or suffer dire consequences. "Oh? How come?"

She glared at me and blinked a few times, with an expression that shouted *how stupid are you?* "Why, he up and died."

Fortunately for me, it was at that time that a second Asian woman approached and in broken English, declared, "I take you now."

Whew.

Following my guide, I crossed the shop, stepping around a variety of machines that looked like they were previously owned by Saddam Hussain, and took my seat in a Lazy-Boy style chair that immediately began to massage my back.

"You like?" she asked.

I nodded.

She pointed at my shoes. "Take off."

I did.

She took a look at my feet, mumbled something that I believe is the Vietnamese word for *amputation*, and then got to work.

With amazingly strong hands for such a tiny person, she grabbed both of my feet an immersed them in a vat of bubbling, soapy, warm water. Now let me tell you: this was very nice. My fears of being recognized or getting shot by Norman's widow melted away.

After perhaps two minutes, she took a seat at my feet, opened a leather case, and extracted a fistful of sharply pointed tools. I frowned. Those didn't look like friendly tools. And they weren't. For the next three years, she sliced off skin (scales? Exoskeleton?) from around my toenails, scraped years of neglect from around the edges, then set to work cutting and smoothing my nails. At one point, she used a power-grinder – the kind I have used to cut pipe - and ground away on the claws protruding from my toes. This was followed by a severe session with a handheld cheese shredder, with which she viciously attacked my dead skin. All in all, it was like having your teeth cleaned minus the drooling and spitting.

But then, life took a decidedly wonderful turn for the better. She put away her torture tools and pulled out a pallet of warm oils and slippery liquids. First one foot and then the other. Surely, Mrs. Norman had read my mind, shot me in the forehead, and I was dead and in heaven. This was *really* pleasant.

After an undetermined passage of time, I was brought back to earth by the Asian woman saying, "All done. Better now?"

Numbly, I pulled on my shoes, paid her a large sum of money for a tip, slipped back into my disguise, and left the shop. As I walked past Norman's murderer, I noticed she had her hands stuck into some kind of microwave oven. Now was my chance. I considered making a crack about Norman's departure – squashed during sex? Shot? Fried and served in a Chinese restaurant? - but passed, remembering a rifled bullet could travel faster than my beautiful feet could take me, so instead, I smiled and departed.

In summary, if you ever want to buy me a gift, get me a gift certificate to Nails Supreme for a "Pettie." And by the way, make it out to John Doe.

Yours Truly,
John (aka pretty feet)

Living Next Door to a Witch

The woman who lives next door is a witch. I don't know much about her. Her name is Zoe something, and her age is somewhere between thirty and fifty. She has long jet-black hair and wears black lipstick and eye-shadow. No, she never stopped by and said, "Hi, I'm new to the neighborhood. Could I borrow a cup of sugar? And by the way, I'm a witch." So, you might ask, how do I know she's a witch?

Well, it started last summer when the wild raspberry crop was nonexistent and hungry black bears came out of the nearby extensive wilderness where they normally live and began nightly patrols of the town streets. They were looking for supper. This meant trash cans got knocked over in the middle of the night, and any tasty treats were consumed. The next morning, all of us trashcan owners would awake to the mess in our yards, and then, mumbling obscenities, pull on our shoes and go clean it up. It was on such occasion that a breeze was blowing and some trash from Zoe's yard blew into mine. Among the detritus were several <u>Witchcraft and Wicca</u> magazines. "No kidding?" I thought, but no big deal. To each their own. After all, there was a time in my life when dubious literary periodicals found their way into my rubbish as well.

But then I began to notice black garments hanging on her clothesline. (Out here in the ultra-dry desert, many people hang out their laundry like my mom used to do when I was a kid.) On Zoe's line, there were black tee-shirts, pants, black hooded robes, and various other black under-garments. Again, no big deal. Some people like dressing in black. Now, lest you think I spend my day spying on my neighbor, I do not. My office, where I now am seated, looks out onto her backyard. Actually, when clothing is hung to dry, it partially obstructs my view of the canyon wall, so I can't help but notice the various black lacy items fluttering in the breeze. As an aside, I never knew witches wore black foam bras and lacy sheer panties. But as it turns out, there's plenty I don't know about witches.

Next in the possible evidence column are the women who arrive on Saturday afternoons for some sort of closed-door meeting. Again, I'm not being nosey but Saturday's are my designated yard-work days and I'm often mowing the lawn or in some way, puttering around outside. The black-clad women arrive in a handful of cars, and without sideways glances and with somber expressions, waste no time dashing from their vehicles into the house next door, not to emerge until long after dark.

You have to understand, our town, East Nowhere, Colorado, is made up of an eclectic population of everything from sullen Navahos to burned-out hippies to poor young families scratching out an existence. The inhabitants here make no effort to dress in any manner that would be called stylish. In fact, the Thrift Store is one of the only two viable businesses on Main Street. (The other is a Wellness Clinic which sells recreational marijuana.) Therefore, a handful of women, dressed from head to toe in black hardly warrants a second look. Again, no big deal.

My conclusion: Zoe and her pals are witches.

Now, in my opinion, having a witch next door is not a bad thing. In fact, we are on friendly terms. We wave and often comment on the weather. Our conversations are generally brief as she always seems to be late for some important date; usually one quick sentence then she hurries off. I'm okay with this. After all, it's probably best to stay on good terms with a witch, as the converse is not attractive. I know this to be a fact. In a past life, I'm pretty sure my ex-mother in law – who looked upon me as fresh dog shit tracked onto her white living room carpet - used to have a voodoo doll of me that she stuck with pins on a daily basis. My evidence? Indirect and perhaps inconclusive, but there is no denying my chronic lower back pains abruptly ceased, never to return, when she died. That episode resulted in an important life lesson: never piss-off someone with magical powers.

Still, you may argue, I have no hard evidence of Zoe being a witch and this may all be a bunch of hooey. Well then, listen to this. Last winter we spent December and January out here. Skiing, snowshoeing, and ice skating were as good as it gets. One morning at dawn, I pulled on my parka and boots, loaded my arms with firewood, and then headed out to my office to fire-up the wood stove. It generally takes about half an hour to heat up the office, during which time I make the coffee back inside the warm confines of our house. By the time the coffee is finished dripping, I trudge back to the cozy office and begin my day. You get the picture.

So here I was, picking my way along the shoveled path with a load of wood in my arms when I stepped in a pile of fresh cat shit. I was not happy and let loose a string of rather creative profanity. Then, feeling the presence of someone nearby, I stopped swearing and whipped around. There standing at the fence which separates our properties was Zoe, wrapped in a black cloak.

"Morning," I said a bit sheepishly as I had just been loudly using the "f" word as a verb, adverb, adjective, and past participle.

Now, you have to understand, in our poor and somewhat shabby little town, cats live seemingly everywhere. Many don't really belong to anyone. In fact, the opposite is true. They inhabit sheds and garages and run-down abandoned stores. Some are fed by the townsfolk – and thus are pets – but many are just part of the landscape, similar to squirrels and pigeons in the park. The cats that had left the treat in my path, which was now squished into the soul on my boot, inhabited Zoe's garage.

"Those cats are becoming a nuisance," she said.

I looked over at her garage. Two cats were sitting on the window sill – the window long gone – staring out at us.

"Not your fault," I muttered, wiping my boot on the snowbank, unsuccessfully attempting to rid my right foot of the poop. "Those cats were there before you moved in. They run wild all over town."

Zoe nodded and glared at the cats. "I'll deal with this," she said, and then hurried off.

I was left bemused. *What did she mean by that? How was she going to 'deal' with them? Was she going to poison them?*

In fact, the cats were not harmed and they are still there, but get this: they don't poop in my yard anymore. They continue to prowl the town and get into noisy catfights from time to time at about 2 A.M., but they take their deposits elsewhere. How is this possible? Unlike dogs and husbands, cats cannot be trained to do anything. Yet, search as I may – and I meticulously did – I cannot find any cat droppings within our fenced in yard. I'm not suggesting Zoe somehow put a non-pooping spell on the cats, but I can't think of any other explanation.

Then there was the jump-starting incident which also took place last winter. It was nineteen degrees and snowing lightly. I was going fishing. Hold on, you might say. Going fishing? In nearby New Mexico is the Navaho Dam, out from which flows the San Juan River. As the water that's being released is from deep in the lake, where it resides at fifty degrees year-round, the river flows merrily down the valley, also at fifty degrees, regardless of freezing air temperatures. The trout that live therein don't care a whit about snow or any of the various winter weather conditions, and feed on hatching insects, totally oblivious to the month of the year. In fact, I prefer fishing the San Juan in the winter as there are far fewer fishermen to contend with. I wonder why?

Regardless, I was happy as the proverbial lark and going fishing. As I loaded my car I spied Zoe hurrying to her auto, which was parked in the drive behind her house. I don't believe she saw me. She jumped in, turned the key, and the sound went something like, "yada, yada, yump." Again, "yada, yada, yump." Then "click." Then nothing.

Now, Mr. Sardonic, who lives inside my head said, "Quick. Get in and drive away. She can call AAA."

But then Mr. Affable, who shares my skull with his unpleasant pal, said, "Wait a minute. You've got jumper cables behind the seat. Just go give her a jump."

"And if you do," replied Mr. Sardonic, "you'll be late for fishing. The insect hatch may be over by the time you get there. Don't be a sap."

"Oh, come on," said Mr. Affable. "How long is this going to take?"

As it turned out, it took an hour. I had to shovel my way into her driveway as the snowplow had left a sizeable pile at the end of her drive. Then, while I was jump-starting her car, the snowplow came by again and dumped another pile of snow, which also had to be shoveled.

I would have thought there would be a modicum of gratitude such as 'thank you', but there was none. In fact, she drove off in a hurry, wheels spinning in the packed snow. I stood there with jumper cables dangling from my gloved hand. Mr. Sardonic said, "I told you so."

So there I was, steam coming out my ears, driving through steadying snow to the San Juan, certain by the time I arrived, the trout would be done feeding and I'd sullenly drive back home.

But get this: the fishing was fantastic! Never before were the trout as hungry and stupid. The big Brown Trout were coming so fast, it nearly became a matter of devalued currency. It was heavenly! Finally, the snow intensified to the point that I had to quit and get while the getting was still good. It was on my way home, with me and Mr. Affable singing a duet, that the thought crossed my mind that there was something surrealistic about the day on the river. A prickling of the hair on the back on my neck feeling came over me. Did Zoe have something to do with this outing of unbelievably great fishing?

Our over the fence relationship has not changed. We still wave and exchange brief pleasantries. On occasion when we do converse, it always quickly heads toward the intersection of Bizarre Boulevard and Puzzling Place. Consider last month at dawn. I had set up my telescope in the backyard to observe one of Jupiter's moons emerging from behind the planet. It was quite a sight and when it was over, I stood back and took in the brightening dawn sky. One block away are two churches: one Catholic and one Baptist. They both have spires with crosses atop. As I watched, a colony of bats was returning home from their night's feeding on nocturnal insects. They all went into some unseen opening in the spire over the Baptist church, and none went into the Catholic Church. A voice from behind me made me jump about a foot. It was Zoe, standing at the fence.

"It's a sign," she said. Then, without another word turned and melted into the darkness.

I was, to put it mildly, and using the vernacular of today's youth, a bit freaked. For the rest of the day I pondered the chance meeting. *What kind of sign? Good or bad?* And I happen to like bats so was it a nod in the direction of the Baptists? I'm still waiting.

Then, a few weeks ago, an afternoon thunderstorm brewed up and at the peak of the fury, an embedded microburst took down two huge trees across the street. Amazingly, neither tree hit anything. One fell across the road, missed all parked cars and the other, fell along the sidewalk, narrowly missing the home it would have flattened.

All the neighbors – except Zoe – pitched in and sawed, dragged, and hauled away the trees. In the end, the town DPW came by and finished the job. I did observe the curtains in Zoe's front window moving but she remained hidden

The next day, I was weeding the flower bed when Zoe bustled by, clearly late for some exorcism somewhere.

I said, "Some storm last night."

She got into her car and began backing out of her drive. I thought perhaps she didn't hear my comment, but as her auto moved by, through the open window, she announced, "It's a warning." Then she drove off.

A warning? I shrugged and went back to my weeding but admittedly, didn't walk under any ladders for the rest of the day. Perhaps I was becoming a bit jaded by the whole witch thing, but then again, you never know.

So, in summary, I've come to the conclusion that living next to a witch is not so bad. They don't play loud music, own barking dogs, or in any way, pry into my business. It could be argued that I'm a lot more prying than she is. Other than the occasional dire prediction based upon swarming bats or falling trees, it's actually quite pleasant. And you know, there could be an upside to this relationship: I may need a magical spell or two in the future.

The Complete and Very Short History of the 1992 Mexican Olympic Men's Hockey Team

Background

In 1988, the sports world became familiar with the Jamaican Bobsledding Team who competed at the Winter Olympic Games in Calgary. Jamaica, where snow has not fallen since the last Ice Age, generally does not compete in winter events. Undaunted, four young Jamaicans (three soldiers and a policeman,) borrowed a backup sled from Switzerland and entered the Olympics to represent their country. The fact that they finished last and nearly killed themselves in a spectacular crash is now forgotten.

And they were not the only unusual entry that year. Eddy the Eagle (aka Michael Edwards) also made the news. The British ski jumper tried valiantly but finished last in every event, and nearly decapitated fans in the process with wildly flailing skis as he flew off the track in the wrong direction. His spectacular, ragdoll style crashes made the highlight films and, for a time, were featured as the "agony of defeat" model used by ABC Wide World of sports.

These were newsworthy stories that captured the imagination of many. Following is an account of one such group that was so enthralled with the concept of being in the Olympics that they actually took action to compete. Well, almost.

March 1988

As usual, on Tuesday evenings, Sid's Bar and Grill was empty. When we piled in at nine p.m., we moved a handful of tables together and took over the establishment. There were usually about twenty-five of us, the number varying from week to week, and as a rule, we behaved ourselves. Roger, the owner of Sid's Bar, (we never did find out who Sid was) was thrilled to see us. In an hour or two he would make as much money as he made all week. It was rare when anyone drank too much because we all had day jobs. The "we" in this tale, was a loose assembly of men and three Russian women, who rented the dilapidated South Road Rink every Tuesday evening to play ice hockey. We started in mid-December and continued into March, depending upon how long the ice making system would hold up. The rink was one of the first New Hampshire rinks built to meet the surge of interest in ice hockey. Soon, newer, bigger, better lit, modern ice-making system rinks were popping up, leaving South Road by the wayside. But to us, it was wonderful - and available! Sure, there were problems. You couldn't leave food in the locker room because the rats would start feasting on your snack before you laced up your skates. The showers were lukewarm at best, and strange things grew out of the drain and up the walls of the never-been-scrubbed shower room. The ice had some peculiarities but generally, it was—well, ice.

We ranged in age from twenty-something to a few old-timers in their late forties, and we had jobs ranging from teacher to engineer to linemen to firemen. We even had one annoying lawyer. Most of us had played high school and some college hockey. Although we all *thought* we were skilled, we weren't. Except, that is, Natasha, one of the Russian women who actually was a professional caliber athlete.

I was one of the goaltenders. The game we played was pond hockey, not NHL ice hockey. For those of you who don't know the difference, pond hockey is played for fun. We chose sides for each game, taking care to keep the skill level on each side even, and to keep the belligerents and hotheads on the same team. Checking, fighting, slashing, pushing, or rough stuff of any sort was not allowed. When someone fell down, the game stopped to make sure the player was okay. Sure, it was competitive, but mostly, it was just plain fun. We were simply a group of guys (and ladies) who loved the game, were still young enough to dream of greatness, and dumb enough to continue taking the lumps hockey deals out.

Back to that fateful Tuesday evening at Sid's in March of 1988. We were into our second beer and the TV over the bar featured a Winter Olympics wrap- up. All the buzz was about the Jamaican Bobsled team and Eddie the Eagle. These guys had represented their countries, albeit poorly, patriotically nonetheless. The topic shifted to ice hockey. The 1988 US team was abysmal and for good reason. They were an amateur squad competing against teams of NHL professionals so it was simply no contest. All the same, they looked proud wearing their jerseys with USA on the front. The show concluded and the TV switched off. We went back to our drinking. I believe the ensuing conversation went something like this:

Jimmy, a likable hayseed from rural Maine, said, "Even I can flop off a ski jump like that character Eddy the Eagle."

Natasha, in her thick Russian accent, said, "No doubt. We have all seen you skate." There was boisterous agreement by all present. She made an ever-so-slight smile, a significant juxtaposition to her normally stoic expression.

Ignoring the guffaws, Jimmy continued. "And the USA hockey team looked like those clowns in the bobsled."

I spoke up. "What do you expect? Our players are college kids and rink-rats, skating against the Montreal Canadians."

It was at this point that big Dave, not known for loquaciousness, uttered those momentous words: "We could play."

Thoughtful silence followed. Most of us viewed Dave, a huge man resembling a clean-shaven Hagrid of Harry Potter fame, as a non-contributor of social niceties. In fact, he generally spoke in short sentences of single syllable words, most of them profane. To refer to Dave as dim-witted is unkind and dangerous. When describing Dave, it would be far safer to label him as the *non-academic* type.

I looked at Dave. "What are you talking about?"

"Hockey," Dave replied. "We could be the fuckin' Jamaican Hockey team."

A few careful, quiet chuckles.

Jimmy swallowed a slug of beer. "One problem, big guy. None of us is Jamaican. Look around, do any of us look Jamaican?"

I pointed at Tony, the annoying *let-me-correct-you-no-matter-what-you-say* lawyer who was a pretty good chap in spite of himself. "Tony does."

"I believe my lineage is African, not Caribbean."

Natasha, who made little effort to hide her amorous feelings toward Tony, said, "Makes no matter. You are a *black* man." What she didn't say was *and a very handsome one as well that I'd love to get my hands upon.*

Jimmy, in mock surprise, gasped, "You are black? When did this happen?"

Tony smiled. "Day before yesterday. Happens to the best of us." Then, turning to Dave, he added, "We can only play hockey for countries wherein we hold citizenry." And then, for good (safe) measure added, "Great idea, however."

Dave studied his beer. "Mexico."

"Come again?" said Tony.

"Some guys on the crew are from Mexico, said Dave. "They can stay here 'cause they went to school." *Roughly translated: Dave was* explaining that some of his coworkers had become American citizens. *"But they go home sometimes."* *Roughly translated: they retained their Mexican citizen status, thus dual citizens.*

"You are correct. Mexico recognizes multiple citizenries even though the United States does not," said Tony with authority.

Jimmy looked delighted. "Great! We can be Mexicans. I think Carlos is Mexican."

Carlos Fernandez, possibly the best all-around player in our group (next to Natasha) and certainly the most fearsome, picked up his head. "What's that, Shit-for-Brains?"

"Aren't you Mexican?" Jimmy asked.

Carlos shook his head in disgust. "Do you think anyone whose name ends in "z" is Mexican? We are commonly known as Hispanics."

Undaunted, Jimmy continued. "We're going to play hockey for Mexico. You can be our spokesman."

Carlos put down his beer glass. "What are you talking about? But before you answer, let's take a little quiz. Do you know *where* Mexico is? Could you identify it on a map?"

While this exchange continued, I turned to Tony. "What do you think? Could we pull it off?"

Tony rubbed his chin. "Theoretically, yes. Becoming a Mexican citizen is not too difficult. But convincing the Mexican government to go along with this plan might be our biggest hurdle. Then, there could be a challenge from the International Olympic Committee. But in theory…" He opened his hands and shrugged his shoulders.

I began to ponder the possibilities and looked around. Carlos had Jimmy in a headlock and, to the delight of those nearby, was testing Jimmy's knowledge of geography. Natasha had pulled her chair close to Tony and was speaking in a hushed tone. Tony, looking none too comfortable, was making frequent and obvious glances at his watch. Dave was licking the inside of his beer glass, trying to extract the last drop. I smiled. These were good people and good friends. We were having fun.

I tried to imagine us, dressed in wide Mexican sombreros and colorful serapes, marching into the Olympic stadium in front of the whole world. I couldn't quite bring that image into focus. It was like visualizing your parents making love. The mental exercise was too much work. It was time to pay up and go home.

April 1988

Although the sports world was enchanted by the Jamaican Bobsled Team and Eddy the Eagle, the Olympic world was not. The widespread attention that Eddy received in Calgary turned into a large embarrassment for the ski jumping establishment. Many athletes and officials felt that he was "making a mockery" of the sport. Regarding the Jamaicans, complaints were filed charging the team with "dangerous incompetence" that created a hazard to competitors and bystanders alike. It is noteworthy that there was no complaint whatsoever from this same Olympic establishment about the continued performance-enhancing drug abuse[1] which we now know was common at Olympic events.

As one frequently quoted source so aptly stated, "I guess having fun like the bobsledders or Eddy did isn't part of the Olympic spirit."

In the end, the attention-seeking pampered prima donnas won. Shortly after the Olympics finished, the entry requirements were greatly toughened, making it next to impossible for anyone to follow in the footsteps of the Jamaican bobsledders or Eddy the Eagle.

Little did we know at the time, this was the least of our problems.

---

[1] The 1988 winter Olympics were no exception. At least one athlete was disqualified for testosterone use. To date, a whopping 538 athletes have tested positive to a cornucopia of "make me run faster" drugs.

May 1988

We decided to have our first official team meeting at Sid's Bar and Grill. As usual, it was mostly empty. Tony, the only semblance of legal civilization among us, took charge. He cleared his throat. "Okay. I think we should get started."

Most of the guys ignored the statement and kept up the level of raucous jocularity.

Tony, "Hey guys, sometime this evening would be nice."

No effect.

Carlos stood up and shouted, "Sit down you assholes and shut the fuck up."

The noise immediately quelled and everyone took their seat.

"Thank you, Carlos," Tony said. "Okay. Thanks for coming. I'm going to keep this meeting brief as we all have jobs to go to tomorrow, plus some of you have rather short attention spans."

A few murmured obscenities and gestures.

Tony opened a folder and took out a sheet of paper. "First order of business...I have here official notification from the United Mexican States, commonly known as Mexico... that we, the undersigned, have been granted permission to represent Mexico in the 1992 Winter Olympic Games to be held in Albertville, France, specifically in the sport of Men's Ice Hockey. We will need to..."

Spontaneous cheers erupted, interrupting Tony.

Let's take a few moments to review how this rather miraculous pronouncement came to be. The short version is simple…it's all about money and connections. In Mexico, if you (1) are willing to part with a rather small pile of cash and (2) know the right person, red tape melts like ice cream in July. Tony is a regional chairman for some international organization of minority-run legal practices that has a chapter in Mexico. A few phone calls and poof, we're Mexicans. This was all Tony's doing. He gets all the credit.

As mentioned earlier, Tony is a practicing attorney who thinks he is smarter than the entire planet, has an annoying habit of finishing your sentences, is intellectually tenacious, and is absolutely the worst (or best, depending upon which side you are on) person to ever tell "you can't do" this or that. He also seems to never weary of arguing inane points in a most energetic manner. In short, he's a really effective lawyer. And a good guy.

The first snag Tony faced was that of our citizenship. To compete in the Olympics for any nation you must be a citizen of that country. Thus, we all needed to become legal Mexicans. Again, Tony took the lead, wading through the paperwork with ease. Although our application process would likely take about a year, we had time. The first step in the process, Tony explained, was for all of us to become landowners in Mexico. It turned out that Century 21 had a branch south of the border. Tony made a few calls, mailed a certified check, and presto, we all owned a hectare (100 meters x 100 meters) of empty land in Durango, Mexico.

"And, as I was saying," Tony continued, "We need to get started immediately on the application of citizenry process. I'm passing around a packet of information for each of you." On cue, I started handing out folders to each of our players. "In the folder is an application. Sign where it says 'your name'. Also in the folder is a liability waiver, sign at the bottom of the page. And finally…"

I must say the words liability waiver hung in the air like a charged thunderhead. It was clear none of us had thought that far ahead. A disquieting mood spread over the group.

"...you all owe me $151.50. This is for filing fees, land acquisition, and pre-paid taxes on the property."

That was the second of his one-two punch. What started out as a beer-fueled fantasy was quickly coagulating into a bureaucratic money pit. Like many aspects of life, it had seemed like a really good idea at the time...

As usual, Jimmy was the first to speak up. "$150?"

"$151.50," Tony corrected.

Jimmy, "I didn't think this would cost us anything."

"Thought wrong," Tony replied. "Did you really believe the Mexicans would pay *us* to play for them?"

The stunned silence had run its course. Everyone spoke up at once, mostly expressing dismay at the cost and the paperwork. The entire adventure was in danger of dissolving on the spot when a miracle occurred.

"I'll pick up the tab." The voice came from the bar. It was Roger, the owner of Sid's Bar and Grill.

Another stunned silence.

"I'll pick up the tab," Roger repeated. He went back to polishing beer glasses with a dirty dishtowel.

Tony broke the silence. "That would be very generous, Roger. You are aware the total is on the order of $4,200? Correct?"

Roger tossed the dirty towel in the corner and reached for another. "Yep. The way I figure it, you guys are soon to be all the talk. If you happen to let it slip out that my establishment here," he beckoned with his hands, "was the place where the whole smear got started, well I think business may pick up. Plus," he went back to polishing glasses, "you've kept me afloat for the last couple years."

Cheers and hoorays and plenty shouts of "What a great guy!" broke out.

Once we settled back down, Jimmy raised another interesting point.

"Ah, excuse me, but we need to maybe, well, talk about one little tiny thing."

Tony and I exchanged glances. Neither of us had ever seen Jimmy be evasive about anything. This was really weird.

Tony asked. "What's on your mind, Jimmy?"

"Well, I don't want to cause any trouble or make a big deal about…"

Carlos spoke up. "What are you babbling about?"

Jimmy pointed at Natasha.

Light bulbs went on throughout the room. Some were dimmer than others but it dawned on all of us, Natasha was a woman. This was men's Olympic hockey.

Silence.

Natasha took this in, her expression showing no effect whatsoever.

What is remarkable is what wasn't said. I would have bet a month's salary that any number of sexual slurs would have been forthcoming but, to the undying credit of the rest of the team, they all kept their mouths shut. Furthermore, Natasha was far and away the best offensive punch we had. She could skate, shoot, stickhandle, and make perfect snap passes. She was our one and only scoring threat. We had a real problem.

Tony was frantically flipping through his file and with an "Ah-ha," he extracted a form. He ran his finger down the first sheet of paper, then the second. Finally, a broad grin spread over his face. We all awaited the pronouncement.

He removed his glasses and said, "We're going to cheat."

This was akin to Santa Claus gaily announcing he is a fraud. Tony was a straight shooter. He was a lawyer. Sure, he might bend the truth (they all do) but he *never* outright lied.

Jimmy found his voice first. "What did you say?"

Tony smiled again and waved his papers around. "According to these new Olympic rules, we will have to pee in a cup. Several cups by the looks of these tests. We will also have to give blood and sign several documents stating we have not taken, nor are we currently taking, a very long list of drugs and substances. Our luggage will be subject to random searches and our contact with the outside world while we are in the Olympic village will be closely monitored. Nowhere here or in anything I have read does it say anything about proving or disproving one's sex."

It was as if the politically correct dam had just burst. A flood of sex-related comments suddenly sprang from the lips of the team like a commotion of seagulls around someone's new-found sandwich. Overheard were exclamations such as "drop pants inspection" and "I'll volunteer to check the women" and "blind group groping" and so on. It went on for a few minutes before Tony held up his hand for order.

"We will proceed until caught. Natasha, you will stay in the background, dress like the rest of us, and keep your helmet on whenever we are on the ice. If someone says anything about it, I will make a big issue about sexual equality and glass ceilings and rattle off some quotes from Martin Luther King and in short, turn the whole event into a 'challenge the establishment issue'." He looked at Natasha and concluded, "It's worth a try."

Natasha beamed at Tony. Her fantasy of jumping his bones was dangerously close to coming true. Tony also realized what was going on in her Russian head and quickly added, "Because she is our best player. Meeting over." He gathered up his papers and left rather quickly.

October 1988

Stunned by the continued attention received by the Jamaican Bobsled team and Eddy the Eagle, the Olympic world, behaving like the spoiled child it was, passed a series of rules and requirements to make sure nothing like that ever happened again. In essence, they required teams who had not competed in previous Olympics (Mexican Ice Hockey, for example) to get an International Ice Hockey Federation (IIHF)and an International Olympic Committee (IOC) ranking. To do so, new teams would have to play in an internationally recognized tournament. Here is the actual verbiage:

"Qualification for the men's tournament is structured around the 2008 IIHF World Ranking. The top nine teams in the World Ranking after the 2008 Men's World Ice Hockey Championships received automatic berths into the Olympics, while all remaining member federations could attempt to qualify for the remaining three spots in the Olympics. In October 2008, the four lowest entrants played off for a spot in the first round. Teams then ranked 19th through 30th played in a first qualification round in November 2008, where the top three teams from the round advance to the second qualification round. Teams ranked 10th through 18th joined the three top teams from the first qualifying round to play in a second qualification round. The top three teams from the second qualifying round advanced to the Olympic tournament."

If this seems difficult to understand, it is. If this seems like a private men's club, it is. What is not written in the gobbledygook above is that the IOC retains the right to advance any team into the Olympic tournament without meeting the prequalification requirement. In other words, let's say a team (like the USA) does so poorly on the international circuit that they would likely fall below the qualification round cutoff. They could and would be elevated to tournament status because, after all, the USA is a huge contributor to the club.

Most sane applicants would walk away from such an organization. Tony, our legal beagle, is not your average sane applicant. In fact, this rather exclusionary mode of operation is precisely what fired Tony to leap into action.

November 1988

"Remember, we are guests here. Behave!" Tony said as we filed into the Officers Club (OC) at Pease Air Force Base in Portsmouth, NH. Being 4 a.m., the club was not yet open for business but because two members of the team were officers in the Air National Guard, we were allowed access to the closed-circuit TV in the OC to watch the first of the qualifying games for the 1989 World Cup Ice Hockey Tournament. Our Mexican team was not yet ready to play, but watching our competition would give us an idea of what we would be up against. This first-round game was scheduled to start at 10 a.m. in Berlin, Germany, which is six hours ahead of New Hampshire.

We groggily took our seats and stared at the dark TV screen. A red light was blinking in the bottom right corner. A technician turned to us and said, "Still connecting. It will be any second now."

I sipped my coffee and looked around. We had come a long way. We were now landowners in Durango, Mexico, our applications for citizenship were proceeding, and passports were in process. The design of our uniforms was still being argued, but at least we all agreed that the national colors of Mexico are green, white, and red. This took a fair amount of convincing because some of the guys are not exactly Rhodes Scholars. No one had yet broached the topic of airfare, but we could tackle that later. So far, so good.

The TV screen suddenly brightened and an ice rink appeared. The technician changed the voice from German to English, turned up the volume and we were in business. Everyone sat up and watched. The game had already started. National teams from Japan and Bulgaria were competing for a spot in the qualifying tournament. The game was only about two minutes old and the score was already Bulgaria 3, Japan 0. I thought there must be some mistake. It is very difficult to score three goals in two minutes. But no, the elapsed time and score were correct.

At this point, a little background information is in order. I learned later that Bulgaria had been arbitrarily bumped by the IIHA from tournament status to a very low seed. It almost certainly had something to do with funding and advertising revenues, but be that as it may, the Bulgarians were humiliated and not happy with their lot. In fact, they were really pissed off. The team from Japan, on the other hand, was really excited about trying out this rather new sport. They brought along their cute little cheering section waving white flags with round red spots, all smiles and behaving quite properly. Another aspect of this particular game that should be taken into consideration as our story unfolds is the relative size and ferocity quotient of each team. The average player from Japan was about 5'6" and tipped the scale at about 125 pounds. As a group, they were polite and relatively gentle in their approach to body checking. The Bulgarians were quite different. Although Cro-Magnons and Neanderthals were first unearthed in France and Germany, there is little doubt that those fossils were Bulgarians who had gotten lost. In fact, it sure looked like their direct descendants were playing for the Bulgarian team. Their guys were huge, fast, and aggressive. Plus, did I mention they were not very happy? The Japanese were in for a bad time.

In retrospect, the entire surreal situation was further exacerbated by the TV announcers who were remarkably bad. The two guys who were handling the TV play-by-play could have been Abbot and Costello, famous for their "Who's on first?" routine. They had a hard time with the names, and they were clearly astounded at the debacle on the ice. At one point, it sounded something like this:

Abbot: "…oh, and another heavy check by Bulgarian Alexsandar Smitspoff on Japanese forward Akemi Mustache…and Mustache is down on the ice."

Costello: "I think it's Mustachi."

Abbot: "Is he hurt too?"

Costello: "No. The Japanese player who's hurt is Mustachi."

Abbot: "That's what I said."

Once they got that straight, they made another observation.

Abbot: "That's the third injured Japanese player who has been taken to the locker room, and the first period is only half over."

Costello: "At this rate, there won't be enough skaters to play by the third period."

Abbot: "And you know, I think the uninjured players who are helping the wounded off the ice aren't returning either. I think they are hiding in the dressing room."

Costello: "Do you blame them? The Bulgarians are crushing these guys. Mustache is still down."

Abbot: "Who?"

The game went on, until near the end of the first period with the score Bulgaria 11, Japan 0, a scuffle broke out.

Abbot: "Take a look at the Japanese bench. Something's happening down there.

Costello: "It looks like the coach and his staff are wrestling with some players. What the heck?"

Abbot: "Look! The Japanese coaches are throwing players onto the ice. And they want nothing to do with it! The players are jumping the boards back onto the bench!"

Costello: "From up here it appears as if the coach is having difficulty getting players to take to the ice."

Abbot: "He'd better get some players on the ice or the referee will give them a delay of game penalty."

Costello: "And check out the Bulgarians. They're laughing."

Abbot: "Do you think the lions laughed when the Christians were tossed into the forum?"

Costello: "Who are the lions?"

Abbot: "What?"

Costello: "Which team is the lions?"

Abbot: "This is a metaphor for what's happening on the ice."

Costello: "What are you talking about?"

Clearly, the two play-by-play announcers would not be invited to join ABC's Wide World of Sports anytime soon.

The Japanese finally managed to get six players on the ice and, for the remainder of the first period, successfully avoided the Bulgarians, the puck, and most importantly, getting crushed. The end of the period mercifully arrived, the horn blew and the Japanese hurried off the ice. A few minutes later, at the beginning of the second period, the Bulgarians took to the ice and skated their warm-up laps. No sign of the Japanese. After a few moments, one of the referees went to the Japanese locker room to get the team on the ice. The locker room was empty. The Japanese were gone.

Abbot and Costello babbled on, clearly at a loss as to what they should be talking about. When it became apparent the game was over, the technician turned off the TV and shut down the system.

For a long time, no one on the Mexican ice hockey team said a word. In unison, we had had a rare opportunity to glimpse future events. It was very likely our qualifying match would be against the Bulgarians, or worse yet, the Latvians who were rumored to make the Bulgarians look like pansies. Hockey on this level was a rough, aggressive sport played for keeps. It was unlikely the Bulgarians would be willing to "take it easy on us."

I could imagine skating over to the Bulgarian bench before the game began and saying, "Hi guys. Listen, we're here on a lark because we think we're funny, and we would really appreciate it if you would dispense with checking and all the rough stuff. What do you think? Could we agree to that?"

Bulgarian response. "Nothing personal, but we are going to kill you, your Mexican coward."

Me. "Well, that's just it. We're really not Mexicans at all. We're actually Americans pretending to be Mexicans." I would smile charmingly.

Bulgarian response. "Oh, that changes everything. We *hate* Americans. We are going to break all your bones, and then kill you."

It was Natasha who finally broke the silence. "Bulgarians are pigs. They like to hurt people. I not playing." She got up and left the room.

One by one, our other players stood, made some flimsy excuse and followed suit. In the end, it was me and Jimmy and Tony and Carlos.

Carlos spoke first: "I'm too old to mix it up."

Tony followed: "Yeah, me too. It was fun while it lasted."

Me: "Sure was."

Jimmy: "Do you think we could be the Mexican curling team?"

Epilogue June 2007

I noticed a "missed call" note on my phone. It was from Tony. His voice-mail message: "Call me."

"Hi Tony, what's up?"

"Does the name Maxious mean anything to you?

"No."

"He is the spokesman for the law firm representing the Sinaloa drug cartel in northern Mexico."

"Okay."

"Are you sitting?"

"I am now."

"My law firm just received a check for $10,000 from the Law Practice of Maxious, Maxious, and Hernandez to cover, and now I'm quoting, 'the cost of immediate and uncontested disposition of twenty-nine hectares of land in Durango, Mexico. The excess payment for land valued at an estimated $2900 US is offered to minimize further contact and correspondence for said parcels of land.' Unquote."

A chill went up my spine. "Wow! What do you think?"

"I think some people have been using our land, and now they want to make things right. Maybe the Mexican government, in their ongoing drug wars, is looking at who is doing what and where they are doing it. I think we do not want to be involved."

"Perhaps we should not offer a counterproposal. Correct?"

Tony chuckled. "It is against my nature not to argue but this time let me put my response in terms we all understand... you bet your ass."

Later, Tony and I had supper at Sid's Bar and Grill. Roger, the owner, bought us a beer and pulled up a bar stool.

Tony: "How's business?"

Roger: "Getting by."

Tony, tapping on the wooden countertop: "Looks like the old bar is showing some age."

Roger: "Yeah, I've been thinking about some renovations. As soon as my fairy Godmother comes across with some cash, I'll take care of it."

Me: "How much to do the whole job?"

Roger scratched his gray beard. "I have a quote for the bar at $7000 and another $2500 for new furniture, mirrors, TV, and lights. I'd guess ten big ones should do it.

Tony and I exchanged looks and nodded.

Extracting a bank envelope from his jacket pocket, Tony said, "Roger, let me introduce myself. My name is Fairy Godmother."

A Road Trip with Aunt Claire

It was a perfect day for a funeral. Although the sun was warm, there was little doubt that autumn was in full swing, complete with fallen leaves being pushed along by a gentle breeze. October in New England is glorious but fickle, with the gray, bitter days of November waiting in the wings. But that particular day was perfect.

Dr. William Sweeny, MD, glanced at his watch, sighed, and then tried to get comfortable on a white, folding funeral chair. Another fifteen minutes and he could depart. He slouched back in his seat, picked a few stray pieces of lint off his black, tailored, pin-striped suit, and raised his face to the remaining sunshine. A warm breeze mussed his shock of prematurely graying hair.

An elderly couple, dressed in appropriate somber garb shuffled to the grave site. Bill jumped to his feet, removing his sunglasses. The man, bald, painfully thin, and shrunken, extended his liver-spotted hand.

"Dr. Sweeny, we are so sorry for the loss of your mother. Caroline was a good woman. She'll be missed."

Bill, at least a foot taller, looked down at him, swallowed a sudden lump in his throat, and smiled. "Thank you. And thank you for coming."

The woman, also diminutive, swept in and gave Bill a hug. "Please accept our condolences," she said in a quavering voice. "And I think it's quite touching how Caroline's ashes will now reside with those of your father." She turned and pointed at the granite marker which read, 'Caroline Sweeny, 1948 – 2018,' and 'Andrew Sweeny 1946 - 2016.'

"Yes, well, that was her wish." Bill studied them both, wondering who they were.

The woman stood back. "The Lord has granted a spectacular fall day for the service. I think Caroline would have been most appreciative for this send-off."

Bill forced another smile. "Again, thanks for coming."

"Still," the woman added, as she turned to depart, taking her husband's arm. "I do miss the bodies and caskets. This business of ashes, well," she shook her head mournfully, "it's just not the same."

Then she and her husband departed.

Frowning, Bill Sweeny replaced his sunglasses and watched them shuffle off. "Bodies?"

When he turned back to the handful of white chairs, a woman was seated in the front row.

"Hello, Billy."

"Aunt Claire! I thought I'd seen you earlier. Where'd you go?"

She pointed a long black gloved arm off to the right. "Do you have any idea how far it is to the restroom? It's hell and gone from here. And in these shoes!" She lifted her foot and wiggled her ankle. Her black leather boots had significant heels. "Come sit with me."

Aunt Claire was smartly dressed in a gray gabardine suit coat and matching skirt. A beaded stylish handbag was resting upon her lap. Her face was shaded by a black Betmar Braided wide-brimmed hat. As Bill approached, she studied him with piercing blue-grey eyes.

"Billy, you're too skinny."

Bill chuckled. "I'd like to think of myself as athletic. And you're the only person alive who still calls me Billy." He took one of her gloved hands in his. "I'm glad you came back."

With her free hand, she reached into her sizable purse and withdrew a silver flask. "Join me?"

He smiled and slowly shook his head. "You never cease to amaze me, and no thanks, it's a bit early in the day for me."

Aunt Claire took a sip and they sat quietly for a moment. "So Billy, what are you thinking?"

Bill pursed his lips and leaned back in the uncomfortable chair. He looked up at the sun. "I guess…I guess I'm kind of sad, but mostly okay."

She extracted her hand from his, removed her hat exposing her full head of striking silver-gray hair, took off her sunglasses, and looked him square in the eye. "I've known you since you were filling your diapers with butternut squash. Even as a little boy, I could always tell when you were lying. You haven't changed a bit. You're lying. Now, how about the truth. What are you really feeling?"

Bill stretched his long legs, chuckling again. "Well, if you put it that way, I suppose I'm feeling relieved. I'm glad it's over. Mom's last six months were gruesome. Cancer is a dreadful way to die. But at the same time, I'm feeling guilty as sin that I'm not overcome with grief or despondency or one of those other synonyms for sad. A strange juxtaposition of emotions I'd say. Make no mistake about it, I'm going to miss her, probably more than I know, but in the end, I was hoping she'd pass quickly." He paused, and then asked, "So there. How did I do?"

Aunt Claire put away the flask and sat for several beats in her prim and proper, erect manner, hands folded on her lap, staring at the grave marker. "That's better. Always tell the truth. And you're right. The last six months were a nightmare for my sister. But you know," She turned in her seat and looked at Bill again, "she didn't die of cancer. She died of a broken heart. She started dying two years ago when her husband of five decades keeled over at the dinner table. I've never seen someone so utterly destroyed by the passing of their spouse. I suppose they really were soul mates. That cancer business, that's just the symptom of a broken heart. If it wasn't cancer it would have been something else."

Bill folded his arms and nodded. "It's not medical science you're speaking of, but likely closer to the actual cause of death that you think. At work, we're studying..."

"I don't think, I know," she shot back. "You hoity-toity, Ivy League doctors think you have all the answers but you and I both know, you're mostly just guessing half the time but can't admit it because you charge too much. When it comes to affairs of the heart, you guys are way out in left field."

Bill nodded again. "Got me there. Hell, I can't even manage the affairs of my own heart."

A few fallen maple leaves tumbled by in the breeze.

"And speaking of that," Aunt Claire said. "What happened to that young woman with the pretty blue eyes and the nice shape?"

"Which one?"

"Don't smart mouth me. You know who I'm talking about. You brought her into my home for dinner last summer."

"Oh, you're talking about Sarah."

"And?"

Bill shrugged. "She wasn't willing to marry someone who works a million hours a week."

"Can you blame her?"

"No, I suppose not."

Another quiet minute passed.

"Do you ever hear from, what's her name, Lorrie? You know, your first wife?"

Bill smiled. "Her name was Lynn. I was never married to a Lorrie. And no, she has re-married to some lawyer, and has a bunch of kids."

"Caroline would have liked a grandchild or two."

"Let's not go there, ok?"

Aunt Claire removed one of her gloves and studied her freshly manicured nails.

Then she said, "I sold my house."

Relieved and pleased with the change of topic, Bill sat up and enthusiastically said, "I heard that! Congratulations! With your house being sold and Mom's also on the market, the old neighborhood will never be the same."

"The people who bought my house want to buy your mother's as well for their elderly parents. If they do, they won't even have to replace the gate in the fence. They'll be able to come and go as we did for all those years."

Bill sat back and mused, as much to himself as to Aunt Claire, "It'll be strange not going there anymore."

"I'm moving to The Villages in Florida."

He turned to his aunt. "This is news. What are the Villages?"

"An adult community. Fifty-five and older. You know the kind I mean. It's a place where old people go who aren't yet ready for the walker and day-time TV."

"Wow! When?"

"Soon."

More silence.

Aunt Claire removed her other glove to examine the nail polish there as well. "I hear, you have four weeks off of work."

"Yep. The office is moving across the street to a newer building. With the exception of medical emergencies, we're closing the practice for a month." Bill gestured to the funeral set up with his right hand. "This sad event marks the first day of my longest vacation since graduate school."

Aunt Claire reached into her pocketbook, removed an envelope, and handed it to Bill.

"What's this?"

"An airline ticket. It's a one-way return trip from Florida to Boston."

"Why…"

"Because tomorrow, you're driving me to Florida."

*   *   *

Without a word or eye contact, the waitress placed a Manhattan in front of Aunt Claire and refilled Bill's coffee, then hurried away. She seemed to be trying to stifle a smile.

Bill stared after her. "An odd duck, don't you think?"

Aunt Claire checked her lipstick with a handheld mirror. "They're all odd down here in the south. Half of them are still fighting the Civil War, the other half are getting inebriated at the car races. Anybody that supports NASCAR racing has the IQ of a toad."

Bill rolled his eyes. "Well, that about covers most of the southland. You may find it difficult to make friends in your new neighborhood with an attitude like that.

Aunt Claire removed the cherry from her drink. "At least they can make a decent drink, which is more than can be said about their food. The steaks were largely forgettable, the vegetables soggy, the salad tasteless, and the store bought apple pie mushy and geriatric. The only redeemable features of this Steak House is its location." She sipped her drink. "What are we, about halfway to Florida?"

"Yes, Rocky Mount is roughly halfway."

She pointed at the sign over the bar. "And what the hell is a Tar Heel?"

Bill folded his hands and exhaled. "It refers to the soldiers from North Carolina who fought in the Civil War. They were reluctant to retreat and their comrades said they had tar on their heels. That's why they stayed. Get it? Tar on their heels? Stuck to the ground?"

"I told you they were still fighting the civil war."

Bill shook his head in exasperation, started to say something but thought better of it. After a pause, he said, "You were quiet during today's drive."

Aunt Claire took another sip of her drink. "Well, as far as I know, I don't talk in my sleep."

"I meant when you weren't sleeping."

"I'm not going to compete with the radio. You had that obnoxious news show on from Massachusetts to North Carolina."

"NPR?"

"That's the one."

Bill sipped his coffee and then frowned. "What's wrong with NPR?"

"National Public Radio? It's the same, tired old rhetoric we've been hearing for fifty years. Continued unrest and bombings in the Mideast. Our nation's economy is heading for disaster. The earth's environment is swirling down the toilet. Our beloved house and senate are at odds with the president. The president is a crook. Nothing's changed."

Bill drummed his fingers for a while.

"*Car Talk* was funny."

"And those guys have retired. Hell, the older brother died. That was a taped show from years ago."

"Good point. Well, *Wait, Wait, Don't Tell* me was funny."

"If you're a liberal. I suspect the other half of our country finds those guys offensive."

They sat silently for another moment.

Then Bill leaned across the table and whispered, "I've been watching our waitress and her pals. They keep staring at us and giggling from behind the kitchen door."

"Ignore them. They're just southern morons."

Bill threw up his hands in exasperation. "Let me ask you something. Why are you so grumpy?"

"You mean more than usual?"

"Okay, yes. More than usual."

"And how would you know what's usual for me? When's the last time you spent any time with me...or Caroline for that matter?"

"Come on, that's hitting below the belt. We've been all over that issue. I'm joking. I'm just trying to make pleasant conversation."

"Well, maybe I'm not feeling all that pleasant."

Another awkwardly quiet moment passed.

Bill said, "I guess that's understandable."

Aunt Claire took another sip of her drink. "I'm going to sorely miss my sister. Her glass was always half full. Mine is always half empty. She was a good woman. She saw the flowers. I saw the weeds. She kept me from falling off the edge. And now…who knows. All my friends are gone now."

Bill nodded.

"And another thing. Are you gay?"

Bill pursed his lips for a long beat, and then said, "You'll have to forgive me but I'm trying in vain to follow the thread that ties this disjointed conversation together." He shook his head and turned his hands palms up. "I give up. And to address your question, no, I'm not gay. Why in the world would you ask that question?"

"I told Caroline I thought you were. She laughed. So you're not?"

Bill smiled and shrugged. "Nope. But would it matter if I was?"

It was Aunt Claire's turn to shrug. "Would it matter to me? Nope. But it's a bit of a mystery why you're still single."

Bill drained his coffee and signaled for a refill. "I was married once."

Aunt Claire waved her hand like she was shooing away a gnat. "And how long did that last? A year? Maybe two? Anybody can get married. Staying married is the trick. Look…you're a doctor, good-looking, and rich. I'd think women would be lined up, wanting to sink their claws into you."

Bill laughed. "Now there's a romantic image!"

"That's me. Claire, The Romantic."

"Well, just to clear up any questions you may have. No Aunt Claire, I'm not gay."

"Well, maybe you should take some time off from work and test the water. Love and companionship are…" Her voice trailed off. For a moment she was lost in a distant memory, but then she concluded with, "You might find there's more to life than being Doctor Billy."

The smirking waitress refilled Bill's coffee, then departed, again without a word. They sipped their beverages in silence for another moment.

Bill asked, "Are you sad to be leaving Massachusetts?"

"Are you kidding? Massachusetts is for rich kids like you. Everything up there is top dollar. There are no bargains in the Bay State for old fixed-income people like me. Make it in Massachusetts… maybe. But keep it in Massachusetts…no way! Plus, the winters are getting colder and longer. You guys keep talking about global warming. That's more NPR and pseudo-intellectual nonsense. It's going the other way. Einstein talked about relativity and how we measure everything from our own point of view. Right?"

Bill folded his arms. "Einstein? Relativity? What are you…"

"I'm right and you know it. As far as I'm concerned, summer has become so short I can sleep through it. My vision of how pleasant or unpleasant the weather might be is my personal relativity and according to Einstein, that makes it a fact…at least for me. And from my point of view, it's damn cold. And dark. And icy. I've had enough. I should have done this years ago."

"Hmm, I'm not so sure Einstein intended his theory to be interpreted that way but each to their own I suppose. But I'm surprised. I thought you were dug in up there. Why didn't you leave before now?"

"Caroline. She needed me as much as I needed her. She was all I had left. Well, *almost* all."

"I see."

"And that reminds me, I have something to discuss with you tomorrow."

"Oh? What's it all about?"

"I said we'd discuss it tomorrow."

"No previews of coming attractions?

"No."

They sat in silence for a full minute. All the while, Bill was watching the wait staff, peeking out the door of the kitchen at them. They were definitely looking their way and smirking. Finally, he started to get up. "Excuse me, Aunt Claire. I'm going to go over and have a little chat with our waitress and find out what's so funny."

She reached across the table and grabbed Bill's shirt sleeve. "Just relax. Sit back down. While you were carrying the suitcases into our room, one of those waitress chickies, the cute redhead with a big chest, sidled over and asked me if you were available. I told her to keep her hands off because I'm a sexual cougar and you are my gigolo."

Bill's eye's popped open wide and he sat bolt upright. "WHAT?"

"Yep. And I told them you were expensive but worth every penny."

* * *

The windshield wipers were barely able to keep up with the pouring rain. Bill leaned over the steering wheel, peering into the morning gloom.

Aunt Claire fiddled with the heat, trying to chase away the dampness. "So tell me, Billy. What is it you do in that research laboratory you spend so many hours at?"

"Lots of things. Most recently, I led a team that developed a breakthrough procedure for administering chemotherapy for certain types of cancer. Our procedure reduces the ill effects of chemo to the point where many patients can receive their full treatment as an outpatient, without nausea and other nasty side effects."

Giving up on the HVAC system, she tightened her sweater. "I see. And are you any closer to finding a cure for cancer once and for all?"

Bill shook his head. "No. We've got a ways to go to pin that one down. But this new procedure, it's a wow. We're going to be really busy getting this on the market. That's one of the reasons our office is moving across the street. We'll need more room."

Aunt Claire looked out the window.

Bill continued. "This new way of handling chemo is going to save a whole lot of pain and suffering, the world over. I'm really proud of my folks."

Still no response.

"You know Aunt Claire, this is really a big deal. An 'atta boy Billy' would be in order here. I'm really proud of this breakthrough."

163

"Is that why you do what you do? For 'atta' boys?"

Bill shook his head in disgust. "I should know better by now."

"What's that supposed to mean?"

A few miles rolled by.

Bill broke the silence. "No matter what I ever did, it was never good enough for you."

"Such as?"

"Even way back in elementary school, you used to drop in after dinner and look over my homework. You always made me correct this or re-write that. You never were pleased with anything I did. It was never to your standards."

"That's because Caroline was too soft with you and her husband was always working. Someone had to check your work."

Bill's face reddened. "Soft? That had nothing to do with it. She was content to have me around, you know – the mom and son routine. The constant whip cracking, that was all your doing."

"And now you're a doctor. If I didn't monitor your schoolwork, you'd be asking patrons whether they wanted paper or plastic at the local grocery store."

"And how about the little league games and school play and cub scouts. You were always pushing me to practice more and try harder and qualify for more merit badges. What I did was never good enough. Maybe a pat on the back would have inspired me as much as the constant kick in the pants."

Aunt Claire folded her hands on her lap and stared out the windshield. "Perhaps, but last time I looked, you seem to be doing quite well for yourself, a big-time research doctor and all. Let me ask you something. Do you remember your entrance essay for admission to Yale? Do you remember what the Dean of Admissions told you?"

It was Bill's turn to go silent and stare straight ahead.

"Let me refresh your memory, he told you it was your essay that got you accepted. I believe the quote was something like… 'he had never read a finer composition.' Surely you remember that?"

No reply.

"And how many times did you rewrite that essay? Let me give you a hint: it's a number between four and six. And let me toss this factoid out to chew on. Do you think I had nothing better to do than to help you get accepted at an Ivy League school, that I knew would open all kinds of doors and create unimaginable opportunities for you to excel at?"

Bill held up his hand. "Fine, but Jesus, Aunt Claire, a 'well done' wouldn't kill you, you know."

"Alright then, 'well done.'"

They crossed into South Carolina in a long period of unbroken silence. Then down around Savanah, Aunt Claire said, "I have something to tell you."

Bill, startled by the announcement, said, "Wha...what? Okay, shoot."

"While getting ready to move, I've been going through all my belongings, tossing out baskets full of stuff I have no idea why I saved in the first place when I came across some old pictures. They brought back memories." She stopped talking for a long time, causing Bill to shoot her a glance.

"And?"

"I had an affair."

Bill gripped the steering wheel to keep from driving off the road. "What? What did you say?"

"I had an affair with Jack McSorely, our neighbor."

Bill blinked several times, cleared his throat, and said, "Look, I really have no interest in..."

"I have to tell you this because everyone else who ever knew anything about this is dead and I have to get it off my chest. You should know this about me."

"Please Aunt Claire, it's ok. Whatever you did..."

"This started before you were born. My late husband, Tom, had been killed by a drunk driver and I was lonely. Jack had lost his wife to some sort of brain sickness the year before and he was also lonely. We got to talking over the fence and one thing led to another."

Bill's mouth fell open. "This is Mr. McSorely, our neighbor to whom I delivered newspapers to every day and shoveled his driveway in the winter for fifty cents? He had that really big black dog, Raven, that always tried to lick my face off. That was the guy?"

"Yes."

"Oh, my God. He lived next door, you lived behind us. You two were...I really don't want to know any more about this, okay?"

Aunt Claire rustled around in her handbag for a minute then extracted a picture. She held it up for Bill to see. "This is one of the photos I found last week. This was me back then."

Bill glanced at the old photo and then did a double take. "Oh Jesus, Aunt Claire, what the hell? That woman is nude! Put that away."

Aunt Claire adjusted her glasses and studied the picture. "I looked rather sexy back then, don't you agree?"

Bill shot another glance at the picture. "Is that you? Is that really you?"

Aunt Claire raised her eyebrows and fixed Bill with a withering glare over her glasses. "Is that so hard to believe?"

"Actually, you look rather..." Bill stopped. "Hold on, where did you have that developed? Back then, drug store film developers wouldn't develop nudes, nor would the camera stores."

Aunt Claire continued to study the picture. "Jack was an amateur photographer. He had a dark room. This was taken before gravity won the battle."

Bill opened his mouth but said nothing. He furrowed his brow, clearly trying to recall the past. "I used to deliver newspapers to McSorely, and shoveled his driveway, and mowed his lawn. You could have been in his house while I was right outside...this is very hard for me to picture."

"We kept our little tryst secret for years. In fact, up until his death ten years ago, only Caroline knew about it. Oh, her husband knew but he made believe it wasn't happening. Denial is very powerful. Our favorite meeting place was a little inn in Vermont, although we had other spots as well. We'd both leave separately for the weekend, to keep the neighbors from suspecting anything, and then rendezvous at the inn. It was <u>so</u> exciting. The anticipation was…" Aunt Claire drifted off, a faint smile on her face.

"Listen, Aunt Claire, I really don't…"

"He'd leave his dog with Caroline and I believe you were saddled with the task of taking care of it. Remember?"

Bill again furrowed his brow, trying to recall those events of his childhood which involved Raven. Then, in an astonished voice, said, "I had to take care of that dog all the time. How many times did you sneak away?"

Aunt Claire said nothing but smiled again.

*   *   *

Moving boxes were stacked in the corner of the kitchen. Aunt Claire had rooted around long enough to locate the coffee pot and two mugs. The beans were ground, the water added and was dripping through the ground coffee when Bill entered, carrying his suitcase.

"Smells good," he said.

"How'd you sleep?" Aunt Claire asked, looking in a box in a futile effort to find some napkins.

Bill pulled up a chair. "Not bad. Of course, I was exhausted after the long drive and could have slept in a phone booth if need be. Thanks for making the coffee. What time does the van arrive to take me to the airport?"

"Soon. About a half an hour. You've got time to sit and visit."

Bill removed a box from one of the chairs and took his seat at the kitchen table. He sipped his coffee then said, "I have to admit, I'm not feeling comfortable leaving you here."

"Oh?"

"You'll be here by yourself in a new home in a new community in a new state, not knowing anyone. I'm not feeling good about leaving you this way."

Aunt Claire chuckled. "Not to worry. At ten this morning I'll be attending the 'Newcomers Welcome Brunch' over at the clubhouse. Then this afternoon is my orientation where I meet all the staff and other newcomers, and then this evening, I've been invited to attend the Mystery Reader's Book Club at the library. I doubt if I'll waste away, pining with loneliness."

"Well, all the same. I'll be a bit worried…"

"I'll be fine."

They sat quietly for a minute, and then Aunt Claire asked, "What are you going to with the rest of your time off?"

Bill squirmed in his chair, took a deep breath, exhaled, and then said, "If I tell you, do you promise you won't poke fun at my plans?"

"All right, promise."

"I'm going on a medical professionals' retreat at a resort in the Berkshires."

No response.

"Well?"

"I promised I wouldn't poke fun."

Bill sighed. "Thank you."

Another minute of silenced passed then Aunt Claire said, "But if I didn't promise, I'd probably say something like… 'now doesn't that sound like a rollicking wild time'…but since I promised…" She sipped her coffee and pretended to find interest in one of the moving boxes.

Bill pursed his lips. "And what else? Come on, get it all out now before I go."

"What are you and your nerdy doctor friends going to do? Run around and stick rectal thermometers in each other?"

"Are you done now?"

"Oh, I'll bet I could come up with a few others but for now, yes."

Bill leaned on the table, staring in his Aunt Claire's eyes to make certain she was listening, and said, "Well if you must know, I've arranged to meet someone there."

Aunt Claire's eyebrows went up. "Someone?"

"Yes, one of my colleagues. One of my *female*_colleagues."

"And is it your plan to discuss something other than rectal thermometers with this female colleague?"

"That is my plan."

"Would I like her?"

"You don't like anybody."

"Would I dislike her less than her predecessors?"

"I think so, but I can never predict."

"Well, this is news." Then, Aunt Claire became quiet, sipping her coffee.

A few minutes passed in silence, then she looked up at the clock and said, "And now, before you go, I have some more news for you."

She put down her cup and stared down at her hands. Then, she fixed Bill with a steady gaze.

"A long time ago," she began, "before my secret affair with Jack McSorely, I was involved with another man. This followed on the heels of my husband's death and I suppose, I was emotionally vulnerable. Regardless, during this brief fling, I became pregnant. Nine months later I gave birth to a boy...which I gave to Caroline."

Silence does not make noise, yet sometimes it is described as deafening. This was one of those times.

Aunt Claire continued. "She had been trying for quite some time to become pregnant to no avail and was getting desperate. I, on the other hand, recognizing my abysmal mothering skills, would not....

She held her hands in an effort to keep them from shaking. "Caroline, on her worst day, was a million times better at being a mother than I, on my best day. And since I'd be just over the fence in your backyard, I could be there and...

Bill quietly interrupted, "And take me to Cub Scout meetings and little league baseball and the circus."

Bill and Aunt Claire stared into each other's eyes. Finally, Aunt Claire said, "I promised Caroline I'd never breathe a word of this to you as long as she lived. And now, well..."

Bill, breathing again, asked, "Why are you telling me this?"

"I don't know."

The van to the airport arrived outside. The driver beeped the horn.

Aunt Claire said, " If you are free, I'd love to have you down here at Christmas."

Bill stood. "It'll take me at least that long to sort all this out."

The van horn beeped again.

Aunt Claire jumped up, crossed the kitchen, opened the door, and shouted, "He'll be right out." Then she turned and faced Bill. "And the answer is yes you know."

"Yes?"

Aunt Claire wrung her hands, and in a tone slightly higher than normal, said, "Yes…I am proud of you. Yes, I'm proud of the work you do. And Lord knows, I've always been fiercely proud of you. I just…

She paused, then took a steadying deep breathe, "…couldn't say it. And I'm sorry I never said the words before. But I am proud of you."

Bill closed the gap between them and they embraced for a long time. Finally, both wiping their eyes, Bill picked up his suitcase and headed for the door.

Aunt Claire said, "So, will I see you at Christmas?"

Bill nodded. "Yes, you will."

Aunt Claire wrung her hands together. "And if you have a woman in tow, I promise to be on my best behavior.

Bill chuckled. "But you break your promises."

"Not this one."

Bill held Aunt Claire in his gaze, and then said, "I'll see you at Christmas."

House Flipping Blues

Chapter One

If it seems too good to be true, it probably is

It was Sunday morning and I had just settled into my favorite chair, a mug of hot coffee at my elbow, and a snappy fire in the fireplace. The weather was uncomfortably cold outside, which meant I would not feel one bit guilty about being a lazy slug and staying indoors to resume one of my favorite pastimes—reading.

I was well into *The Canterville Ghost* by Oscar Wilde, when my wife Doris came bustling in.

"Nick," she began excitedly. "Take a look at this." She held aloft the real estate section of the local newspaper, *The McPhee Star*.

I sighed. "Well, good morning to you, Doris. No, I wasn't doing anything important, so sure, go ahead and interrupt my veritable emergence into the haunted castle at *Canterville Chase*."

"Where?"

I held up the hardcover book I was reading.

"Oh, I see." Doris replied. "Sorry to bother you, but I found just what we've been looking for: a house on the lake."

I slid a bookmark into my book, snapped it closed, and reluctantly laid it on the end table next to my chair. "No. If it's in the real estate section of the paper, it's what *you've* been looking for, not me."

My wife and I had recently retired to the quiet little hamlet of McPhee, Colorado. Doris, like me, was a retired college professor from Arizona State. We had long planned for this next phase of life, and as Lt. Colonel George Custer said on June 25, 1876, as he rode along the Little Bighorn River in Montana, "So far, so good."

By way of introduction, I'm Nick Weatherspoon and I was three years into my retirement — retired with a full pension from my job as Professor of English Literature at Arizona State — when this strange tale began.

I suppose I look the part of a former professor: I'm tall, have a mop of unruly white hair, wear tweedy jackets, smoke a pipe, and continue to battle a few extra pounds. The latter, of course, is due to my ongoing quest for the perfect table wine.

My idea of retirement is, first and foremost, to read anything and everything that I was too busy to read when I was working. Once, in a moment of temporary insanity, I mentioned to Doris that I thought I might like to buy/fix/sell houses in my retirement. Big mistake.

Conversely, Doris, retired professor of business accounting, is tall and angular. Her hair resembles that of Albert Einstein, as do most aspects of her personal appearance, and her idea of retirement is to do *everything*. Owing to her boundless energy, she is actually trying to accomplish this impossible task. Sitting and reading is not even on her list, which, for some couples, could be a reason for conflict, but because we really and truly love each other, it isn't. Still, it does result in an occasional heavy sigh. The house on the lake was one of these times.

I sighed heavily.

Undaunted, Doris plowed on. "There's a house down on the lake with three acres and two-hundred feet of frontage, for sale, and it's going for a song."

I made my fingers into a tent. "How much is a song?"

"Two twenty-five."

"Lakefront property, three acres, lots of frontage, all for two twenty-five? What's wrong with it? Is it sitting on a nuclear waste dump site? The land alone is damn near worth more than that."

"Exactly," Doris said, re-firing with enthusiasm. "Let's go take a look."

"When?"

"Thirty minutes?" she asked.

My shoulders slumped.

The term fixer-upper has plenty of leeway. As we walked through the lakeside house with the realtor, I frantically jotted down notes that I hoped would aid in my case for walking quietly away. Doris, on the other hand, was bouncing from room to room with the excitement of a six-month-old Labrador retriever. She loved everything. I could only see endless projects costing incalculable dollars.

Fast forward one week. After hours of discussion, meetings with contractors, and frequent heavy sighs, we bought the house.

Chapter Two

First Encounter

I brushed the snow from my shoulders, stamped the slush off my boots, and stepped into the tavern. It was early in the evening and the usual four guys, dubbed the *townie bar quartet* by Doris, were hunched over their beers at the bar. Otherwise, the pub was empty, or so it seemed.

Denver Ted, the owner, was emptying the dishwasher, stacking pint glasses on the shelf beneath the bar.

"Hey Nick," he said, looking up from his task. "What brings you out in this weather?"

I held up an empty gallon jug. "Fill 'er up." The next day was the Super Bowl and I needed to be prepared. A growler of beer for me and Doris ought to do it.

Denver Ted stood, wiped his hands on his apron and pointed at the taps. "The usual?"

I nodded.

Ted Johansson, also known as Denver Ted due to his passion for the Denver Broncos, was a wiry, diminutive man with bad teeth and very little hair. Although short in stature, he was fantastically strong and could hoist full kegs of beer around with seemingly little effort. Should a beer-soaked customer become unruly, Denver could—and did—heave them onto the street as easily as tossing out the cat. But Denver Ted's greatest asset was his heart. He loved everyone and when one of his regulars walked thru the door, he'd light up with one of those whole face smiles that shouts *I'm really glad to see you.* As he refilled my empty growler jug, he asked, "Who do you like in tomorrow's game?"

We idly chatted as if we had inside information and knew what we were talking about. What neither Ted nor I noticed was a dark shape peering in from the front window; then it was gone.

"What's this?" Ted asked, "I hear you bought that house on the lake?"

"Yep," I replied. "We'll be starting work out there on Monday."

Denver Ted nodded as he topped off the growler, wiped the jug clean, and slid it across the bar to me, adding, "It's about time we get some snow. This drought has all but emptied the lake. And good luck with the house."

I tossed a twenty Ted's way, turned up my collar and headed for home.

Stepping outside the warmth of the tavern felt like getting slapped across a frozen cheek with a hand of stinging wind. It had freshened out of the north and was pushing thick snow in its path. Hunching my shoulders, I trudged off in the direction of our home.

Roughly one football field from the tavern was an abandoned two-story inn. Renovations had long ago stopped due to lack of funds, and now it had taken on a sickening downwind lean. One day soon the whole thing would come crashing down. Next to the inn was a squat, empty store that recently had been a yoga studio. That enterprise had lasted almost an entire summer. As I approached, both buildings loomed in the fading light, their black windows yawning wide in the silence of the falling snow. Then, a dark figure stepped out of the alley between the buildings, blocking my path. Instinctively, I stepped off the sidewalk into the snow-covered empty street to avoid colliding with the person.

"Hello Nick," the dark figure said.

I stopped and shielded my eyes from the snow. Then I cautiously leaned forward to get a better look.

The dark figure was huge! And, as best as I could determine, it was a woman. Long strands of blond hair blew in the wind, plastering themselves across her face. She had a scarf tied around her head and wore a tent-sized overcoat.

"Sorry to startle you," she said, holding up a mittened hand in a weak wave.

I stared for a moment, and then asked, "What can I do for you? And who are you? Do I know you?"

She smiled. "Can ya' spare a minute or two?"

I frowned and thought *Are you shitting me?* "Look," I began with forced patience, "I'm not buying anything, don't need to find Jesus, and would rather not hear why I should vote for you, or sign your save-the-world petition. In fact, my focus right now is to get home before I freeze to death."

The woman pulled the scarf tighter around her head. "It's about the house on the lake."

I blinked away snowflakes from my eyelashes. "What about it?"

"I need you to do a favor for me."

I stared at the woman through the swirling snow. "Who are you?" I asked again.

She smiled for a second time. "No time for that now, but I'll explain when it ain't so flippin' cold. I just was wondering—when are you going to start work on the house?"

My brain was yelling at me: *Just turn and walk away.* But my feet weren't buying it. My instincts were telling me this was not a bad person.

"Not sure," I lied. "Maybe on Monday. What's this all about?"

But without another word, the woman turned and ducked back into the alley, walking into the shadows.

Silence.

Again, my brain was yelling: *Go home, NOW!* But my feet had other ideas. The alley was shrouded in total darkness, and there was nothing but an abandoned parking lot at the other end. *Where could she be going?* Against the warnings from my brain, I cautiously entered the alley. The snow crunched underfoot as I padded along. Finally, a ghostly glow of fading daylight emerged. I paused and peered out from the alley. Nothing. No one. Looking down, I noticed her footprints – which were swiftly filling with snow – led out into the empty lot. I followed, but then they abruptly stopped. There I stood, in the middle of what once was a parking area for long-gone guests, looking down at a set of tracks. And they went no further.

Chapter Three

The Spiritual Occupancy Field Agents

The snowstorm quit after midnight, dropping just a few inches of powder that hardly dented the ongoing drought. Then the Super Bowl came and went, proving, as usual, to not live up to the hype. Finally, it was Monday, bone-chilling cold with a bright blue sky.

Doris's sister in Denver was having a hip replaced, so Doris volunteered to help with the recuperation. Much to my chagrin, she would be gone for a few weeks, more likely a month or more, so I decided to busy myself with our new investment—the house on the lake.

I hadn't mentioned my chance meeting with the huge woman to Doris, partially because I didn't want to alarm her, and partially because I was not really sure it had actually happened. *Was it a dream? Could I have simply misinterpreted the encounter? People don't just vanish into the night.* Still, the encounter left me a bit uneasy.

When I arrived at the house on the lake, I loaded my sled with tools and firewood, but then paused. Just to be sure I was alone, I walked all around the perimeter looking for tracks in the snow, but there were none. Then I unlocked the back door and went it.

"Hello!" I shouted into the dark, empty house.

I waited.

No sound.

Feeling a tad foolish, I walked into the living room and kindled a fire in the massive wood stove. Then, as a precaution, I doubled back into the kitchen and locked the back door. I stood, rubbed my hands together trying to warm them, and took a look around. Back in 1918, the house had been constructed twenty miles away in a town that was now under water. When the construction of the reservoir was approved in 1985, homeowners in the soon-to-be-displaced community were given the option to disassemble their houses and move them to a new location. The owner of this home, a Horace Clumprider, purchased the parcel of land on which the house now stands, then took apart the building, board by board, and reassembled it in its present location. And now, Doris and I owned a dwelling that had been built a century ago, following building practices of that time. In some cases, the results were eye-popping, with hand-hewn crown moldings, custom windows, and solid wood doors. Other aspects of the old house were not so appealing: scant insulation, leaky plumbing, and knob and tube wiring that was dangerous and cumbersome.

I stood in the kitchen and surveyed our new investment. The walls were covered with peeling wallpaper, the faucet was dripping, and the cracked ceiling was water stained. The 'to-do' list was as long as my arm. I sighed longingly and wished I was in my leather chair, sipping coffee, and diving into some long-forgotten classic literary work.

Then I heard someone clear their throat. I froze. "Hello?"

"Hello," came the response, a woman's voice, from the living room.

With leaden feet, I crept down the hallway toward the living room. By now, the wood fire in the old cast iron stove was crackling away, chasing the chill from the vacant dwelling.

There, seated on an ancient claw foot sofa that had come with the house, was the same woman I'd met a few nights back. She was positively enormous, almost obscuring the sofa's faded floral slipcover. She looked to be three hundred pounds and over six feet in height, and she still wore the tent-sized, moth-eaten overcoat she'd had on in the snowstorm. Her scarf was gone, revealing a massive tangle of long blonde hair. She held her hands out in the direction of the wood stove. Her face was round and smooth and her eyes were bright blue. She smiled in a kindly fashion and nodded my way. "Mornin'," she said. "Nice fire. Feels good on the old hands."

I blinked a few times, swallowed, and then asked, "Who are you?"

"The name's Molly Williehouser. And you, of course, are Nick Weatherspoon."

"How do you know that? Have we met?"

"Well, no. Not all formal like, except for the other night on the street. As for how I know you, well, I don't really, but I read your name on the papers you left back on the kitchen table."

I turned around and looked down the hallway. There, piled on the kitchen table were the purchase and sale documents from the closing on the house.

I opened my hands. "What are you doing here?"

"Now, that's a dandy question that'll take some explainin'." Molly moved her bulk over a bit, the sofa groaning in protest, to make room. "Come sit down."

"I think I'm okay over here," I replied, casting a glance at the back door, just in case.

"Suit yourself," she said with a shrug. "So, here's the tale. Back in eighteen-ought-three, a prospector by the name of Lopez came up this way from Mexico and built a sod and stone house right here on this spot. He was lookin' for gold I guess, and if you go out the back door," she pointed toward the door I had come in through, and where my car was parked. "That old fallin' down building out there was his original house. The stonework is all that's left but in my business, a dwelling is a dwelling."

"Your business?"

Molly looked up, her bright blue eyes wide. "Why I'm a Spiritual Occupancy Field Agent, I am."

"A what?"

She chuckled, her bulk shaking slightly, causing the sofa to groan ominously. "You could call me a ghost if you'd like. Same thing."

"A ghost," I said in a whisper, leaning back against the wall to steady my wobbly legs.

"Yep. Technically, I'm supposed to be out back in that original building, but this here house is much homie, if you know what I mean."

"But why...?"

"'Cause ole Senior Lopez built his homestead on that there spot. He didn't know it at the time, but right out the back door, hardly a watermelon seed spit away, is a sacred spot—a kiva actually—that once was used by the Anastasi high priests. And when someone desecrates a shrine, like by building a house on top of it, why one of us Spiritual Occupancy Field Agents gets assigned." She frowned. "It's not really much of a job, but it's one of those entry level things for us new folks."

"How long have you...?"

She nodded. "Since eighteen-ought-three when Lopez moved in. He didn't like me one bit and high-tailed it back to the old country. Bein' full of superstitions, he wasn't about to stick around. But, as for me, I'm stuck here until I get sprung."

"Until you get sprung?" I repeated in a whisper. The realization that this was not a dream, and that seated across the room from me was a ghost, made me feel woozy.

"You don't look so good," Molly said. "Come on, take a seat. I promise I don't bite."

Thinking *Oh what the hell*, I wobbled over and plopped down. Again, the sofa moaned.

Molly gave me a once over. "You might want to get a drink of water, or maybe something a bit stronger."

I waved my hand dismissively. "Sprung as in no longer here?"

"Yep. Once the property, in this case, a shrine, is restored back to its intended purpose, we move out. Of course, there are other ways."

"Oh?"

Molly nodded. "I hear there are some folks, witch doctors, and voodoo priests, who can perform a ceremony and chase us Field Agents away, but most of the time, things go very badly and the chasers get chased and get cursed to boot, which is a really bad thing to have happen." She shook her head somberly.

"Great, just great." I closed my eyes and rubbed my temples. "So, let me get this straight. I just bought a haunted house and you, the ghost, are not leaving anytime soon."

"Well," Molly replied, "technically, I'm assigned to that stone building out back."

I sat quietly for a few beats, and then said, "I guess this is why the place was priced so low."

Molly chuckled again, shaking the sofa. "Yeah, they—the previous owners—really didn't like sharing their property with a Field Agent."

"Wonder why," I mumbled.

We sat together in silence. The only sound was that of the fire snapping away in the stove.

Finally, when my head stopped spinning, I got to my feet, turned to Molly, and said, "I'm going home now."

I drove home in a daze, had two stiff belts of bourbon, and went to bed.

The next day, I came back. Ghost or no ghost, there was work to be done. Doris had hired a contractor to bring the house up to code, so at the very least, that work had to be completed. And now, with a ghost in residence, the sooner the better. Plus, Molly didn't seem at all scary. In fact, she was sort of pleasant.

My first assignment on the project was to measure doors and windows and take the dimensions to the local building supply shop so they could begin fabrication. Our goal was to retain the ambiance of the one-hundred-year-old, Southwestern style home as much as possible. If we were lucky, we could use standard fit items and nestle them into the hand-hewn frames and window sills. If we had to go the custom route, our costs would skyrocket. Fortunately, the wiring and plumbing upgrades would be out of sight, and not affected by our goal to keep the Southwestern 'look'.

When all this work was done, we'd tackle the final tasks of removing the God-awful wallpaper, sanding the floors, and painting. But, first things first: I needed to get those measurements.

As I drove the five miles to our investment home, a zillion question swirled around in my head, not the least of which was how would the contractors feel about working with Molly the Field Agent hanging around?

I came in the back door and shouted, "MOLLY?"

No answer.

Then I walked into the living room and took a thorough look all around to avoid surprises. No Molly. *So far, so good.*

A few minutes later, I was on my knees in front of the wood stove kindling a blaze to take off the chill. As I added a few substantial pieces of scrub oak, a dense wood that burns long and hot, I sensed the presence of someone in the room.

Without turning, I asked, "Molly? Is that you?"

"Not hardly," replied a man's voice.

I jumped to my feet. There, standing alongside the sofa with the floral print slipcover, was a thin man who looked to be about twenty-five. He had spiked blond hair, a gold hoop earring dangling from his right earlobe, and wore a long, black tweed topcoat with brown loafers and no socks. He was absorbed with his nails, which he was shaping with a file.

"Sorry to startle you, darling," he drawled, "but I strenuously object to being called Molly."

I blinked. "And you are?"

"Dylan St. Jean," he said without looking away from his nails.

I leaned against the wall. "Are you a ghost?"

"I prefer Spiritual Occupancy Field Agent," Dylan said, then looked up and shot me a scornful glare.

"Another one," I muttered to myself. "Where's Molly?"

Dylan tossed back his head and took a few casual steps toward an old dusty bookcase. "The whereabouts of Her Immenseness is not my concern."

I scratched my head. "So, what are you doing here?"

Dylan stopped, put on his scornful glare again, and cocked his head. "I am the rightful occupant of this dwelling. And you, sir, are an intruder."

"Yeah, yeah," I said, folding my arms across my chest. "I've heard it all before."

"From The Fat One, I presume?"

"You know," I said, brushing the wood ashes from my hands. "That's not very nice. I like Molly better than you."

"Humph," Dylan grunted. "And I suppose she told you she was assigned to this house?"

"Well, no." I said. "She said something about being assigned to the broken-down shack out back."

"Correct," Dylan said with a feeble wave of his hand. "That's where she belongs, and that's where she should stay. I am the rightful Agent of this house."

I folded my arms across my chest. "So, let me get this straight. There are two ghosts on my property, one out back and one in here?"

Dylan walked to the bookcase and studied a few of the books. "I was assigned when this house was built in nineteen seventy-five by that Clumprider character..."

"Who?"

Dylan sighed audibly. "Horace Clumprider. The hopeless chap who moved a house from the town that was to be flooded purchased this land and rebuilt the very dwelling we are currently occupying. And this house just happens to be atop an ancient sacred shrine that once was used by the high priests of ancient peoples."

"But what about Molly? Couldn't she have haunted..."

"We don't haunt. We simply occupy."

"Okay, okay. Couldn't she have *occupied* both houses since they're virtually side-by-side?"

Dylan shook his head, disgust was written all over his long, lean face. "No. These are two very different violations. The rules are very clear on these matters."

"Rules?"

"Rules. Surely you don't think we simply show up willy-nilly with no rhyme or reason."

"Can't say I ever gave it much thought."

Dylan took out his nail file and began working on another nail.

I put another log into the stove. "And by the way," I asked. "Are there any more of you *agents* living here on my property?"

"No, just The Large One and myself. And let me assure you, this is not *your* property."

I nodded. "Okay. Point taken. I'm cool with that. And believe me, I'm going to fix this place up and sell it as fast as I can, so whether it's mine or not hardly matters."

Dylan filed a nail. "Ah yes; they come, they go, and we are left in here. Believe it or not, I actually feel sorry for you guys."

Dylan turned his back on me, quietly saying, "There is another way."

"Oh?"

But without another word, Dylan tossed a scarf around his neck, shoved his hands deep into the pockets of his topcoat, and left the living room, walking into what once must have been a library.

Curious, I waited a few seconds, but no explanation was forthcoming. So, I followed Dylan into the library; except, Dylan was not there.

Before going home, I walked out back to the broken down old house. All that was left were four stone walls and a tangle of fallen-down roof beams. The crisp air smelled of wood smoke and not a sound could be heard.

"Molly?" I said.

Nothing.

I stepped inside, through an open doorway. "MOLLY?" I called again, louder.

After a full minute of silence, with the sun dipping behind the canyon wall and the shadows slipping out from their hiding places, I turned to leave. There, blocking my path, was the immense bulk of Field Agent Molly Williehouser.

"Yikes!" I shouted, backing away, holding my hand over my heart. "You scared the crap out of me."

Molly grinned. "Just doin' me job."

I chuckled. "Good one. Say, do you have a minute?"

Molly grinned again, "Got all the time in the world."

I pointed over my shoulder at the house. "I'm freezing out here. The wood stove is still warm. Can we go in there to chat?"

We settled in as we had the day before, side by side on the groaning sofa, and I recounted how I'd met Dylan. Molly responded, "An unpleasant little gnat, ain't he?"

"Yeah, he is."

"Actually, he's not all bad," Molly said. "It took about twenty years but we've finally come to what you might call an *almost* friendly relationship. I think he's basically an unhappy guy that came to a really sad end, so it's left him a bit prickly."

"Oh?"

Molly rocked slightly back and forth, her round, kind face displaying an expression of pain and sorrow. "Dylan had this lover, see, some guy named William, who wanted to break it off, but Dylan wanted to work it out. So, one day, William poisoned Dylan."

"No kidding!"

"Nope. And as Dylan died, his guy just got up and left the room without another word. Dylan's last vision was that of his lover's back, walking away, closing the door behind him."

"Wow!" I exclaimed. "That's awful."

Molly kept gently rocking but said no more.

After several quiet minutes, I asked, "If it's not too personal a question, how'd you die? You don't have to answer if you don't want to."

Molly smiled, her eyes twinkling. She gave me a kindly once over. "No, not personal at all, but thanks fer bein' sensitive to my feelins'. We don't get much of that." She shifted in her seat and said, "Nothin' exciting. I toppled off our raft when we were crossin' the Ohio River. The water was swollen with snowmelt and floodin' the banks. We hit a submerged rock causing the raft to jolt and I went flying off into the freezing waters. I was dead due to shock long before my lungs filled with water." She stopped smiling and her face once again took on a sad expression. "They never found my body. Broke my daddy's heart."

"Wow," I said softly. "When was this?"

"March of eighteen twenty-nine. My family was headin' west."

More sorrowful silence.

I tossed another log on the fire. "When we met, that night in the snow, you said something about a favor. Remember?"

Molly nodded. "I do."

"And?"

Molly sighed. "I'm still trying to work out the details with Dylan. He can be difficult. We'll need his cooperation on this matter, and in the past, he wasn't willing. He might be this time, though"

"When was the last time?"

"Thirty-eight years ago."

I thought for several beats, then asked, "What's the significance of thirty-eight years?"

"Has to do with the moon."

I snapped my fingers. "That's right. The moon's year only repeats itself every nineteen years. So, thirty-eight years is two moon cycles."

Molly beamed at me. "You're pretty smart!"

"Not really, I just read a lot. That's what us English professors do."

Molly rocked back, the sofa squeaking with her movement, "So then, Professor, let's see if you can figure this out. What was different, back two moon cycles ago?"

I pursed my lips. "Let's see, it's two-thousand seventeen so thirty-eight years ago was nineteen seventy-nine. You were here back then, and Dylan was too, because he arrived in nineteen seventy-five, correct?"

"Correct."

I looked at the ceiling, thinking hard. "Let's see, two moon cycles ago, let's see…" Then it came to me. "The lake wasn't here! It wasn't built until nineteen eighty-five."

"Correct again, Professor. Not bad."

I jumped up, opened the front door of the wood stove, and using a metal poker, stirred the ashes. "So then, what's the favor?"

"Better put another log on the fire, 'cause it's complicated."

Chapter Four

Big Mistake

The next morning, Molly and I met at the house. I brought the required one-hundred-foot tape measure, a shovel, and a pickaxe. Per Molly's instruction, I measured out from the right front corner of the foundation of the main house, due east, onto the dry lake bed. I went out one hundred and ninety-three feet and marked the spot. There, I started digging.

Being mostly hardened clay and silt, the surface broke up with a few hits from the pickaxe. I was down about a foot when I hit something solid with a "clink."

I looked at Molly, and she smiled.

Even though the temperature was hovering at ten degrees, I was starting to sweat. Moving crusted earth is hard work.

I stopped and wiped my brow. "I wouldn't object to a little help," I said.

She shrugged. "Can't."

"Can't?"

"As Field Agents, it's strictly hands off. Sorry."

I sighed, and then went back to work.

In short order, I uncovered stonework that formed a circle about fifteen feet in diameter.

I stood back, examining my work and catching my breath. "You don't want me to dig this out do you?"

She shook her head. "No. Not all of it. But how about you dig down to the floor in just one spot?"

I walked to the approximate center of the circle and began to dig. Again, once the crust was removed, the digging became fairly easy. It was lake-bottom silt with few rocks.

When I was about knee-deep, Dylan showed up. I stopped digging.

Molly smiled. "Well, hello there, Mr. Sunshine."

Dylan studied the circular kiva. "We're not getting back into name-calling now, are we?"

"Nope," she said. "Those days are behind us. Just trying to lighten up the moment."

His perpetual scowl softened. "So, this is it," he said.

Molly nodded. "Yep."

"Think it'll work?" he asked.

"Worth a try," she replied.

I was working on the dry lake bed, about one hundred feet in from where the lake had receded. The lake, what was left of it, was covered with thick ice. Ice fishing shacks dotted the lake's surface, and one in particular, the closest one, was perhaps another hundred feet away from us. While Dylan and Molly examined my work, three men emerged from this nearest shack.

"Hey," one of the men yelled. "You can dig all you want but you're not going to catch any fish there! You have to be on the ice."

The other two men howled with laughter. Even though it was early in the day, it was likely all three had been drinking.

I ignored them and went back to digging.

The ice fisherman continued. "What are you going to use for bait? Mud balls?" More laughter.

I kept digging.

"Hey you, I'm talking to you!" Clearly, the yelling man didn't like being ignored.

Dylan looked over at the three ice fishermen and, with a casual wave of his hand, a gust of wind suddenly came up, blowing clouds of snow from the ice, and sending the ice fishermen scurrying back inside their shack. Then he waved his hand again, and a second, more powerful gust of wind materialized. This one was powerful enough to tip the ice fishing shack on its side and send it sliding across the lake. From where I stood in my hole, I could hear the men shouting with alarm as their shack swept away from us, gliding further and further until their yells faded completely. Finally, it came to rest on a frozen mud flat about a mile away.

Molly, unfazed by the ice fishermen, peered down into my hole. "Just another foot or two ought to do it."

Sure enough, when I drove my shovel into the silt, I hit something solid. I cleared a fair-sized spot. This was the floor of the kiva; hard-packed clay from a long, long time ago.

She looked at Dylan. "What do ya' think?"

He shrugged. "Should work."

Molly smiled again.

Chapter Five

Spill the Beans

Three days later, I met the public relations spokesman for Indian Affairs in Cortez, Colorado. His name (I never did figure out if it was his first or last name) was Shilah. He was perhaps forty, and for a native, unusually tall and slender. He was a member of the Mountain Ute tribe, wearing the customary long braided black ponytail. He rose to meet me.

We shook hands and Shilah said, "Please, take a seat. What can I do for you?"

I took a deep breath. "Recently, my wife and I bought a house on the lake as an investment property. We were planning to renovate the dwelling, and in the spring, put it back on the market for sale. As it turns out, and unbeknownst to us, the house was constructed on a sacred site that was probably built and used by ancient Pueblos during the Pueblo One Period, I've been told, and, well, I'd like to sell it back to you."

Shilah stared at me, not saying a word.

I plowed on. "There are two kivas on the site; one behind the house and one out front, on the lake side of the house. With the lake down, the second kiva is now accessible. The arrangement of the one I've seen is round, which dates it before the modern Hopi whose kivas were square."

He continued to hold me in his gaze.

I checked my notes. "According to my sources, the two kivas are connected with a type of mystical force, and they are both illuminated when a particular 'super' moon rises. The ancient peoples were able to use the force for healing purposes. You can see for yourself next Tuesday when the full moon comes up."

Shilah sat stone-like, hardly blinking. Finally, he said, "Many questions. The first one is, how do you know it is a sacred site? Next, who are your sources?"

I smiled faintly and thought, *okay, here goes.* "You may not believe this, but both the house and the kiva out back are haunted by ghosts. They told me they are there because the site was violated, and they'll be there until it goes back to the rightful owners. They also gave me all the information about the kivas."

He held me with a steady gaze.

I thought sure I was about to be asked to leave. After all, if someone came into my office and told a similar tale, I'd be calling security to escort the nut case off the property. I started to get up, saying, "Thanks for your time."

Shilah motioned with his hand, "Sit, please. How much are you asking?"

I was astonished. "Excuse me?"

He folded his hands. "Let us say for talking purposes that our experts in such matters verify that what you are saying is true; what would the purchase price be?"

I sat speechlessly. Finally, I asked, "You mean to tell me you believe my story?"

Shilah smiled. "No, not entirely, but let's move past that. After all, who in their right mind would make up such a tale? So, maybe we need to hear what you have to say. But you must understand before we go any further, we'll need to verify your claim. And if what you say is correct, ghosts or no ghosts, we may want to acquire such a site. Now, I have to make a few calls and I'll get back to you."

Chapter Six

Work Goes On

The next week brought a bevy of activity at the house: windows and doors were replaced, all wiring and plumbing were brought up to code, bathrooms were totally rehabbed, the existing hardwood floors were sanded and refinished, leaks around the chimney were patched, ceilings were repaired and redone. Painters painted and laborers labored. In short, much of the house received a facelift.

All the while, Molly and Dylan hung around, causing workers to constantly mutter about how the house felt cold and creepy. Curiously, they couldn't see the Field Agents. And it wasn't like they tried to hide or be quiet. Dylan and Molly were constantly bickering like an old married couple.

Dylan watched the painters. "That color will never do," he said to Molly.

"What's wrong with it?" she replied.

"Boring, and look; it clashes with the sofa."

"Everything clashes with that sofa," Molly replied, walking over and plopping down upon it. The squeaking protest of the sofa was heard by one of the painters, who shot a tremulous glance at it, then went back to painting.

"What would you know about colors and patterns," Dylan quipped, planting his hands on his hips. "Just look at that carpet you insist upon wearing."

"What's wrong with my coat?" Molly replied indignantly.

And so it went, day after day, but other than shooting frightened looks at mysterious sounds, the workers saw and heard none of it.

One afternoon, after the ceiling plaster crew departed, I asked Dylan, who was standing motionless, staring out the window, "How come I can see you and they can't?"

"Well, sweetie," Dylan replied with his customary disinterested drawl, "it's because you can. Most people can't. It's that simple. Nobody seems to know why. Almost everybody feels ghosts are a bunch of hooey and those that claim to see them are a bit touched, but the simple fact remains—it's because you can."

Dylan strolled around the living room, inspecting the new ceiling. "You're the first person I've ever met that can. The question then becomes: is it a gift or a curse?"

Chapter Seven

Magic in the Moonlight

The canyon wall across the lake was formed when the Colorado Plateau was sliced by the San Juan River. The plateau continued to rise, and like the crust on a hot apple pie, cracked here and there. One such crack was due east of the two kivas. It was a vertical crack, nearly straight up and down. This orientation allowed - once every nineteen years – a line of glowing moonlight to be cast upon the far shore, which is where the kivas were dug. Just prior to the moon clearing the canyon wall, a beam of moonlight connects the two kivas.

The "super" moon had now cleared the canyon wall and the line of moonlight had faded and disappeared. The two religious tribal leaders who were standing in the illuminated kivas when the two circular pits were connected by the beam of moonlight, had hastily rejoined the small group of regional tribal representatives. From where I stood, a respectable distance away, I couldn't make out the words but I could hear the tone; it was rapid and excited.

Dylan and Molly were by my side.

I pointed at the group. "What's happening?"

Dylan, hands deep in the pockets of his topcoat as always, said, "From the sound of it, the two religious tribal leaders have determined that in fact there are plenty of spiritual vibes. And now, they are sharing their findings with the tribal movers and shakers."

Molly chuckled, her face aglow in the light of the moon. "Movers and shakers? Not sure if that's proper Ute or Navaho speak."

"Honestly," Dylan said with exasperation "just a figure of speech."

I watched. "What happened when that shaft of moonlight connected the kivas?"

Molly shook her head from side to side. "Not sure, but I could feel something. It was powerful. Couldn't you?"

I blinked a few times. "Nope."

Dylan nodded in the direction of the tribes. "But they did."

Finally, after about an hour of discussion, the tribal spokesman, Shilah, broke from the others and strode to where I stood. With the bright moon illuminating his face, he said, "We accept your offer to sell this property."

Chapter Eight

Home Again

I settled into my favorite chair, a mug of hot coffee at my elbow, snappy fire in the fireplace, and prepared to pick up where I'd left off with Wilde's *The Canterville Ghost*.

With her sister well on the way to full recovery, Doris was driving back from Denver and should be arriving before nightfall. This left me with a few hours to kill.

I stared at the fire, yellow flames hungrily licking up the sides of a small stack of split scrub oak logs, and thought about the events of the past three weeks. The newly renovated house was now a multi-tribe religious center, and the crumbling stone structure out back was once again an important kiva, a sacred shrine. Contractors had been paid in full, and our bank account – thanks to quick work by the regional tribes - was about where it had been before the house on the lake came into our lives.

I stared at the words on the page to no avail. What would I tell Doris? As far as she knew, the renovations were underway and we'd be flipping our investment soon. The wild ride with the Field Agents and moonlit kivas was an incredible tale. Would she believe me? Would I believe her, if the shoe were on the other foot?

Still, what was paramount in my mind had nothing to do with the house or contractors or Indians. Instead, I thought about Molly and Dylan. The kivas were now back in the hands of the rightful owners, so they were released from their 'Field Agent' assignments. But where were they now? What would become of them? There were, of course, no answers to these questions, only more questions.

I sipped my coffee and eventually, picked up my book and resumed reading.

Pond Hockey

Out here in Colorado, December 2017 will be remembered as snowless and cold. Unless the weather changes pretty soon, there will be no skiing or snowshoeing this year. However, these conditions freeze local lakes and ponds which invite those of us who love the outdoors to lace up our skates and get out and play hockey. The game we play is aptly named *pond hockey*.

For those of you who don't know, there are two types of ice hockey: the traditional NHL style contest and the game we play on a frozen pond. They are significantly different. Consider the following:

The Google definition of ice hockey, the sport played by the Montreal Canadians and Boston Bruins, is as follows:

> *A fast contact sport played on an ice rink between two teams of six skaters, who attempt to drive a small rubber disk (the puck) into the opposing goal with hooked or angled sticks.*

Here's how pond hockey differs:

1. Fast? Not hardly. Pond hockey might be frantic and energetic but certainly not fast. Many players wear skates that don't fit and simply cannot skate very well (if at all). Skating fast is out of the question. Some, in fact, don't even have skates so they

play in their snow boots. Fast? Nope. Imagine how fast *you* could move on the slippery ice, dressed in winter garb with hats and scarves and heavy boots.

2. Contact sport? In pond hockey, the only contact occurs when two (or more) players accidentally collide, or, more commonly, when a player loses their balance and falls – sometimes spectacularly – to the ice. For example, during the game, we played on the Winter Solstice, Jake, the largest player on the pond, performed one of those feet-go-way-up-in-the-air maneuvers and landed flat on his back. The ice boomed and reverberated back and forth the entire length of the pond. We all held our breath, hoping the ice wouldn't give way and watched to see if Jake was okay. Fortunately for Jake, he'd already consumed four beers and came away unscathed. The next day was a different story but nothing a few hits of Aleve couldn't handle.

3. Ice Rink! Ha! Our rink is the pond. Ice rinks have Zamboni machines that shave the ice surface to a glass-like smoothness, applying a film of warm water in its wake to further melt any imperfections. Conversely, frozen ponds have cavernous cracks, rough spots of all sorts, and frozen footprints where some idiot walked across the pond when it was still slushy, thus capturing their boot prints like dinosaur tracks forever etched into the prehistoric mud. All of these imperfections add to the challenge of the game and as the puck often moves "pinball" style across the pond, accurate passes are damn near impossible.

4. Two teams of six skaters? Wrong again. The game is played by whoever happens to be at the pond: parents, grandparents, big kids, little kids, dogs, girls, boys, etc. And the roster is fluid. If one side is dominating the other, we switch a good player with a not-so-good player to even things up. I believe the scientist who authored the concept of the "Chaos Theory," was inspired by watching a game of pond hockey.

5. We don't use a hard rubber puck which hurts like hell when it hits your shins, knocks teeth out, and wreaks havoc when it collides with a player's face. Just check out the Frankenstein-like faces of goalies from the forties and fifties. Our puck is the kind used in street hockey; bright red and made of plastic so as not to damage the player who takes it off the chin, privates, or any other unprotected area.

6. Equipment? Little or none. There are some of us who use traditional hockey sticks, others use make-shift home-made devices that more resemble over-sized golf clubs, and goaltenders often use snow shovels. Come to think of it, a snow shovel does a pretty fair job of blocking the goal. Any other traditional ice hockey equipment such as padded gloves, shin pads, fancy blockers pads, etc., are non-existent.

But the biggest difference between NHL style ice hockey and the game we play on a frozen pond is what I call the *fun factor*. I've played hockey for about sixty years on many different levels. All of the organized hockey games and leagues I've suited-up and played in – from Pee Wee all the way up to Adult Men's Leagues - were grimly serious. On the other hand, the sounds heard along a pond when a game is in full swing are not shouts, crashes, and angry expletives, but laughter, squeals of delight, and barking dogs. The sounds of pond hockey form a cornucopia of pure joy. This type of activity, played by young and old alike, is as good as the game of ice hockey gets.

For those of you who have experienced getting out there on a winter afternoon, you know what I mean. I raise my stick in salute to you!

Forty-Seven

Gasping for air, I looked up at the clock. Less than a minute was left in the game. I spat on the ice. Still some blood from an earlier high stick.

The public address system droned on; "…and the men's hockey league will resume next October. Have a great summer."

The faceoff was just outside their zone. My hip and elbow were protesting from the last shift and the collision behind the net. "Rally!" I mumbled unconvincingly. "Just one more shift."

But when the referee dropped the puck, the nightmare resumed where it had left off last time I was on the ice. The rest of the players moved like a movie run in fast motion. Everyone, red shirts and white shirts alike, instantly accelerated to high speed. I was left behind, reaching as would a child trying to catch a spinning carousel but unable to grasp the colorful horses as they shot past.

The play ebbed and flowed around me but my feet seemed to be stuck in wet sand. All I could do was face the play and dig down deeper moving my legs, trailing the action. Suddenly, a misdirected pass hit a skate and pin-balled onto my stick. Instinctively, I turned up the ice. The lane was clear and I had two full strides on the nearest white shirt.

"Turn it on," my brain screamed. "Skate for Christ sake!" But my legs weren't listening. The once well-oiled machine was running on empty. I was three strides across the blue line when a strong white shirted shoulder drove me off my unsteady legs into the boards. The impact pushed any remaining air from my lungs and I went to the ice. Hard. My vision blurred for an instant. Looking up from my prone position, my eyes focused on something very different.

A tall skater with an orange and black jersey broke into the clear. He was moving in well ahead of the pursuit, all alone. The Vermont College goalie set himself for the confrontation. Two Vermont defensemen were being left behind. With a quick shift to the right, the tall skater flipped the puck over the sprawling Vermont goalie.

Stick and arms raised in celebration, he was swarmed by his jubilant teammates. The crowd roared as Columbia Tech had now taken the lead over heavily favored Vermont College. The Columbia Chiefs would win this game and advance to the playoffs for the first time in the history of this newly formed hockey team. The crowd yelled and banged trash can lids. The din would have hurt the ears of the players if they weren't so pumped. How they cheered. God, how they cheered.

"Hey man, you ok?"

I looked up into the face of a white-shirted player. He was so very young. Was I actually skating against kids? Was that fair? Surely the adults could skate circles around these peewees. Then I remembered; he was the player that took me hard into the boards.

"I sure didn't mean to check you that hard. You just sort of crumpled. You ok?" He asked again.

Somebody behind him yelled, "Nice going asshole. This is a no-check league, remember?" The referee and players from both sides were gathered around. The kid looked amazed and said, "I hardly touched him."

I sat up. "I'm ok. Just taking a little rest." Then, trying to get up I realized maybe I wasn't all right. Two redshirts propped me up and skated me to gate leading to the locker room. "There's only a few seconds left. Want some help getting to the shower?"

"No." I replied. "I'm fine."

I sat on a locker room bench quietly, stripped to the waist. My elbow was swelling and my hip was throbbing so insistently I couldn't lean over to remove my skates, socks, or any other gear. I just sat there, waiting for the game to end. Waiting for my teammates. Waiting to tell them.

The locker room smelled of disinfectant, Dial soap, and cold concrete. I held a cold beer against my swollen lip and leaned back against the wall. "They all smell the same," I mused. "They always have."

Thirty-two years prior, Chicory High School won its first Western Massachusetts Hockey title. In the winning game, a tall swift skating freshman had scored three goals. Back then, the ultimate prize wasn't the cheering crowd or even future sports scholarships. The true Golden Fleece was a letter "H" and uniform number on the school jacket. In high school, when peer pressure is absolute, status is all there is. Somehow, in all the yelling and whooping of the post-game celebration, the swift-skating freshman had forgotten his hard-won symbol of victory behind in the locker room. Later that evening, when the arena was empty and dark, he returned to recover his prize. There, in the dim light of an empty locker room, he first noticed the odd smell that permeated every hockey locker room wherever he went. For years, that odor would faintly linger on his jacket. And that same smell would trigger memories of victories, celebrations, and momentary greatness. And status.

Outside, on the ice, the horn blew signifying the end of the game. "They'll be coming through that door soon," I thought. "I'll tell them then." But I didn't.

The team showered, told bawdy stories, insulted each other, and in general acted like the over-grown little boys we were. The younger guys were the first out the door, heading for the local watering hole. The not-so-younger guys were the next out; a bit less effusive but looking forward to the frosty beer just the same. In the end, it was just Jim, another veteran of about 25 post-college hockey seasons and me. We shouldered our duffle bags and left the locker room.

"Stopping for a cold one?" He asked.

I dropped my duffle bag and looked out at the now empty rink. "No. Not tonight." I limped over to the stands and sat down. "I think I'm going to hang around here for a little while."

Jim looked across the rink where a chubby man in a plaid coat was driving the Zamboni onto the ice. There were no more games. There was nothing to watch. He looked back at me, examining my face.

"Tough night," he said. Not a question, just a statement of fact.

"You got that right."

"You don't look so good." He added.

I tried to smile. "Thanks."

After an uncomfortable pause, he continued. "Are you hanging 'em up?"

I watched the Zamboni making its first turn. The chubby driver had lit his cigar creating a cloud of white smoke.

"Yeah. I wanted to tell the other guys but..." my voice trailed off. "I suck. You guys will do better without me. This is a game for kids. Starting tonight, I'm not a kid anymore."

Jim pursed his lips and started out at the ice. "You're full of crap as usual. You'll be back. He shouldered his duffle bag and picked up his hockey stick. "You're right about this game getting harder. I'll ache for half the summer." He turned and walked to the exit door, turned, and yelled, "I'll call you tomorrow."

I sat in the bleachers about three rows up. The new water shimmered on the ice behind the Zamboni, just like a January rain on a woodlot pond. A pond just like Ondrick's Pond.

Coming up the hill behind old man Ondrick's barn were twelve boys and one big brown dog. They had played hard all day just like they did every winter Saturday. They were a tired-looking bunch; red cheeks, unbuckled overshoes, and unzipped coats... but their hearts were happy and souls content. Among the group was little fancy equipment. Some of the hockey sticks had been mended by handy fathers; screws and tape holding the fractured pieces together. The game had been played with all the energy twelve young boys can expend. It was hockey in its simplest form. No frills. No winning or losing team. No spectators banging trash can lids. No hockey jackets with an "H" sewed to the sleeve. Just one big brown dog barking encouragement and licking your face when you fell down. It was perfect. And although they didn't know it then, this was the best it would ever be. It was hockey at its finest. Anything that followed would be a futile effort to recapture those Saturdays on Ondrick's Pond.

"Hey you!" The chubby man with the plaid coat was shouting at me. He had completed resurfacing the ice and was putting away the Zamboni. "I'm closing up. Time to move on."

Gathering my duffle bag and hockey stick, I limped down the bleachers and left through the exit door at the far end of the rink. The chubby man was right; it was time to move on.

Bunny's Day in the Sunshine

The sky was a uniform gray like the wash of a watercolor painting. The first flakes of snow were already drifting down. The car radio droned on, "...Panama's leader General Manuel Noriega surrendered to United States authorities this morning..."

My teenage daughter Michelle looked at me and moaned, "Can't we listen to some music now?"

"I thought we were going to take turns?" I replied.

She folded her arms and stared out the window.

I turned off the radio and said, "There. Silence is always better than world news."

We drove on for a few more blocks.

"So this is your hometown," said my daughter breaking the quiet, still gazing out the car window. "How long has it been since you've been here?"

"Um, let's see. I'd say about fifteen years since I came through this end of town."

"What's that over there," she asked, pointing to a snow-covered field.

I looked out her side of the car. "It's a commemorative park, marking the spot where the old textile mills used to be. They burned down one night when I was a real little kid. What a fire! Lit up the whole sky. Burned for days."

"Hey, Daddy, stop! Look at those kids. They're building an awesome snowman."

Pulling the car to the curb, I asked, "Awesome?"

We watched a handful of frosty-breathed children dressed in colorful winter coats pushing a huge snowball. A large man lifted the sphere of packed snow and set it atop another. He then stepped back and clapped his hands.

"Check out that guy," she said. "He looks kinda weird."

I leaned across the front seat to get a better look. "My God," I exclaimed. "That's Bunny. I can't believe he's still around."

"Who?"

"Bunny. He's hung around this field since before my time."

She searched my face for the expected punch line.

"No kidding," I continued. "This park is the town's little league baseball field. When I started playing baseball, I was about eight. He was there then. Bunny's always been there. You see, he's retarded…or *challenged* as we now say. I suppose in a sense, this field is his home."

"Oh." Michelle stared at the activity on the ball field, Bunny clapping his hands and helping the children. "Gee, that's kinda sad," she added.

"No honey, not sad. Take a look at him. Does he look sad to you?"

"No, I guess not." She didn't sound convinced. "What's that red jacket he's wearing? I wonder what it says on the back."

"It says: CHAMPS - 1959 TIGERS: B TEAM 1, A TEAM 0."

"Wow! You can read that from here?"

"Nope. My team gave it to him."

"Really? Your team? How come?"

"Well, it involved two little league baseball teams, the TIGERS A and the TIGERS B. Every year, they played for the town championship. Bragging rights."

Michelle turned in her seat to face me. "You mean there were only two teams in the league?"

"No, of course not," I replied. "There were lots of teams but only two from town."

"Oh."

"So anyway, they always played at the end of the season and the A team, which was made up of the rich kids, always won. Incidentally, I was the catcher for the B team. The A team had uniforms and spikes and team pictures and jackets. All we got were hats. Just the same, it was a good crew and we had fun. Our first baseman was the only black kid in Chicory. Our shortstop was a girl and back then, a girl playing baseball was unheard of. She was a great fielder and quicker than lighting but couldn't hit to save her life. Our left fielder smoked Camel cigarettes and our pitcher Jimmy (or *Giggly* Jimmy as he was known behind his back), was so fat that when he fell down, he looked like a turtle on its back trying to get up. Once he fell down on the ball while trying to field a bunt and the guy got a triple out if it before I could roll Jimmy over to get the ball. We lost most of our games but like I said, we had fun."

Michelle looked back out the window. "And what about Bunny?"

"Well, there's a bit of a story about that. It was 1959 and the day before the big game. Chrissy, our shortstop rode her bicycle to my house. I was just finishing my newspaper route…"

"Hey, Kenny. Hear the news?"

"Sure did! The White Sox clinched the pennant!"

She hopped off her bike. "Not that. We need a new pitcher. Jimmy's got the measles!"

"Get out."

"No really! His mom says he might miss the first day of school, too."

I thought for a moment. We had eleven players on the roster but two were still at summer camp and with Giggly Jimmy down with the measles, which left eight. We might have to forfeit the most important game of the year! I looked at Chrissy and solved the problem the same way we solved all summer problems.

"Wanna play whiffle ball?"

"Yeah! First ups!"

"Okay but I'm the Yankees."

"You're always the Yankees..."

"But the next day arrived and we were still without our pitcher. It was almost game time and our coach was getting desperate, smoking one Lucky Strike after another. He called the A team coach and asked if we could play with eight instead of nine."

"What did he say?" Michelle asked.

"He said we would have to forfeit."

"What a dweeb!" She exclaimed.

"Well, perhaps." I answered, not exactly sure what a dweeb was. "But then a miracle occurred. While we were warming up, a ball got by me and rolled over to Bunny, who was standing by the backstop. He was at all our games. Actually, he was sort of our mascot. We bought him popsicles and gave him the stale bubble gum from the packs on baseball cards. Anyways, he clapped his hands and picked up the ball. He was a huge man and his fingers encircled the ball like mine would a golf ball. Then, in one swift motion, he fired it back to me. Let me tell you, that ball had some zip on it!"

"Zip?"

"Zip. Speed. You know, a fastball."

"Oh."

"So I tossed it back to Bunny and told him to do it again. He did. And again and again and again. Then I called the coach over ..."

*"Hey, coach. We got us a pitcher. Watch this." I tossed the
ball to Bunny and shouted, "Come on Bunny. Speedball!"*

*As before, with one swift motion, a white blur and WHAP,
right into my catcher's mitt.*

*The coach said, "Do it again." We did. And finally, after
several more times, he said quietly, "Well I'll be dipped in
shit."*

"After he saw what Bunny could do, he walked across the diamond
and spoke to the A team coach. Then the two coaches met with the
umpire. The A team coach was so sure his team would win, he waved
off any objection to our new player. A few minutes later the meeting
was over and our coach returned, smiling and said: "Let's play ball."

"But then the A team coach made a big mistake. Just as we were
taking the field he turned to his players and said in a loud voice, "Look
at your opponents. A colored, a girl, and a retard! What a bunch of
losers!"

His team laughed.

We didn't.

Being a catcher, I walked out to the mound to calm my pitcher
who of course was Bunny."

*"Don't pay any attention to them. Just throw the speedball.
Okay?"*

*Bunny looked at me and just for a second, his face lost its
dazed, drifty expression and became sharp and determined.
He nodded.*

I walked back to the plate and crouched down.

"BATTER UP!" yelled the ump.

The first A team player came to the plate. He was grinning.
His coach yelled, "Go easy on 'em Johnny. Just a homer!"
They laughed some more.

Bunny wound up and fired. WHAP. And again. And a
third WHAP.

"STRIKE THREE! YOU'RE OUT."

"The A team coach wasn't laughing then, or the next inning, or the next. As a matter of fact, he was downright serious by the time we came to bat in the bottom of the last inning. The score was 0 – 0. I led off with a weak ground ball which the third baseman booted so I made it to first. The next two batters struck out. Then Chrissy came up. She hadn't gotten a hit all season but nonetheless, everyone was standing and yelling for her. I can still to this day, clearly remember the look in the eyes of the A team coach when she hit a sharp line drive to left field that fell in for a hit. I rounded second and slid safely into third. This was unbelievable. First and third, two outs. We had a chance to win! But then Bunny came to the plate.

"Was he a good hitter?" Michelle asked, nodding to the huge man in the snowy field, awkwardly clapping his hands.

"Hardly. Take a look out there. His coordination hasn't improved with age."

Bunny was trying to push a large snowball but tripped and fell face first into the snow. No matter, he got up laughing and clapped his hands.

"So there we were, Bunny at the plate. His first two times up he never swung the bat, being called out on strikes both times. He stood there, gripping the bat like he was holding a flag while marching in some parade. But again, like when Chrissy came to the plate, we were all screaming and jumping. And then, with two strikes against him, he swung at a ball way out of the strike zone and to the amazement of anyone within hearing distance, nudged the ball over the first baseman's head. I ran home and we won the game. It was unbelievable. Everyone was hugging and yelling.

"Wow," Michelle said quietly. "What did the other coach do then?"

I looked out into the field where it was now snowing steadily, and let the question linger.

"Dad?" Michelle asked. "You ok?"

"Yeah. I was just remembering." Then I continued. "The other coach ran to the umpire and began talking real fast, all the while beaconing to an open page in his Little League Rule Book. After a few minutes, the umpire called for our coach to join them. Even from across the infield, I could see the three faces: the A team coach, arms crossed, wearing a smug smirk; the umpire trying to remain impartial but looking pretty damn pissed off, and our coach whose shoulders slumped and stayed that way. We all quieted down and watched. Finally, the umpire turned to the A team coach and said in a voice loud enough for us all to hear, "Happy now?" Our coach shuffled back to where we waited and took a seat on the bench. He lit another Lucky and began.

> *"Boys," he began, "and girl, you just played the best game of the season. You played your hearts out but I'm afraid we didn't win. Officially that is."*

> *An uproar of "What? How come?" and other similar protests rang out. The coach let us have our say for a few drags on his smoke then held up his hand. We fell silent.*

> *He looked around, catching all our faces. "It's true. Even though we beat 'em fair and square, their coach told the ump Bunny's too old to be playin' in this league. The ump had to give the game to them 'cause we broke the rules."*

> *More uproar. Same as before, he gave us a minute or two then said, "Now, no more of that. I want you all back here,*

at this very spot, at nine tomorrow mornin'. Okay? Can everyone make it?"

"Yeah, sure, okay. Tomorrow morning."

"Well, the next morning we were all back at the ballpark like we were told. Bunny was there but he wasn't clapping his hands or anything. He just looked sad. We all told him it wasn't his fault but I think he felt he let us down.

Then the coach showed up. He was carrying a big shopping bag. Without any fanfare or speech, he reached in and pulled out a new, bright red athletic coat, the kind we used to wear back then with leather sleeves and snaps and really cool cuffs. The coach held it up, then turned it around and showed us the back. It read CHAMPS - 1959 TIGERS: B TEAM 1, A TEAM 0. He told us he could only afford one coat so we'd all have to take turns wearing it."

"Wait a minute," Michelle interrupted. "Just one coat?"

"Our coach was somebody's grandfather who had nothing better to do. He certainly didn't have a pocket full of money. In retrospect, that one coat probably set him back a bit."

Michelle nodded.

"Anyways, we just stood there, not really knowing what to do. Then Chrissy spoke up and said Bunny ought to wear it first since he pitched a perfect game. We all chimed in and agreed. So the coach walked over to Bunny and helped him into the coat."

Michelle gasped. "What did Bunny do?"

"Well, first his face brightened up. Then he started to clap his hands and dance all around. But then he did something I'll never forget. He cried just like a baby and went all around from player to player, hugging each one of us. And you know, even at nine years old we all realized those were tears of joy.

None of us took turns wearing that coat. The next season we moved on to new teams and in some cases, new neighborhoods but Bunny stayed here, waiting for the next crop of kids. You know,

I'm kind of proud that it was my team that provided his day in the sunshine. I don't think he has ever removed that coat. That's it he has on out there now."

Michelle stared out the window. The snow had now covered the windshield. She turned in her seat and said, "Daddy, let's go say hi. You know, wish him a Merry Christmas. He'd probably be really happy to see you."

I shook my head. "Bunny has no long-term memory. Do you know what that means?"

Michelle said, "I think so."

"So he can't remember what happened last week, let alone twenty-nine years ago. No, let him be. He's happy out there."

The snowman was now four tiers high and huge in girth. The minions in snowsuits and rubber boots had now taken to throwing snowballs. Bunny clapped his hands in encouragement.

I started the car. "Let's go. Your grandmother's going to be worried."

Authors Note: Andrew 'Bunny' Conroy died on October 3, 2012. He was seventy-two years old and a local legend. When his apartment was cleaned out, hanging on a rack by the back door, was a faded, threadbare red athletic coat with leather sleeves. On the back were the words:

CHAMPS - 1959 TIGERS: B TEAM 1, A TEAM 0.

The Last Laugh

The Queen Anne's lace parted as I strode through the field that led down to the river. I arrived just in time to spot a fisherman pulling himself out of the cold water. His soaked clothing clung to his body.

"Hey buddy," I called. "Are you okay?"

"Yeah. Wet and cold but otherwise in one piece." He removed his hat and wrung it out.

"What happened?"

Gesturing to the footbridge that crossed the river, he said, "There's a cable broken at mid-span but you wouldn't notice it if you weren't aware of it, and I didn't. The planks gave way, dumped me into the water, and then sprung back into place."

As he emptied his waders, I studied the bridge. It was a pair of cables with foot planks laid crossways along with a couple of handrails. On either side of the small river was a concrete block footing, holding the swaying arrangement in place. I'd been across it many times and had planned on crossing it this morning. From where I stood, it appeared to be as sound as ever.

Apparently, the wet fisherman read my mind because he said, "Come on. I'll show you where the break is."

I followed him out onto the bridge. About halfway across, he stopped and cautiously pushed on the next plank with his foot. It swung downward then sprang back up.

I whistled. "Looks like a perfect man-trap is there ever was one."

"You got that right. Imagine my surprise," he said grimly. "Good thing the water's fairly deep down below. That fall could've hurt something other than my pride."

I peered down at the swirling dark waters. "We ought to put up a sign."

"Not me," he said, retreating from the bridge. "I'm freezing. I'm heading home."

"Take care."

After he left, I sat on the bank pondering the situation. I couldn't in good conscience wander off without putting up some kind of warning. But then again, I did come here to do some fishing, not be a gatekeeper. I knew I had nothing in the car I could use as a sign and a quick scan of the immediate area turned up nothing. Then a trout gobbled-up an unseen bug off the surface of the river. A minute later, it happened again. And again. Suddenly, I had forgotten all about the bridge.

Studying the water, I eventually saw what the trout were eating: ants. These were big black ants with wings. Apparently, they were swarming somewhere upstream and some were falling into the river, washing down into the pool beneath the bridge.

Tucked in the corner of my fly box were two hand-tied flies that imitated black ants. I took out the first one, tied it onto my leader, and cast to the nearest rising trout. Immediately, a foot-long Brown Trout grabbed my fly. I reacted too fast and snapped off the fly in the mouth of the fish.

"Damn," I muttered. Tying on my second and last ant, I made another cast. This time when the trout struck, I was more careful. And the next time, and the next.

The surface was fairly covered with ants and the trout were responding accordingly. By then, both the angler and the angle had worked ourselves up into a frenzy. Trout were popping everywhere and I was being selective with my targets, casting to only the biggest feeding fish. I guarded my last ant fly with my life. Then it happened.

I got careless and snapped-off the fly in the bushes behind me. After a futile search of the alders, I glumly sat back down on the river bank.

"Gawd damn!" said a gravelly voice from behind.

I turned and faced the new arrival. There stood a small, roundish man with an unfiltered cigarette pinched between his lips. A brown knit watch cap sat atop his head. He held a fly rod in his hand.

"Just once," he lamented. "I'd like to have this place to myself. Always some joker here before me." He shook his head in disgust.

Looking upstream and down, there was no one else in sight. He was referring to me. I guess I was the joker.

"Fish here, Gramps," I said. "I'm all done for a while." I beckoned to my rod leaning against a nearby tree.

Shaking his head again, he asked, "Who you callin' Gramps? I could walk your tail off without breakin' into a sweat. Hell, if I was your age, I wouldn't be sittin, I'd be fishin'. And why ain't you working? It ain't no weekend. You young kids are everywhere these days. Don't your generation work no more? What's happened to our country?"

I pondered the barrage of questions for a moment. Obviously, the rude man was planning on some solitude but I got in his way. Too bad but it is a free country. But I just couldn't resist answering his final question.

Looking him in his beady little eyes, I said, "My generation? Why, we're all on drugs or worse yet, hooked on fly-fishing."

He scowled at me, twitching his cigarette as he pondered his next verbal assault. "I'll bet you weren't in the service, right?"

"Wrong."

Ignoring my response, he continued. "I'll bet you drive one of those Jap cars, right?"

"Got that one right."

"See what I mean?"

"No."

Again ignoring my response, the cigarette man looked out at the river. He was clearly shifting his tact. "Look at that damn river," he growled. "There's no fish here like there used to be. The state doesn't stock like they used to. Damn politicians."

I gazed at the river in amazement. There, not two casts from where he stood, were several plump trout merrily slurping ants. I couldn't contain myself.

I pointed at the fish. "What do you call those, Gramps?"

He spat out some stray tobacco without removing his cigarette – a pretty good trick, actually. "That's nothing' like what use to be here. Christ, we'd never even think about killin' a trout 'till it was two foot or better."

"Maybe that's why they're not here anymore."

"Bah. It's the state's fault. And I'll tell you somethin' else,…"

And so it went that fine spring morning. That little chubby man ran down not only my generation and the state fish and game department, but also the governor, president Regan and his wife, Mr. Gorbachov (for being some sort of co-conspirator with Regan), Walt Disney (something to do with Bambi), Ted Williams (for catching all the Atlantic Salmon), the Danish fishing fleet (for killing those remaining salmon Ted William's missed), and various long-haired environmental types (for reasons that eluded my best efforts to understand).

"…your type doesn't know what work is. We worked like dogs…"

I found this man both annoying and amusing. Could life be so bad as to color one's perspective so darkly?

"…and if your generation would get off their duffs,…"

During his tirade, he continuously fidgeted with his fly rod and kept stealing glances at the river, and then he'd look my way on occasion. I believe he was checking not to see if I was paying attention, but to see if I had noticed the fish feeding. Finally, it hit me: this was an act! If he complained and insulted me long enough, I was apt to get up and leave. Then, he'd have what he wanted in the first place: solitude.

Suddenly, with the abruptness in which it began, the dissertation on all that is ill ended. Apparently, he was convinced that I wasn't going anywhere so he decided on plan two: get to the best spot quick! He and I had both spotted a large trout feeding against the far bank. Without so much as a, "so there!", he headed across the bridge.

As I watched him purposely stride across the bridge, I suppose I really should have warned him about those planks. I really should've.

September's Song

Turning into the campsite, that déjà vu feeling of never having left always takes me by surprise. So many things are unchanged from year to year. All the familiar faces are here, their canoes and tents and campfires occupying the same places as always. Our spot under the tall White Pine had been left vacant in expectation of our arrival. The seasons of sharing the same campsite had made friends of our neighbors. And now, their handshakes are firm, their welcomes sincere.

We methodically go about the business of setting up camp. There is a controlled haste to our actions, for no matter how often we have been here before, there is no denying the excitement of finally being at the river after having journeyed for so long. When all is ready, the aluminum rod cases are taken from the truck and the rods are removed and assembled. My father and Uncle Hank have been making this September pilgrimage to Northern Maine for 40-odd years. Yet, as we pull on our waders and hip boots, their eagerness rivals that of my fishing partner Mike, here for his first trip. Dressed in sweat-stained hats and bulging fishing vests, we shuffle down the path that leads to the river.

Like something too-long stored, the kinks are slow in coming out of my casts. The line flows overhead with awkward angularity but it feels good to be fishing again just the same. The first cast settles easily not only on the water but on my mind as well. My attention focuses on my streamer fly. I will it to swim fishily but it refuses; more evidence of my lack of practice. Once, on a June fishing trip several years ago, my first cast took a three-pound salmon. But this is not June and the autumn river does not yield so easily. My second cast feels better than the first but the results are equally unproductive. The awkwardness is almost gone by the third. This will be the charm, for sure.

But it isn't.

And so it goes.

The fishing today is more a matter of driven compulsion than genuine pleasure. And after a score of fruitless casts, the elation that held the road-weariness at bay for the past hour gives way to exhaustion. The road that connects the outside world of decisions and deadlines, to this place that is wilderness Maine, is nine hours long. When I finally return to camp, I find I'm the last one back.

In the dusk that creeps out from the woods, the Coleman lanterns can be seen in the surrounding camps. Tradition dictates that my father and Uncle Hank tend to the cooking. Their good-natured badgering of each other is a continuous, never-ending fixture in camp. Mike and I provide the firewood and attend to any other necessary tasks. The urgency of our earlier efforts is absent now, as evidenced by the glass of whiskey close by each elbow.

Supper is announced. Wood smoke, the open air, and the voracious appetite one develops in the wilderness combine to make each supper an event. Leftovers are unknown. The final course is a homemade apple pie from my aunt's kitchen. Careful storage kept it undamaged for the six-hundred-mile journey. But now, within a few short minutes, nothing is left but a few crumbs.

We clean up the pots and dishes, tidy up our camp, then get on with the business of renewing old acquaintances. Ted comes by in a tattered felt hat and a six-day-old stubble beard, as always. Ace regales us with his guide's tales of clients with 'buck fever' and 'big ones that got away'. The others join us. The coffee pot perks and a bottle is passed, but the main course on these September evenings is the conversation with old friends.

Purposefully, I draw my seat up next to Ralph's. I once read that Jack Nicklaus returns to his boyhood teacher each year and takes instructions in the rudiments of golf just to keep from drifting too far from the basics of the game. My guru is Ralph. He catches big fish consistently. The first to leave camp in the morning and the last to return at night, he couples his persistence with a thorough mastery of the basics of fly fishing. Ralph explains his success with a few simple truisms, such as, "Keep your fly in the water, and keep it moving." His advice seems oversimplified until I consider the amount of time I spend fishing when my fly is *not* in the water and *not* moving.

I look around the campfire at the circle of faces and try to see myself through their eyes. Twenty years ago I was a kid my father brought along on fishing trips. It was exciting for a boy to be in their company then, as their stories seemed so much larger than life. I smile at the thought and realize it is just as exciting to be accepted as one of them now.

The dawn mist covers everything: the rods, the table, even the spent moths lying by the lantern. My sleeping bag beckons for me to stay, competing against the wet and chilly morning, but outside, the river also calls to me. Yawning, I sit up, undecided until I the smell of frying bacon drifts through the tent. There is no denying the power of that aroma. Within minutes, I'm outside, fully dressed, and engaged in breakfast conversation over the rim of a coffee cup.

"Today's the day," we all agree.

"Fishing's been slow but they lowered the gate at the dam a few inches during the night," reports Ace. Indeed, the throaty sound of the river is markedly different with the increased flow. This, everyone agrees, will improve our luck and "bring up the big salmon." Optimism and coffee seem to go together in fishing camp mornings.

My father and Uncle Hank drive up to the dam. There is little debate that the rips below the spillway hold more salmon than any other stretch of the river. But they also attract the most number of fishermen.

Today, I pass on the dam. Instead, I fish a place called the Warden's Camp. It's a spot I've been fishing, in my mind, all during the previous months of waiting. The swift water is a serious challenge to any fisherman but it's worth the trouble. The place even looks the part; rapids tipped with white foam against a background of dark fir and spruce.

The first time I ever fished this water behind the abandoned Warden's Camp, I was negotiating my way around some beaver slashings on the far side of the river when I met an old hunter and his setter. They might well have stepped out of a Burton Spiller classic. Perhaps the fact that neither of us saw a rival in the other's presence allowed us both to be candid. I swapped pipe tobacco for sour wild apples and we chatted about the whereabouts of salmon and woodcock. He smiled when I confessed an envy of his woodland wisdom; I smiled when he confessed his envy of my youth. We parted with a handshake. His memory remains part of this special place and I pause each time I fish here, straining to hear the tinkle of his setter's bell.

After a few hard touches of frost, the river takes on a different complexion below the surface as well as above. The big spawners are in. Such is their single-mindedness in autumn that mature salmon can't be bothered with trivial matters such as eating. The fly patterns that appealed to their appetites during the spring are ineffective now. Yet, for some unknown reason, a big gaudy streamer fly will occasionally provoke a vicious strike. I tie of the biggest streamer in my fly box.

A Landlocked Salmon, *Salmo salar Sebago*, even a small one, is an exhilarating fish to catch. The first fish to take my fly is not a salmon but instead, a brook trout. In his breeding colors, he is astonishingly beautiful. In the fall, the trout season is closed on Maine Rivers, so this fifteen-incher is carefully released.

Mike fishes with me today. His perfect casts run out in smooth, tight arcs. Realizing full well that bottom fishermen take more salmon with their weight streamers, Mike continues to use finesse techniques with unweighted flies. Others may catch more fish, but few derive more pleasure from their fishing.

I happen to glance downstream just as a salmon breaks water in a short leap. I smile and return my attention to placing my fly behind a midstream boulder. After a moment, I wonder if Mike saw the jumping fish. Glancing downstream in his direction, I see him climbing over a deadfall with his rod held high. It takes another long moment for me to realize the two events are connected. As I watch, the fish makes another leap and a white line shoots out of the rod, into the river. Mike is already into his backing and scrambling to keep up with the salmon.

Quickly reeling in and laying my rod aside, I grab my landing net and set off to help Mike. I remember to hang my hat high atop a streamside sapling after I've gone a dozen steps. It's not unusual to end up half a mile downstream from where the fish was first hooked, and only the memory of other anxious searches for mislaid gear prompts me to mark the spot.

Mike has moved around the bend in the river, out of my sight. I climb over the deadfall where I last saw him, moving as quickly as cumbersome waders permit among the rocks and boulders on the river's edge. I catch up with him about a hundred yards downstream; standing in mid-river, just over his waders. His rod is held high over his head to clear a snag of mid-river brush. Although his backing has been regained, Mike is locked in a deep-water standoff with a salmon on the far side of the snag.

I balance my way out along a horizontal tree trunk and take the rod from my partner. Suddenly the fish makes a run back around the snag, taking half the backing with him. If it were my salmon, I'd be whooping with excitement. Instead, I feel like I've been entrusted with something important and hang on doggedly. Having worked its way free of the snag and back out into deep water, I pass the rod back to Mike with a sigh of relief.

The salmon makes a short run upriver and makes a final spectacular leap that carries him end-over-end. Mike keeps the line tight and a few moments later, I ease the landing net under his first ever salmon.

We measure and weigh the fish, take a few photos, and hold it upright in the current so it may regain its strength. Of my fishing acquaintances, only Mike shares my belief that trophy fish should be returned to the river. It's a practice that I've often wished I could apply to my autumn bird hunting.

The salmon swims away sullenly, disappearing in the deep water darkness. Mike claps me on the shoulder and laughs a "thanks." Turning upriver, we start off to find a red hat hanging atop a streamside sapling.

My father and I spend a day drift-fishing along a serene stretch of the river. We take turns with the canoe paddle. I am in mid-cast when he whispers, "Hold it," and points to what appears to be a school of fish paralleling our course. When they break the surface, I recognize them as otters. They follow us for about one-hundred yards, playing a game of tag which takes them under the canoe. As they move in and out of our shadow, I find my doubts about their abilities to catch a fish quickly dispelled. Then, as suddenly as they appeared, they're gone. I reel in to take up the second paddle. We have to put this stretch of water behind us. Enjoyable as the performance was, it has ruined any fishing we might have had.

It's my father's turn to fish. He casts smoothly and accurately, expertly working the deadfalls and boulders. As we drift by the mouth of a brook, I see his rod tip jump.

"There's one," he says in a whisper and retrieves his line for another cast. I ease the anchor into the water and watch my father find the range. I find myself holding my breath. There is a sudden rise of his rod tip, but for a moment, nothing happens. Then a swift-moving, small wake begins behind the point where the line enters the water, followed instantly by the one-note complaint of the reel's drag. The fish goes deep across the bow of the canoe then shows himself with two spectacular leaps that leave me dumbfounded. He's huge! Three jumps later, the salmon succeeds in snapping the tippet but leaps once more for good measure, the large Gray Ghost stream visible in his mouth. For a half-minute, we sit motionless, eyes glued on the dissipating ripples caused be the giant salmon's final leap. Ted brought in a salmon a few years back that tipped the scales at six pounds so we both knew what a six-pounder looked like. My father's was bigger. Much bigger. Yet, following the loss of the fish, there is no angry outburst from my dad. Instead, a shake of his balding head and a smile.

Were our positions reversed, I'm not certain that his son could have demonstrated as much class.

*   *   *

There has to be a reason that a bunch of grown men will pack up and drive nine straight hours in a cramped truck, then sleep outdoors and swat bugs for a week. When asked, I usually say it's all for the sake of catching a salmon. That, at least, is the simple version of the correct answer. A more complete reply would have to include, among others; the Canada Jays and the Red Squirrels that quickly make off with any unattended food in camp, the fledgling Red-Breasted Mergansers and American Goldeneyes on the river, the family of porcupines that chewed out the side boards of the outhouse, the otter family that so enchanted us on that afternoon. So would the Pine Marten I saw one day. And part of the answer would have to include the inky blackness of the sky when the nearest streetlight is fifty miles away. And of course, there's the complete absence of styrofoam cups and beer cans that litter everything everywhere. The river? Well, of course the river. The evenings of old stories and genuine laughter with old genuine friends. But of all the reasons I come here, I count as paramount the opportunity to share it with the man who first showed it to me years ago.

The northern lights put on a show in the night sky during our last evening in camp. I linger long after the others return to their tents, fascinated by the green curtains of light that dance between Andromeda and the Dipper. Both the starlight and the aurora are reflected in the quiet pool below camp. I close my eyes, wanting to record the scene but my mind is already filled with images from the past week on the river. I recall and recount them all, one by one, as I watch the display and realize that the melody the river plays in the background is also part of each of them. It is September's Song.

We say our farewells. There are the usual idle promises of holiday get-togethers and correspondence, but we all know we'll not see nor hear from one another until we come to the campsite next September. If the fishing has been less than spectacular, it matters little. I'm taking back a full measure of what I came here for. I light my pipe and take a last look around the campsite. If I pause until the others grow impatient, it is because I know that as soon as I climb behind the wheel, I'll begin the long journey to next September.

The Revenge of Russel's Sister

I sat at my desk, staring at my computer. Nothing was happening. The characters of my novel had taken the day off and not told me. They simply weren't there. When I looked up, my sixteen-year-old daughter was standing in the doorway to my office.

"Have you ever been in trouble with the law?" she asked.

"Well," I leaned back in my chair. "Once. A long time ago. But it wasn't serious. Why do you ask?"

Ignoring my question, she asked, "What did you do?"

I scratched my chin. "I don't think I want to tell you."

She folded her arms across her chest. "You've always said I should learn from your mistakes. How can I know what I'm not supposed to do if you won't tell what mistakes you've made?"

I smiled and studied my daughter. She made a good point. "Well," I said, realizing I was trapped. "Pull up a chair. It's a rather long story."

She did and I began.

"Back where I grew up in Massachusetts, there was a policeman named John Stock who was a real dirt ball. Everyone in town hated him. Even the other cops on the force would avoid him. One day, a few friends and I tried to fix his wagon. Well, it didn't go as planned and we sort of got in trouble."

"Sort of?"

I put my feet up on my desk. "I guess you could call it trouble. But it was all worth it. Like I said, he was thoroughly loathed by one and all. For example, he'd get kicks out of sneaking up on parkers and taking flash pictures, and then send them to the kids' parents. You would know anything about parking now, would you?"

"Of course not."

I gave her one of my fatherly glares then continued. "Anyway, I was twelve when Stock got my friend Russel's sister pregnant. Now, this in itself isn't unusual. These things happen, but Stock denied any part of it, claiming he never went near Russel's sister. The whole town knew he'd sneak over to her house every day, but no one knew how. He was supposed to be on-duty when those rendezvouses took place so he had an alibi. Also, you have to understand that a few years back, this sort of thing created a major league scandal in a small town."

"Well, there were four of us that hung around together back then, including, of course, Russel. And we weren't real happy about Stock and this thing with Russ's sister so we decided to get even. The problem was how."

"Our first real hurdle was to figure out how Stock could be in two places at once. If we could somehow prove his involvement with Russ's sister, we felt we could nail him. But Stock was no dummy and he, a former high school football star, was more than a match for us physically. That meant we had to rely upon our wits, which put us in real trouble. But we got some help from an unexpected source."

I sipped some of my coffee, which by now had grown cold. "It all started when the gossip about the scandal was at its peak. Russel and I had plans to go fishing. After all, we couldn't let a little thing like family disgrace spoil our weekly fishing trip. I was to meet Russel down by the river…

"Hi Rus."

"Howdy." Russel stepped cautiously down the path, hopping from stone to stone. He was dressed in old, patched dungarees and a formerly white tee shirt. He was tall, or perhaps, sort of stretched like twelve-year-old's can be. His hair was mussed

as usual. In his hand, he held his fishing rod; hook baited and ready for action.

"You bring the cigarettes?" he asked.

"Yep," I replied, touching my shirt pocket. A twig broke up the path from where we stood. "Who's that?"

Russel sighed. "My cousin from Tennessee."

The pig-tailed girl, face covered with freckles, emerged from the bushes. She looked to be about our age and like most kids back then, was skinny with bony knees.

"She's a girl," I whispered to Russel.

"No kidding."

"You showed a girl our secret spot?"

"Look, I had to bring her along. My mom made me."

The girl stepped forward. With a definite haughty air, she announced. "My name is Thelma. I'm Russel's cousin. His sister's going to come to stay with us until she has her baby."

Russel shot a killing look at his cousin then turned away. For the next minute, we stood silently, embarrassed, trying to figure out what to say next.

"Marlboro?" I asked, extending a pack of cigarettes – swiped from my older brother's car – toward Rus.

Thelma put her hands on her hips and in a Miss Know it All fashion, stated, "They'll make you sterile!"

I frowned. "My father says that's not true. He smoked them for years and I'm here."

Thelma, ignoring my rebuttal, quipped, "Too bad that guy Stock didn't smoke them."

Russel whipped around. "Shut up, you ass!"

"Just making an observation," Thelma responded airily.

After a few more minutes of strained silence, Russel announced, "We've got to get Stock. I'm serious. We've got to make him pay."

I spit on the ground. "Damn right. I heard my mom and dad talking and they said he's been a problem for the whole town and this time should be fired. That is, if someone could prove it."

Russel's jaw tightened. "If only we could figure out how he got into my house while he was supposed to be somewhere else, we could nail his fat ass."

Thelma cleared her throat, and in a surprisingly timid voice, asked, "Why don't you ask your sister?"

"Yeah, right," replied Russel sarcastically.

"What a stupid idea," I added.

After another silent minute, Russel turned to me. "Maybe that's not such a bad idea."

"So what happened next?" my daughter asked.

"Well, Thelma was right. Russel's sister knew the whole story and was more than happy to spill the beans once she learned we were trying to nail Stock."

"But how was he doing it? How did he manage to be in two places at once?"

"As it turns out, it was rather clever, especially for John Stock," I said. "First, he'd park the police cruiser alongside the highway. "Then, when there was no traffic and the highway was clear, he'd place a mannequin dressed in a police uniform behind the wheel of the car. At a pre-arranged time, Russel's sister would come by and pick him up. The rest is history."

My daughter nodded. "I see. That way everyone thought Stock was on duty. Okay, but that doesn't explain how you got into trouble."

I smiled. "That is more complicated. Russel thought we ought to go to the police chief with the mannequin story. But the other two guys we chummed-around with, Ray and Tom, didn't agree."

> *"Whose bright idea was that?" asked Ray, commonly known as The Weasel.*
>
> *"Mine," said Russel.*
>
> *Tom, a cocksure smart aleck, scoffed. "You been sniffin' glue or something? When the chief gets done laughing, he'll throw you out into the street. Do you really think he's going to believe you? I know he won't cause he's my Uncle Bill's boss and he hates all kids. Have I ever told you guys about him?"*
>
> *Ray wiped his nose with the back of his hand. "Yeah, about a million times."*
>
> *"Up yours, you jerk," Tom retorted.*
>
> *Thelma, who had been quietly standing back, stepped forward. "Well then, what do you think we should do?"*
>
> *"And who are you?" asked Ray the Weasel.*

"I'm Thelma, Russel's cousin from Tennessee. So, what do you think we should do?"

We all fell silent. Then, Ray the Weasel came up with the best idea of his entire weasely childhood. He said, "I think we gotta steal that dummy and present it to Tom's Uncle Bill. That way he'd have some evidence to take to the chief."

We all stared at the Weasel, blinking in disbelief.

He grinned his evil grin. "Boy, I'm a regular Perry Mason."

Tom scoffed again. "You look more like Della Street."

"Oh listen to the funny man," snapped Weasel. "You ought to be on Ed Sullivan." Then he jumped on his bike, saying to Tom, "We gotta ride, remember Einstein? I told my mom I was comin' right home. You comin'?"

Tom climbed on his bike. "Yeah, yeah. I'm comin'." Over his shoulder, he called, "See you guys later."

Watching Weasel and Tom ride off, trading insults, Russel asked, "What do you think?"

I shook my head. "I know it sounds good but think about it. What are we supposed to do? Just walk up and take the dummy?"

Thelma opened her arms like some evangelist preacher. "Why not? I'm sure by now, Stock's got another girlfriend and he's probably pulling the same stunt. We know where he parks. Let's go and have a look." Then, looking back and forth between Russel and me, she added, "You're not scared are you?"

*No freckle-faced southern girl was going to call me a coward.
"Not me," I announced.*

"Me neither," Russel said with not a whole lot of conviction.

*"Okay then, let's go," Thelma said, leading the way back up
the path.*

*"Hey Russ," I whispered. "When's she going back to
Tennessee?"*

"Not soon enough!" he whispered.

"Did you really take the dummy from the cop car?" asked my
daughter.

"No, but not for lack of trying. Well, to be truthful, it was Thelma
that gave it a go. I can still see her, strolling right up to the police car…

*I pushed aside a branch, which obscured where Russel and
I were hiding. Thelma was striding right up to the parked
cruiser.*

"My God, Rus, look at her. She's got the balls of a bison."

*"That's cause she's a girl and knows that nothin' will happen
to her if she gets caught. I'd be that brave too if I was in her
shoes," replied Russel. Then, with a touch of pride, he added,
"Plus, she's my cousin."*

*Thelma was peering into the car. From where Rus and I
were hiding, it sure looked like Stock was seated behind the
steering wheel. She knocked on the window, and called out,
"Hello? Mr. Policeman?"*

Nothing.

Then she knocked and called again.

Still nothing.

Turning our way, she signaled for us to come.

I looked at Russel. "We're gonna die, you know."

He just nodded, his face a strange shade of pale green.

Thelma signaled again and then planted her hands on her hips.

This time we obeyed.

"Help me get this dummy out of the car!" she whispered.

"Okay," we whispered back.

"Why are you whispering?" Thelma asked.

"Cause you whispered first," Russel answered, again whispering.

"I did not!"

"You did so!"

"Children, please!" I said. "Shall we?"

Thelma reached for the door and gave it a mighty pull, but to no avail. I was locked! Swiftly, we tried all the doors but no luck.

"Shit!" I said, drifting into profanity which for a twelve-year-old was serious.

"Double shit!" said Russel. Then, with a definite squeak in his voice, exclaimed, "And here comes Stock!"

Thelma and I shot a glance up the road where Russ was pointing. Sure enough, Stock was making his way back toward his car. He was keeping to the shadows to avoid being seen, his head on a swivel to watch for oncoming traffic. Fortunately, he hadn't spotted us yet. At Olympic class speed, we dashed away through the woods, never stopping until we were safely crouched down behind Russel's garage.

Russel, his face now gone the color of morning fog, said, "I - pant, pant – don't think he – pant, pant – saw us."

Thelma and I, also gasping for air, nodded in agreement.

"What do we do now?" asked Russel.

We all looked at each other. There were no answers, not yet.

I leaned back in my chair. "I suppose the whole story would have ended right there if it were not for Weasel and Tom. They accidentally spawned the final idea. The next day, we were down by the river, skipping a few stones and smoking some of our parent's cigarettes. Thelma filled-in Weasel and Tom regarding our failed adventure at Stock's car the previous afternoon. Russel and I were pretty intent on fishing and had moved down a little way, just out of earshot…

"Wow," exclaimed Tom. "You really went right up to Stock's car?"

Weasel wiped his nose. "Are you deaf as well as stupid? That's what she just said."

The turning to Thelma, he said, "No kidding? You really went right up to the cop car?"

Thelma was staring at a lit Marlboro cigarette, held at arm's length. "Cough Cough. Why do you guys smoke these things? They taste awful!"

"Smokin's not for girls anyways," Weasel announced, a cigarette held by his thin lips, bouncing as he spoke. "It's a man's sport. It's cool."

Tom skipped a flat stone eleven times before the individual bounces slurred together and ceased. "Okay Mr. Cool, let's see you beat eleven."

Responding to the challenge, Weasel began searching the shoreline for the right stone. "I'd have loved to see you at Stock's car. That must've been great. Too bad you don't have a picture. That really took balls." Then he stooped over a picked up a stone. "This here's a beauty!"

Tom shook his head. "Boy, you're really rude."

"About what?" Weasel replied.

Thelma snapped her fingers and smiled. "That's it!" she exclaimed.

"About balls," Tom said, ignoring Thelma's eureka moment.

"Balls?" asked Weasel, wrinkling his long skinny nose.

"Yeah balls," Tom said. "Girls don't have balls or hadn't you noticed, Birdbrain?"

"That's it!" exclaimed Thelma again to herself.

"Well," Weasel retorted. "Listen to Mr. Know-it-all. Of course I know girls don't have balls."

"Where's Russel and Kenny," Thelma asked excitedly.

Weasel and Tom were too deeply engrossed in their anatomical discussion to notice Thelma.

Tom was saying, "If girls don't have balls then they can't take balls to do something."

Weasel said, "You are a moron. It's that thing our teacher is always sayin'."

Tom frowned. "They say lots of things."

Weasel scratched his head. "It's a..., it's a...figure of something."

Tom shook his head no. "Figure of speech? No sir. I think it's more about..."

Thelma left the debate and set off to find her cousin. By the time she located the two fishermen, she could hardly contain herself.

"Russel! Kenny! I've got it! We don't have to get the dummy. This is even better. Tom's uncle is a cop, right? And Ray's mom still works in that clothing store, right? And Kenny, your dad's the photographer for the paper, right?"

Russel and I nodded.

"Okay," Thelma continued. "Listen to this."

The plan was actually quite ingenious. It involved some tricky timing and required a lot of things to go right. You see, what Thelma had in mind was to arrange, via an anonymous letter, for my dad and Tom's uncle, the cop, to be hidden nearby, waiting for something big to happen.

Meanwhile, after "borrowing" a female mannequin from Ray's mom's clothing store, we'd dress it up in some rather suggestive attire. Tom and Weasel, being well beyond their years with electrical stuff, would lift the hood and turn on the siren and blue lights. Down comes the hood. Then, Russel and I would place the sexy mannequin on the hood of the police car in a compromising pose. And away we run! From behind the bushes come the photographer and Tom's uncle. Stock, slithering back to his car, would be as good as dead. Sounded good. What could go wrong!

What could go wrong? Well, for starters, we didn't know Stock had broken up with his latest girlfriend – a small but important detail.

Thelma looked up and down the paved route where speeders often got nabbed. "Okay, go ahead. No cars coming."

The five of us crossed the highway and went straight for Stock's car. Russel and I leaned the scantily clad mannequin – bra, panties, garter belt nylons; wonderfully exciting stuff for a twelve-year-old boy with hormones awakening - against the car and began adjusting her arms and legs. We needed to prepare her for her resting pose on the hood. Meanwhile, Weasel and Tom popped the hood and went to work. Thelma stood guard.

Straightening the fantastically smooth and silky lace nylons, I glanced at the mannequin inside the car. "Boy," I thought. "It sure looks real."

Next was the wig. It had to be attached just so. Again I looked at the police mannequin. "Huh?" I thought. "I swear its head was turned the other way a minute ago."

Finally, the positively hot negligee. With the garment properly aligned, Thelma had to attend to that duty as none of us had any idea which was front, back, up, or down, I glanced at the police mannequin for the third time. This time it grinned an evil, toothy grin that I wouldn't see again for several years, not until Jaws was released.

"OH SHIT!" I yelled.

"What?" asked Russel.

"OH SHIT!" I repeated, too paralyzed with fear to say anything else.

Stock, however, was anything but paralyzed. He grabbed his nightstick and leaped from the car shouting, "HEY YOU LITTLE BASTARDS..."

But he never finished his sentence. The siren and blue lights sprang to life, temporarily staggering the stick-brandishing Stock. Now it was our turn to leap and leap we did; straight up, about face, and full speed ahead. The race was on. And by the way, where the hell was my dad and the town cop?

My daughter held up her hand. "But wait. What about the mannequin?"

"Well, for reasons that were never adequately explained, Russel wrapped the mannequin in a bear hug and carried it with him as he dashed across the highway. With its wig and marvelous negligee flapping in the breeze, it looked like the battle flag of the Light Brigade. As he ran, Russel eventually realized his extra baggage was slowing him down so he handed-off the dummy to Thelma who passing him on the right. Thelma, wanting no part of the mannequin-carrying detail, passed it on to me. I, in turn, passed it to the closest runner, which by then was Stock, who tucked our lady dummy under his arm like a football and plunged on.

"So there we were, five terrified kids, running for their lives, hotly pursued by an enormous, nightstick-wielding, dummy carrying policeman, about to cross the highway. Then, via what I firmly believe was divine intervention, circumstances took a sudden shift from the desperate to the absurd. Old man Garzinski, local poultry farmer, nearly deaf and ornery as a poked hornets' nest, was driving back to his farm with his truckload of fresh chicken manure. His was so intent on listening to a blaring polka issuing from his radio, that he didn't spot the gaggle of kids and the irate cop about to cross the highway until it was too late. Even empty, the aging truck likely couldn't have maneuvered around us but with a full load, there was no hope. He slammed on the brakes and veered hard to the right, which rolled the truck on its side, ejecting an entire load of odoriferous cargo onto the road. The manure, which was about fifty percent liquid, came at us in a two-foot brown wave. We all went down; the five of us, Stock, and our wayward mannequin. I can't recall if I swam, crawled, or staggered through the morass but I managed to be on my way again quickly. I remember passing the perplexed town cop and my father, who was busy clicking pictures for the newspaper. I suppose I should have said hello but all things considered, escape from a crazed Stock was my top priority."

"If we would have paused and turned around, we would have been witness to a four-car fender-bender, a spreading slick of disgusting chicken manure, and right in the middle of the mayhem, a pretty good fight between old man Garzinski and Stock. The fight turned out to be a draw with both men a bit bloodied. Under normal circumstances, Stock should have dropped Garzinski quickly, but holding fast to the erotic mannequin, Stock could only punch with one hand."

My daughter was spellbound. "So you guys escaped?"

"Nope. At nine o'clock the next morning, we were lined-up in front of the chief's desk. Our parents were all there, occupying the chairs in the back of the room.

> The police chief silently eyed us, clearly at a loss of how to proceed.

> "Who's the ringleader of this gang?" he asked.

We all studied our shoes. Finally, in a timid voice, I said, "I guess I am, sir."

Thelma glared at me. "What do you mean, you are? It was my idea."

Russel cleared his throat. "Yeah, but I'm the one who started it all."

Weasel wiped his nose. "But you guys were nothing without my brains."

Tom shot his pal an amused stare. "Oh sure. Listen to Mr. Humility here. Let me ask you this Einstein, who hot-wired the siren and lights?"

Weasel turned and faced Tom. "Yeah, but who knew how to pop the hood, birdbrain."

Tom flushed. "Don't call me Birdbrain, Jerk!"

"OKAY! ENOUGH!" shouted the chief impatiently. "Let me try again. What were you people doing around Officer Stock's cruiser yesterday?"

At precisely the same time, Thelma and I offered answers. Unfortunately, they were different.

"Eating berries."

"Picking flowers."

The chief frowned. "What's that again?"

"Eating flowers," I said meekly.

A few muffled snickers came from the back of the room. The chief lit a Camel cigarette and studied us through squinted eyes. After what seemed like an eternity, he finally said, "There are only two more weeks left of this summer, and then, you'll be back in school. If I so much as see any of you between now and then, I'll put you in the slammer for a week. IS THAT CLEAR?"

We all answered at once. This time, we all said the same thing: "Yes, Sir."

"But what happened to Stock?" asked my daughter.

"Not sure exactly. I heard our episode was the final straw and he got fired and pretty much run out of town. Somebody said he ended up selling used cars in the Bronx, but that may have been just talk. One thing for sure, no one missed him."

"And how about Russel's sister? What happened to her?"

I shrugged. "Again, not sure but I think her part in the adventure ended happily. Russel said while she was in Tennessee, she met a soldier and they ended up getting married. Last I heard, they were doing fine and were raising their own family."

I paused, then asked, "Now why this sudden interest in my past criminal career?"

"Well," my daughter began, not meeting my eye, "about last Friday night. The police chief would like you to call him today."

Ole' Wrinkle Neck

"But Dad, it's going to be dark soon!"

"I don't care. Maybe next time you'll remember. How many times do I have to tell you to close the barn door? I'm sick and tired of searching for our animals all over the countryside. Now get your jacket on and go find our cow!"

The screen door banged shut behind me as I stepped outside. The sun was already dangerously low, painting the scattered clouds with a final splash of yellow and orange. Ole' Wrinkle Neck, the family cow, had slipped away again. She was a good milker, never kicking or resisting when the pails had to be filled but unlike most of her species, she loved to roam. And now I had to find her. And it was getting dark! Young boys often find themselves in that twilight zone of youth wherein admitting any fear of the dark is unheard of yet, is *very* real. I was no exception.

The usual thoughts of running away preoccupied me as I drifted through the barnyard towards the garden. I was halfway to California, out on the highway, thumb out to hitchhike, when a voice startled me back from my travels.

"It can't be that bad."

I looked up to see my ancient grandfather in the asparagus patch. He was cradling tonight's harvest in the crook of his arm.

"Huh? What can't be that bad?"

He slowly straightened his long back and walked to where I stood. His wrinkled face softened. "Your expression would curdle fresh milk. Surely the world's problems aren't weighing you down just yet. Now make yourself useful and take this asparagus from me."

We took the fresh spears to the porch.

"I gotta go Gramp," I said. "I gotta go fetch Wrinkle. She took off again while I was in the barn."

He cocked his head in a listening way, looked out at the deepening shadows, and adjusted his glasses.

"I could use a walk," he said. "Maybe I could join you in your quest for our runaway. That is, if you'd like some company."

"Oh, could ya?" Then, regaining my composure, I added, "I'm not afraid of the dark or anything, but it *is* a nice evening for a walk."

He brushed aside a nonconformist lock of white hair, cleaned his wire-rimmed glasses with an old red handkerchief, and echoed, "It is a lovely evening."

It didn't take us long to find Ole Wrinkle Neck. She was down by the brook where the white clover grows in profusion, covering the hillside that leads to the old orchard. Just, incidentally, where Grandpa said she'd be. The cow surrendered without a struggle and soon, we were on our way back to the barn.

As we stepped to the rhythmic beat of Ole' Wrinkles cowbell, the spring peepers were tuning up for their evening concert. Mists were beginning to creep out over the meadow, and the sweet fragrance of lilac joined the ever-present aroma of old cow.

"Gramps, can I ask you something?"

"Yep."

I took a deep breath. "Some kids were talkin' in school last week about God and stuff. Well, Martin Biggs, you know him, he's the one who always spits, says there's no such thing. He says if there's a God, then I should prove it."

"What did you say to that?"

"I told him he was a jerk."

"Did that settle it?"

"That he was a jerk?"

"No. I mean about proving the existence of God."

"I guess not."

We walked in silence for a minute or two. A couple of bats, out for their evening patrol, swooped low, intercepting a few unseen insects for dinner.

I said, "Biggs says there's no such thing as heaven either. He says some old people made it up cause they're afraid of dying."

"What do you think?"

"I think Biggs is a jerk."

We had come to the family graveyard, a place I stayed clear of when the light faded. Grampa handed me the cow's lead and said, "Hold this for a second."

He walked straight to Grandma's tombstone, stooped, and then removed a handful of weeds that had sprung up around the marker. With some effort, he straightened and returned. Taking the cows lead, we resumed our homeward journey.

We walked in silence for some time, past the corn, around the rhubarb, until the yellow lights of the farmhouse appeared up ahead.

I broke the quiet. "There is a God, isn't there?"

Grandpa stopped and looked down at me. Then, he turned and scratched Ole' Wrinkle between the eyes, gazing back into the darkness towards the graveyard. I couldn't see his eyes but I sensed he was looking at a time a long way from here.

"Your Grandmother used to say that whenever mankind took charge of anything, it'd quickly become disorganized and reduced to chaos. But every spring, in some orderly way, flowers come up when the freezin' stops. And birds show up when the leaves come out so they can hide their nests. And the cows have calves when the grass turns green. Something, or perhaps someone, keeps everything in order and man certainly has nothing to do with it. Your Grandmother was a simple woman who didn't claim to know much about church or the

Bible or Heaven or Hell, but she strongly believed that something way greater than you and me, was behind those ever-present miracles. I suspect God has something to do with that."

As we approached the barn, I could see my dad puttering around the harsh light of the Coleman lantern. Every now and then he'd stop and peer nervously into the darkness. I turned to my Grandfather and he handed me the lead to Ole' Wrinkle Neck. Then I did something that this twelve-year-old wasn't accustomed to doing: I hugged him. I hugged him tightly. I didn't know it then but it would be the last time I ever did such a thing, for he would join Grandma a short time later.

Grandpa said in a soft voice, "Now go."

Wiping my eyes, I led Ole' Wrinkle Neck into the barn.

Worm Hole

Chapter One

A Bad Day for Ryan Wiggins

Attorney Ryan Wiggins sat in Trial Room Number Two of the First District Courthouse, impatiently drumming his fingers on the massive oak attorneys table. He looked at the huge clock with Roman numerals and ornate hands above the jury bench. It was ten minutes before five, much too late to get started. Another day wasted. Another day without billings. He silently took two Rolaids from his shirt pocket and popped them into his mouth.

Finally, the judge removed his reading glasses and looked up.

"Mr. Wiggins?"

Wiggins jumped to his feet. "Yes, your honor."

The judge, a mere skeleton of a man with a few wisps of gray hair covering his liver-spotted skull, glared down at the attorney standing before him. His fierce brown eyes shown with impatience. "This petition is incomplete. The Greenwich District Court will not take up this matter until you produce a document that is capable of becoming a court record. Surely you are up to that task?" He held up the document he'd been reading, and then tossed it down in disgust. "A first-year law student can do better than this. Try again and submit your work to my court for consideration. We'll set another court date after the holiday recess. And this time," he studied the crestfallen lawyer standing in front of him and paused. The ticking of the clock seemed to rise to a crescendo. "And this time, get it right."

With that, he stood and left the courtroom.

Wiggins pulled on his overcoat and stared out the window. The snow was coming down heavier than ever. Traffic on the street below had slowed to a crawl, a stream of red taillights fading into the distance. The drive home was going to be a long, arduous task.

He walked down the stairs and paused before stepping outside to wrap his scarf and button up.

"Forget something?"

Wiggins turned and faced James, the front door guard, a huge bald black man with a snow-white mustache.

"What's that?"

James blinked and then repeated. "Forget something?"

Wiggins shook his head no. "No. Why do you ask?"

"You were just here a minute ago. Ducked in then ducked out without saying a word. Now, here you are again."

Wiggins frowned. "I wish I was. I've been upstairs in court." *Getting my ass reamed.*

"No sir," James said, slowly shaking his head. "You was right here." He pointed at the door.

"Whatever."

Snow in Greenwich, Massachusetts comes in two basic consistencies. On rare occasions, when the temperature is in the twenties, it can be powdery and light, drifting into white waves and blowing around like autumn leaves. It's the Currier and Ives kind of snow and makes you think of Christmas and hot chocolate. But most of the time, such as on that particular evening, the air temperature flirted with thirty-two degrees, making the snow heavy and wet, clinging to everything, pulling down wires and branches. To make matters worse, when compressed such as underfoot or under tires, it became extraordinarily slippery. Driving through this variety of winter weather was akin to pushing through mashed potatoes. Stopping in these conditions was 'iffy' at best. Rear end collisions were common, which further slowed progress. Outside, horns blew and tires spun.

Wiggins picked his way down the courthouse steps, hanging onto the wrought iron rail for dear life, then turned and headed for the parking garage. The high-pressure sodium streetlights created cones of light, snow coursing down through the blue-white illumination. Outside of these cones, it was pitch black.

He shuffled along the sidewalk with head down, leaning into the blinding snow, moving in and out of the lighted cones. As such, he failed to notice the dark figure slip out of the shadows and follow his path, staying about fifty feet back.

When Wiggins reached the garage, he headed for the third deck. A creature of habit, he always parked in the same spot, thus eliminating the need to remember where he had left his car at the end of the day. He stamped his feet to remove the slush, brushed the snow from his hat and shoulders, and then started up the stairs. As most commuters had cut out early, taking heed of the predicted snow storm, the garage was mostly empty. His footfalls echoing on the concrete steps drowned out the sound of another person coming up behind him.

Reaching his car, the last one on the third deck, Wiggins unbuttoned his coat and dug out his car keys. Then he paused. An uneasy prickly feeling swept up the back of his neck. He turned around and spotted a man walking toward him. At first, Wiggins thought he was looking at a reflection of himself, as one would see in a plate glass window on a city street. The approaching man was uncannily similar.

"Hello Ryan Wiggins," the man said as he drew near. He smiled and removed his hand from his coat pocket. In it, he held a small, thin rectangular device, which he raised and pointed at Wiggins.

"Nothing personal you understand," the man said, and then pressed a button. An orange light shot out from the device and hit Wiggins in the chest. The car keys slipped from his fingers and dropped to the deck of the parking garage.

Chapter Two

Visitors

Six months later, the hot, humid weather settled in for a long visit. In Massachusetts, tropical weather is not unknown but an extended period of the sticky stuff is an anomaly, generally despised and loudly denounced by the locals. However, small-time vegetable farmers like me, who grow peppers and tomatoes and cantaloupes, welcome it as it kicks the plants into high gear and yields skyrocket.

It was still early in the day and the sun had mercifully not yet cleared the oak trees. I needed to fill the order from Julio's Grill, a Latino restaurant in nearby Greenwich. Diego, the phenomenally rotund cook, paid handsomely for any and all peppers, especially the New Mexico Long varieties. My plants were drooping to the ground under the weight of the crop. This would be a fine cash day. I picked with both hands, dragging the harvest basket along behind.

It is always interesting to examine what pops into your head when attending to a mindless task. The content can be an emotional barometer of mental health at the time. For example, if you find yourself giving some poor soul a thorough and sharp tongue lashing about some social slight or off-handed comment, you are likely in a not-so-good frame of mind. Conversely, if your focus is on which trout stream to fish in the evening and what fly to use, you are probably in a better place. That's where I was. Just at dark, the trout would go on a feeding frenzy making fishing wildly exciting and my hope was to be there when it happens.

As was my habit, I was singing softly to myself. I found it kept the demons away. The pepper basket was overflowing, and I needed to go to my barn to fetch another. As I walked along the garden row, my thoughts drifted to that evening's fishing. I was just about done finalizing my fishing plans when behind me, I heard someone clear his throat. I whipped around. There, outside the deer fence which surrounds my garden stood a man and a woman.

The man bore a striking resemblance to me: tall, thin, gray hair and mustache, blue eyes. He wore a wrinkled white cotton shirt and blue jeans. The woman was not so tall but also thin, with curly brown hair, attractive, and wearing a neatly pressed black tee shirt and white shorts. She held a briefcase to her chest, arms crossed.

"Sorry to startle you," the man said, holding up a hand in a weak wave. "You appeared to be deep in thought. And if I'm not mistaken, that song…the song you were singing…was *"Turn, Turn, Turn"* by the Byrds. Right?"

Ignoring his correct identification of my song, I mumbled, "I was and you did." Brushing garden soil from my hands and straightening my stiff back, I asked, "What can I do for you?"

The man and woman exchanged looks. The woman asked, "I hate to interrupt your harvesting but could we have a moment of your time?"

I studied them both.

"Look," I said. "My focus right now is to finish picking before the heat and humidity crank up. Plus, you are in my yard, on private property, so - and don't take this personally - why don't you go back the way you came and find someone else to chat with."

The woman waved at a pestering mosquito and said matter-of-factly, "We have come to arrest your neighbor and need your assistance."

I blinked a few times. "What?"

She cocked her head slightly and patiently replied, "Your neighbor, Ryan Wiggins, has violated a number of laws involving security and exchange of trusts. Further, he is under suspicion for grand theft and murder one. And now, he needs to be brought back home to stand trial."

Again, I blinked. "Wiggins? You've got to be kidding me. And what does this have to do with me?"

The man smiled and shooed away a pesky horsefly. "It's a long and involved story. Can we go somewhere to talk? These bugs have taken a liking to us."

It was then that I looked more closely at the man. It was like looking in the mirror! If I had a twin brother, he was him. But I don't, at least to my knowledge. Or maybe I do. This was very confusing.

"Are you the police?" I asked, stalling for time to think.

The woman said, "In a sense, we are. I am a prosecuting attorney and my assistant," she nodded to the guy that looked like me, "is an apprehension agent."

"Do you have identification?"

More waving and slapping at bloodthirsty insects. "Can we go somewhere else? Please?" she asked.

We walked the short distance from the garden to my back deck and pulled up three chairs, still damp from the overnight dew. I would have offered my guests something to drink except I was still suspicious and didn't want them to get too comfortable.

"Okay," I said, wiping my hands on my already dirty jeans. "So what's your story?"

The woman placed her briefcase on her lap and began, "Your neighbor..."

"No, no," I interrupted. "Who are you?"

The woman nodded toward her partner, who in turn leaned forward, elbows on knees, and began. "My name is Bartholomew Andrew Russell and I'm, well, I'm *you* from another dimension. And by the way, call me Bart. I hate Bartholomew. Way too formal."

I took another deep breath, scratched the back of my head, and thought, another whack job religious zealot.

"Look," I said. "I'm a busy guy and although you probably mean well, you have to leave. Right now. OK? Understand? Out!" I pointed to the street.

The man smiled faintly, holding me in his gaze, and said, "Let me try another approach to convince you that we're legitimate. A long time ago when you were a little kid, you removed the caution sign from a construction hole on Broadway Street and an unsuspecting car drove into the hole. Remember that? You have felt terrible about that stupid prank ever since. And let's see, how about this one. One of your newspaper customers used to, when her husband was away, give you more than the customary twenty-five cent tip on Friday paydays. Remember her? And then there was that huge tire you and our pal Joey Reynolds, rolled down the hill that flattened the town building. Remember that infamous night?" He stopped and held me in his gaze.

I was stunned. Those were my deepest secrets. "How the fuck..."

"Look at me," he continued earnestly. "I am you. You are me. We live in different parts of the cosmos but are the same person. I know all your secrets because they are my secrets as well." He paused, then smiled broadly and said, "I've got an idea. How about we drop trousers and compare our private parts?"

The woman cleared her throat and interrupted with, "I don't think that will be necessary. I think Mr. Russell gets the point. Just give it a minute to sink in."

I sat back in my chair and tried to figure out if this was a dream or if I had finally lost my mind.

The woman reached into her briefcase and extracted something that looked like a plastic poker chip with a USB stick protruding from it. She handed it to me. "I am Federal Attorney Meredith McNally and this is my electronic business card. If you plug it into your laptop, it will give you all my identity information including pictures, references, and other information pertinent to this case.

You are not losing your mind and we are who we say we are. And we need your help."

The man extended his hand and said, "Call me Hank."

Dazed and confused, I shook his hand. "Hank? I thought you said..."

The man, Hank, sat back and chuckled. "As you know, my Dad, who of course was also your Dad, was Hank Russell. We went everywhere together and people began to refer to me as "Little" Hank. As time passed, they dropped "Little" and I became Hank. It stuck. Didn't this happen to you?"

I shook my head 'no,' and slowly got to my feet. "I'm going to make some coffee."

Chapter Three

Worm Hole

It was no surprise that Hank took his coffee the same way I do – black. Meredith chose tea. We sat quietly for a few minutes. They - patiently waiting to resume our conversation; me – staring at my coffee in a state that can only be described as 'bewildered.'

Not a hint of a breeze was blowing. Another sultry day was in the making.

After a few sips of much too hot coffee, I put down my mug and asked weakly, "Tell me again where you guys are from."

Hank and Meredith once again exchanged looks, and then Hank said, "Let me try."

He put down his coffee cup and began. "You fashion yourself as an amateur astronomer, correct? I know this because I do, too."

I nodded.

"So, you've heard of the various theories of parallel universes. Right?"

I thought for a moment. Parallel universes were right up there with the string theory and other such babble. "I never paid much attention to them. They sound like some half-baked fantasies from pseudo-intellectuals who try to sound intelligent at parties."

"Well," Hank replied, "At least one of those theories is correct. We are living proof of it."

I raised my eyebrows. He seemed to know what I was thinking.

"As far as we know, there are a whole lot of parallel universes out there. And now we have discovered how they are connected."

"Oh," I said with mock sincerity. "And how's that?"

Hank picked up his coffee. "Here's where it gets a bit weird. In our solar system which, incidentally, is exactly, or almost exactly, the same as yours, way past Pluto's orbit is something called the Oort cloud. Ever hear of it?"

"Yep. And I believe it's actually known as the Opik-Oort cloud. And it's just another theory. Correct?"

Hank smiled. "Not anymore. It's real. It's huge. And that's where some of the wormholes are."

I shook my head. "Oh, come on. You're not telling me wormholes actually exist?"

Hank nodded again. "Yep. And that's how we got here." He sipped his coffee and leaned toward me. "They are energy whirlpools, like the ones in a draining bathtub."

I looked at the woman, Meredith, to see if she was buying this tale. She was studying my face.

"I can see," she began earnestly, "that you don't believe a word of this and are wondering who we are and what we are all about."

"That's about right," I replied.

"Neither of us is a scientist," she said. "I'm an attorney and Hank is a Federal Agent. So exactly how all this science works is a bit of hocus-pocus to us as well. But let *me* try to explain." She looked at Hank who raised his eyebrows and again sat back in his chair as if to say 'let's see if you can do any better, Miss Smarty Pants.'

Meredith folded her hands on top of the briefcase which lay on her lap and began. "What Hank says is true. The wormholes in our, and *your*, Oort cloud were created by several dying stars swirling around each other."

"Those would be White Dwarfs," Hank interrupted.

"Thank you, Hank," Meredith quipped, then turned back towards me. "Like I was saying...somehow, this swirling around creates an energy tunnel which links our parallel universes. Please don't ask me how because even the scientists are at a loss to understand...but it works."

"I thought," I said, "these wormholes were supposed to be time travel portals. Now you're telling me they connect different dimensions?"

Meredith looked at Hank who shrugged, and then she continued. "Strange as it sounds, yes. If there are other wormholes that offer time travel, I am not aware of them. So far, we have not heard anything about them being discovered. What we do know is, as of a few years ago, we have started making rather routine journeys through the various wormholes without any ill effects. And that brings us..."

I held up my hand. "Hold on. So you guys from your supposed parallel universe are much older than us. I mean your civilization has been around for a lot longer. Right?"

Meredith thought for a moment, pursing her lips, and then said, "No, that is not true. I believe every parallel universe discovered to date is exactly the same age. We have been told they all were formed at the same instant. But as I said, neither of us is a scientist."

It was my turn to lean forward. "Then how," I began, "is it possible for you to travel way out to the Oort cloud and take the shortcut which landed you here? We here on my Earth can't even remember how we sent a man to the moon. I think we lost the plans for the rocket. Travel to Mars is still a fantasy. Travel to this," I waved skyward for effect, "Oort cloud would be impossible with existing technology. And furthermore, where's your spaceship?"

"Ah-ha!" Hank replied with some energy. "Excellent questions. You see, your Earth and our Earth might be the same age, but technologically we're at least one hundred years ahead of you."

"How convenient," I replied. "And how did this happen?"

"Gavrilo Princip," Hank said.

"What is Gavrilo whatever?"

"Who, not what," Hank replied. "He is the assassin that on June 28, 1914, in Sarajevo, shot Archduke Ferdinand of Austria. Remember him from world history class?"

"Rings a bell. But what does he have to do with..."

"This happened here on your Earth," Hank said. "But on *our* Earth, when running to the motor car to shoot the Archduke, Gavrilo tripped over an untied shoelace and fell flat on his face and in the process, shot himself in the foot. Guards jumped him and tossed him in jail, never to be heard from again. Since it was this big event that triggered WWI here on your Earth, that catastrophic European event never happened on our Earth."

"Time out," I said. "So we're not exactly parallel universes anymore? Isn't this a rather significant divergence? I thought we were exactly the same?"

Meredith spoke up. "We are still sorting this out as well. Don't forget, we might be ahead of you technologically but, as you may imagine, there's a mountain of unanswered philosophical, social, and moral questions yet to be addressed. And with regard to exactly the same - take you and Hank for example - you two may look strikingly similar but take a good look. I think there are some very slight differences."

Hank and I stared at each other.

Hank said, "Are you sure you don't want to compare private parts? Maybe there's a significant deviation there."

In spite of my distrust for these two, I chuckled. But Meredith rolled her eyes and shook her head in disgust. "I see there is no difference between your maturity levels. You both share the same sophomoric sense of humor." She resumed. "Even from where I sit, I can see slight differences in gray hair patterns, skin blemishes, moles, and the wrinkles around your eyes."

Hank said to me, "She's a real charmer, don't you think?"

"But according to our scientists, slight deviations," she said, plowing forward, "do not seem to affect the entire planet as a whole. At least so far."

I scratched my head. "This seems a bit like double talk to me. What about this Butterfly Effect that science fiction writers love to dabble with? You know what I'm talking about, the ultimate effect of a minuscule change. Doesn't that fit in here somewhere?"

Hank got up and, a bit presumptuously I thought, went into my house, and soon returned with more coffee. He said, "You are touching upon a hotly debated topic. The current thinking is called the Beach Sand Corollary which goes something like this:

> *Go to the beach, pick up a handful of sand, and throw it in the ocean. According to the Butterfly Effect Theory, the world will never be the same as a result of this action. But according to the Beach Sand Corollary, the effect of moving an infinitesimally small amount of sand, of which there is a near infinite amount, will be insignificantly small at the time of occurrence and totally insignificant in the long term.*

Hank looked at Meredith. "That's the gist of it, correct?"

"I believe so," she replied.

I sat back and tried to absorb the Beach Sand Corollary.

Hank, sensing my confusion, leaned forward and said, "The physicists refer to individual events as *markers*. They say, on a given planet, during a twenty-four hour period, there are a nearly infinite number of markers. Follow?"

I nodded.

"And if you change just a few of these markers," Hank said. "The effect, on the whole, would be infinitesimally small. Sort of like your chances of winning Megabucks or Powerball. Yes, you have a chance of winning, but statistically, you don't have a prayer. Right?"

I nodded again.

"So in the long run, the divergence between your Earth and my Earth, well, is not so much. And in fact, you guys are about to make a few changes that will once again close the technological gap."

"We are?" I asked. "Such as?"

Meredith cleared her throat. "We cannot tell you, for legal reasons involving non-disclosure laws."

"Too bad," I said.

Jumping in, Hank said, "That would be like knowing which horse was going to win tomorrow's race. A fellow could make a few dollars off such information."

Then, after pondering the topic for a moment, I said, "All right. So, let's get back to the guy who shot himself in the foot."

Then I paused and thought about the Bosnian Serb terrorist who tripped on his shoelace. I was not so sure about how that huge event could be explained away by the Beach Sand Corollary. I needed more time to think that over. Then, I circled back to my original question. "But how did he give your Earth a technological leap of one hundred years?"

Hank exclaimed, "Ah yes, the oft-discussed technological gap! Think about it. What would have happened on this Earth if there was no World War One? Both your Earth and our Earth got the twentieth century off to a good start and the first decade saw great strides, but then, your Earth spent most of the balance of the nineteen hundreds fighting not one but two world wars, struggling through a crippling depression, spending all your time and energies dreaming up ways to kill each other, then trying to fix everything that was blown up or destroyed. The social ripples of those cataclysmic events continue even to this day. What if this didn't happen?"

Hank leaned towards me, clearly warming to the topic. "Let's face it; on this planet, World War One was, at the very least, a major contributor to the Great Depression, and was a *direct* cause of World War Two. By all accounts, the depression of the thirties set civilization back at least a decade…perhaps two. Then bring on World War Two. Look what resulted from that murder fest. The world was deeply divided between the East and the West and on the doorstep of total annihilation. Under the dark clouds of those events, how much forward progress did your civilization make? The untied shoelace of Gavrilo Princip made quite a difference between your Earth and ours. At least in the short run."

Hank paused to let those thoughts sink in while I sat quietly and scratched the stubble on my chin.

"Okay," I said. "This well-rehearsed history lesson is really interesting and all, but I have to ask the question. How did you get here, or maybe more to the point, where's your spaceship?"

Hank looked at Meredith who sipped her tea. He said, "It's a fair question you know. I told you he'd want to know."

Meredith said, "Show him."

Chapter Four

Sticks and Stones

The three of us stood, and then Hank led the way. We walked down from the deck, across my backyard, around a cluster of small trees, and then out into the field where my garden was struggling in the mid-summer heat and unpicked weeds.

Hank stopped and pointed at the garden. "There it is."

I blinked a few times and looked at Meredith for clarification, but she was waving at a buzzing horsefly.

"Where?" I asked.

"There," Hank repeated.

I exhaled a disgusted breath and thought, I knew it. Whack jobs. I said, "I didn't expect to see a Flash Gordon rocket standing there but somehow, I have a hard time believing you travel through space in my garden. Next, you're going to tell me the tomatoes are really a wormhole, right?"

"Not your garden," Hank replied. "Just beyond it. Hovering above the dirt road."

"Is this like the Emperor's New Clothes?" I asked, not making any effort to hide my sarcasm. "Do I have to be smart to see it?"

Hank bent down, picked up a golf-ball size rock, and handed it to me. "Give it a toss," he said. "At a spot about ten feet above the dirt road."

I looked at him with raised eyebrows, then cocked my arm and threw the stone. The stone followed a curving trajectory then "bang," hit an invisible barrier, stopped, and dropped.

I put my hands on my hips and studied the empty space above the dirt road. There was nothing there. I bent and picked up a second stone and repeated the action. Again: 'bang.'

Still, in disbelief, I strode to my garden, grabbed my walking stick which always stands at ready, awaiting a stroll down to the lake, and walked to the spot at the dirt road where the stones had come to rest. Walking around, I poked my stick skyward, always hitting something about ten feet up. At one point, I couldn't hit anything, so that must have been the edge of this invisible object. I worked my way all around, roughly outlining this supposed spaceship, and then, covered with sweat, quit when I came back to my starting point. Whatever it was, it was about the width and length of two tractor-trailer trucks, side by side.

I looked back at where Hank and Meredith were standing in the shade of an oak tree. Hank was smiling, arms folded across his chest in an 'I told you so' stance. Meredith was swatting at a pesky bug.

We returned to the deck and as they sat in the shade of the umbrella, I ducked inside and came out with three bottles of Snapple Ice Tea.

After taking a swig, I asked, "How?"

Hank also took a swig and studied the bottle. "This is good," he said with a note of surprise, "We don't have this on my Earth. And then, addressing my question, said simply, "Cloaking."

"Cloaking?"

"Sure. Your military is nearly there. They make airplanes that are invisible to radar and submarines that disappear in the ocean. Recently, scientists are making Harry Potter invisibility cloaks in their laboratories. It won't be long before your scientists put the two together and come up with a cloaking device similar to that one out there." He pointed back towards the garden.

"But...." That seemed to be all I was capable of saying.

"You don't have to make an object disappear to make it invisible," Meredith said. "You simply have to block the visible light emanating from the source. We have the technology to selectively choose which wavelengths of light we need to suppress. It's really quite simple."

Hank snickered. "There, clear as mud. Like I said, cloaking."

I looked back at the field and then returned my gaze to Meredith. "I thought you said you weren't a scientist?"

Meredith said dismissively, "I read a lot."

Hank chuckled and added, "All the time."

I thought about submarines and airplanes and Harry Potter. And I thought about the invisible thing out there over my field. Intellectually, it almost made sense. Emotionally, no way. Then a thought popped in. "Can I go in?"

Hank scratched his chin and stared off into space. Meredith studied the Snapple bottle. A long moment of silence passed.

"I'm sorry," Meredith said, "but we can't let you do that."

Disappointed, I looked from one to the other. "Because?"

"Well," Meredith replied, "this will become clearer shortly. I think at this point, we have sufficiently overwhelmed you. And by the way," she looked at Hank, "we have some pressing business to attend to."

Hank took out his phone and checked the time. "Yikes," he said. "You're right." He turned to me and said, "See you tomorrow, or maybe the day after at the latest. Now, please stay here and don't follow us."

I put down my drink. "Where are you guys going? What's this about my neighbor?"

They stood and Meredith said, "Your neighbor – Ryan Wiggins – is not who you think he is. The man that lives in that house came from our Earth and replaced the Ryan Wiggins that *used* to live there. We will be back soon."

She smiled, perhaps sympathetically owing to my dazed and confused look, and then they left the porch, strode across my backyard, and rounded the corner behind the trees. They were headed out back to my garden. I sat for a moment pondering all the new information I had just received, and then leaped up, exclaiming aloud, "Please stay here? Like hell I will!"

I jogged down across my lawn but when I turned the corner around the small copse of trees and looked out to my garden, Hank and Meredith were nowhere to be seen. I looked all around – nothing. Puzzled, I ran to the dirt road, picked up a stone, and gave it a toss. This time the stone passed through and fell harmlessly back to Earth.

Chapter Five

Rules

When I awoke the next morning, I lay in bed, recalling the events of the previous day. There was a surrealistic feel to the images in my memory and I began to question whether they were real.

Then I heard voices.

I got up and went out to the balcony off my master bedroom. There, down below on the deck, seated in the comfortable chairs were Meredith and Hank.

I couldn't believe my eyes. *Who were these people and what did they really want with me?* "Just go ahead and make yourselves comfortable," I said sarcastically.

Hank looked up. "We did. Also, I took the liberty of making some coffee. You're running low and will need to buy some more next time you go to the store. Get that good stuff from Trader Joes. Come on down. We're planning the day."

A few minutes later, I joined the two invaders from space on my deck. The day was already hot and the humidity soaring. No air was moving. We huddled around the table, in the shade of the patio umbrella.

Meredith brushed a limp curl off her forehead. "I have a thought. Would you mind taking us for a ride to Greenwich? We can use that time to discuss why we are here. Plus, we need to check on something."

Other than gardening and trout fishing later in the evening, I had nothing else on my 'to do' list. Plus, my continued befuddlement had given way to curiosity. "Sure. Let's go. Maybe you can also explain why you have contacted *me*."

We piled into my Honda Element – Hank in the back, Meredith in the front with me - and took the back roads to Greenwich. The car's air-conditioning was most welcome.

"So," I began, "I have lots of questions. Where to begin, where to begin. Okay, how about this one: why I can't go into your spaceship?"

"Here on your Earth," Meredith began, adjusting her seatbelt and gripping the armrest tightly, "I believe you have an agency known as the Securities and Exchange Commission. Correct?"

"Yes."

"Do you know why they exist?"

"Umm. Maybe," I replied, scratching the stubble on my chin in thought. "I think they guard against things like insider trading so we mere mortals can't get rich."

Meredith nodded. "Yes, that's one of their many functions. And if you were to receive a well-placed 'tip,' you, of course, could become wealthy armed with this knowledge. And this would be unfair to all other potential investors. Correct?"

Hank leaned forward from the back seat and said, "Except that rule does not apply to our wonderful senators and congressmen, who supposedly need this advantage to augment their paltry salary, those poor boys."

"And allegedly," I said, catching Hank's eyes in the rear-view mirror, "this helps jump-start emerging industries our government deems in the country's best interest. What a crock!"

"We diverge and are getting off track," Meredith said, still with a death grip on the armrest and sitting up rigidly. "And PLEASE, keep your eyes on the road in front of you. Look out for that car coming out of the side street."

"Relax, relax. I see it."

In spite of her discomfort with my driving, Meredith plowed on with her explanation. "Suffice it to say, there are reasons why investors should not receive unfair advantages in an open market. Now," she turned in her seat and faced me. "Consider technology and science. We, on our planet, have decided that the same type of rules and restrictions must apply."

I squinted through the windshield, trying to work that out. "Not sure I follow."

"What she's saying," Hank said from the back seat, "is, if we took you aboard our Ship, you might steal all our secrets then build one in your shed for nefarious reasons."

"Hey, nefarious. Good word," I replied.

"You sound surprised!" Hank quipped.

"Please," Meredith said rolling her eyes at our banter. Suddenly, she braced herself as if an impact was imminent and exclaimed, "You are much too close to the car in front of us! LOOK OUT!"

I shot her a glance and said, "No I'm not. What's with you, anyway?"

Hank chimed in from the back seat. "We don't drive our own cars back home. Our cars drive themselves. We just sit back and leave the driving to IBM Auto."

I turned at looked at Hank. "No shit!"

"PLEASE!" Meredith shouted. "Watch the road in front of you!"

"All right, all right," I replied. Then, added with a smile, "Just relax. I don't crash much."

Meredith sat rigidly on her side of the front seat, breathing rapidly, and not finding me the least bit humorous. After she stopped hyperventilating, she picked up her explanation where she left off. "Our policy is to allow other planets to evolve at their own pace. Interference of any sort is strictly against the law. These policies and laws are called the ICC or Interstellar Code of Conduct."

"I see," I said. "And I understand. But I have to tell you, I'm curious as hell. What sort of propulsion system do you guys use?"

Hank spoke up from the back seat. "There are two, and they work in unison. We've figured out how to turn off the force of gravity and, in doing so, can drift freely around the universe like a big bubble. So then, all you need is a steady push, even a really small push, and after a little while, you can go really fast. Our propulsion system is an ion exchange drive. Real slow off the line but it can accelerate forever. Pushes 90% the speed of light."

"You can turn gravity on and off?" I asked.

Hank leaned in. "Do you remember way back in college when we studied gravity and electromagnetism? I think it was freshman physics. Do you remember the equations?"

"No."

"Well, if you did you'd remember they were the same basic equation except for the constant. Does this ring a bell?"

"No,"

"Well, dig out your Physics 101 textbook and take a look. Here's how it works. Just as electromagnetism can be turned on and off, so can gravity. It just takes a huge amount of energy applied in the right place. For example, let's say you wanted to send an aircraft carrier to the moon. All you'd have to do is turn off gravity surrounding the *USS Nimitz* and give it a push. Off it goes. When it leaves the Earth's gravitational field and starts to pick up the moon's force, turn off the gravity blocker and let the gravity of the moon pull you in that direction. You can just imagine how fast you can get moving when you play the gravity game."

"Wow! No kidding!" I said. "But back to the speed, you guys travel at. What about Einstein's theory that mass begins to increase as you approach…"

"That will do," Meredith interrupted sternly. "This is exactly what I was just saying."

Hank tapped me on the shoulder and said, "We'll talk later."

"You will not," Meredith chided, shooting a glare at Hank, who sat back and looked out the window. "And now," she said, moving forward, "as to why we are here. We have reason to believe your neighbor, Ryan Wiggins, has flagrantly broken several of our ICC laws and needs to be brought back to our planet to stand trial."

I nearly drove off the road which caused Meredith to once again brace herself for a crash.

"Are you sure you have the right guy?" I asked, "This is Wiggins, Ryan Wiggins? The guy who lives next to me? He's dumber than a box of rocks."

Hank chuckled from the back seat and said, "That's him all right."

I continued, "He's the guy who keeps changing the boundary markers of our property, trying to grab some of my land. He's an idiot!"

"Perhaps," Meredith said. "But perhaps not. Take the next left, and then turn into the parking lot."

Just beyond Drum Hill, across the Greenwich line, we pulled into the parking area of a modern three-story office building.

Meredith pointed to the side of the building. "Go around back and park in the shade along the rear of the lot. Back into the parking space."

There were a few cars scattered in the lot. I backed into a space in the shady back row as directed. In the front row was a white Mercedes.

"See that white car," I said. "That's Wiggins's."

"We know," Meredith replied, visibly more relaxed now that we were not moving. She pulled a strange device from her briefcase. The device looked like an Android phone but it was longer. She typed a few commands on the screen then pointed at the building, aiming it at an upstairs window. The device chirped a few times, beeped once, and then went silent.

"You know?" I asked.

"Yes," Meredith replied. "We've been following him now for about two weeks."

"Two weeks?" I asked incredulously. "I thought you just...where have you...two weeks?"

Meredith, ignoring my incredulity, fiddled with the over-sized Android.

"Still nothing?" Hank asked from the back seat.

Meredith frowned and said, "Oh, I believe it's there all right but the signal is too faint to hack into for verification. He must have it hidden." Then she placed the device on the dashboard of my car and sat back.

"What's that?" I asked.

Meredith stared at me, obviously trying to decide whether or not to tell me.

Hank spoke from the back seat. "So there, Miss Law and Order, what are you going to say now?"

I looked from Hank, who was smiling, to Meredith, who was frowning.

Finally, Meredith said, "All right. I'll tell you only what you need to know, but be aware, what I'm about to tell you must go no further."

"Oh, get off it," Hank said from the back seat. "Who's going to believe him? What's he going to say? Two people just arrived from another dimension in an invisible spaceship to arrest a fugitive from interstellar justice. And oh, by the way, one of the space people was me from this different dimension. Would *you* believe him? Hell, I wouldn't. There are days I'm not so sure I believe what's going on."

Meredith turned and faced Hank. "So why don't we give him a joy ride in our ship and show him what it can do?"

I sat up straight. "Oh, wow! Could you?"

Meredith, still facing Hank continued. "And while we are at it, we can make him a copy of the plans for the propulsion system for him to sell to the highest bidder."

"Not a bad idea," I said.

Hank held up his hand. "Okay, okay. I get the point. But if we expect him to help us, he needs to know what he's getting into."

"Help you do what?" I asked.

Meredith continued to glare at Hank. "That's why I said 'need to know'."

"Um, excuse me Boys and Girls," I said, reaching for the door handle. "Do you want me to step outside and let you guys..."

"No," said Meredith. "We're fine." Then she turned and looked at me. "Clearly, some of this is new ground for us as well, and we continue to work out the wrinkles. This discussion about what we can say and how far we can go, this is ongoing and new ground for us. I'm not sure there's a right or wrong answer and we have precious little guidance from our home office but all the same, we do have a job to do. And we *are* going to need your help."

"You keep saying that," I replied. "Help with what? What is it you need from me?"

Meredith glanced back at Hank then fixed me with her blue eyes. "*You* are going to capture Ryan Wiggins."

"WHAT?" I shouted. "Why me? You want me to do WHAT?"

Hank snickered in the back seat and said, "Don't worry. You'll have plenty of help."

"Why doesn't that make me feel better?" I asked sarcastically.

Chapter Six

Ryan the Rodent

Once I calmed down, Meredith put away her over-sized Android and said, "We're all done here for now. I'm getting hungry. How about lunch?"

Hank, from the back seat, agreed. "Yeah, good idea. Let's get out of here before Wiggins looks out his office window and spots us lurking back here. How about Antonio's for lunch?"

As I started the car, it dawned on me what Hank just said. "How do you know about Antonio's?"

"Don't forget, we're from the same neighborhood. They have the same hole-in-the-wall location on our planet as well. The best Italian food around, right?'"

"That's the place," I said, driving out of the parking lot and cranking up the air conditioning. "And what's this about computers driving your cars?"

Hank said, "It's just the same as your airliners. They essentially fly themselves. The pilot just goes along for the ride. Cars will be next."

I scratched my head, which caused Meredith to shoot me a concerned look. I quickly put both hands on the wheel, smiled at her, and asked Hank, "Are you sure about that? I mean the bit about airplanes flying themselves?"

Hank shrugged. "If they are not totally controlled by an auto-pilot, they will be soon."

"Hank, please," Meredith exclaimed.

I caught Hank's eye in the rear-view mirror and he winked.

Enfield was two towns over and, being the middle of the day in the middle of the week, there was practically no traffic. Tempting as it was to do otherwise, I took extra care to drive at the speed limit and stayed way back from other cars to avoid tailgating. That seemed to put Meredith at ease. While we were in transit, we chatted about food on their Earth versus on my Earth.

"It's about the same," Hank said. "We have developed a synthetic salt that's a whole lot better on the blood pressure but that's about the only major difference. And of course, there are constant battles between vegans and normal people, but no big deal."

"Hmm," I mused. "No major breakthroughs. So, do some people still smoke?"

"Yep," Hank replied.

"And how about cancer? Have you guys figured out how to cure it?" I asked.

"Nope," said Hank.

"Huh," I said. "So tell me again. How do you know about Antonio's?"

Hank chuckled. "Back home on my Earth, I live three doors down from Antonio's, in the white house with black shutters. I'm a regular."

Meredith said, "And I live in Dallas but come up this way for meetings in Boston. That's where our office is. Based upon Hank's recommendation, we've eaten at Antonio's on occasion."

"Small world," I said quietly, privately speculating about the coincidence of us all living nearby. Then I realized if Hank was me on his planet, it's not much of a stretch at all since he lives nearby. "So, Hank," I said, catching his eyes in the rear-view mirror. "How come you don't live in my house in Lytleton? I thought we were sort of the same guy."

"I did," he said, looking out the window. Then after a pause, added, "Until my wife died."

"Oh," I replied softly. "I'm sorry."

"Drunk driver killed her. That was before all our cars were driven by computers." He paused then added, "Same fate for both of our wives."

We drove in silence for a minute or two.

I turned onto the side street and pulled into the shade of a huge Linden tree. I was about to say "We're here," but, then, they already knew it.

As we climbed out of the car, I offered my hand to Hank and said, "Hey Man, I didn't mean to..."

"Not to worry," Hank said, cutting me off. "I moved over there," he pointed to a small white house across the street, "After she was gone, I couldn't stay in Lytleton any longer. The house had too many memories. Too many ghosts."

Meredith drifted away, taking a sudden interest in some flowers growing along the edge of the sidewalk.

Hank was staring at the small white house he inhabited on his earth. "What about you?" he asked. "Is it tough living in the house where she lived?"

I nodded and whispered, "Yeah."

The demons came floating back. My brain shifted from the pastoral setting of a small New England village to the dark, silent hallways of my house at four in the morning. The pit of my stomach knotted, the emptiness returned.

I didn't sleep well anymore and after lying in bed, eyes open, watching the second-hand sweep the face of the clock over and over again, frequently got up and shuffled aimlessly around the house.

It had seemed so innocent.

"I'm running to the store to pick up some nutmeg for the pie," she had said. "Do you need anything?

"Just your hands on my skin," I replied.

"Later." Then she pecked me on the cheek and then left.

That was it. That was the end. All that followed was a nightmarish blur.

I took several deep breaths and wiped my damp eyes.

And then it passed. The demons retreated.

"Wow," I said. "It must be tough to visit me in your old house?"

Hank put his hands on his hips and continued to stare at the white house across the street. Clearly, he was mulling over my question. "Strangely, no. I'm surprised that it isn't but have no real explanation as to why. But no. It's okay. I'm okay."

I asked, "How did it happen? I mean what…"

Hank shook his head slowly. "Out of the blue. I mean, one minute she was there, running to the store to pick up a bottle of wine, and then she was gone. She never came back."

Silence.

"Strange," I mused. "It was nutmeg for me."

"Nutmeg?"

"Yeah, she was heading out to pick up nutmeg. My version of your wife buying wine."

Hank shrugged. "Parallel universes are strange. We both got off to the same start but things diverge rapidly."

Meredith, sensing the moment had passed, walked to where we stood, touched Hank's shoulder, and quietly said, "Let's go have lunch."

She handed Hank a Chicago Cubs baseball cap and dark sunglasses, then spotted the questioning look upon my face. "It's better," she said, "that you don't look alike. Less attention, fewer stares.

Antonio's was an aging, former sandwich shop that with vast popularity, transformed into a trendy bistro. Tables were jammed into every possible location creating a crowded but cozy atmosphere for patrons. An upscale wine shop was attached to the west end of the restaurant and owed its existence to Antonio's *bring your own bottle* policy. Parking was a problem but the local police rarely issued tickets owing to a back-door understanding that involved trading biscotti and tiramisu for traffic violation tolerance.

We took an outside table and sat under a large umbrella. There was no one else seated nearby. We all ordered panini and drank bottled water.

After our food was delivered and the waitress departed, Meredith took out her over-sized Android, tapped a few buttons, and laid it on the table.

I nodded toward the phone. "What's up with that gadget, anyway? And what was it you were trying to track in Wiggins's office?"

"This device performs many functions for us," Meredith replied. "When we were parked behind Wiggins's office, I was trying to locate a stolen super-computer which we strongly suspect to be hidden in his office. Currently, it is masking the sound of our voices. Our conversation will not be able to be recorded or eaves-dropped on by any nearby listeners or hidden mechanical listening devices."

Hank looked around. "I don't think there's much danger of that," he said, raising his eyebrows.

Meredith sighed. "If you recall our training, our marching orders are to mask all our movements and conversations. We must minimize our impact on our guests."

Hank held up his hands. "Understood, understood. Just stating the obvious."

Meredith took a tiny bite from her sandwich and chewed. When she swallowed, she said, "You never know if somehow, perhaps via a security device, we are being watched and listened to. Even if it's accidental, it could be damaging."

"Again," Hank said, "just making an observation. And not to put too fine a point on it, but the application you just employed, it's not masking our conversation."

Meredith stopped chewing and stared at the Android device.

Hank said, "I believe what you just did was shut down electronic signals within a ten-meter radius."

As if on cue, a patron came out of the restaurant, got in his car, and tried to start it. Nothing happened. After a few frustrating attempts, he then got out, muttered a few well-aimed curse words, and went back inside.

Hank pointed at the Android. "You need to hit # *send* for the audio jamming to work. First hit *delete* to undo the electronic shutdown."

Meredith did so.

A moment later, the patron re-emerged with a young waitress in tow. He handed her the keys, she got in, and the car started right up. As she got out of the car, she said, "See Dad, I told you it likes me better than you." The man, red-faced, got in and drove off.

Hank looked at me and said, "We're still unfamiliar with all the applications on our new multi-purpose gizmo."

Meredith glared at him but said nothing.

"Well," I said, changing the topic, "Perhaps this would be a good time to let me in on what's going on? You know, fill me in. Especially, since I'm the guy who's supposed to nab the bad guy. Isn't that what you said? So, what's going on?"

For a moment, Hank and Meredith poked at their food and said nothing. Neither knew how to proceed. Finally, Meredith looked at Hank and said, "You tell him."

"Well," began Hank, "Here's the story. About six years ago, Ryan Wiggins, one of our Low- Level, Intelligence Desk Jockeys, went missing along with one of our highly sophisticated, portable, analysis computers known as an IBM 245. Stealing one of these little babies is a very serious crime. These are essentially a supercomputer in a small package. They can perform some rather unbelievable tasks which, if used by some bad guys, can be really troublesome. I can't get into the details, so you're going to have to trust me about this. Curiously, if it were just Wiggins that went missing, it'd be no big deal. Good riddance. But the 245 - not so. We actually missed the computer before anyone missed Wiggins."

Meredith began to smile but caught herself and looked away.

"If you recall," Hank said, "that was about the same time your neighbor, Ryan Wiggins changed careers from flunky divorce lawyer to superstar investment counselor, correct?"

"Beats me," I replied. "I can't stand the man. Whenever I'm in his presence, I quickly glaze over. All he ever does is pontificate and boast about himself."

"Well," Hank continued. "That's the way it worked out. We already checked. His financial turnaround was sudden and nothing short of amazing. His track record in the financial world is perfect. He's like a baseball player that bats one-thousand. Apparently, no one questioned why. And in spite of what you might think, Wiggins is no fool. He pays his taxes and follows the rules. Your IRS has no beef with him."

I took a bite and chewed. "So?" I said through a mouthful.

Hank leaned on his elbows, closing the gap between us. "So, maybe because it's not the same Ryan Wiggins."

Meredith slyly looked all around to make sure no one was snooping. Even with the sound jammer, she wasn't taking any chances.

Hank said, "We have reason to believe our Ryan Wiggins arrived here six years ago, made your Ryan Wiggins go away and, armed with the IBM 245, is cashing in by knowing future events."

I stopped chewing. "What do you mean 'made Ryan Wiggins go away'?"

Hank shrugged.

I pressed on. "You mean like murder?"

Hank and Meredith again looked uncomfortable and became silent. Then Hank said, "Well, our Ryan Wiggins is still missing and your Ryan Wiggins has never shown up, challenging his replacement. So I think maybe yes. Maybe murder."

Meredith leaned over the table and said, "We'll be able to verify our suspicion when we take him back home. Our law enforcement scientists can examine the memory of a probable cause suspect."

"You're kidding," I exclaimed, a bit too loud.

Both Hank and Meredith shhhh'd me. Meredith continued the Wiggins story. "This is not too different from the DNA analysis that has now become commonly accepted evidence in your courts. The next logical step, which by the way, your law enforcement researchers are about to develop and utilize, will be to examine brain cells taken from the memory center of the cerebral cortex. These cells store short and long-term memories. If you know the approximate time frame of an event, you can essentially read a suspect's memory. This makes convictions fairly straightforward. It's really quite simple when you know where to look."

"Wow," I said. "I bet the ACLU had a few things to say about that!"

Hank smiled and shook his head. "They still do. The battle continues but our Supreme Court upheld the use of this technique... for now."

"Holy shit," I mumbled. "Wiggins a murderer? Who'd a thunk it."

"Exactly," Meredith said and sat back.

"So," I began after a moment's pause. "Why don't you just bust into his office and arrest him?"

Meredith raised her eyebrows and held me in her gaze for a moment. "We, of course, have thought of that but there are at least two problems. First, we need to make sure he has the stolen property in his possession. That is the IBM 245 we discussed."

"But before," I interjected, "you said you picked up a faint signal. So it's got to be there."

"It is *likely* it's there...but exactly where, we don't know," Meredith replied. "We have to be sure. We would look awfully foolish if we charged into his office only to find out his fish tank aerator or hamster lamp was creating the signal. We have to be sure."

"The second problem," she said after a pause, "has to do with positive identification. We must be sure he is the Ryan Wiggins from our planet. We would be in very serious trouble if we haul the wrong Ryan Wiggins back through the wormhole to our planet Earth. And we will be able to prove this one way or another by analyzing his memory. Again, we have to be sure, beyond a shadow of a doubt. Plus, our laws prohibit us from acting unless we have probable cause which later turns out to be accurate. If our supposed probable cause turns out to be false, we will lose a lot more than reputation and credulity."

I wondered what she meant but left it alone. I took another bite of my sandwich and chewed for a while. Then, after wiping the crumbs from my face, asked, "So I still don't get where I fit in. Why don't you guys just swoop in and haul him away? What do I have to do with snagging Wiggins?"

Hank leaned forward again on the table. "You're going to trap him. I can't do it because even though we look alike, I haven't been his neighbor for the last twenty years or so…but you have. You guys have a history, maybe a bit strained but a history none the less. If I made contact with him, he might get suspicious right away if I don't react the same way you would to hot buttons for this or that. Get it?"

"No. If you guys are correct, he was actually your neighbor longer than he was mine."

Hank nodded. "Good point but let's take into account recent events I'd have no knowledge of."

I thought for a moment. "Like what?"

"Well," Hank replied, "you tell me. What interface have you had with him in the last four years or so?"

Again, I thought for a moment. "Well, he's been bugging me about cutting down some trees that shade his pool, but surely…"

"Bingo," Hank exclaimed, a little too loudly, causing Meredith to say "Shhh!"

"Bingo," Hank said again, quieter. "That's just the type of detail I'm talking about."

I took a deep breath and exhaled slowly. "Okay I guess but I still don't…"

Meredith leaned in and interrupted, "You are going to meet with Wiggins at his office and discuss hiring him as your financial advisor."

"WHAT!"

"Shhh! You are going to make an appointment and go talk to him about your retirement funds. He has become quite successful at that business, primarily due to the IBM 245, and may welcome the opportunity to demonstrate what an uncanny investor he has become. Let's face it, impressing a neighbor is high on some people's list of ego boosters."

"What!" I said again, but quieter.

Meredith continued. "And during this process," Meredith continued, "he's likely to slip up and give us something we can use as hard evidence. Plus, he'll most likely have to use the IBM to consult with."

I held up my hand. "Give *us* some information? I thought you said it would be me that had to meet with him. What's this *us?*"

Meredith again said "shhhh." Then she said, "I'll be working as his temp secretary in the adjacent office and Hank will be nearby, listening in."

"I see," I replied. "You guys are setting a trap all right. And I'm the bait." I simmered for a few beats, and then said, "Why don't we just do it this way: once he slips up and you have what you need for evidence, you send me some kind of signal and I'll punch him in the face, take him down, and you guys can rush in and take over"

Meredith and Hank exchanged looks. She frowned. "He's far more dangerous than you think he is."

"Wiggins? He's a big marshmallow."

"Perhaps the Wiggins that you have known but not this one."

Hank leaned closer. "Now I don't want to scare you but I think you should know what we know."

Chapter Seven

The Collection Agency

Hank took a deep breath and began, "Two years ago, back through the Wormhole to the other planet Earth, the one that Meredith and I call home, we had infiltrated an organized crime gang that believe it or not, eventually led us to Wiggins here on your planet Earth."

Meredith said, "We're still piecing the story together but we're rather certain that this is the way it transpired."

Hank folded his hands. "We had a plant on the inside, way up in the organization. In fact, he was their CPA. His name was Glenn…"

"Did you say *was*? Like in the past tense?"

Hank grimaced. "Yes, like in the past tense. Things got rough and people got hurt. But let me tell this story and maybe you'll understand what we mean about the Wiggins we're about to take down. This is the way we think it went on the other planet earth…"

The meeting in the parallel dimension took place in a third-floor penthouse apartment above Michele's French Bakery in Strock's Corner, South Carolina. Two men sat on a cozy balcony, cantilevered out over East Main Street, overlooking the town. They sipped black coffee and enjoyed almond Croissants from the bakery downstairs.

A device roughly the size of a nickel was attached to the wrought iron railing. It beeped softly every minute, announcing the 'all clear' notice. It was an electronic jamming module designed to shield the conversation from any other eavesdropping devices that may be present or aimed at the balcony from afar. Two men patrolled the rooftop across the street, one scanning the horizon and the other watching the street below for anything that looked suspicious. Three heavily armed employees, disguised as businessmen, were reading the newspaper in the bakery. Should anything be spotted by the rooftop guards, the employees would spring into action and deal with any problems. A local police officer, also on patrol, slowly patrolled the block in his cruiser, watching for anything suspicious.

Robert J. Glenn CPA, a spindly, geeky looking man in his thirties with short cropped dark-haired, removed his wire-rimmed glasses and sat back in his chair.

"So that about does it for my quarterly report. In summary, business on all fronts is stable and our profits continue to grow at a healthy rate. We've eliminated the problem over on the coast and to cover our tracks, contributed heavily to the police retirement fund. That's all been taken care of. As directed, we've placed one of our new hires well up in the bank organization and he'll be giving us a heads up before the next merger. We have cash available, ready for a massive stock purchase. That will be very profitable. Our supply of product remains secure and we've contacted some new clients in South America for potential new outlets. In short, this has been a good quarter."

Details were deliberately vague. The rule that applies to this type of meeting was no names, no specifics. Details are available by other, more secure channels when required. In other words, nothing that could link the participants to anything explicit could be spoken. As sophisticated and complete as the various defenses against intrusion were, other people – law enforcement or competitors - may be just as sophisticated.

The man seated across from Glenn was Tony Piazzini. He nodded and sipped his coffee. Everything about Piazzini was perfect. From his styled black hair combed straight back, to the black onyx with diamond rings, to his white silk shirt covering a muscular linebacker's frame, it was all perfect. Even his shoes were polished to the degree that one's face could be reflected in the black leather. Piazzini oozed power and wealth. He silently watched the people on the sidewalk below.

Glenn gathered up his report, and then cleared his throat. "There is one more thing."

Piazzini raised his eyebrows.

"Some time ago, I think it was five or six years before I joined the organization, you asked to be informed if we ever located a certain person of interest."

Piazzini held Glenn in his gaze.

Glenn took out a pen, and wrote RYAN WIGGINS on a piece of note paper and slid it across the table.

Without any perceivable change in his expression, Piazzini silently studied the note for a long minute. Then he took out a cigar lighter, flicked the device until a blue flame shot out like a miniature jet engine, and burned the paper. When the ash had drifted down to the street below, Piazzini stood and went inside.

The next week, on a hot, humid, late afternoon, Tony Piazzini visited with his mother and younger brother Vito. She, the matriarch, lived in an impressive, circa 1837 mansion on North Elm Boulevard, a quiet street in the upscale Magnolia Acres neighborhood on the south side Chelmsford of North Carolina. They sat on the front porch; she sipped sherry while the Piazzini boys smoked cigars. The quarterly review, which had been held inside, away from prying eyes and ears had covered all facets of the family business, from potential issues to emerging opportunities. At the conclusion of the meeting, they reconvened outside. This was when and where more personal topics were discussed.

"I want to take a little trip," Tony Piazzini said.

Mama Piazzini, tiny, ancient, crippled with arthritis, spoke in a faint, husky voice. "I thought you'd want to do this. I don't think this is a good idea."

Vito stood, walked to the ice bucket and removed two beers. Handing one to his brother, he sat back down. "We have people to do this sort of thing."

Tony took a swig. "This is personal."

They sat silently for a few minutes, each with their own thoughts.

Mama sipped her sherry. "You are needed here."

Tony tossed his cigar into a brass spittoon. "Are you ordering me not to go?"

"You are being foolish," she said, holding up her empty snifter. On cue, a stocky man dressed in black from head to toe, dashed out from inside the house, refilled her glass, and then retreated back inside.

Vito stood again, paced nervously for a moment, and then sat upon the railing directly across from Tony. "This is different. Wiggins..."

"No names," Mama croaked.

"The mark," Vito continued, "is not exactly down the street. He's a few trillion miles away. Why don't you let our people take care of this one?"

Tony drained his beer. "I want to do this. We've been patsies with this guy. If the word gets out..."

"It won't," Vito countered. "I just say the word and he disappears. We have people inside the space agency."

Tony stared off into the distance. Again all was quiet. Then he shook his head no.

"We have a reputation. It's about respect. This guy thinks he outsmarted us. The word gets around. We need to treat this one special. I want to watch his eyes as he sucks in his last gasp. I want to do this myself. It's personal."

Both men fell silent and turned toward mama. She took a healthy swallow of her drink, raised a shaking hand, and then pointed a bony finger at Tony. "Okay. You do this. But no more. Capisce?"

"Capisce."

Chapter Eight

Can't Go Wrong

Back on the other planet Earth, the next day, Tony took the private jet to Cape Canaveral, Florida. As he left the aircraft, an attractive, dark-haired woman met him at the bottom of the stairs. She held a large umbrella aloft, and Tony ducked under. The grey skies had opened up and the rain was falling in sheets. Thunder rumbled nearby. She was dressed in a raincoat, buttoned to the neck, and wore spiked high heels. As they walked to the private terminal, huddled under the umbrella, her arm in his, she said, "This weather front has delayed your flight until tomorrow. Perhaps you would be interested in checking out my new condo over on the beach."

"What happened to your apartment in Miami?"

"Oh, that. Too small. Plus, I wanted something a bit more..." she paused and squeezed his arm, "...interesting. You'll see."

More thunder.

He smiled.

She nudged him. "What are you thinking?"

Tony said, "I was just wondering what you are wearing under that raincoat?"

"Why, nothing. Nothing at all."

The storm departed overnight and the next day was clear and warm. Tony said goodbye to his friend and then took a space agency shuttle from the main terminal to the waiting spaceship.

The *ship* was nothing like any NASA rocket ship from *our* planet Earth. Instead, it appeared to be a series of submarines all linked together, covered with solar panels, and a quiver of arrow-like antenna sticking up in all directions. It covered about one football field, gleamed in the sunshine, and patiently hummed as if ready to go. Various hoses and cables were connected to the sprawling complex, filling tanks and charging batteries.

It was one of six freighters the space agency used to travel into deep space, usually via wormholes, and perform a variety of tasks such as the construction of docking platforms and supply stockpiles in lonely outposts. For space travelers, these outposts served the same purpose that islands did for ancient mariners who sailed the Pacific Ocean: places to resupply and fix whatever needs fixing.

In the newly discovered parallel system - where Ryan Wiggins had fled to – an outpost was being constructed, from which, the agency could observe the other planet Earth. The location of this outpost was a large chunk of ice. This was a comet that was captured into an orbit around the sun, almost exactly the same distance away as the Earth but on the opposite side of the sun. Thus, it was not yet discovered by Earthbound astronomers and a convenient place to hide from astronauts and cosmonauts. This comet, as well as asteroids and a variety of planetoids, were sometimes called Trojans. In short, these were bits of this and that, captured by gravitational fields, and floating around the solar system.

Why did a comet make a perfect outpost? Because the propulsion system used by modern spacecraft used deuterium and tritium as fuel – both being isotopes of water – so building a docking station on a huge ice ball was perfect. The Trojan, known as SN23b, would provide fuel, fresh water, and a safe place to hide.

A young, clean-cut black man was waiting for Tony and quickly whisked him away. They entered through a hatch labeled

AUTHORIZED PERSONNEL ONLY. Then Tony followed him down one corridor, through another hatch, and then took a right into a small compartment. The space was very similar to a first-class berth on a cruise ship. Against the wall, there was a something that looked like a cocoon with pillows and blankets inside the mesh, a compact bathroom, a wall-mounted flat television, a small table with a refrigerator tucked underneath, a closet, and a few other odds and ends. They each sat in a padded chair – all legs velcroed to the floor - and the guide closed the door.

"My name is Joe Wilson. I'm the systems technician on this freighter. And as you know, I also work for your brother Vito."

"Freighter?"

"Yes. This ship will be traveling through a wormhole and docking on a Trojan which circles the other planet Earth behind the sun. Follow?"

"No," Tony said. "I didn't understand anything you just said. Do I have to?"

Wilson frowned. "Not really. All you really need to know is it'll take us about three days to get there."

"You mean *this* is the spaceship?"

Wilson nodded.

"Just out of curiosity, how do you plan to get all this off the ground?"

"Simple. Just turn off the gravity waves that are keeping it on the ground. You didn't know that?"

"I wouldn't have asked the question if I did. Now, you mentioned three days. What am I supposed to do…?"

Wilson pointed at the sink. "There are sleeping pills marked SLEEP in the cabinet over the sink. The only other pills in there are Dramamine IV. Hopefully, you won't need those. Once we get underway, I recommend you take two of the SLEEP pills. They are space travel drugs. Each pill knocks you about for about twenty-four hours. When you wake up, we'll be getting close to your destination."

He paused, frowned, and then asked, "Didn't Vito brief you about any of this?"

"No, and when I come back, we're going to have a little chat about that. All he said was I'd be in good hands and not to ask too many questions. But back up. I'm curious. What's this about a freighter?"

Wilson waved his arm all around. "That's what we're sitting in. This is a freighter, owned by the 3M Corporation out of Minnesota."

"*This* is a spaceship?"

"Yeah, I know what you mean. It sure doesn't look like one. Gone are the days when spaceships resembled something out of a Flash Gordon movie. Now, we just build these things on the ground, turn off the gravity waves coming out of the Earth's molten iron core, fix upon the moon or sun, and off we go."

Tony blinked a few times.

"It's a helluva lot easier and safer. And faster, too. We can reach our end of the wormhole in about thirty hours."

"If you say so. And I will be sleeping during this?"

"Yeah. It really would be better if you didn't leave this room until we're there."

Tony looked around. "Food?"

"In the refrigerator." He paused. "Now, I've got to get up to the bridge. Get comfortable, watch a movie if you want but when you're ready, grab a bottled water from refrig and take two pills. And remember to strap yourself into the hammock. We're going to be weightless very soon. And follow the directions about using the toilet carefully. They're printed on the wall over there. If you don't...well, just follow the directions. You'll be all right. I'll be back to brief you on what happens next. If you need me, hit the black button," Wilson pointed at a box on the wall, "and say seven-two-seven. That'll get me."

Tony repeated, "Seven two seven."

Wilson got up, went to the door, opened it, and looked up and down the hallway. "All clear. I'm outta here. Keep this door locked. Sleep well."

Then he closed the door and left.

Two days later, Joe Wilson tapped on the door. Nothing. He tapped louder. After a few beats, the door swung open and pea soup green Tony Piazzini floated by.

Joe floated in and shut the door behind him. The room smelled strongly of vomit. "You okay?"

"Do I fucking look okay? That toilet over there sucks your face off."

Tony was referring to the negative pressure commode. Basically, when you sit on the seat, or in this case, stick your head in, something that looks like a plastic shower cap wraps itself around you, and then the business end of the toilet opens and pulls a negative pressure on the bare bottom or puking face. It is roughly the sucking pressure of a vacuum cleaner. This works well unless you don't quite make it on time when the moment arrives. If you are slightly off target, air born unpleasant stuff floats around. This makes things even more unpleasant which hastens the return cycle. In Tony's case, the two days of sleep were fine but upon awakening, space sickness hit him like a meteor.

"There's no way you can go through with your..."

"Don't tell me what I can or can't do. I'm here on business and I aim to get it done."

"Look," Wilson said. "If you still want to go, fine, but let me tell you what you're in for. In two hours, you are going to slide into Chessie and ride to Earth and back.

"What's Chessie?"

Chessie, named after Chesapeake Bay Retrievers, was one of four small, utility vehicles attached to the freighter. They are quite similar to the deep submersible Alvin used to explore the ocean depths. These mini-modules were used to leave the mother ship and repair any damage from micro-meteors, replace software on the solar panels that fail during the trip, and in general, attend to anything that has to be done outside the freighter. They can also be used for trips to the Earth for other reasons or other planets as needed. Like all spacecraft, they have the ability to cloak and turn off gravity waves.

"Think of it as your taxi to and from Earth."

"How do I drive it?"

"You don't. It'll be programmed. You're just going along for the ride. But if you want to wait until…"

Tony grabbed onto the door to the closet as he floated by, stabilized himself, and then pointed a finger at Wilson. "I'm going," he growled. "End of discussion."

"Okay, okay. I'll have everything ready," Wilson replied. "You'll be departing in two hours. Your man is at home."

"And you know that how?"

"We've got satellites circling the Earth. His car is parked in the driveway."

"Spy satellites? Don't the people who live down there spot them?"

"No. Our surveillance satellites are tiny, about the size on space junk." Then, cautiously, added, "His wife is likely going to be home as well."

Tony shrugged. "No problem."

Wilson drifted across the room to the TV and picked up the remote. He pressed a few buttons and the screen lit up. Breathing through his mouth to avoid smelling the airborne vomit, he said, "Look here. You'll be landing in the backyard of Ryan Wiggins at five in the morning. We're going to set you down right here." He pointed at the screen. The landing spot for Chessie was marked with a red X. "The back door is here, alongside the swimming pool. You can do what you want but it may be the best way in. Plus, most people leave their back door unlocked. Once you are inside, you'll have to find his bedroom."

"I know what to do," Tony said impatiently. "How much time do I have?"

"Ah that. Good question. One hour. The freighter will orbit Earth once but only once, to take some ozone readings in the upper atmosphere because…"

"I don't care what you're doing. Back to me. One hour should be more than enough time. Then what happens?"

Wilson shrugged. "Chessie will take off, catch up with the mother ship, and dock right back where it started. You climb out, pop a few sleep pills, and we go about our business."

Tony nodded. "Sounds like a plan."

"One thing that's really important. Make sure you're back in Chessie in an hour. If anything goes wrong and you need to abort, get back to Chessie. It's programmed to return, with or without you. If you miss the return…well, don't miss the return."

"Because?"

"Because there's no coming back for you. You'd be stranded on a planet Earth different from the one you call home."

Chapter Nine

The Two Iron Finally Works

Two hours later, climbing aboard Chessie, Tony slipped into the contoured pilot seat and buckled in. Wilson was hanging upside-down in the access hatch. "The countdown has begun. Sit back and enjoy the ride. Remember where you land. You won't be able to see this ship once you're out and about. And make sure you are buckled in one hour after you arrive. That clock on the dashboard will start counting down to liftoff the moment you touch down."

"I know, I know."

"Got everything you need?"

Tony patted himself down. Revolver with silencer tucked on the right side, curved razor knife on the left. "All set."

"Safe travels." Wilson then backed out and like the automatic doors at grocery stores, the hatch slid shut.

Ten minutes later, Chessis lifted out of its cradle, accelerated, then flipped over and dove into the atmosphere. Simultaneously, Tony's stomach flipped over and he resumed his dry heaves.

The journey to the surface of the Earth was similar to a water slid ride at an amusement park. Down he went, sliding into the cloud cover and then popping out the bottom. At about five thousand feet, Chessie leveled off and the rate of descent slowed. The sun had just come up over the eastern horizon. Finally and ever so gently, Chessie set down on the far side of the swimming pool. As it did so, it nudged a deck chair, tipping it over. The falling chair made a slight "doink" as it hit the patio block.

It just so happened that at that very moment, Ryan Wiggins was in the upstairs bathroom, located in the rear of the house with the window open, sitting on the can, reading Sports Illustrated. The faint "doink" caught his attention. Often, the deck chairs were tipped over in the morning. This was the result of Barred Owls perching on them, watching for mice. Hoping to catch a glimpse of an owl, he peered out the window. What he saw was not an owl. It was a vaguely familiar man, suddenly appearing about five feet above the pool deck.

"What the fuck?" Wiggins whispered.

As he watched, the man climbed down from something invisible, and then turned and faced the house. The rising sun lit up half his face.

Wiggin's eyes opened wide. He thought *that's Tony Piazzini! What the hell is he doing here?* Then Tony removed a gun from the inside of his coat. *That's what he's doing here.*

Gun in hand, Tony, still a bit wobbly from the dry heaves, stood quietly for a minute, scoping out the backyard. Pool, hot tub, chairs with towels draped over the backs, and bingo, the back door. He walked around the pool and tried the doorknob. It was unlocked.

Inside the house, Wiggins wasted little time. Without attending to the necessary paperwork, he pulled up his boxer shorts, padded barefooted downstairs, and then down the cellar stairs as well, grabbing a two iron from his golf bag which was stored in the basement as he ran to the door. He knew in a flash that this was not a social call. He hid behind the cellar door, golf club raised over his head, ready to strike, and waited.

His work at the ICC - on the other Earth - had been a cover for his *real* job, which was a racketeer for Tony Piazzini and his organization. Within the law enforcement agency, large sums of money had to be shifted into various accounts to pay for ongoing operations, bribes paid to informants, purchase of illegal goods to ensnare the bad guys, and other such activities that required piles of cash. Wiggins was the money mover, a task he performed smoothly and efficiently. In fact, he was so good at his job that his work was rarely scrutinized. Lost among the enormous cash payouts that came and went on a regular basis were a few minor allocations into bogus accounts created by Ryan Wiggins on behalf of the Piazzini organization. Being relatively small dollars, they were overlooked and unnoticed. After a while, these 'minor allocations' added up and Wiggins's personal status within the Piazzini organization grew. He began receiving invitations to golf tournaments, trips to the Caribbean, and was included in the many social functions that prior, were only for the organizations elite. He was on good terms with Tony Piazzini and they struck up a friendly relationship.

It was sometime during those lavishly good times that the winds of change began to blow into the sails of Ryan Wiggins. He began to feel like he had become a key player in the organization. The real power, of course, lay within the family, but he felt he was now in the second tier. Next, he began to gamble. Horses, dogs, casinos. They became his obsession and the cost of this entertainment skyrocketed. It was then, to cover these costs that Wiggins simply dipped into the river of cash that was flowing into the organization. Another change that altered the way he viewed the world was prompted by a secret ICC investigation that due to his position in the ICC, Wiggins became aware of. Wormholes and the other planet Earth had just been discovered when an ICC insider decided to steal a spacecraft from the space agency and take off to the other Earth, taking on a new identity and cashing in on the technology gap. The new space technology was evolving so fast, the security could not keep up. From Wiggin's point of view, this was an opportunity to strike out on his own. He had just begun working towards that goal when he learned - via a tip from a friend in the organization – that Tony Piazzini had caught wind of Wiggin's misappropriation of the organization's funds, and was going to pay him a visit. Before that happened, Wiggins put his plan into action. He bribed his way into the space agency, stole a ship, and the rest was history. And now, there he was hiding behind the cellar door, awaiting the long overdue visit from Tony Piazzini. There would be no conversation or negotiation. Life was too good.

Tony pushed open the door and stepped into the basement. As he paused to let his eyes adjust to the darkness, Wiggins swung viciously and hit him above the right ear, splintering the graphite shaft of the golf club. Tony's legs buckled and down he went, his gun clattering across the floor. In a flash, Wiggins was on it and picked it up. Ever so casually, he walked back to the moaning Tony Piazzini, aimed the gun at his chest, removed the safety, and fired six times into his upper body. Then, while blood was still spurting out of him, Wiggins rolled him up in the indoor-outdoor carpet and dragged him outside, all the way around the pool, and over the spot where he had seen Tony climb out of. He extended his arms and felt around, trying to locate the cloaked spacecraft. After a few steps, he found it.

Then he ran to the garden shed and took out a bag of powdered lime, and returned to the ship. He threw several handfuls in the air and some of it landed upon Chessie, creating a vague outline of the spacecraft.

He climbed up and the hatch automatically opened. The controls slightly resembled those in the ship he stole six years prior, and the glowing dial near the GPS screen indicated the cloaking mechanism was engaged.

He could see a digital clock on the dashboard that counting down. To what? Takeoff? Banking on that assumption, he 'omphed' Tony's body up onto Chessie, then lowered him into the seat, buckled him in, and stood back thinking. Murder weapon! No need keeping this around. He slid the gun back inside Tony's jacket. Then he ran back to his house, grabbed the bloody golf club, returned, and tossed that inside the spacecraft as well. He smiled, thinking, *never could hit a two iron*. The clock was then at 29:00.

Wiggins climbed down, the hatch sliding shut on its own, and went into the house. He scrubbed his hands with hot soapy water, taking care to remove the blood from under his fingernails, and then made himself a pot of coffee. Steaming mug in hand, he went back outside to watch what would happen next. Again, he climbed onto Chessie. Again the hatch slid open. 05:22. He jumped down. The hatch slid shut.

While he waited, he looked around and made a mental list of things to do. The blood-soaked carpet would have to go. He would cut it up with pruning shears, then load all the pieces – and the shears - into recycle bags and take them all to the town landfill today. He would have to wash down the floor and pool deck with bleach. As his wife was sleeping off another two bottle binge, she wouldn't emerge until noon. With a little luck, he would have the place all clean and evidence-free by then. Not a bad plan.

Wiggins picked up the deck chair that had been knocked over, alerting him to Tony's arrival, and sat down. He didn't have long to wait. The spacecraft clicked a few times, hummed, and then lifted off. The powdered lime quickly fell off the shell of Chessie, and then it disappeared. Ryan sat quietly, sipped his coffee, and tried to image where the craft was heading. It was too small to be heading very far. There must be a mother ship up there somewhere. In a short time, the ship carrying Tony's body would arrive back where it came from. And then what? Would somebody else come looking for him? Maybe he should have kept the gun.

Wiggins drained his coffee and got up. After the rug was disposed of and the floors were washed, he was going to take a ride. He knew of a gun dealer in Kittery, Maine that would sell a handgun with no questions asked. It was time to start carrying.

Chapter Ten

Two Fewer Bad Guys

Vito Piazzini and his mother sat on the front porch of the family mansion on North Elm Boulevard in South Chelmsford. She sipped sherry while the Vito smoked a cigar.

Mama Piazzini, tiny, ancient, crippled with arthritis, spoke in a faint, husky voice. "I knew in my heart that Tony shouldn't have gone, yet I let him go. This is my fault."

"Come on, Mama. You know it's not. He would have gone no matter what you said. That's how he was." Vito held up his hand and a stocky man dressed in black from head to toe, dashed out from inside the house.

"Whiskey," Vito said. After he was served and the man retreated inside, he continued. "But, we'll make things right."

"Make things right? What can you do to bring back my Tony?"

"Nothing. Sorry."

She paused, lip trembling. "You aren't going now, are you?"

"No, not me. We have people inside the space agency who attend to such matters. I'm going to make a few calls."

They sat in silence for a few minutes, soaking up the last rays of the afternoon sun.

Mama asked, "Who is this Ryan Wiggins?"

"He worked for Tony and for a while, was a good soldier. But then he got greedy. Happens all the time."

Mama stood and slowly shuffled to the door, but before she went inside, she turned and said, "Kill him."

The next day, Ryan Wiggins had a motion detecting sensor attached to the back of his house. But instead of having it connected to a spotlight, he had it attached to an interior silent alarm. If anything larger than a gray squirrel came into the pool area, he would receive an urgent message and series of soft beeps on both his phone and his laptop.

He also bought a case of Greenthumb Wasp and Hornet Killer, a liquid spray capable of killing a flying insect at twenty-five feet or more.

He also bought a Hot Shot DuraProd Rechargeable Livestock Prod with 32-inch Flexible Shaft and plugged it in.

He also made some minor modifications to all the doors of his house.

And of course, he started carrying his forty-five caliber handgun with him wherever he went – including to bed.

He thought about warning his wife about the possibility that bad people may be coming around with the intent of murder, but then he thought better of it. With a little luck, she would go down in the expected melee. That would kill two birds with one stone.

A month later, Newfie, the two-seat version of Chessie - named Newfie in keeping with the tradition of naming the support spacecraft after the various breeds of retriever dogs, this time the Newfoundland Retriever – lifted away from the freighter and headed for Earth. On board were two heavily armed men, hired to not only kill Ryan Wiggins but dismember his body with a chainsaw and spread the pieces around his patio. Once again, they had an hour to accomplish the task and felt confident it would be a simple job.

As with Chessie the previous month, Newfie set down at five A.M. on the pool patio and the hatch slid open. Two men climbed out, guns drawn, and headed for the back door. It was a cloudy morning and the air was still. It had rained earlier and the patio was wet. The first man reached the door, turned to the second man and whispered, "Ready?"

The second man nodded and the first man reached for the doorknob. Immediately, two-hundred twenty volts shot through his hand, up his arm, down his torso, and out his feet into a grounded, metal-wire foot mat. The mat was wired to the basement iron water pipe, creating a wonderful circuit for electricity to follow. Because the muscles of his hand contracted with the flow of electricity shooting through his body, he could not let go. It didn't matter because, in roughly five seconds, his heart had stopped, his breathing had ceased, and he was already dead. The second man jumped back, clearly surprised by the vibrating, spasmodic man in front of him. Knowing a little something about electricity, he knew not to reach out and try to pull him away. He never heard Wiggins coming up from behind.

"Hello there," Wiggins said jovially.

The second man whipped around and got sprayed in the face with Greenthumb Wasp and Hornet Killer. He grabbed his face in agony and his knees immediately buckled. Writhing in pain on the ground, he again did not see Wiggins approach. Utilizing his fully charged Hot Shot DuraProd Rechargeable Livestock Prod with 32-inch Flexible Shaft, Wiggins zapped the man on the leg, causing the victim to violently convulse, his entire body lifting from the stone. Wiggins zapped him again. Same results.

"Who sent you?" Wiggins asked evenly, but the man was in too much pain to respond. Wiggins zapped him again, this time in the crotch.

"Was it the Piazzini gang?" The man was screaming now. "That's okay. I already know." Wiggins said with a sigh, and then zapped him in the chest, stopping his heart.

With the first man dead, lying on his back, smoking, right hand blackened, and the second man twitching his final twitches, Wiggins put away his cattle prod and the can of Wasp spray, turned off the electricity to the doorknob, and took out a bag of powdered lime. As he did with Chessie, he covered Newfie with white dust, and then dragged both men to the spacecraft. Once they were buckled in – taking notice that the countdown was now at 12 minutes and still ticking, he went into the house and came out with a piece of paper. On the sheet was the following note:

To the Piazzini gang:

The next time you send someone to kill me, I'm going to send back an explosive device so that when they dock on whatever ship you are in, it will blow you to pieces. This is your final warning.

RW

PS: Just so you know, I would have done it this time but didn't have time to acquire a bomb. You've been warned.

He then pulled out his Bostitch Heavy Duty Staple gun and stapled the note to the first man's head. He climbed down off Newfie and surveyed the scene. *Good. No mess to clean up this time,* he thought.

When the dashboard clock reached zero, the spacecraft clicked a few times, hummed, and then lifted off. The powdered lime quickly fell off the shell of Newfie and then it disappeared.

Wiggins checked his watch. He still had time to get the golf course, meet his foursome, and make his tee time.

Chapter Eleven

Hatching the Plan

Back at Antonio's in Enfield, Hank finished his Wiggins tale and sat back in his chair, concluding with, "This guy's a major league bad man."

Meredith pursed her lips and thought for a moment, and then said. "And, yes you are."

I blinked. "I am what?"

"You asked if you were the bait in a trap. In a manner of speaking, you are correct. You are the bait."

By the time we finished lunch, it was late afternoon. Meredith suggested we swing past Wiggins's office on our way home. I still wasn't feeling too kindly, being the designated piece of cheese in this half-baked plan, so I agreed to the detour with a less than enthusiastic endorsement.

"What for?" I asked.

Meredith put away her sound masking phone and said, "Information gathering."

Hank, sensing my growing frustration, added, "It'll just be a quick stop. I'm sure she has a good reason."

"Don't put words in my mouth or thoughts in my head," Meredith quipped.

I was starting to heat up and it wasn't from the stifling weather. "Have you guys ever done this type of thing before?" I asked.

"Well," Hank replied, standing and stretching, "Sort of. Well, not exactly."

Meredith said, "Actually, no."

"Great," I said. "That's just fucking great."

"The reason," Meredith began, "I want to swing by Wiggins's office is to gather enough data to make his apprehension a smooth operation wherein no one gets hurt."

"Yeah, like me," I replied. Then I asked, "What if I don't want to do this? I mean, you guys just show up and assume I'm willing to risk my ass to help you out. Then you tell me this is new terrain for you. What if I want out?"

Meredith looked at me. "Just say the word and we'll never bother you again. I know this is a lot to ask and you'd be justified to walk away. Is that what you want?"

I fell silent.

Hank, sat back down at the table and said, "This guy we're talking about is not the same Ryan Wiggins who you have the boundary dispute with. This guy likely murdered the Ryan Wiggins you know. He's a really bad man. And with your help, we think we can drag him home and make him pay for his crimes. Here's the fly in the ointment: if you choose not to help us…and Lord knows you'd have good reason to walk away…I don't think we can get the job done. We'd have to dream up another approach, and that would take time. And maybe in the meanwhile, we'd be reassigned to some other case and off we go. And if that happens, you live next to Wiggins the murderer. But that's not the point. We want to bring him in. If you help us, we can do it. If you walk…"

I looked up and watched a red-tailed hawk circling overhead. The Wiggins I knew - my neighbor - was a buffoon and a bully. He liked pushing people around, using the threat of court action like some kind of weapon, to get what he wanted. His latest was when he challenged the unanimous decision by the neighborhood to put in speed bumps in an effort to get people to slow down. Kids were always playing in the road and sometimes, outsiders would drive way too fast. Speed bumps would slow them down. But Wiggins threated us all with court action if we proceeded. His opposition to the plan had nothing to do with public safety. For Wiggins, it was a matter of banging the exhaust system of his car if he went over them too fast. He simply did not want to slow to a crawl to make it over the bumps without damage. So instead, he bullied us all into backing down, and cars kept whizzing around the neighborhood. That was the unlikeable Wiggins I knew. But this guy from the other planet Earth was different. I thought about my options for a minute, stood up and then said, "Let's go."

We drove to Wiggins's office, pulled around back, and parked. Wiggins's white Mercedes was gone.

Meredith opened the car door, looked at me, and then asked, "Coming?"

"What? Where?" I asked, getting out. "And what about him?" I said, pointed at Hank in the back seat.

Meredith, heading for the office building, said, "How would it look if two of you walked into the building? Plus, you are acquainted with Wiggins if he returns from wherever he is."

I closed the car door and ran to catch up. "And what if we run into Wiggins? Who are you supposed to be? My sister?"

"Okay, your sister works," Meredith replied.

"You don't look like my sister."

Meredith stopped and turned toward me. "Has Wiggins ever seen your sister?"

"Well," I said, thinking about the question. "No. Not that I..."

"Then just go with it," Meredith replied, resuming her purposeful stride toward the office. "It's bad enough I have to deal with Hank's questioning and second-guessing everything I do but now I have two Hank's to answer to."

I wanted to yell "TIME OUT" and call the whole thing off but somehow, I'd been sucked along into this adventure and wasn't sure how to get out and maybe...was curious to see it through. Plus, I'd be delighted if Wiggins took a pie to the face. So I trotted along beside Meredith and closed my mouth - at least for the moment.

We took the stairs to the third floor, spotted the door with the letters <u>Ryan Wiggins, Attorney at Law; Investment Counselor</u> stenciled on the glass and stepped into the waiting room of Wiggins's office.

There was the usual, five or six cloth covered chairs (all empty), a couple faded mundane seascape prints on the walls, a pole lamp or two, a round glass-topped table with a messy array of magazines, an inexpensive Staples sale desk, and a receptionist. She was maybe twenty-five or thirty years old, chubby, purple hair, two or three nose piercings, some sort of jagged metal rods stuck through her ears, black lipstick and matching eyeshadow. Even though she had earbuds stuck in her ears, the steady throb of some rap music could be heard from where we stood, ten feet away. She was reading a book. Behind her was a closed door with a sign affixed, stating RYAN WIGGINS, PRIVATE.

After about a minute, she looked up, stared at us like a lizard examining a fly, snapped her gum a few times, and then said in a dead-pan voice, "Mister Wiggins is gone for the day."

Meredith stepped over to the desk, smiled, and said, "That's fine. We wanted to speak with you."

I looked at Meredith, scratched my chin, and thought, '*We did?*'

"WHAT?" The receptionist replied over her music, obviously annoyed.

Meredith pointed at her ears. To my astonishment, the receptionist removed the earbuds and fiddled with her iPod, turning off the drumbeat. I thought sure we were going to receive the one-finger salute or some such response.

"That's better," Meredith said. "Now, as I said, we are here to see you, not Mr. Wiggins."

The receptionist cocked her head. "Me?" She snapped her gum.

"Yes," Meredith replied. "I'm Meredith McNally. We run a catering business and we're here to make preparations for Mr. Wiggins's surprise party."

"Huh?" The receptionist asked, clearly dazed and confused.

"Yes," Meredith said with a smile, "to be held the day after tomorrow."

"Day after tomorrow?" the receptionist repeated. "But I didn't..." Snap. Snap.

"May I sit down?" Meredith interrupted.

"Yeah, sure." Her face changed from stupefied to bored. Snap.

Meredith pulled up one of the cheap office guest chairs and motioned for me to do the same. Once seated, Meredith again smiled sweetly and asked, "And I'm sorry, I didn't catch your name."

"Caitlyn," the receptionist replied. "With a C." Snap.

"Okay Caitlyn with a C," Meredith said with a warm and charming smile, "The day after tomorrow, several of Mr. Wiggins's friends are throwing him a surprise anniversary party here at the office."

Caitlyn wrinkled her pierced nose. "I didn't know Mr. Wiggins had any friends."

"Oh," said Meredith, a bit taken aback. Then quickly recovering, said, "These are old friends. From school."

"Whatever," Caitlyn said, now back to being bored.

"And you get the day off!" Meredith said enthusiastically.

"I do?" Back to being stupefied.

"With pay and," Meredith reached into her briefcase, "with this bonus." She handed Caitlyn a one-hundred dollar bill.

"Kick ass!" Caitlyn replied, accepting the bribe. "But what about..." Snap. Snap.

"What about your temp agency?" Meredith interrupted. "They don't have to know. And on the day after tomorrow morning, I will tell Mr. Wiggins you are not feeling well and I am filling in for you."

"Kick ass!" Caitlyn said, with almost a smile. "Anything else?" She asked, closing the book she was reading, 50 Shades of Grey, and putting it in the desk drawer. She turned off the desk lamp.

"Well, I think we have covered the arrangements," Meredith asked with surprise. "But wait. Are you going somewhere? I will need to know how to get in here in the morning."

Caitlyn looked at her watch, an oversized dial mounted on a super wide, fluorescent orange plastic wristband. The face of the watch was somewhat like that of Alice Cooper. The hands of the watch were two lizard tongues. "I'm outta here. Know what I mean?" Snap. Snap.

"But it's only 3:30," Meredith said. "I thought the office hours, as printed on the door, were 8 to 5?"

"Yeah, well Mr. Wiggins see," Caitlyn began, "He never comes back after lunch, know what I mean? I was still here because I was just at a bitchin' part in the book and lost track of the time. I usually bolt at 2." Snap.

"Do you like the book?" Meredith asked. I looked at her in surprise, thinking, '*Why the chit chat?*'

"It's wicked awesome," Caitlyn replied. "Except for the spanking shit. I don't get off on that. Know what I mean?"

"Yes," Meredith replied earnestly. "I'm not fond of S&M either."

"I mean, the bondage shit is way hot," Caitlyn said, with almost a bit of enthusiasm. "But who goes in for spanking? What's that all about? Know what I mean?" Snap. Snap.

"Yes, I do and I agree," said Meredith. "But you know, in the next book in the series, Fifty Shade Freed, there's not as much."

My mouth dropped open. I looked at Meredith and asked incredulously, "*You* have read..."

Meredith shot me a 'keep your mouth shut' glare, and then turned back to Caitlyn. "So about the day after tomorrow. How do I get in? There must be a key or lock of some sort."

Caitlyn pointed at the door. "The keypad on the wall in the hallway...code 123 then pound-sign. You know, the tic-tac-toe thingy." Snap.

"Okay," Meredith said evenly. "123 then the tic-tac-toe thingy. Got it. And how about Mr. Wiggins's office. I see there is a keypad on the wall next to his door. What's the code for that one?"

Caitlyn shrugged. "Don't know. He keeps it secret. I never go in there."

Meredith nodded. "And what time do you normally get here?"

"Eight. Mr. Wiggins won't show up 'till about nine." Snap.

Meredith nodded. "Okay. And what do you do here for him? I mean to say, what is your job here?"

"Well," Caitlyn said, thinking deeply, "I'm supposed to answer the phone and keep his what-cha-ma-call it book," she pointed to the black-covered appointment book, "but hardly no one ever calls except his bimbo wife and she calls about a million times a day, you know what I mean?... and since the grab ass thing, Mr. Wiggins keeps his own appointment book." Snap.

"The grab-ass thing?" Meredith asked.

"Yeah, but we got it straightened out." Snap. Snap.

Meredith sat up straight, folded her hands over her briefcase, and said. "Tell me about that."

"Oh, it was no big deal," Caitlyn replied. "When I first took this gig, about a year ago, Mr. Wiggins was always touching me. You know, hand on my shoulder, my arm, rub my back, all that shit. You know what I mean? Gave me the creeps. Then one day, he came back from playing golf in the morning...I think he had a few drinks because his face was all red and he was goofier than normal... and he grabbed my ass. I told him if he ever touches me again, my boyfriend will cut off his fucking balls. He never touched me again. Know what I mean?" Snap. Snap. Snap.

"I do," said Meredith. "You do know there are laws that protect you from that sort of thing."

"Yeah," Caitlyn replied nonchalantly, "But I got my point across. Plus now, how can he fire me? Think of it this way...if the word got out that a big deal investment what-ever he is, fondles his help..." Caitlyn held up her hands in a palms-up gesture. "I got him by the balls. Know what I mean?" Snap.

"I do," Meredith said again. "But be careful with that. Don't get hurt."

Caitlyn looked at Meredith with something that resembled affection. It was a tiny smile from the corners of her mouth. At least I think so but it was hard to tell with the black makeup and piercings. Caitlyn said, "I have some awesome friends that look out for me. You know what I mean. But thanks."

Meredith and I left the office - and Caitlyn with a 'C' - and strode purposefully toward the parked car where Hank was taking a mid-afternoon nap. I waited until we were halfway across the parking lot, out of earshot of anyone in the vicinity, and then asked, "What the hell was that all about? What's this about you catering a party? What's going on the day after tomorrow?"

Meredith stopped and turned toward me. Patiently, quietly, she said, "Are you done now or do you have any more questions?"

"I don't know yet, but those will do for a start," I replied, unable to shake the unpleasant feeling that I was sliding down a slippery slope.

Meredith said, "Let's get in the car and head for home. I'll explain along the way."

The hot, humid weather had evolved into a late day thunderstorm which was breaking upon us as we drove. True to her word, Meredith answered all my questions on the drive back to my house. The answers, however, did not make me feel any better.

When she finished, I stared at the road through heavy rain and oscillating windshield wipers. Then I asked, "You mean to tell me, you're making this up as you go?"

Meredith thought for a moment then replied, "Let's rephrase that as modifying the existing plan to incorporate the circumstances."

Hank leaned forward from the back seat and said, "She's making it up as she goes."

Meredith shot him a disgusted look and responded with, "I haven't heard any great ideas from you."

Hank, ignoring her reply, asked, "What time is Bart's appointment?"

I gripped the steering wheel in alarm and asked, "What appointment?"

Meredith paused then said, "Ten o'clock should work."

"Hey! Hold on," I said. "What's this?"

Meredith looked at me. "Remember earlier when we were talking about you meeting with Wiggins? That will be the day after tomorrow at 10."

"But…" I said.

Meredith overruled my objection and said, "Just go in, sit down, and tell him you heard how well he's doing for his clients and you'd like to discuss moving your retirement portfolio to his care."

"And what does this have to do with capturing Wiggins?" I asked.

Hank said, "We're hoping to locate the stolen computer in his office. That will give us the evidence we need to take him back. We know it's in there somewhere but he's got it hidden behind some kind of shielding device."

I felt a knot forming in my stomach. "So really what you're saying is *I'm* being sent in to locate his computer, right? And what am I supposed to do? Tear apart his office while he's talking to me?"

Hank sat back and said quietly, "We're working on that."

We drove in silence the rest of the way home.

I pulled together a garden salad for a light supper, as we were all still full from lunch. By the time we sat down to eat, the afternoon thunderstorm had run out of steam. The setting sun had crept back behind the trees and the deck was once again in shade. The evening was humid but pleasant.

Meredith nibbled on a cherry tomato then said to me, "Let me put your mind at ease. If we don't pick up a strong signal from his office while you are meeting, nothing will happen. You will go home. I'll close the office in the afternoon. And we'll think of something else." She paused and watched me for a reaction. When I didn't look comforted, Hank spoke up and said, "Not to worry. We're not expecting you to overpower Wiggins then ransack his office. We'll do all the heavy lifting. You're just our spy. Okay?"

I nodded. Although the idea of hitting Wiggins's arrogant, smirking face with a solid, right-cross was rather appealing, it really wasn't realistic. Plus, if he turned out to be the real Wiggins from this planet and not the missing Wiggins from the other Earth, I'd probably end up in jail for assault. Still, it might be worth it to get in one good punch. Hmmm. No, as an adult, punching someone in the face is not an option. I let it go. "Okay," I said. "I'm okay with that."

With supper about over, we sat back and relaxed. Hank and I drained our second Sam Adams Lager while Meredith, deep in thought, sipped a Bogle Chardonnay.

Chapter Twelve

Strange Coincidences

Murphy's Pub on Palmer Street in North Sayer is an aging bar and grill that has never made it big – for good reason. It is poorly lit, the furniture is sticky, and the food should be served with a side of Rolaids. As a rule, the beer on tap is flat and all the wine comes from bottles with screw tops. A hint of stale smoke lingers from the days before tobacco was outlawed. The wait staff is surly and the regulars are exactly what you would expect: unshaven, weathered, and permanently hunched over their drinks.

Caitlyn Mendoza sat alone in the booth all the way down on the left. She was no longer snapping her gum, had pulled on a Red Sox shirt, and was watching the front door. A bottle of Sam Adams sat on the table in front of her.

At eight P.M., Lieutenant Brian Kelly of the Camden Police Department walked in. Medium height – perhaps 5'-6" – but stocky and solid. He sported a clipped goatee, professionally groomed short brown hair, wore a plaid shirt with open collar, and smartly pressed chinos. The blue blazer he wore barely hid his sidearm. The barflies checked him out, recognized him as a cop, and went back to their stale beer.

329

Kelly walked directly to the booth where Caitlyn sat and slid in across the table from her. He opened his coat, removed his identification, and held it up for Caitlyn to read. He said, "Kelly, Camden PD."

Caitlyn took her time, reading the ID, looking from his picture to his face, then pulled out her identification, saying, "FBI Special Agent Caitlyn Mendoza."

Kelly nodded, looked around, and then said, "Not exactly a five-star gourmet dining establishment."

"Perhaps," Caitlyn replied, eyeing Kelly steadily. "But a perfect place for a meeting if you don't want to be seen. I assume there's nothing like this in the hoity-toity upscale town of Camden."

"You assume correctly," Kelly replied.

They sat quietly, eyes locked in a tense test of will.

Kelly leaned forward. "Thanks for agreeing to meet with me. Let's get right to it. Your boss, Director Joe Stevens, is an arrogant, misinformed, incredibly unpleasant asshole. I wouldn't piss on him if he was on fire. But you're different. I've seen you in action and the word on the street is you're okay. I know this is a bit unusual for the F'ing BI – perhaps an anomaly - but it is what it is. So I've got some information that may be of interest to you. This is my attempt at reaching out to a fellow law enforcement officer and perhaps work together, in spite of our long-standing distaste for each other's organizations."

Caitlyn said nothing.

A waitress resembling a toad waddled to the table. She glared at Kelly. "Menu?"

Caitlyn said, "He'll have a bottle of Sam Adams Lager. And please bring me another."

When she left, Caitlyn said, "Never order anything here that comes in a glass or on a plate."

Kelly nodded. "I'll keep that in mind."

The toad returned, put two bottles of beer on the table, and then departed.

Caitlyn asked, "Who blew my cover?"

"Blew your cover? No one. Your cover's intact."

"Oh?"

Kelly took a sip of beer, wrinkled his face, and put down the bottle. "I don't see how people drink that stuff. As for your undercover work, you are safe. You're not thinking the FBI gave a lowly town cop any information, do you?"

Caitlyn shrugged.

Kelly made a tent with his fingers. "They didn't. They never do."

"So, if you didn't go through my boss, how did you find me?"

"Do you remember," Kelly began, "the drug bust that went down about four years ago? It was that ring set up by the Hurley brothers from Fall River and it involved all the suburban towns up this way."

Caitlyn nodded.

"Well," Kelly continued, "I was on the case at the time, representing Camden. And I remember you, as a brand spanking new FBI field agent, did a helluva smooth job coordinating all the towns and agencies. You worked with difficult personalities and somehow, convinced them to work together. But most importantly, you stayed in the background and let the local police chiefs get all the WJZ TV time. They looked good but you and I both know you did all the heavy lifting. That's contrary to the normal mode of operation by your employer, the FBI."

Caitlyn shrugged and took a pull on her bottle of Sam. "Our job is to put away the bad guys. We can sort out the atta-boys later."

Kelly smiled. "Refreshing. Are you sure you work for Stevens?"

Caitlyn stared at Kelly. "So you were going to tell me how you found me."

"I have this thing about faces and names. It's my strong suit."

"Congratulations," Caitlyn said.

Kelly continued to sit ramrod straight, hands unmoving on the table. "So then I get this new case last month. It involves your boss, Ryan Wiggins. And we set up a survey of his office, and watch who comes and goes. And guess what we see? Lo and behold, who comes out but Caitlyn Mendoza; purple hair, piercings, and all. Incidentally, not my style but each to his or her own."

"So I get to thinking, why is this rising star for the FBI, working as a receptionist for our person of interest? Was she fired by her dumb ass boss after laying low during the Hurley drug bust? Probably not. I would have heard about that. So what's the other alternative? I'd guess the FBI has some interest in Wiggins and perhaps, they've inserted you in. How's that for sleuthing?"

Caitlyn smiled for the first time. "Stevens was rip-shit at the way I handled the Hurley case. He would have loved to send me to Antarctica to count penguins but the result was a big score for all of us, and his boss ended up looking pretty good. So since he couldn't get rid of me, he did the next best thing – I was assigned to an undercover gig in Greenwich. It doesn't get any better than that." She took another swallow of beer. "Now, let me ask you a question. Why is a cop from Camden working in Greenwich?"

Kelly narrowed his eyes and pursed his lips. "It's both professional and personal, which of course, brings us to why we are here. Recently, a financial advisor from one of those big investment companies paid Wiggins a visit. I suppose his job was to snoop around and try to find out why the highly successful Wiggins was making all the investment firms look like kindergarteners. That night, he did not come home. Now, a year later, he's never been seen nor heard from again. Since he's a resident of Camden, I've got the case in my inbox. That's the professional side of the coin. The personal side – he was my brother-in-law. And my sister is slowly going out of her mind. They've got two kids who I've all but adopted, but still, the question remains, where is dad?

So I do my police investigator thing and find out his last known contact is none other than Ryan Wiggins. I call my pals at Greenwich PD and they're too budget-strapped to do much but would welcome my involvement. I talk to Wiggins who has a conveniently poor memory and sheds no light on the situation. I send out an APB for my missing man and get a call from my counterpart at the Newfields PD.

He can't help me find my man but – get this – he also has a financial guy missing. This missing person was from Becket's Investments Inc. and has been gone for two years. His last known contact was – you guessed it – Ryan Wiggins. Now, this guy even sent his wife a text, saying he'd be home late because he has a dinner date with Wiggins. Never came home. Once again, Wiggins has no recollection of this person, their meeting, or their dinner. Coincidence? Nope. My instincts tell me Wiggins has a lot to do with these two missing persons. Couple that with the fact that they were both snooping around, trying to discover the secret to Wiggin's success."

Caitlyn swigged her beer and held up two fingers. "Two murders."

Kelly nodded.

"Jesus," Caitlyn muttered. "And I thought I was chasing a fraud and money racketeer."

Kelly opened his hands and held them palms up. "That's what I've got. Can you add to my story?"

Caitlyn leaned back in her seat and exhaled. "I wish I had something solid for you. I got involved because somebody way up the food chain in the Securities and Exchange Commission called somebody way up the line in the bureau and asked to have Wiggins tailed. Apparently, his investment counseling record is off the chart."

"And?"

"Nothing. He's straight. The IRS says he's perfect with his taxes, no known record, no suspected insider sources, and other than being liberal with his groping hands, he appears to be playing it straight."

"Shit," Kelly said quietly.

"There *are* two curious aspects of Wiggins that I have no idea what they have to do with anything, but curious just the same."

"Oh?"

"First, he changed dramatically about six years ago. We've been looking into his past and conducting some interviews, and it seems that he used to be mister gregarious. Always throwing parties, and trying to be the joke-telling, slap you on the back, have another beer, neighborhood big mouth. Then – like I said – about six years ago, he suddenly withdrew, stopped hosting gatherings, and in short, left the party scene. That's also when he changed from a bumbling incompetent lawyer who was barely making enough to survive, to mister stock market wizard whose net worth is zooming."

"Interesting."

Caitlyn continued. "And second, he seems to be able to disappear."

Kelly raised his eyebrows.

Caitlyn leaned even closer, her voice barely above a whisper, and said, "The son of a bitch simply cannot be followed. Say what you want about the bureau, but we are pretty damn good at tailing people. This guy, sometimes he leaves the office, gets in his car, and bingo, it's gone."

"The car is gone?"

"Yep, we put a tail on him and he drives somewhere – different places – turns a corner and when we get there, he's gone. Happens on a regular basis."

"Have you put a bug on his car?"

"Several."

"And?"

"Nothing. They go blank. We replace them, have 'em checked out, and they're fine. We put new bugs on, same thing."

Kelly made a tent of his fingers again and sat quietly. Caitlyn leaned back in her seat and drained her beer.

After five silent minutes passed, Kelly asked, "I need your gut feel. Is this guy Wiggins capable of murder?"

Caitlyn looked Kelly straight in the eye, and said, "Absolutely."

Chapter Thirteen

Who is this Guy?

The next day, Lieutenant Brian Kelly CPD, called his sergeant Denise Hopper into his office. He tossed her the file on Ryan Wiggins. "I need you to do some sleuthing. This guy graduated from Western New England Law School in '82. I think there were about seventy-five students in his class. Call around and see if you can find a classmate that remembers him, and – more importantly – has stayed in touch with him."

Hopper was not your typical police sergeant. She was a bit plump, gray hair pulled back in a braid, half-moon reading glasses, and a kindly face that who be better suited for someone's mom that stayed at home and made cookies. It was this matronly demeanor that evoked easy conversation and in some cases, the outpouring of information not normally gathered by cops in the interview room. She was perfect for investigating affairs of the heart.

She took notes on her tablet. "What am I looking for?"

Kelly shook his head. "Don't know but there's something fishy about that guy. Maybe even dangerous. We need to learn more about him."

"What's he done?"

"Nothing we can prove. Yet."

Of the students who she actually spoke to, most had only a vague recollection of Wiggins. Academically, he had finished last in his graduating class and was unremarkable in all other aspects. He had a reputation as a party boy who drank too much and usually embarrassed himself. Hopper was on student number seventy-one when she struck gold in the name of Attorney Nichole Larkin.

"Yes, I knew Ryan Wiggins, or at least, thought I knew him."

"Would you care to elaborate?"

"Not over the phone."

"Okay. Where then?"

"I'm coming out your way tomorrow to for a conference in Eastford. It's at the Eastford Regency. Is that near you?"

"Yes. A few towns over."

"How about we meet tomorrow afternoon?"

"I can do that. I'll check and see if there's a lounge in the hotel. If there is, let's meet there.

The watering hole in the hotel was called Clair's Tavern. Sergeant Hopper met Attorney Larkin in a booth along the rear wall, far from the noisy bar and potentially eavesdroppers. Hopper ordered a diet coke and Larkin ordered a glass of wine.

After introductions and the required chit-chat, Sergeant Hopper got right to it. "So you said you knew Ryan Wiggins."

"Actually, I said I *thought* I knew Ryan Wiggins."

Hopper got out her tablet to take notes but Attorney Larkin shook her head no. "Let's keep this off the record. No quotes. No names. Okay?"

"Fair enough."

Larkin was a tall, attractive woman carrying a few extra pounds. Her blond hair was pulled back, she wore little markup or jewelry, and no wedding ring. If it is possible to do so, she looked like a lawyer. She studied her glass of wine. "We met in college. I was married at the time and he had a girlfriend back home, somewhere near Boston. We worked together on some class projects, often well into the evening. Usually, we'd wrap up out sessions with a drink or two. Or three. And then, one thing led to another and we ended up in bed together." She exhaled, frowned from the memory, and then continued. "Neither of us wanted to change our home status so we kept it quiet. It was our secret. Then it happened again. And again. But then we graduated and went our separate ways, and I thought that was that." She sipped her wine. "Then, a year or two later, we bumped into each other at a lawyer's conference in Cambridge. And yep, you guessed it." Another sip. "Have you ever seen the movie with Alan Alda entitled *Same Time Next Year?*"

Hopper nodded. "I have. That's the one where they meet each year to carry on an affair?"

"That's it. Well, that's what we did. We'd meet each year at a country inn somewhere in Vermont and for one weekend a year, we'd pick up where we left off." She looked across the room but her eyes were focused upon something a long way away. Another sip of wine. "Then, I guess it was six years ago, I didn't hear from him. We always touched base before our getaway weekend to confirm where we were going, but that year, nothing. So I called him at his office, and when we spoke, he said he had no idea what I was talking about. Then I got in my car and drove to his office and showed up at his door. He said, and this is a quote, 'Who the hell are you?'" She smiled painfully. "Can you believe that shit?"

Hopper slowly shook her head.

"I didn't know what to do so I turned around and left feeling, I think the word is bewildered. And hurt. And rejected."

They sat in silence for a while. Finally, Larkin drained her glass and motioned to the bartender for another. "I guess that makes me a woman scorned, doesn't it?"

Hopper opened her hands. "No reason offered?"

"No nothing. It was as if he was looking at a total stranger. But you know..."

The bartender brought another glass of wine and took away the empty.

Larkin continued. "You know, I get this feeling he really didn't know who I was. I don't think it was an act. The Ryan Wiggins I knew was transparent. You always knew what was happening inside his head. He had this habit of forcing a smile and rubbing his chin when he was buying time. And he had watery blue eyes that in spite of the fact that he was not the brightest bulb in the bag were kind and sparkled, and ready to start partying at the drop of a hat. That Ryan Wiggins I met for that last time..." She slowly, sadly shook her head. "His eyes were ice cold and there was no trace, not even a hint of a smile on his face." She leaned across the table, held Hopper's eyes, and said in a low voice, "I know this is impossible but that guy wasn't the same Ryan Wiggins I knew all those years."

Chapter Fourteen

Topless Ginger

The next day I got up at about six, went out back and threw a stone. It followed a curving trajectory then "bang," hit an invisible barrier, stopped, and dropped to the Earth.

I put my hands on my hips and studied the empty space above the dirt road. There was nothing there. I bent and picked up a second stone and repeated the action. Again: 'bang.'

They were back.

A voice from behind said, "If you're trying to dent our spaceship, it won't work."

I whipped around and there, standing in the doorway of my shed, were Hank and Meredith. Looking at Hank was like looking at myself in a mirror except it wasn't me. It was unsettling.

"You know," Hank began, "This shed is a great place to play chess. I can see why you and your pals gather here."

I was so focused on Hank, wondering if I *really* looked and sounded like him, that I didn't hear what he said.

"I'm sorry, what did you say?"

"Your shed," Hank repeated. "I like it."

I crossed my arms and asked, "What are you guys doing in my shed?"

Meredith said, "We awoke early and didn't want to wake you just yet, so we were taking a tour of your garden and yard, and this," she beckoned towards my shed, "rather odiferous man-cave."

I blinked a few times and studied my visitors; Meredith looked the same; neatly pressed white blouse, black crop pants, arms wrapped around a briefcase. But looking at Hank, he really *did* look like he just got out of bed: his hair was mussed, his wrinkled shirt half in/ half out of his pants. Subconsciously, I began tucking in my shirt and smoothing my hair.

"You want some coffee?" I asked.

Hank stretched and yawned. "Thought you'd never ask."

We sat on my back deck and drank coffee and tea. Even though it was early morning, it was already hot.

"So," I began. "Today's the day I meet with Wiggins. Right?"

"Change of plans," Meredith said. "Yesterday, I checked with Caitlyn, his receptionist, and she told me Mr. Wiggins will be playing golf today. Your meeting has been moved to tomorrow."

I put down my coffee cup. "What if I'm busy tomorrow?" I asked.

"Are you?" Meredith asked.

"No. But you could have asked."

Hank snickered.

We sat quietly for a minute, and then Meredith said, "I suggest you pay your neighbor's wife Ginger a visit."

"What? Why would I want to do that?"

Hank leaned toward Meredith and said, "I told you that would be his reaction."

Meredith exhaled. "Dealing with one of you is bad enough, but now I have to put up with two." Ignoring Hank, she said, "First the why. Because his wife, Ginger, would know if this was the same Ryan Wiggins she married. As I have already explained, we need to be certain. As for the what, just go over, knock on her door, and pay her a social call."

Hank said, "Look, this is easy as pie. With Wiggins off golfing today, you just drop in and pay her a neighborly visit. No big deal"

"Why don't *you* pay her a neighborly visit?" I asked.

"I'm not her neighbor."

Meredith interrupted, "He's right. You do *know* his wife, Ginger, right?"

"Not well. We've chatted a few times in the past. Not too much lately, since me and her hubby have been feuding. And besides, how would she know the difference? I mean, if the new Wiggins is exactly the same as the old Wiggins…"

Meredith almost smiled. "She would know."

I opened my hands and looked to Hank for support, but he just smiled.

"Women know these things," Meredith said again.

I drummed my fingers on the table. "Oh sure, next you're going to tell me women have this sixth sense about these things…"

"They do," Meredith said.

"Well," I stammered, "I'm not so sure…"

"Nonetheless," she said, interrupting my weak argument. "We'd like you to do this. And you're the person to do this, not Hank. You know all the details of the history that has transpired over the year – Hank does not. Plus, we have some business to attend to today."

Feeling a bit ganged up upon, I sulked for a moment. Curiously, I felt myself getting sucked into this mystery and was now wondering about this guy Wiggins and who was he really. After a moment, I said, "All right. I'll go over and borrow a cup of sugar or something. And incidentally, where did you go yesterday? And where are you going today?"

Meredith set down her teacup, stood, and picked up her briefcase. "Let's just say…other business."

"Like what?" I asked. "What could you possibly be needing to do on this planet Earth? Christmas shopping? A yard sale somewhere?"

Hank stood and smiled. "I'll give you a hint: you don't think your pal Wiggins is the only fish in the sea, do you?"

341

Meredith shot a glance at Hank. "That will do."

Hank punched me lightly in the shoulder. "See you tomorrow, bright and early."

Then they left.

I moped around the house for a couple of hours, feeling used and abused. I had planned to get in a whole lot of fishing, plus some gardening, poker, and a little chess. Now, it was clear I was getting sucked into an investigation of a neighbor I didn't like, for some people I didn't know, for reasons that were still not clear. Other than my weekly chess game, my plans had drifted away like smoke from a campfire. Yet, there was a germ of curiosity starting to grow. What *was* my neighbor up to? And better yet, who was this guy *really?* Could he be as dangerous as Meredith and Hank said he was? If he was, should I keep arguing with him about the trees that separate our houses? And if he was, I needed to help send him back to where he came from. I finished my third cup of coffee then headed next door.

The Wiggin's house was a large, boxy colonial. The pool out back was surrounded by a tall privacy fence. I went to the back door and knocked. Nothing. I knocked again, louder.

"I'm out back, sweetie," came a woman's voice from the pool area. "You're early today. Come on in."

I opened the gate to the backyard, stepped in, and announced, "Ginger, it's Bart from next door." Suddenly, I felt the need to have a reason to be there. I never just drop over. "It's about you spotlight that lights up your pool. It's been left on all night for weeks," I lied unconvincingly, a smile plastered on my reddening face.

Propped up on a Chaise Lounge, wearing only black bikini bottoms, dark sunglasses, and a large, designer floppy sun hat, was Ginger Wiggins.

She was a tall, green-eyed, voluptuous redhead who ten years ago was a *wow!* And even though the passing years, countless bottles of wine, and way too much idle time had taken a heavy toll, she still had an aura about her that cooed *I'm pleasant to touch.*

Next to where she lay was a half-empty bottle of white wine. She removed her sunglasses and stared at me, blinking. Clearly, I was not who she was expecting. Then she reached down, picked up the bikini top, and tried to cover her breasts. Unfortunately, one side of the bikini had turned inside out so there she sat, holding the disheveled garment with one breast covered with black fabric but the other with the white lining on the outside.

I averted my eyes to the pool and said, "Perhaps I should come back some other time."

"Nonsense," she said. "Come in, come in. Sit down. We haven't spoken for a dog's age."

I did so.

She held up a bottle of 2008 Didier Dagueneau Silex wine. "May I pour a glass for you?"

"No thanks."

She topped off her glass and pushed the bottle my way. "Help yourself if you change your mind. Now, to what do I owe this pleasure?" Her words slurred slightly. I figured she was already a six out of ten on the drunk-o-meter...and climbing.

I took the bottle from her and studied the label. "Wow! This is very fine wine, and pricey, too. What does it go for?"

She made a dismissive gesture with the hand that had been holding the top half of her swimsuit in place, allowing one side to slip down. Her bikini now resembled a sagging Venetian blind with one string broken. "I buy it by the case," she said. "I think it runs about one hundred dollars a bottle."

I returned the bottle, trying not to stare at her exposed breast.

She caught my eye and looked down, noting her disheveled attire. "Oh what the hell," she said and tossed the top into the pool. "You don't mind, do you?"

"No."

"So," she said, taking a liberal swallow of wine. "What brings you over here on this fine day?" Before I could think up an adequate answer, she snapped her fingers. "Ah, I think I know why you're here.

And since Ryan is out playing golf somewhere, it's just the two of us." She smiled seductively. "Would you care to take a dip?"

"Tempting, but no thank you. Honestly, I'm really quite flattered, but I'm here to talk about another topic."

She took another liberal swallow of wine and smiled again. "Are you sure? The water is quite refreshing." Sweat beaded up on her skin, gathered together and ran down between her breasts.

Suddenly, I was aware of my shallow breathing and a quickened pulse. I sat perfectly still, in a trance, waiting for the outcome of an internal battle which was in full swing. On one side of the struggle were the forces of logic, loyalty, and the all-too-fresh memory of my wife. The opposing forces were made up of lust, carnal sins, and reinforced with the small but powerful band of *what the hell* stormtroopers who show up from time to time and wreak havoc with an otherwise normal but boring life. There were attacks and retreats, then counter-attacks. Neither side was giving an inch. Casualties were heavy. Finally, galloping onto the battlefield, the *don't be an idiot* cavalry charged in and sent lust and all his pals packing.

I snapped out of my stupor. "Tempting but no. Actually, Ginger, I'm here to ask you about Ryan."

She frowned. "Oh, him."

"I know this sounds a bit personal, but how are you guys doing?"

"Doing?"

"You know, how is your relationship? I know it's none of my business but..."

Ginger made a *who cares* wave of her left hand while with her right hand, she took another mighty swing of wine. She gazed at the pool. "Not so good," then she looked back at me. "Don't get me wrong, I get anything I want. I drink only expensive French wine, wear $300 sun hats, drive a BMW, and spend one weekend a month in the Berkshire Health and Beauty Spa. In short, anything money can buy. But Ryan..." She shook her head. There was a touch of sadness in her eyes.

"The blush is off the rose?"

She chuckled. "He moved into the spare bedroom years ago. I believe we can safely say the rose bush is dead."

I leaned forward on my seat. "How many years ago?"

She shrugged. "Let's see…it was…hmm…"

"Six?" I asked.

She nodded. "That's about right?" Another gulp of wine. Another refill. The drunk-o-meter was now at seven.

"And what about Ryan. Has he changed much?"

She nodded again. "He's become nasty. He's a mean old man. Say, isn't that a line from some Beatles song?"

"*Mean Mr. Mustard*, from their Abbey Road Album," I replied.

Ginger looked at me and blinked. "You *know* that?"

Ignoring her question, I said, "I know what you mean about him being a mean old man. And he certainly has become a real pain in the ass about our shared property line and those trees over there." I pointed at the row of white pines that separated our house lots.

"He never touches me anymore," she said, as much to herself as to me. She took another swallow. "And he scares me."

I sat up straight. Here, sitting in front of me within arm's reach was a mostly naked, quite attractive, mostly drunk, seemingly willing woman. Yet, my feelings for her suddenly shifted to pity and fear for her safety. She wasn't a rocket scientist and certainly, not someone I'd seek out at a cocktail party but basically, she was okay. And perhaps in danger.

"Ginger, are you safe here?"

"Oh sure," she scoffed. "He never lays a finger on me. I'm certain it's just my imagination. When you live by yourself, you imagine all sorts of things. But there are times…"

Ginger stopped. We both turned toward the gate. A vehicle had pulled into the driveway. I got up.

"That'll be Francis," Ginger said, shooting a glance at the large outdoor clock hanging on the wall. "Right on time."

"Francis?"

"He delivers my dry-cleaning. Be a good sport and let him in for me, will you please? And maybe you'll want to hang around. After all," she smiled her seductive smile again, "I hear two men are twice as nice."

I walked over and opened the gate. There stood Francis. His skin was the color of coffee with two creams, his hair black, wavy, and slicked back. He wore several gold chains around his neck and had large biceps. His aftershave or body perfume was strong enough to kill mosquitos. He looked at me with a mixture of confusion and fear.

Stepping aside, I opened the gate wider, beckoned to Ginger, and said, "Next."

Then I walked home.

Chapter Fifteen

Setting the Trap

The next morning, I was lying in my bed in that half-awake/half-asleep zone, trying to recall this bizarre strange dream I had had. It had something to do with two visitors from a parallel dimension who wanted to arrest my neighbor. Then, someone opened the drapes in my bedroom, letting sunlight stream in. It was Meredith.

"Time to get up," she said.

"So you weren't a dream?" I asked.

She turned from the drapes, looked at me, and said, "No, not a dream. I hope you don't mind but we let ourselves in. Hank made coffee downstairs. We should get moving." Then she paused for a moment, pushed a stray lock of hair from her forehead, and added, "We really appreciate your help with this matter. I know this can't be easy for you and in fact, a bit risky. I just want you to know neither Hank nor I take you for granted. Thank you." She then turned to leave, took a few steps, but then stopped and about-faced.

"I need to ask you something," she said.

"Okay."

"It's a personal question about Hank. And since you are about as close as possible to being Hank without being so, perhaps you can shed some light on my concern."

I scratched my head tried to shake the sleep cobwebs from my brain. "I guess so. What's on your mind?"

"You and Hank married the same woman back in 1991. But in the interim period of time, both your wives died. You know about that. Correct?"

"I do." I frowned and thought, *this is kind of early in the morning to be hitting me with this.*

"Forgive me for prying but were you devastated when your wife was suddenly taken from you?"

I really had to go to the bathroom but couldn't because Meredith chose this moment to dive into this rather puzzling topic. I crossed my legs under the covers to buy myself some bladder time."

"Well, yeah. Big time." I replied, "Why do you ask?"

Meredith walked over to the slider and looked out the window. "I was surprised at how quickly Hank returned to work. Sure, he acknowledged the loss but somehow, I thought that perhaps, he may have…" She stopped, unable to formulate the words.

"Ah," I said. "So I get it. You're asking me because I'm sort of Hank, to find out if we have any feelings or simply are cold-hearted trolls. Right?"

She whipped around. "That's not what I said nor meant. It's just that…"

I held up my hand in a stop position. "No problem. It's actually a good question. Let me ask you this; how long has it been?"

Meredith said, "Since Hank's wife died? Let's see, it was two years last month."

"And in that time, has Hank hooked up with another woman?"

"No," Meredith said. "And by 'hook-up,' I assume you mean 'had a date with.' The answer is no, not that I know of."

I really had to go and couldn't wait much longer. I had to make this quick. "Listen," I said. "Here's the deal. Hank was and probably still is deeply in love with his wife. And since his wife was the same as my wife, he probably feels like I do…that replacing her is not an option. So he is living his life still committed to her which is like, the greatest compliment ever. Follow? And about him coming back to work too soon without doing all the grieving stuff, that's because we men suck at showing emotions. I mean, we really suck. We'd rather suffer in silence than ask for help and show, heaven forbid, any weakness. And that's why you women outlive us men because you keep nothing inside. Any opportunity to let it all hang out is fine for you guys, even to perfect strangers. But us men, no sir. Suck it up and be a man. That's the way we were brought up. And all this pain, it eats men alive. That's why many guys die young. It's really, really, stupid, I know, but them's the apples. Understand?"

Meredith studied me but said nothing. I couldn't read her.

So I said, "Look, it's really nice that you are concerned about Hank, but if you are waiting for him to break down and tell you how gut-wrenching lonely he is, you may wait a long, long time. Now let me ask you something. Are you interested in Hank?"

Meredith stiffened. "Professionally, of course, I am. It is appropriate for..."

Again I held up my 'stop' hand. "Don't give me the professional crap. You know what I mean."

Meredith didn't answer but instead, went back to staring out my slider.

"So you are," I said. "I thought so. And if I were Hank, I might be receptive to a little loving. It's been a while. So maybe you stop being Miss Know-It-All and warm up a bit. I mean, you're attractive and," I paused, unable to think of an inoffensive way of saying shapely, "all that. You care about him and I'll bet if you let him know, well, who knows? Something inside Hank may reawaken."

Meredith, without turning, asked, "Didn't you just say he's still in love with his wife and replacing her is not an option?"

"One step at a time," I said. "Don't get ahead of yourself. If I'm hearing you correctly, you're talking about maybe a date or two to see where it goes. Replacing someone's soul mate is way down the line. That whole topic is complex and I'm certainly no expert. And I doubt if in Hank's heart he'll ever replace his wife, my wife, but affairs of the heart are not additive. It's not like filling a bag with apples. The heart doesn't work that way. I think there may be room for another. I don't know for sure, but I'd bet I'm right. Now, if I don't get to the bathroom very soon, I'm going to wet my bed."

Meredith turned and looked at me, and then smiled. Then she turned and left my bedroom.

A few minutes later, bladder mercifully empty and still trying to sort out the conversation with Meredith, I made my way downstairs and poured myself a coffee. Hank, dressed in workman's coveralls with the name Superior HVAC Repair stenciled on his back, was standing in our latest addition to the house: an airy family room with cathedral ceiling, leather furniture, and a big screen TV.

He said, "I like the changes you made to the house."

It took me a few moments to absorb what he said. Of course! He had lived in this exact same house up until recently when his wife died. In his version of our lives, this room was still a screened in porch. The changes had been made after he moved away.

My brain was not yet fully awake yet so I was a bit slow on the uptake. I sat down and sipped my coffee. Hank came and joined me at the kitchen table.

I asked, "Is this weird for you? I mean, being in your house?"

He shrugged. "Not too bad. Some pangs. I find, looking around, you know, I miss my wife. Those were good days."

"I thought so," I replied. "I spend a fair amount of each day aching. That's what the farm is all about. Keeps me busy, which keeps the demons at bay."

Hank caught my eyes and nodded. '*Enough said*,' I thought. 'That's enough for now.' Then, changing the subject, asked, "What's with the coveralls?"

"Part of Meredith's plan," he said, grinning.

"And speaking of which," Meredith said while washing out the coffee cups at the sink, "It's time to go."

The day started off as the last one ended: with more surprises. When we left the house at 7:15 am and walked outside, there, parked in the driveway, was a Chevy van with the words Superior HVAC Repair painted on the sides.

"Where did this van come from?" I asked.

Meredith, climbing into the front seat, tersely said, "Our ship. Now please, get in. We don't want to be late."

"What?" I said, climbing into the back. Hank was in the driver's seat. "Where? This came from your *ship*? How did…"

"Later," Hank said, pressing a 'start' button. The van backed out of the driveway.

It took a few minutes before I realized what I was seeing: the van was driving itself. From the outside, it was no different from our run-of-the-mill working vehicles which are a common sight in our towns and cities. But from the inside, it was WAY different. First, Hank wasn't driving. It was driving itself. Yes, there was a steering wheel and all but it was essentially on cruise control: making turns, using the turn signal, merging with traffic, etc. I couldn't believe what I was seeing.

"What the hell?" I said.

"What?" Hank replied, turning around to look at me.

"What are you doing?" I yelled. "Watch…cars…look out…"

Hank laughed. "Oh this," he said. "Not to worry. This baby is really a safe driver. Much safer than any human."

"Just the same," I said. "Could you at least pretend you are driving and watch out the front windshield?"

"Fine," Hank said, again laughing. "Look ma, no hands!" He put his hands over his head.

Meredith peered at Hank over her reading glasses. "Put your hands on the wheel. Other drivers will become alarmed."

"Thank you," I said from the back seat. "How does this…?"

Hank caught my eyes in the rearview mirror and said, "Radar. Haven't you been in any cars with the backing-up radar?"

"No."

"Well, they're out there on some of the newer models. The car tells you when you are too close to an object. There is also an automatic parallel parking gizmo in some of your cars. Ford calls it their 'Active Park Assist.' Essentially, the car parks itself. This is simply the next evolution of the same thing…only the controlling device combines a sophisticated GPS navigator with the rolling radar. It's just around the corner for you guys here on this Earth. I think BMW will be the first to introduce…"

"Hank," Meredith interrupted with a fair degree of exasperation. "Please. We can't be divulging that sort of information."

Hank chuckled and said, "Hey Bart, for the record, disregard what I just said."

I sat back and said, "Consider it disregarded. Not to worry. BMW's are way out of my price range. But if this is to work, don't all cars have to have it to avoid each other?"

Hank scratched his head. "No, I don't think so. Take us for example. We are on auto right now, smoothly avoiding other vehicles and staying on the road. It takes a while before you totally trust the auto-drive system, but so far, so good."

I mulled over the idea of self-driving cars, and then asked, "Does this system avoid traffic? You know, are your roads choked with rush hour snarls?"

Hank shook his head. "Nope. In fact, we don't have many roads anymore. Our cars ride on a thin strip of magnetic tape. It's called electromagnetic suspension. Simply put, a thin rail is turned into an electromagnet, positive pole up. We build cars with a similar strip, turn it into an electromagnet, positive side down. The positives repel each other and the cars ride on electromagnetic suspension. You guys are already experimenting with this technology. I believe it's being used on some high-speed monorails. It's really a piece of cake. Think about it. No more tires, shocks, struts, roads to repair, highway bridges, gas stations, nothing. Just a thin strip leading from your garage to the nearby road, merging into the nearby highway, and away you go. Computers figure out the best route. No traffic. No hassles."

"Wow!" I muttered. "Can you zip right along?"

"Yep," Hank said. "Our passenger cars top out at about 180 km/ hr. while our trains and ground transports approach 700 km/hr. Think about it. No friction to slow you down."

I did think about it. It sounded great, like some fantasy land ride in Disney World. Then, coming back to Earth, I asked, "And what about this baby?" Next to me, in the space between the two bucket-style back seats, was a black tower of some sort with lots of blinking lights. It hummed and clicked.

"Is this your droid like the ones in Star Wars? You know, R2D2?"

Meredith turned her seat; it swiveled around and faced me. "Not as far from the truth as you might imagine. It is our activity monitor. It is known as an A.S. Shrike. We have already programmed today's plan and it will advise us as the events unfold as to the probability of success. In some cases, it will suggest a course correction. It's really quite handy." She was absently twirling her pen with her fingers.

"Help me Obi-Wan, you're my only hope," I said. Then, looking over my shoulder at a large red cart in the cargo bay, I asked, "And what's that? A Star Wars Land Speeder?"

"That's my toolbox," Hank said from the driver's seat. Then he added, "And please excuse my back. I'm pretending to be driving."

I looked again at the large red cart. It *was* a toolbox complete with caster wheels, drawers, extension cords, and all the other odds and ends piled high on your basic mechanic's tool chest.

"What are you planning to do?" I asked.

Hank said, "Hopefully, it will all be clear shortly." Then he added, "We're here."

We parked in the same spot we did the previous day, way in the back of the parking lot behind Wiggins's office. His white Mercedes had not yet arrived. Meredith grabbed her briefcase and said, "You two don't go anywhere. Bart, I'll give you a call at about 9:45 for your appointment." Then she opened the door and got out. Reaching in her briefcase, she extracted something that looked like a St. Christopher's medal on a silver chain. She handed it to me.

"Wear this," she said. "It's a listening device. It is tuned into the Shrike's frequency. Every word will be recorded. Plus, if you need us, we'll know about it and if necessary, move fast."

"Well," I said. "Thanks, I guess."

Meredith shot a glance at the office building, paused, and then said, "Time for me to go." She was back to twirling her pen.

"What's with the pen?" I asked.

Hank chuckled. "That's one of her nervous habits. She used to be a majorette in a marching band?"

"Really?"

"No," she said. "Let's focus on the job before us."

Hank saluted. "Yes, boss."

"May the force be with you," I said, trying to lighten up the tense mood.

She looked at me over her reading glasses, considering something for a moment – perhaps scolding me- but instead said, "I'll see you at 10 am." With that, she turned, crossed the lot, and entered the building.

Hank and I sat in silence for a few moments, and then he asked, "How are you doing with all this?"

I shrugged. "I wanted to go fishing last night. Maybe I'll get to go tonight."

"Are you worried about this whole take-down unexpectedly blowing up in our faces?"

I thought for a moment and said, "Before you arrived, I probably would have said yes. Now, with you showing up and convincing me you are a Xerox copy of me, and all the other stuff about wormholes and parallel universes," I shrugged, "Shit, this rumble with Wiggins pales in comparison."

Hank chuckled.

I said, "I've been thinking about this whole deal. Seems to make sense, what you're doing as cops and all that. But something else; why can't you give me a head's up about what's coming my way?"

"Because you might get it into your head to try to stop an event and in doing so, could end up doing something stupid. And maybe make it worse."

I frowned.

Hank drummed his fingers on the steering wheel. "We're still trying to figure out this your earth, our earth thing. We're under strict orders to not disclose anything to you, here on a parallel earth, which may alter the course of events."

"But what about that beach sand whatever it was you guys quoted?"

Hank shrugged. "Good question. That fact is; we simply don't know how much we are screwing things up by meddling in a parallel earth. Let's take our wives for example."

I raised my eyebrows.

"They both died but it was three days apart. What if I would have contacted you after my wife died, and warned you of the impending event. What would you have done?"

I sucked in my breath but said nothing.

"Exactly," Hank said. "What *could* you have done? And then what?"

We sat in silence for a moment, each alone in our thoughts. What would I have done? Locked her in the house? Taken away her drivers' license? How would that have changed our lives?

Then Hank spoke, snapping me back to the present. "And you asked why we picked you? Well, simple. In this case with Wiggins, you are the main man because he's your neighbor. And yes, we checked you out just to be sure we could work together."

"Work together? Why couldn't we? I mean, if you can't work with yourself..."

"Precisely. But don't forget, some people are their own worst enemies. In yet another earth, something you know nothing about, I can't work with me. We clash."

My mouth opened and for a moment, no sound came out. Finally, "Another planet Earth? In another parallel dimension? No shit?"

"No shit."

Silence.

After a few beats, I said, "Meredith really cares about you, you know."

Nothing.

"And you'll never be able to replace your wife, but..."

Still nothing. For the first time, I noticed the deep wrinkles emanating from Hank's eyes. Unconsciously, I touched my own face, feeling for the same lines. They were there.

"And I'm not sure any of us should be alone, and caring about someone else won't diminish your feelings for your wife."

Hank continued to stare.

"Just thought I'd put in my two cents."

After a moment, Hank said softly, "I'll think about it."

Again we sat quietly, then, changing the subject, I asked, "Can you tell me more about your spaceship? Especially the drive system?"

Hank smiled and some of the wrinkles disappeared. He said, "Well, in spite of what Meredith says, I'll tell you what I know." Hank explained how the device that turns off the force of gravity works and in fact, seemed quite simple. It requires setting up a force field around an object, such as a spaceship, then energizing it to the point where gravity is neutralized. Force fields are nothing new. We have been using electricity to make electromagnets...a force field...for years.

"Then," Hank said, "we zap this force field with a whole lot of energy which neutralizes gravity for the object inside the force field. Get it?"

"I think I do," I replied.

"Well," Hank continued. "Here's the trick. The force field has poles, you know, north and south?"

"Okay," I said.

"And at the poles, it can be opened at will. Like opening a window in this big, gravity-neutralizing 'beach ball' surrounding the spaceship. And this opening window, which we call a porthole, continues to feel the gravity of whatever it is opened to. So if we open the porthole and the moon is up there, the moon's gravity will tug us up off the planet Earth and away we go."

"You're kidding!" I said.

"Nope. Works like a charm. Pop open a porthole facing the sun or the moon and you've got liftoff. It's smooth and gentle, like going up in a hot air balloon."

"Okay," I said. "So you get pulled up off the ground and you're heading to the moon. How then do you keep from crashing into the moon, or worse yet, the sun?"

"Close the porthole and turn on the ion exchange engine. This little fusion powered baby pushes out a steady stream of ions and we, being weightless and frictionless, are propelled the other way. Remember one of Newton's Laws...every action results in a reaction? Well, that's us."

"Fast?"

"Nope. Not at first. But because the acceleration, small as it is, is constant and there's no friction from air once you leave the atmosphere, we really get cranking in no time. After about two hours, we're going at cruising speed."

"Which is?"

"About 500,000 km/hour."

"Holy shit!" I exclaimed. "That will make the moon in what... about an hour?"

"Yep," Hank replied. "And Jupiter in 6 days...if we don't use gravity assist."

I mused, "I think I've heard of that. That's using the gravitational field of the planets to pull you along, like that carnival ride, Crack the Whip. Right?"

"That's the one," Hank replied. "We use Jupiter to fling us out into the Ort Cloud, towards the Wormhole."

I smiled. "You're making all this up, right?"

"Come along!" Hank said. "And see for yourself."

"Can I?"

"No. Sorry."

At about 9:15, Wiggins arrived, parked his car and went into the office.

"There's your man," Hank said.

I nodded and then asked. "Fusion?"

"What?" Hank replied.

"Your spaceship's ion exchange driver. You said it was energized by fusion."

"Oh that, yes."

"And when did fusion come along?"

Hank thought for a moment and scratched his head. "Don't know. Before I was born. Sometime in the late thirties, I think."

"Holy shit," I mumbled. "You guys are way, way ahead of us."

"Only in science and technology," Hank replied. "The rest is about the same."

After a moment of mulling this over, I asked, "And you have a fusion reactor on your spaceship? You know, the one that's in my backyard, hovering over my garden?"

"Two actually," Hank replied. "One for the force field and one that drives the exchange system."

"Well that should make my tomatoes grow," I said. "And what do you use for fuel?"

"Deuterium – Tritium. This is found in…"

"Water," I interrupted. "And where are you getting water in outer space? There are no gas stations floating around out there. Or are there?"

Hank smiled and nodded. "Yep. You've got one orbiting in Earth's orbit on the other side of the sun."

"Come on," I said.

"They are called Trojans. Both asteroids and comets can be captured by planets and pulled into their orbits where sometimes, they remain relatively stationary with respect to the planet Earth. Haven't you heard of them?"

"Maybe," I said.

"Well, there's a big ice ball comet, about one hundred, eighty degrees around Earth's orbit which is where we pick up our water for fuel. You haven't discovered it yet because it's always on the other side of the sun from Earth. We're in the process of building an unmanned docking station on it as we speak. It's like having an Exxon Station out there!"

At 9:35, the black AS Shrike said, in a mechanical monotone voice, "All is well. Wiggins buys the story. He has been told Bart will be his 10 am appointment."

"Wow," I said. "So that's how you do it. But what about cosmic rays? Aren't they a problem?"

"Not as long as the force field is energized."

We fell silent and waited.

At 9:50, the Shrike again squawked, "Time for Bart's meeting."

I felt my stomach tighten. I looked at Hank and said, "Well, here goes."

Hank extended his hand, and said, "Go get 'em." We shook hands and off I went.

Chapter Sixteen

The Almond Brothers vs The Beatles

I entered the office. Meredith was sitting behind the desk, reading a memo of some sort. "May I help you?" she asked.

Puzzled, I looked at her.

She looked back at me, her eyes wide with exasperation, and repeated, "May I help you?"

"Ah...um...yes," I stammered. "I have a 10 o'clock appointment with Wiggins?"

Meredith glared at me over her glasses. "And who should I tell MISTER Wiggins you are?"

I nodded and thought, 'okay, okay, I get the point.' "Please let MISTER Wiggins know Bart Russell is here for his 10 appointment."

Meredith pressed the intercom button. "Mister Wiggins, your 10 o'clock is here."

The door to Wiggins's inner office flew open and there stood Ryan Wiggins: wide smile, splotchy red face, curly blond hair. His Hawaiian shirt was unbuttoned one button too many, three garish gold chains hanging around his neck. His belly stretched the shirt like an overfilled balloon around the waistline. "Well, hello neighbor!" he exclaimed a little too loudly. "This is a pleasant surprise. Come in, come in."

I did as I was told and entered his office.

It was a bit smaller than the reception area but unlike the 'on-the-cheap' decor of the outer office, this one was lavishly, garishly, over-decorated. The walls were covered with official-looking diplomas and certificates, numerous framed pictures (all with a smiling Wiggins at the center, arm around this dignitary or that famous person) took up all available wall space. A collection of Boston sports teams bobbleheads were lined up on one window sill, and jammed upon the other window was a huge aquarium. One large fish swam in slow circles, pausing each time it came around to hungrily eye the office occupants. Three overstuffed leather chairs were jammed in, one behind a gargantuan highly polished oak desk, the other two awaiting guests. A full set of golf clubs stood at ready in the far corner, and a full-size rendition of a bronze nude woman stood in the near corner, arms uplifted, clearly serving as a coat/hat rack, an umbrella hanging from one of her over-large nipples, Boston Red Sox hat perched on the other. In the other corner was a small refrigerator which also served as a bookcase.

Wiggins noticed me gawking at his nude woman coat rack and said, "What do you think? I picked her up for a steal at Jack and Jill's Nightclub's going out of business sale. Great, isn't she?"

I was trying to think of how I could verbalize my extreme repulsion of this woeful attempt at eclectic decoration that belonged in the bathroom of some seedy fraternity house, but was at a loss for words.

"Yeah, really classy," I mumbled. "And what's with the fish?"

"That's Mr. Teeth," Wiggins said enthusiastically. "He's a full grown Piranha from the Amazon River. Isn't he lovely?"

"Yeah, if you like creatures that gang up on you and rip you apart. A real charmer."

"Well, sit down, sit down," Wiggins exclaimed, ignoring my not so complimentary comments. "Make yourself comfortable."

We both took our seat and Wiggins, smile about to break his phony face, asked, "So Bart, to what do I owe this truly wonderful surprise visit?"

I gritted my teeth and thought, 'if I jumped up, I could hit him five good shots before he knew what was going on,' but instead said evenly, "I'm here to hire you to manage my retirement funds.

"I am so-o-o-o honored," Wiggins said. "This is indeed…"

I held up my hand in the stop position. Thankfully, Wiggins stopped in mid-sentence.

"Wiggins," I began, "Let's get one thing straight. I don't like you and you don't like me so let's cut the shit, okay? I'm here to make money and for some reason, you seem to be good at this business of investing. So let's get down to it and stop wasting your time and mine. How does this work?"

Wiggins sat back in his chair. The smile instantly vanished from his pudgy face but to his credit, he didn't look shocked or surprised at my candor. He licked his lips and then nodded.

"I see," he said. "Fine. I like direct." Then he leaned forward, and folded his hands on his desk and began. "Fine," he repeated. "Here's my pitch. My fees and the terms of our agreement are non-negotiable. First, you pay me fifty-grand up front. This will be either cash or a personal check made out to my offshore corporation. That's my cost, no refunds on this. Then I invest a minimum of $500,000 for a five-year term. Now, you can have every cent of the $500,000 back at any time. Just say the word. Even if the stock market takes a dive. You can have all your money back, except the fifty –grand of course. As your nest egg grows, I take 25% of the profit. This is done annually, on the one year anniversary of the investment. In other words, you make 75% of the gains with no downside. There is no risk to you. Again and I repeat, you can take your full investment nugget out at any time. Every cent. If you choose to stay the course for the five-year contractual arrangement, you can then take out the full investment amount plus 75% of the profits. And as I'm sure you know, I've been averaging 47% growth per year. No one has ever opted out. In short, my clients are doing very, very, well."

It was my time to sit back in my chair. "Let me get this straight," I said. "For fifty grand, you take my retirement nugget and guarantee the principal no matter what the stock market does?"

Wiggins sat back and opened his arms wide. "I'll bet the big brokers can't match my offer. Plus, I absolutely guarantee growth that will beat the market. Absolute money-back guarantee!"

I sat quietly for a long two minutes, giving the appearance of thinking about the terms of the agreement. Then said, "All right, what do we do next?"

Wiggins opened his top drawer and extracted a folder, from which he took out a handful of forms. He pushed them across the table to me.

"These are," he said, "IRS forms. We have to keep everything above board. We keep Uncle Sam apprised of all our investments." He smiled his full-faced, toothy smile for my benefit.

"Except for the fifty-grand?" I said. "Right? That's just for Uncle Ryan."

The smile again vanished from his face. "Fill out the top sections only," he said, ignoring my question. "Want some water?" He got up and went to the refrigerator in the corner.

"Sure," I replied, reading the paperwork. These were the usual I9 tax forms. I picked up a pen and as is my habit, began to hum to myself.

Wiggins took our two bottles of water, placing one on my side of the desk. He then went over and stood by the window, absently staring out while I filled out the forms.

"That song," Wiggins said. "That's my favorite. Ramblin' Man by the Beatles."

I shook my head no. "Allman Brothers."

"Pardon me?" Wiggins asked. "The Beatles recorded Ramblin' Man on their Abbey Road album."

I sat back. "Like hell. It was the Allman Brothers on their..."

Behind me, the door flew open and Meredith stepped in. In her hand was the oversized Android. She pointed it at Wiggins, pressed a button, and zap! A stream of red light flew out of the device, missed Wiggins wide left by about two feet, and smacked the Jerry 'Rem Dog' Remy bobblehead, blasting the bobbing head to pieces, the body falling off the window sill.

Wiggins stood by the window, mouth agape. He stared at the broken souvenir then glared at Meredith, and then shouted, "SOMETHING IS WRONG WITH YOUR PHONE!"

Unfazed, Meredith pushed a few more buttons, aimed the phone and again, a stream of red light shot out and again, missed Wiggins, this time wide right by two feet. The recipient of this errant shot was Mr. Teeth, the piranha, who flew up out of the aquarium, did two and a half flips, then fell to the floor, never to bite anything ever again.

Wiggins screamed. "MR. TEETH! OH MY GOD!" Then he grabbed a six iron from his golf bag, advanced upon Meredith, and shrieked, "GIVE ME THAT PHONE BEFORE YOU HURT..."

This time, Meredith didn't miss. The third stream of red light hit Wiggins square in the chest. He staggered backward a few steps, hit one of the guest chairs, and fell over backward, his legs sticking skyward, his tongue lolling comically out of his mouth.

I jumped to my feet and looked at Meredith. "WHAT THE HELL ARE YOU DOING?" I shouted.

Meredith walked around the chair, stooped, and with some effort, rolled Wiggins over onto his back. "He'll be alright. He's out for about an hour," she said standing. "The Beatles made famous Ramblin' Man on my planet Earth. The Allman Brothers did it here on your Earth."

I blinked a few times at Meredith, and then it hit me. "WHAT? YOU JUST SHOT HIM WITH YOUR LASER BEAM BECAUSE HE GUESSED THE WRONG MUSIC ARTIST? I *ALWAYS* GUESS THE WRONG ARTIST!"

"Stop yelling and go meet Hank at the freight elevator," Meredith said. "And yes, he made a tell-tale mistake with the incorrect artist so I temporarily stunned him with the Taser app on my phone. And you have nothing to worry about, that was merely static electricity, not a laser beam. And this is why." She walked over to the refrigerator and gave it a pull. It rolled out from the wall far enough to reveal an upright computer. "This is the IBM 245 we have been looking for. He had it well shielded behind the refrigerator. Quite ingenious I might add. Now if you would, please go give Hank a hand."

Mechanically, my legs began moving. My brain was still in 'trying to absorb' mode while I walked out of the office, across the hall, to the freight elevator. After about a minute, the bell 'dinged' and the door swung open. Out came Hank in his coveralls pushing the rolling toolbox.

"Hey mister," Hank said with a smile. "Want your air conditioner fixed?"

Still stunned, I walked with Hank. Together, we pushed the over-large tool chest to Wiggins's office.

Walking into the reception office, Hank turned to me and said, "Turn off the lights in this outer office, lock the front door, and then come on back."

Again I did as I was told and by the time I joined Hank and Meredith in the inner sanctum, they were running diagnostics on the IBM 245.

Hank looked up. "Bingo," he said. "We have our man. Now, give me a hand."

While Meredith fiddled with the IBM, Hank walked over to the cart, turned a key and the top opened out like a cigar box.

"Help me lift our friend here," Hank said.

Still, in an information overload daze, I did as I was told. Me on the feet, Hank on the arms, we lifted fat Wiggins up and into the tool chest. He almost fit. We had to fold him up a bit to get all of his appendages inside. Then, Meredith stood, walked over to the chest and zapped Wiggins again.

She looked at me and noting the alarm on my face, said, "He's fine. He'll be out for about eight hours. We'll be far, far, away by the time he awakens."

Hank chimed in. "And don't worry. This box has many well-hidden ventilation holes. We need to keep him alive for a while. Once the ICC Commission gets thru with him, he may wish we didn't."

I plopped down in one of the chairs. Hank went about the business of securing the rolling cart. Meredith unplugged the IBM, removed a folded cloth case from her briefcase, and began fitting it over the IBM, clearly making it ready for travel.

"Um," I said, "Excuse me but what's going to happen when ole' Wiggins here doesn't come home tonight?"

Hank pulled a large envelope from inside his coveralls. "I almost forgot," he said, then tossed it to me. "Take a look."

I opened the envelope and took out some large glossy photographs. They were all of a disgustingly out of shape, stark naked Ryan Wiggins and some shapely, voluptuous, not-at-all disgusting nude young woman in a variety of sexual positions. Both participants were looking toward the camera. They appeared to be posing.

"Where the hell did…" I asked.

Hank shrugged. "Photoshop."

"So these aren't real?" I asked.

Hank paused and looked at me. With great earnest, he said, "Never, never, believe what you see in a picture." Then he motioned to the desk. "Put those back in the envelope and put the whole thing in his top center drawer. Put it under some papers like he was trying to hide it."

"Unbelievable!" I muttered.

Meredith took the photos and envelope from me and did as Hank suggested. She said, "After a day or two, the police will be notified about Wiggins being gone. They will come here to snoop around and find these pictures. They will then put two and two together and tell his wife he has likely run off with another woman."

"Wow!" I said. "I wonder how she'll take the…"

"Take the news?" Hank said, finishing my sentence. "She'll pretend to be mortified but really, she'll be ecstatic."

"How do you…" I began.

"We've been watching," Hank replied. "Mrs. Wiggins has been spending frequent afternoons with the hunk of a delivery man who works for that bring-to-your-door dry cleaning company. Haven't you noticed the truck in your neighbor's driveway? Quite a lot of dry cleaning I'd say?" Hank said with a grin.

"As a matter of fact I..." I said.

"Plus," Meredith cut in, "She has already been making some plans with a divorce lawyer in Newfield. Three calls last week alone."

"How do you..." I began.

Meredith said matter-of-factly, "The AS Shrike in our vehicle has been listening."

Hank closed the lid of the tool chest and said, "She'll be thrilled. First, she'll be a rich widow free from this clown. Second, she'll hire some brain to track down Wiggins's private account in the Cayman's. If she can get her hands on that pile, you'll never see her again. And just think; no messy divorce. Just another missing husband for society to gossip about. Not to worry. This is going to be a very, very good day for Mrs. Wiggins. Now, let's get out of here."

Meredith took a look around and reassembled the office. She took the appointment and address books, Wiggins's phone, and laptop computer. As they left, she turned off the lights and closed the door.

As we arrived at the freight elevator, the door swung open and a man in coveralls stepped out. "Who the hell are you and what are you doing here?" he asked, clearly agitated. "I don't recall having any problems with our air conditioning."

Meredith stepped forward and politely asked, "And you are?"

He crossed his arms across his chest and stood his ground. "Nope. I asked you first."

Just then, the other elevator door swung open and out stepped Caitlyn with a "C." She held up a badge: "FBI. Special Agent Caitlyn Mendosa, Boston office."

Chapter Seventeen

The Turkey is Cooked

Meredith extracted a badge from her briefcase, held it up, and said, "Federal Attorney Meredith McNally, ICC, Dallas Office. We just apprehended Ryan Wiggins and intend to bring multiple racketeering charges against him, and possibly three first degree murder charges as well."

I was tempted to whisper to Hank; 'might be Dallas all right but not Dallas from *this* universe' but refrained due to the fact I was really scared.

Caitlyn screwed up her pudgy face. "You just bagged Wiggins?"

Meredith nodded.

Caitlyn snapped her gum a few times, thinking. "Can you make it stick?"

Meredith put away her badge. "Mr. Wiggins will not be returning to this office again. Ever."

Caitlyn pointed at the guy in coveralls who got off the freight elevator. "That's field agent Carter. We've been watching Wiggins for almost a year and have gotten nowhere. Not so much as a parking ticket. We know he's dirty but don't have anything but a gut feeling. At this rate, we'd never nail him. We've been looking for an excuse to walk away from this one…and you just gave it to us. He's all yours."

Then she looked at Hank and me. "And who are those guys? The Bobbsey Twins?"

Hank waved. "Hank Russell, Federal Apprehension Agent.

I just waved meekly, holding my breath and hoping there would be no more questions.

Caitlyn smiled and said to her field agent, "Well Carter, this is our lucky day. We can finally close this one." Then she turned to Meredith. "With all the budget cuts and sequestration crap, we're way too thin. If you want this turkey, he's all yours. Just get him off my turf."

Meredith said, "We are on our way."

Caitlyn said to her field agent, "Let's go pack up our toys." Then for our benefit, added, "We bugged Wiggins's office and need our hardware back. Again, budget cuts."

As we rode down the elevator, I asked, "Why didn't the FBI chick..."

"Caitlyn Mendosa" Meredith corrected.

"Yeah, her, why didn't she ask who the ICC is?"

Meredith smiled. "Have you any idea how many agencies your federal government employs? There is no way any one person can be familiar with them all."

"Good point," I said. Then I asked, "But what if she didn't buy it? You know, what if she challenged you?"

Hank opened his coveralls. There, resting in a holster was an oversized Android. He nodded towards Meredith and said, "Unlike Annie Oakley here, I hit my target the first time."

Chapter Eighteen

Good Bye, For Now

While the van drove itself back to my house, Meredith and Hank busied themselves with a detailed checklist of 'to do's'. Pensively, I sat in the back seat and stared out the window.

Upon arrival, instead of pulling into my driveway, Hank directed the vehicle to drive itself around my house, out back to the far end of my garden.

When we arrived at a predetermined location that seemed to be okay with Hank and Meredith, they told the car to shut down, which it obediently did. We all got out and stretched. Even though it wasn't noon yet, the day was getting hot already.

Meredith took a step towards me and extended her hand. "I want to thank you," she said, with a genuine smile, "For the help. I'm not sure this would have gone so smoothly without you."

"What? You're leaving?" I asked. "You just got here."

Meredith again smiled. "We have to go. Our cargo is, shall we say, time sensitive."

"How about you come in for a quick beer?" I asked.

Meredith extended her hand again. "Thanks, but we really have to go."

We all shook hands and I mumbled something like, "It's been my pleasure."

Then she looked at Hank, winked, and then said, "Why don't you two jokers take a short walk. I have to program our Shrike for departure."

Hank motioned with his head for me to follow. Taking this all in, I wondered 'now what.'

We walked over to the row of blackberries and silently picked a few. Then, Hank, glancing back to make sure Meredith wasn't looking or close enough to overhear our conservation, said in a quiet voice, "Listen. You really helped you know. Meredith is a master of understatement. We couldn't have pulled this off without your help. And through all these confusing thirty-six hours, you never once asked 'what's in it for me?'"

I shrugged. "I guess I forgot to."

"Yeah, bullshit," Hank said. "You just got sucked along and in the end, realized we are for real and maybe, this was the right thing to do."

I shrugged again and said, "Yeah, I guess so." Then I asked the question that had popped in and out of my head several times but I never got around to asking it. "Where's the Wiggins that use to live over there?" I pointed in the direction of my neighbor's house.

Hank shook his head. "Don't know, but we'll find out. He's most likely long gone."

"Gone?"

"Dead."

Meredith waved to Hank who held up his index finger, asking for one more minute. Then he put his hand on my shoulder and turned me away from Meredith. "I got to go so I'll be quick. If I were you, I'd buy some IBM stock."

"I already own 200 shares…"

Hank interrupted. "I mean *REALLY A LOT* of IBM stock. Very soon, they're going to buy a company the rhymes with moogle, then the new joint company is going to buy SpaceX, and then some really cool things are going to happen. Got it? Understand?"

I nodded yes and we walked back to where Meredith was waiting. Much to my surprise, she gave me a brief but warm hug, and then got in the van. Hank reached around me and gave me a manly sort of bear hug. He shot a glance back at my house, nodded, then climbed into the van. He rolled down the window and said, "I almost forgot. Would you be willing to do this again? Ole Wiggins here isn't the only criminal from our Earth that's living here. What do you think?"

"Absolutely not!" Then I smiled and said, "Let me think about it."

Hank waved and said, "Well then, it's goodbye, for now. Now please stand back."

I returned the wave and stood back.

The van started up and from somewhere over my tomatoes, the faint hum of a motor running could be heard, followed by the unmistakable sound of a hydraulic lift yawning open. The van rolled forward and vanished, followed by the same hydraulic sound. This time, the sound was that of a loading ramp closing up. Then there were some faint sounds resembling those of computers starting up, followed by a gentle whooshing noise. Followed by silence.

I waited for a minute or two then stooped and picked up a stone. I gave it a heave into the empty space where their spaceship had hovered for the last two weeks. This time the stone passed through and fell harmlessly back to Earth over there somewhere.

I probably should have stood there for a while, contemplating what I had just experienced. After all, it isn't every day you get to… oh well, you know the story. No need for me to repeat myself. But instead, I had an important errand to run. I had to go buy a whole lot of IBM stock.

REBOOT

The following are the first seven pages from my next book, **REBOOT**. Consider this a preview of coming attractions.

Chapter One

Black Tuesday

"Your wife is having an affair with my lover."

Roberto 'Rob' Santos looked up into the smooth face of a tall, thin black man. "Excuse me?"

The man pulled up the mink collar of his full-length black leather coat. "I said your wife Nicole is having an affair with my lover, William. And it's been going on for more than a year."

Rob studied the man standing in front of him outside Boston's Finest Coffee shop on Newbury Street. It was snowing lightly and the sidewalk was crowded with bundled-up people going to work on this typical January Tuesday morning. The man had huge brown eyes, impressive diamond earrings, and gold wire-rimmed glasses. He was much taller than Rob, who was an even six feet, but he appeared to be thin and slight of build. His leather coat hung off his shoulders as if attached to a stick figure. Snowflakes alighted on his perfectly coiffed hair, pausing before melting.

As was his habit, Rob Santos began each day by ducking into Boston's Finest for a coffee and a *Wall Street Journal*, which were always waiting for him by the time he reached the counter. The routine is always the same: Karen, the ageless owner flashes her disarming, ice-melting smile - hands Rob his paper and coffee - he hands her a ten dollar bill - she pushes the change his way - he points at the Jimmy Fund jar - he says "God bless you," - and he leaves.

What made this not a typical January Tuesday morning was the tall, pretty, black man standing in his path.

Rob Santos continued to gape up. "Wha...What did you say?"

The black man's eyes filled. "My William has taken his love elsewhere. You may know him as your wife's personal trainer. I know him as my reason for living. And now..." Tears flowed down the man's smooth cheeks. Then, without another word, he turned and swiftly strode away.

The black man's words kept replaying in Rob's head as he sat in his downtown office. Like all seeds planted in fertile soil, the idea of Nicole having an affair began to sprout. Yes, she did have a personal trainer named William, and yes, she had been training under his instruction for what? At least two years now. And sex with his wife of sixteen years had steadily fallen off from *very infrequent* to *extremely infrequent*. And when it did happen, it was not exactly wild and crazy. Still, there was nothing unusual about that. Most of his friends complained of the same thing. And yes, his wife spent one weekend a month at a health spa. Was this a cover for a weekend with her lover? Until this very moment, he had never doubted any part of her story. How could he check up on her without being too obvious? Then an idea popped into his head: call the spa in the Berkshires to verify first, that it exists, and second, that Nicole actually goes there. Rob scrolled through his Outlook emails and bingo...there it was. Contact information for the spa in case he needed to reach her when she was away. He dialed the number.

"Good morning. This is the Berkshire Beauty Retreat."

Rob sighed in relief. It *did* exist. He said, "Hello, my name is Rob Santos. My wife, Nicole Santos, spent the weekend of December sixteenth at your spa. She has misplaced her wallet and we were wondering if, by any chance, she left it there?"

"This is the answering service for the Berkshire Beauty Resort. The facility is closed for the season. It will reopen in April. Shall I get a message to the owner?"

"Closed? When did it close?"

"Right after Columbus Day weekend, sir."

"You mean it was not open, let's see…" he scrolled backward, through the Outlook calendar. "You mean it was not open November 17 and 18, or on October 15 and 16?"

The woman was silent for a moment. Then, with a definite note of apology to her tone, she said, "I'm sorry sir, but no. They are closed for the winter."

Rob closed his door for the lunch hour and stared out the window at the Boston skyline. One advantage of being a Senior Vice President with a corner office is that you can close the door for privacy without raising suspicion. The door remained closed until, at two-thirty, a loud knock brought Rob back from his desolation.

He sat up, straightened his tie, and shouted, "Come in."

The door opened cautiously and in stepped Manuela, his staff assistant. She closed the door behind her. Manuela Gonzalez was very pregnant and looked decidedly uncomfortable. A striking woman with coal black hair and eyes to match, perhaps thirty, she was due to go out on maternity leave in three weeks. There were whispers around the office wondering if she would make it that long. Waddling across the office, she took the guest chair in front of Rob's desk. She had a file folder in her hand. She peered at her boss, tilting her head slightly, a puzzled look on her face. "Que pasa, boss?"

"Having a bad day."

"You missed the staff meeting."

Rob put his head into his hands and moaned. "Oh shit."

"No worries," Manuela said. "I covered for you. Got a minute?"

"What am I going to do without you?"

Manuela stared at her plump fingers. "That's why I wanted to talk with you."

Rob adjusted his glasses. "Okay…shoot."

She handed the folder she'd been holding to Rob. "In today's meeting, the budget summaries were passed out. Take a look."

Distractedly, Rob flipped through the folder. He shrugged.

Manuela stood and rubbed her lower back. "Look at the bottom of page two."

Rob did. "JESUS CHRIST!"

"Exactly!" Manuela replied, wincing with pain. "What do you think's going on?"

Rob adjusted his glasses again and studied the page. "Our expense account is frozen. What's this all about?"

Manuela plopped herself back into the chair. "I asked the same question and was told: 'irregularities, violation of company policies, just cause for an internal investigation', a bunch of vague garbage."

Rob removed his glasses. "That's bullshit. I review all the expense charges when they come in. My guys are straight shooters. Whose account are they looking at? Any specifics?"

"Confidential, confidential." Manuela said. "It's the ole' *let's hide it in the cloak of confidentiality* trick. How convenient."

Rob was coming alive. "We can't do our job unless our lobbyists can wine and dine the politicians at the state house."

"Exactly," she said again. After a pause, she said, "Now, let me ask you a question. And don't take this personally. I'm a short timer so I can be bold. Plus this kid in my belly is a really big pain right now, so I'm a little short on patience and diplomacy."

"Ask away."

"Who do you think is behind this - and why?"

Rob shrugged. "My guess would be one of those nerds in internal auditing."

"Maybe," she said. "But maybe not." She stared at Rob for a beat then asked, "How old are you?"

"What? What does that have to do with…?"

"No really. How old are you? And how many years have you worked here?"

Rob sighed. "Let's see, I'm forty-six and have been here for…" he looked at the ceiling for a moment, "twenty-two years. Why?"

"Because," Manuela said, with some heat, "you're pretty damn naïve. By now, if you haven't figured out how the wind blows in this place, you're hopeless. Don't get me wrong, I've never met a more considerate man, and as a boss, you're the best. But Goddammit, can't you see what's going on?"

Rob opened his hands and said, "What are you…?"

Manuela leaned back in the chair. "Come around here and help me put my feet up."

Rob did as he was told. He removed her shoes and lifted her swollen feet up to the desk. "Better?"

She nodded. "Haven't you wondered why you got this promotion last year?"

"Because I'm the best there is at corporate tax code?"

"That had nothing to do with it." Manuela was rubbing her bulbous belly. "Think, Amigo, think. You're married to the CEO's beautiful daughter. Life is good for you. You're gorgeous, with a great bod. All the women dream of jumping in the sack with you. You're the golden boy. Then the old man croaks, and pronto, you get promoted to Senior Vice President. But the project you're given, influencing politicians to simplify the tax code, is impossible. The Democrats in Boston will never simplify *anything* and let's face it, they own this state. Then, out of the blue, your discretionary expense funds are frozen. Now, you can't do your job. You can't possibly succeed. You've been set up to fail!"

Rob got up and walked to the window, staring out, but seeing nothing. After a while, in a quiet voice, he asked, "Okay, let's assume you are right, and I have to admit, what you say makes sense. But why?"

Manuela continued rubbing her belly. "Because our new president, known around the water cooler as Cleavage Claire, hated your father-in-law."

Rob turned around. "What?"

"Your father-in-law was a pompous, self-absorbed pig, and you know it. He promoted Clair Anderson to President so he could keep a close watch on her tits. He thought he was getting some kind of 1950's secretary with high heels and red lipstick. But Claire had other ideas. She wanted to be God. So, both parties were disappointed. Claire refused to be poked and prodded, and your father-in-law wouldn't take no for an answer. The results? They fought incessantly and despised each other. If he hadn't dropped dead, he certainly would have trumped up a reason to fire her skinny ass. You didn't know this?"

Rob shook his head. "How do you know it?"

She shrugged. "How do you *not* know it? And now, guess what? She's going to take out her revenge on you because you are the old man's boy."

"No shit?"

"No shit."

Rob shook his head. "I had no idea." He went back to staring at the Boston skyline. "How long do you think I have?"

Manuela lowered her feet from the desk, and slowly stood up. "I have to pee. I'd bet you'll be fired at the end of the second quarter. You got less than six months. Maybe less."

Later on that fateful Tuesday, a beleaguered and browbeaten Rob Santos went home early to his lavish home in Carlisle and was surprised to find his two daughters at home. They should have been in their dormitory at Philips Andover.

"What are you guys doing home?"

Danielle, the sixteen-year-old, shrugged and said, "Mom will tell you." Then she and her sister left the kitchen and headed upstairs to their rooms.

Rob saw the message button glowing on the house phone. It was the Dean of Students from Philips.

"Hello, Dean Mason? This is Rob Santos returning your phone call."

At the conclusion of the call, he ran up the stairs, two at a time, and pushed open his daughters' bedroom door.

"Can't you knock?" Amy, the fifteen-year-old snapped.

"You've been expelled!" Rob said, trying to keep the rising anger out of his voice. "You both have! For bullying."

"Whatever," Danielle said dismissively.

"WHATEVER?" Rob yelled. "This is serious. The Dean told me the school is considering involving the police. Who is Carol Murrow and what the hell have you two been doing?"

"Listen, *Roberto*," Amy began.

"Roberto? Whatever happened to *Dad?*" He paused, breathing hard, trying to regain his composure. "The dean says you two have seriously hurt some of your classmates."

Amy muttered, "Dweebs."

Danielle, without taking her eyes off her iPhone, said, "Mom said you'd take their side."

"THEIR SIDE? WHAT THE…" He stopped, paused, took a few steadying deep breaths, and then asked, "She knows about this?"

Amy said, "Well, yeah."

Rob again paused, and then asked, "Where is your mother?"

Danielle, who was texting, ignored her father. Amy, also involved with her iPhone, mumbled, "At the gym, of course."

Rob thought about going on a rampage and smashing their iPhones, computers, and all the rest of the expensive shit they lived within. Then he thought about smashing the empty skulls of those two insolent, spoiled, brats…but regained control. That was when he realized he despised them both, his own children. He had been excluded from their lives a long time ago. And now, it was painfully true: these two young women were evil.

Without another word, he stepped into the hallway and quietly closed their bedroom door.

Artwork

The leading illustrations for *The Innkeeper* and *The Door in the Tree*, as well as the cover, were created by Gina Noelle Ash.

By pleasant happenstance, Gina's husband plays center field on my softball team, and when I mentioned I was looking for an artist, voila!

As it turns out, Gina is an accomplished, award-winning artist. Her website is www.GinaNoelleAsh.com. Take a look! You'll be impressed.

Thank you, Gina!

Questions for Group Discussion

As a young lad in junior high school, some of my textbooks – geography, and history if I recall – had sections in the rear of each chapter, entitled something like "Topics for Further Study." These were a series of question about the material covered in the preceding chapter, designed to inspire and encourage the student to dig deeper into these topics. I remember thinking, "Who in their right mind would want to do this?" There were scores of far more interesting items to 'ponder,' such as baseball, fishing, and some of the girls who sat close by. Nonetheless, many textbooks came equipped with such questions.

Now, a half-century later, here I am writing such a section for my book. In the unlikely circumstance you decide to use my book as the focus of a group discussion, the following are suggested discussion points.

Have fun!

- *The Innkeeper.* What age would you return at? Would you marry the same person? Would you behave as did Judy Johnson and Linda Vincent? Hmm. What's the first thing you would do as a younger you? Perhaps as important; what would you not do again?
- *Nasty Jake.* When it comes to barnyard animals of any sort, count me out. I've wrestled with pigs, been pecked and bit by roosters and geese, and been butted by goats. How about you? Got any tales of adventures at Farmer Brown's yard?

+ *Joey Lonzack.* The death of anyone close is tough, but when a childhood pal passes, it forever remains a mystery. Have you ever wondered, as I did, why them and not you? Are we guided by some sort of master plan, or is life just the roll of a dice?

+ *A Kiss is Just a Kiss.* Can you remember your first smooch? Dad, wherever you might be; I sure do wish you would have taken me aside when I was starting to grow whiskers and given me a few pointers on the fine art of kissing. Then again, maybe we all have to go through the embarrassing first tries – and failures - to make us good at it.

+ *The Door in the Tree.* What's behind the door for *you?* Is it positive or negative? Does it terrify or delight you? Hmm.

+ *The Mysterious Christmas Package.* Where would you go with this scenario? Would you share with your spouse? I suspect some of us would have tossed the package into the trash and slammed the cover shut. Another consideration: would you be offended? Especially if the panties were extra-large, would you automatically assume someone was implying you were getting fat?

+ *The Serendipitous Arrival of the S.S. African Queen.* Who would come to rescue you?

+ *The Murder of Giovani "Big Cheese" Manicotti.* This is a game. Which character would you be best at?

+ *I Got a Pedicure.* These are wonderful! Women already know this but many guys do not. If you choose to surprise your male partner with a gift certificate to your local pedicure shop, and they scoff at it, please send it to me!

+ *Living Next Door to a Witch.* Now, this is really interesting. Do you know – or have you known – any witches? How would you know? What questions would you ask of them to prove themselves? And to the point, can they do magic?

+ *The Complete and Very Short History of the 1992 Mexican Olympic Men's Hockey Team.* If you were to go to the

Olympics, what event would you compete in? Are you exceptional at anything that could be an Olympic sport?

+ *A Road Trip with Aunt Claire.* Do you know anyone who has experienced this type of stunning surprise? How did it go? How do you think you'd handle it?

+ *House Flipping Blues.* It seems like everyone has a story about buying a house that is haunted, cursed, or in some magical way, special. These make good stories, even if most or fabrications. Heard any good ones?

+ *Pond Hockey.* Have you ever played? I have played this variant of the sport all of my life. It's simply terrific. Do you have any tales of pick-up sports activities?

+ *Forty-Seven.* Alas, all good things must come to an end, and for me, it was ice hockey. I still dream of playing. Do you have anything similar?

+ *Bunnies Day in the Sunshine.* Back when life was simpler and some guy hanging around a ballpark was not viewed as a sexual predator, this fellow nicknamed 'Bunny' was part of my life. I learned that people like him were just people, like you and me. Have you had a similar life lesson?

+ *September's Song.* Do you have a very special place? For me, it was going fishing with my Dad in northern Maine. How about you?

+ *The Revenge of Russel's Sister.* All kids get into mischief. This is a yarn about such an adventure. I'll bet everyone alive today has a similar tale, don't you?

+ *Ole' Wrinkle Neck.* Some of us were blessed with caring grandparents who were kind enough to listen. Were you? And a more difficult question; are you one?

+ *The Last Laugh.* Oh, revenge is sweet. Sometimes. Got any tales of when it was? Or how about, got any tales of when it wasn't?

+ *Worm Hole I.* Can you imagine meeting yourself from another dimension? What would you say? What would you want to know about the near future?

Thank You!

As the stories contained herein were written over a period of forty years, I've got plenty of people to thank. Just about everyone I know has been tapped at one time or another to read my writing and provide comments. You folks are part of a long and distinguished list of good friends. Thank you one and all for your support. My life is richer because of you.

Special thanks to Mary Weaver who, in addition to reading every word I write, has patiently hammered away at me about my tendency to misuse apostrophes and my seeming disregard of the rules of capitalization.

Thanks to the best writing teacher on the planet, David Daniel, and my wordsmithing champion, Melanie Aves. What you guys do is pure magic.

Then there are Marcy Abbott, Andrea Long, and Jen Adams, all who have read, reviewed and edited some of the work herein – thank you!

Thank you, Scot Campbell, an extraordinary editor as well as fine gentleman who urges me to explore the English language. And he also wears a kilt!

Carolyn Lands offered direction and guidance regarding the hierarchy of the Native American societies. Thank you!

And lest I forget my long-time fishing pal, Mike Tenbus, who has read just about everything I've written and offered thoughtful commentary. Thanks, Mike.

And of course, thank you to my loving and extraordinarily patient wife, Ann, who has spent every morning listening to my ramblings concerning my latest and greatest writing ideas. I am indeed blessed.

9 781982 208479